All God's promises

All God's Promises

Will the last
of the lost be found?
Will Karl discover for herself
that all God's promises
are true?

A Prairie Heritage, Book 7

VIKKI KESTELL

Faith-Filled Fiction™

www.faith-filledfiction.com | www.vikkikestell.com

A Prairie Heritage, Book 7
©2016 Vikki Kestell
All Rights Reserved
Also Available in eBook Format

BOOKS BY VIKKI KESTELL

A PRAIRIE HERITAGE
Book 1: *A Rose Blooms Twice*, **a free eBook, most online retailers**
Book 2: *Wild Heart on the Prairie*
Book 3: *Joy on This Mountain*
Book 4: *The Captive Within*
Book 5: *Stolen*
Book 6: *Lost Are Found*
Book 7: *All God's Promises*

GIRLS FROM THE MOUNTAIN
Book 1: *Tabitha*

NANOSTEALTH
Book 1: *Stealthy Steps*
Book 2: *Stealth Power*
Book 3: *Stealth Retribution*

ALL GOD'S PROMISES

A Prairie Heritage, Book 7
by Vikki Kestell
Also Available in eBook Format from Most Online Retailers

So many unanswered questions.

Who am I really? Kari wondered again. *I am not KariAnn Hillyer. Not KariAnn Granger. They tell me my real name is KariAnn Thoresen Michaels. But who is that person?*

She frowned. *And where are my sister and brother? Who took them? Where are they now?*

"Lord, my uncle and my cousins urge me to trust you. They say that you will help me through this difficult transition. And they say that *you* know where Elaine and Samuel are, that I can trust you—that in you the lost are found! I am so new to this faith thing, though. It is hard to believe you will find them after so many years."

~~~

Kari pledges her considerable fortune toward the search for the social worker who, thirty-three years earlier, took three-year-old Elaine and infant Samuel from the scene of an accident—the same accident that killed Kari's parents—and sold them in an illegal adoption.

And she is not alone in the search for Elaine and Samuel. Private investigators Anthony Esquibel and Owen Washington join efforts to unearth the identity of the social worker and trace the adoptions of Kari's siblings.

Will the *last* of the lost be found? Will Kari discover for herself that all God's promises are true?

HYMNS

I Need Thee Every Hour
Lyrics, Annie S. Hawks, 1872
Music, Robert Lowry, 1872
Public Domain

Silent Night
(*Stille Nacht, Heilege Nacht*)
Joseph Mohr, 1818
Public Domain

It Is Well with My Soul
Horatio G. Spafford, 1873
Public Domain

SCRIPTURE QUOTATIONS

DEDICATION

This book is dedicated to
our eleven wonderful grandchildren:
**Ben, Damion, Eddie, Josiah, Noah,
Miriam, Jael, Abbi, Maqinzy, Nate, Aubri,**
(and still counting)!
You bring us such joy!
I pray for you daily to know Jesus, the only Savior,
and serve him with your whole hearts.
May you be fruitful branches in his eternal kingdom.
May you walk all of your lives in
All God's Promises.

ACKNOWLEDGEMENTS

Many thanks to my esteemed teammates,
Cheryl Adkins and **Greg McCann**,
who give selflessly of themselves
to make each new book the most effective
instrument of God's grace possible.
I love you.

COVER DESIGN

Vikki Kestell

TO MY READERS

This book is a work of fiction,
what I term Faith-Filled Fiction™.
While the characters and events are fictional,
they are situated within the historical record.
To God be the glory.

𝒫ROLOGUE

July 1991

Kari fell asleep that night, comforted by a peace her understanding could not fathom. She slept deeply until, in the dark, early hours before dawn, she began to dream.

In the dream, she stood on the road that ran east from Søren's farm, out onto the prairie. From far down that road she spied the dust of travelers coming toward her. They walked, some together, some singly, all with their eyes on her.

Then she saw her mother and father. Their faces radiant and joyous, they stretched their arms toward her.

Mommy! Daddy!

Daddy reached her first and she could smell the familiar scent of his cologne on his collar before they touched.

Always, at this point in her nightmares, before his arms reached her, she would awake, filled with that unseen dread she knew only as *The Black*—the dense curtain that hid something vital she could never grasp or recall, something she struggled to remember but could not, the thing that terrified and grieved her so deeply.

But this time, this time Daddy's arms curled around her, and she sank onto his shoulder. She was again six years old and he was comforting and holding her. Kari wept in exquisite joy. She clung to his neck, burying her face in the scratchy hollow below his jaw.

Daddy! Kari felt she could not get enough of his strength, his warmth, his love. She would never let him go. And she would never need to face *The Black* again.

But she was wrong. The old nightmare began to intrude.

It was dark—so dark! She was on the side of a black, moonless highway. Daddy and Mommy had put her far away from the narrow shoulder of the road, far from the faint outline of their car, broken down on the edge of the highway.

"Wait here where it's safe," Daddy had said. "Watch over them for us." He had hugged her before he and Mommy went back to the car to try to fix it.

Kari had stayed close by her charges—just as Daddy had asked.

Until the blinding lights of the semi-tractor and trailer swept down on her parents and carried them away.

The grinding of the truck's brakes jangled in Kari's ears—the wheels as they locked and screeched on the roadway, the tires as they squealed and shredded, followed by the hideous rending of metal. The sounds of the collision went on and on until there was only silence.

Silence and darkness.

In her dream, Kari lay curled into a ball in the dirt and weeds trying in vail to push the sights and sounds from her mind. With her eyes squeezed shut, she clung to Daddy's neck, clung as hard as she could, blocking out the horror. Blocking out everything. Everything.

Then strong hands pulled at her, trying to pull her away from Daddy.

"No!" Kari protested. She clung harder and squeezed her eyes shut.

"Kari," Daddy whispered. "Open your eyes."

He wanted her to look? Look at *The Black*?

"No, Daddy! I don't want to!" *No! I don't want to, Daddy!*

Daddy's mouth breathed in her ear; his voice grew insistent. "Please, Kari. Open your eyes."

"No, no! I can't!" Kari squirmed and burrowed deeper into his shoulder.

"*Kari! Open your eyes!*"

Kari's eyes flew open. Unseen hands ripped her from the comfort of Daddy's arms where she had, in her imagination, hidden from the horror she had witnessed.

She looked around. She was no longer near the side of the highway in the dark. She was in a room, a brightly lit room, struggling, trying to reach—

Those same unseen hands restrained her, but for the first time she could see what she strained *toward*: A man bending to pick up a tiny girl with curly brown pigtails; a woman holding an infant in her arms.

The man spoke to the person gripping Kari, holding her back. "We do want this little girl and the baby boy, but I'm afraid, well, we don't want *her*," the man insisted, thrusting his chin toward Kari, "She's too old and likely too set in her ways. We don't want her."

"Don't worry; it won't be a problem," the faceless woman restraining her declared. "She's been catatonic since we picked her up, night before last. Hasn't said a word until now, in fact. We'll send her into foster care. She's so traumatized she likely won't remember a thing."

"What about their family? Won't someone come looking for them?"

The woman laughed, sounding confident. "Nope. We found the father's address book. The only emergency contact was some church denominational headquarters back east. We called them.

"Turns out the Grangers were *missionaries* and have been out of the country for years. The woman from the church headquarters said that neither of the parents had any family."

She temporized. "Well, the woman we talked to said that the man *did* have an uncle but that they had no record of his name or where he lived. Apparently, Mr. Granger and his uncle were not close. Hadn't been in contact for years. The situation is perfect, really."

"But what if someone from that church calls back, asking more questions?"

"Oh, we've already sent them a letter. Thanked them for their help; told them we'd located the uncle and that he had made provisions for the burial and the children."

"What about the police?" the man demanded.

"Stop worrying. I have an arrangement with the officers at the scene; I will pay them, too. They will 'neglect' to put the two smaller children into their reports. They will only mention *her*."

"Yeah. We don't want *her*," the man frowned, "but what if she talks?"

"She won't talk." The woman shook Kari and twisted her arm. "You hear me, little miss? You aren't going to remember any of this, got it? If you tell anyone about this, I'll make you wish you hadn't been born."

She slapped the side of Kari's head with her palm and jerked on her arm when Kari cringed and whimpered. Kari tried to pull away but the woman yanked her close. She leaned into Kari's face.

"Look at me!" the woman hissed.

Kari stared, terrified, into the woman's face. She gagged on the woman's cheap cologne infused with cigarette smoke and noted her hard eyes and harder mouth and the plastic tag pinned below her collar . . .

"That nice man and woman are going to give your sister and brother a good home. But if you *ever* mention your sister or brother to anyone—*if you ever say their names*—well, very bad things will happen to them. Do you hear me? In fact, if you ever even *think* about your sister or brother again, I will know it, and I will have that man and woman *throw your sister and brother in a river to drown*."

She shook Kari. "Nod if you understand."

Kari, a deep, dark tunnel opening before her, somehow nodded. Then the tunnel swallowed her and the darkness was spilling over her, filling her mouth and eyes with thick sand until she was choking and retching, until consciousness began to fade.

The woman turned back to the man, "See? She won't say a word. Now give me the money."

9

Kari struggled up from the dark tunnel and tried to scream, "No! You can't take them away! You can't take them!"

They ignored her. Did they even hear her? Or was she screaming her protests only in her own mind? She tried to open her mouth but the dark— *The Black*—flooded in.

"No!" Kari struggled against the suffocating feeling of sand clogging her throat and managed to croak again, "No!"

And then she *was* screaming. "No! You can't take my sister and brother!"

Kari's shrieks woke the house. A frantic Max thundered down the stairs and reached her locked door first; Søren was right behind him.

"Break it, Papa! Some 'un's hurting Kari!" the terrified boy shouted.

Søren's shoulder popped the flimsy lock and he spilled into the room; Kari was sitting up in bed, still shrieking. Max, scared nearly out of his skin, fell to his knees sobbing—something he would vigorously deny later on—as Ilsa arrived at Kari's door.

Wide-eyed, Ilsa watched Søren sit on the bed and wrap his arms around Kari. He held her, rocked her, and repeated her name. "Kari! Kari, it's all right. Kari, it's just a bad dream. Kari!"

Kari's screams dwindled and she relaxed into Søren's embrace. Instead of shrieking, she babbled.

"I saw, Søren, I saw! Daddy made me look and I saw *The Black*! I saw them!"

Ilsa sat on the edge of the bed facing Søren and took Kari's hands. "You had a bad dream, Kari. You are safe. We have you."

"Yes, Kari. It was a bad dream," Søren repeated. Max crept up onto the bed and put both his hands on Kari's arm.

"Please be all right, Kari," he sobbed. "Please be all right!"

Kari made an attempt to calm herself, conscious of Max's young, impressionable heart. She shuddered and took a gulping breath. "But, Søren, Ilsa, it wasn't just a dream. I remembered!"

"Remembered what?"

"I remembered what happened after they told me Daddy and Mommy were dead! The police took us somewhere and there was a woman. And then a man and a woman, a couple. They-they said, "We don't want *her*! But we want the little girl and the baby!"

It was so clear in her mind now—so very clear. Kari made herself breathe slowly. "Søren. Ilsa. They took them."

"Took who, Kari?"

"They took my little sister and baby brother," Kari whispered.

Søren and Ilsa exchanged baffled looks.

Hours and many cups of coffee later, Kari remained adamant and critical of herself. "All these years! I forgot them all these years! *How could I?*"

Søren finally believed her. "Kari, you were a child. You watched your parents die—you were traumatized. It's not your fault."

"But—"

"Listen, Kari. If someone took your brother and sister, then we'll find them. We will start an investigation."

"I remember . . . seeing some sort of tag on the woman's coat. A name tag. *Marge* something. It started with an 'S.' *Marge S.*"

Søren touched Kari's face. "All right, then. Owen found you; we'll have him start looking for this woman, this *Marge S.* She had to be a social worker, right?

"And we'll get that guy you used in Albuquerque—what was his name? Anthony something? He's an investigator, too, yes? If this woman was a social worker the year your parents died, there can't be many with the name of Marge, can there? And there would have to be a record of your brother and sister's adoption the same year somewhere in New Mexico, right? We will find it."

"But what if we don't find them, Søren? I have forgotten them for so long! What has become of my little sister and baby brother?"

"Do you recall their names, Kari?"

Kari blinked and her brows drew down. "Funny you should ask. I have forgotten them all these years, but . . . but it feels like their names *should be* right on the tip of my—oh! Sammie! My baby brother's name is Samuel, but we called him Sammie!"

"And your sister?"

Kari nodded. "I think . . . Elaine! Yes; Elaine and Samuel. How could I have forgotten?"

"Kari," Ilsa said quietly, "They aren't babies any longer. You said your sister was three and you were six? She would be, what? Thirty-five, now? Your little brother would be thirty-three? They aren't children anymore. They aren't in immediate danger."

Kari considered what Ilsa had said. "I-I know you're right. But I'm having trouble seeing them . . . grown."

She thought a moment longer. "And now that I remember them, it means I am not the sole heir of Peter Granger—his estate does not belong exclusively to me."

Kari turned to Søren. "I had already been praying about using my inheritance for God's glory. I still intend to do that with my portion, but now Clover and his firm will need to make provision for Elaine and Samuel in the probate, too."

"Those are their names? Elaine and Samuel?" Ilsa asked.

"Yes," Kari whispered. "Sammie was only a baby."

Søren nodded. "Kari, your homecoming is the answer to decades—*generations*—of prayer and trust that the 'lost are found.' But maybe . . . maybe we should take a wider view."

Ilsa, Max, and Kari looked to Søren to explain.

"Maybe you are the firstfruits of our family's faith, Kari."

He took her hand and set his jaw in determination. "You are the first to be found, but the others are coming. Until then, we trust The Lord—and we never stop searching. Because *we know* that in God the lost are found."

PART 1

For Jesus Christ, the Son of God,
does not waver between
"Yes" and "No."
As God's ultimate "Yes,"
he always does what he says.
For all of God's promises
have been fulfilled in Christ
with a resounding "Yes!"
And through Christ, our "Amen"
(which means "Yes")
ascends to God for his glory.
(2 Corinthians 1:19, 20, NLT)

$\mathcal{C}$HAPTER 1

AUGUST 5, 1991

T he screen door slapped closed behind her as Kari ran down the porch steps. She crossed the farmyard, paused near the pump, and drained the last of the coffee from the mug she held.

In the hour before dawn, Kari had helped Max feed and milk the cows and goats, feed the chickens and gather their eggs, and muck out the stalls. Now morning chores in the barn and outbuildings were done, and she had a few minutes to herself before Ilsa called them to breakfast.

The sun was cresting the horizon at her back; its heat warmed Kari's shoulders, warning of the scorching day ahead. Showers had pummeled the ground the night before, leaving mud and puddles in their wake, but the glowing ball of fire rising in the sky east of them was already wicking the moisture from the earth, shrouding the rain-soaked fields in mist.

Kari's gaze fastened on a point unseen, west, across the misty pasture. *It's all right,* she thought. *The haze will burn off quickly.*

Besides, she knew the way by heart.

With wisps swirling around her boots, Kari strode down the slope, away from the house and far down the pasture, until she reached her destination.

Kari had made a habit of spending this precious part of each morning the same way—standing on the bank of the stream that separated Søren's farm from the abandoned homestead on the other side.

She found her usual vantage point. The creek bank was strewn with wild poppies. Their long stems lifted sleepy crimson heads to greet the rising sun; their furled buds peeked above the mist that swirled across the ground and about Kari's feet.

Kari often sat among the poppies in the late afternoon, but not this morning, not while the soaked earth was surrendering its moisture. Instead, she stood on the bank of the stream and peered across its dancing water to the other side. Through the mist, she spied the shape of the little house that, these many generations later, was still standing, although near to falling down.

The remains of Rose's house, she thought. *Rose and Jan's home. Where they raised their daughter, Joy.*

Joy.

Joy, my grandmother.

My real *grandmother.*

Those three words still stunned her. With shaking fingers, Kari wiped cobwebs from her eyes and wished the empty mug she clutched in her other hand still held steaming coffee.

"Must have more coffee," she muttered. A moment later she added, "Actually, what I really must have is more of you, Lord."

Of the many revelations of the last three weeks, finding Jesus had been the best. The most . . .

Earthshaking.

Life-changing.

Awe-inspiring.

Finding Jesus has changed everything!

She snorted under her breath. *Actually, he found me, 'cause I sure wasn't looking for* him!

And then the chuckle caught in her throat and became a sob. *O Jesus! I am so glad you found me! When I think of the intricate thread you spun to guide me to you, your hand is evident.*

It is nothing short of a miracle.

A miracle?

Yes, a miracle.

And the precious land across the creek was hers now. Rose and Jan's falling-down house was hers now.

Someday I will build a house near theirs and spend part of my life looking from the other side of this creek.

That idea boggled her mind, too.

So much has changed.

Too many aspects of Kari's life had changed in such a short period of time, and she struggled daily to process it all.

Only four months ago, Kari had been nursing the wounds of her husband's betrayal and their subsequent divorce. The divorce, finalized in January, had required her to sell their home in Albuquerque and split the proceeds with David, the man who was now her ex-husband. But Kari had nowhere to go after the house sold.

She had been flat broke, without a job or the prospect of one. She had been balancing on the sharp edge of desperation.

I didn't even have enough money to rent an apartment until the sale closed and paid out. And the proceeds from the sale of the house, once they paid out? That money would have kept me for a mere six months.

And then a letter had arrived. A letter from *Brunell & Brunell, Attorneys at Law*, New Orleans. The words still burned in Kari's memories.

. . . If you are KariAnn Alicia Hillyer, born in 1952 to Michael D. Granger and Bethany M. Granger, and legally adopted by William and Eleanor Friedman in 1961, would you kindly contact our offices at your earliest convenience?

Brunell & Brunell has been managing Mr. Peter Granger's estate for many years now and we are most anxious to settle it.

Cordially,

C. Beauregard Brunell, Managing Partner

Brunell & Brunell, Attorneys at Law

Kari stared with unseeing eyes into the distance. The memory of the disdain she'd felt as she read that letter remained with her, strong and vivid.

This has to be a joke or a scam, she had reasoned. *I mean, what kind of nut names their child 'C. Beauregard,' for heaven's sake?*

But it had been no joke. It had not been a scam.

The man named in the letter as Peter Granger had left the sum of his earthly possessions to his estranged nephew, Michael Granger. Apparently the breach between Peter Granger and his nephew, which occurred when Michael was in his early twenties, had been deep—so deep that uncle and nephew had never spoken again.

Years after their parting, however, Peter Granger had regretted his actions and had sought to be reconciled to Michael. Although Peter had spent large sums on private detectives, the investigators had been unable to locate Michael. Peter Granger had died in 1964, leaving all he possessed to his nephew—or, should his nephew have died, to his nephew's offspring.

As the attorneys of Brunell & Brunell had explained to Kari, this Michael Granger had been *her father.* That meant that she, Kari, was the sole heir to Peter Granger's estate.

Why had it taken so long for the attorneys to find her?

Kari sighed and rehearsed the details. Again.

Kari's father and mother had died on the shoulder of a New Mexico highway when a truck crashed into their disabled car. The year had been 1958, and Kari had been six years old.

Unable to locate any relatives to take custody of Kari, the State of New Mexico had placed her into the foster care system. Later she had been adopted by Nell and Bill Friedman. Even later, Kari had married David Hillyer. Their seven-year marriage had ended when David announced he was leaving Kari.

It wasn't until this past January, when The Albuquerque Journal published Kari's divorce decree, that Brunell & Brunell's in-house sleuth had, at last, located the heir to the Granger estate.

And so, in a matter of days, Kari's situation had been dramatically, irrevocably altered. Kari had inherited Peter Granger's home in New Orleans and the entirety of his estate—an estate so large that its size, at first revelation, had bewildered and terrified her.

"It still terrifies me."

Kari shuddered. Her grip on the cold, empty coffee mug tightened. "O Jesus, please help me to make peace with all these changes."

The size of the Granger estate was not the only change Kari was adjusting to. No, it had been only the beginning, for then, mere days later, Kari had discovered a journal—the journal of one *Rose Thoresen*.

Kari had been acquainting herself with Peter Granger's sizable house. After she had explored every room on both floors and in the attic, she had decided to see what secrets the old detached garage held.

To Kari's immense delight, the garage had housed a classic, candy-apple-red Cadillac Coupe de Ville—securely covered and mounted on blocks. Under its wraps, the car was in like-new condition.

According to the attorneys of Brunell & Brunell, Peter Granger had bought the car off the showroom floor in 1959 when he was 87 years old. However, because of his advancing years, he had not driven it much.

When their client passed away in 1964, his attorneys had found the car in a neglected state, its tires flat and ruined. They hired a specialty company to remove the car's wheels, set the chassis on blocks, drain the car's fluids, and secure a custom-fit cover over it.

After Kari discovered the vehicle, her attorneys had the Caddy towed to a classic car restoration company. When the company delivered the restored, ready-to-drive Coupe de Ville to Kari, she had been thrilled.

Classic Caddy!

But as much as Kari loved the Caddy, the vehicle had not been the garage's most meaningful treasure. In the attic above the garage, Kari had found an old trunk filled with her grandmother Alicia's evening gowns—beautiful relics of the 1910s and 20s. Kari had lifted each dress from the trunk with love and care, exclaiming over their exquisite beading and lace work.

But under those gowns? At the bottom of the trunk, concealed by boxed hats, shoes, and handbags, and tied up in a diaphanous silk scarf, Kari had found a small cedar box. The box was locked; glued about its girth was a paper seal with the year "1957" scrawled across the paper in a shaking hand.

The date on the seal had puzzled Kari, for Alicia Granger, whose belongings filled the trunk, had died in 1927. Everything in the trunk—with the exception of the cedar box—predated the sealed box *by three decades.*

Someone had hidden the little cedar box away. Someone had, quite intentionally, placed the box where it would not easily be found.

Kari had searched for and discovered the tiny key that fit the lock on the cedar box—it was glued to the underside of the trunk's lid. Once she had unlocked the box, she found a velvet bag. In the bag were two items: a sealed envelope and a small red volume, its binding faded and cracked with age.

The ink on the envelope had faded over time; nevertheless, Kari was reluctant to break its seal until she knew to whom the envelope had been addressed.

The book, however, was not sealed. The inscription inside the brittle cover read:

Rose Thoresen
My Journal

The journal's opening date was April 25, 1909.

Eighty-two years ago!

Although Kari had no idea who this Rose Thoresen had been or why her journal should be at the bottom of Kari's grandmother's trunk, the account recorded in the little book became the most precious, most important portion of Kari's inheritance.

"O Rose!" Kari moaned as her fevered mind traced the details of the last three weeks.

Because of you, my life has changed.

Kari had devoured the words penned in Rose's own hand. What Rose had written during a two-year period had set Kari's heart afire. But when Rose's account ended abruptly on April 12, 1911, Kari could not relinquish the woman or her words.

She longed to know more about this Rose Thoresen: What had become of her? How had her journal ended up in Peter Granger's attic, buried beneath Alicia Granger's clothing? And what of Palmer House, the home in Denver Rose had described with such passion? What had become of the girls who had lived there?

. . . And what of the God Rose loved and served?

Kari had to find answers to the questions that burned within her.

Less than four weeks ago, armed with the scant few clues the journal provided, Kari had left New Orleans en route to Denver in search of the mysterious Rose Thoresen. Rose's journal had led Kari to . . . *such grace!*

Rose's journal had led Kari to Palmer House and the elderly woman who still lived there and could personally speak of Rose Thoresen.

Rose's journal had led to the revelation of a heartbreaking event of decades gone by, an event that had defined the families it touched.

It had led to the faith-filled prayers of generations.

It had led to the infant boy who was lost—and to his daughter *who was found*.

And it had led her to Jesus!

I found you, Lord. I found you! Because of Rose's journal, I found you, and I found the truth about myself. I found my real family—three uncles and a gazillion cousins and dear friends.

You stripped away decades of deceit, Lord. You showed yourself to be faithful to those who trusted in you, but . . .

But I still have so many unanswered questions.

Questions like, who am I really? I am not KariAnn Hillyer, not KariAnn Friedman. I am not even KariAnn Granger.

Peter Granger was not my great-uncle. Alicia Granger was not Peter Granger's sister-in-law, was not my father's mother, was not my grandmother.

They tell me my father's real name was not Michael Granger but Edmund Thoresen Michaels, and that he was stolen from his parents, Joy and Grant Michaels.

They tell me that my real name is KariAnn Thoresen Michaels.

But who is that person? Who is Kari Michaels? Kari wondered again.

She shuddered. *I am drowning in change; I am mired in uncertainties.*

Kari stirred from her deep reverie. She blinked and sucked in deep, reviving breaths. Her reflections always ended here—frozen. Stuck at this place of unanswered questions and concerns.

The concerns were not only for herself, either, because the startling revelations of the past week had unlocked another door, the door to Kari's earliest childhood remembrances.

For her entire life, a mental fog had imprisoned Kari's memories—particularly her recall of the night her parents had died. Now, like the morning haze that surrounded her on this creek bank, that fog was lifting away under the intense light of truth.

Her lost memories were returning.

Kari sighed. *It is almost too much, Lord. Too much—and yet not enough.*

As far back as Kari could remember, she had suffered nightmares and debilitating anxiety attacks.

The attacks came on her whenever she dreamed of or tried to recall her parents, whenever she sought to remember their touch, their voices, or even their faces. Or if she thought about the night they died.

For when she dreamed or thought of them, *The Black*—a dark, terrifying curtain—would engulf and smother her. Once she was caught in the grip of a full-on panic attack, the episode usually ended in Kari losing consciousness.

To avoid these attacks, Kari had taught herself not to think of her mother or father. She had learned not to think or speak of the night they perished.

But eight nights ago, *The Black* had lost its hold over her.

Eight nights ago, Kari had been dreaming of her father—his comforting voice, the familiar smell of his suit, the scratchy roughness of his cheek on hers. As usually happened, the precious moments were interrupted and Kari was soon caught in the suffocating clutches of another nightmare featuring *The Black*.

This time, though, her father had *not* disappeared. He had encouraged her to fight the dark curtain.

"Kari," Daddy had whispered. "Open your eyes."

He wanted her to look? Look at *The Black*?

"No, Daddy! I don't want to!" *No! I don't want to, Daddy!*

Daddy's mouth breathed in her ear; his voice grew insistent. "Please, Kari. Open your eyes."

"No, no! I can't!" Kari had squirmed and burrowed deeper into his shoulder.

Her father had been insistent.

"Kari! Open your eyes!"

Inside the dream, Kari had opened her eyes—and she had remembered.

She had remembered the truck hitting her parents and their disabled car on the side of the road. She had remembered the sirens and flashing lights, the police coming and finding her.

She had been unresponsive to them. For hours, perhaps days, activity had swirled around her, but she had been locked in her own body, unspeaking, unmoving.

"Catatonic," she'd heard a woman say from a far distance. "She won't talk."

That same woman had assured the man and woman holding a little girl and an infant that Kari would not present a problem—except that Kari had woken then, screaming, "No! You can't take them away! You can't take them!"

The woman had shaken Kari and twisted her arm. "You hear me, little miss? You aren't going to remember any of this, got it? If you tell anyone about this, I'll make you wish you hadn't been born."

She had slapped the side of Kari's head with her palm and jerked on her arm when Kari cringed and whimpered. Kari had tried to pull away but the woman had yanked her close.

"That nice man and woman are going to give your sister and brother a good home. But if you *ever* mention your sister or brother to anyone—*if you ever say their names*—well, very bad things will happen to them. Do you hear me? In fact, if you ever even *think* about your sister or brother again, I will know it, and I will have that man and woman *throw your sister and brother in a river to drown.*"

That was Kari's first encounter with *The Black*. The darkness had spilled over her, had filled her mouth and eyes with the choking sensation of thick sand, and had stolen the very breath from her body—until consciousness had faded.

But in the dream eight nights ago, Kari had, after thirty-three years, remembered. Now that she saw what lay behind the curtain, *The Black* would never again hold her in its death grip.

I remember my little sister and baby brother now.

For the umpteenth time she berated herself. *How could I have forgotten them? How could I have not remembered them all these years? How could I?*

She frowned. *And where are they? Who took them? Where are they now?*

O Lord, I'm so grateful to be free of The Black! *I am so grateful that you are restoring my memories of Sammie and Elaine. So grateful for everything.*

She took a slow, deep breath. "But it is time. Time to start looking for them."

Kari strode up the slope toward the farmhouse, her long legs eating up the yards. When she glanced toward the top of the field, she spied Max's blonde hair next to the pump. His slumped eight-year-old shoulders told her that Søren had forbade Max from interrupting Kari during her morning ritual.

He spotted her and brightened. "Hey, Kari!"

"Hay is for horses," she teased.

Max eased under her arm and they walked the remaining distance to the house in companionable silence. The boy fit against her side as if he had always been there.

I am learning to love Max, Kari thought. *It will break my heart to leave him.*

She knew he felt the same. She also knew he harbored an unspoken hope that Kari and his papa, Søren, would "get together."

Lord, I am learning to feel something for Søren, too. Kari shrugged the thought away. *No, it is much too soon to go there. My life has been a mess for years. I don't need emotional entanglements to complicate it. Besides . . .*

And Kari's thoughts returned to Elaine and Samuel.

Max and Kari passed Kari's Coupe de Ville, parked close to the house. Søren's friend Jeff had delivered the Caddy last evening. The repairs—to replace the smashed windshield and fix the dented hood, both caused when a bale of hay fell from Søren's truck onto Kari and her car—had taken longer than two weeks. Now, as Jeff had promised, Kari's car was "as good as new."

Kari brushed her fingers across the chrome on the fender as she and Max passed by. They climbed the back porch steps and, with the screen door slapping closed behind them, entered the open kitchen.

Søren's sister, Ilsa, smiled from the stove. "Perfect timing. Breakfast is ready."

"I'll wash up."

Kari walked from the kitchen into the living room on her way to the guest room and paused at the old family photographs lining an entire wall. Her fingers touched the glass covering the portrait of Jan, Rose, and Joy when Joy was around Max's age.

Kari sighed. "Ah, Rose." Then she brightened. "Oh! That reminds me."

A few minutes later, Kari stepped over the bench and took her seat at the table. Søren bent his head to pray. "Lord, we thank you for this bountiful food. May it strengthen us and may we use our strength for your glory. Amen."

"Amen," Ilsa, Max, and Kari murmured in unison.

They were silent while Ilsa passed around the platters of bacon, potatoes, eggs, sliced tomatoes, stewed apples, and pancakes. Even Kari took more than she had been accustomed to eating—accustomed, that is, before she came to visit Søren and Ilsa.

I eat more because I help Max with his chores—and it is hard, demanding work.

Good heavens, they've turned me into a farm girl!

She realized she'd laughed aloud when three heads swiveled toward her. "Sorry. Thinking aloud."

Max grinned at her, and Kari couldn't help it. She ran her thumb down Max's cheek.

"I'm gonna miss you." She hadn't meant to say that aloud, either, but it came out anyway.

Max's face fell. "Me, too," he whispered.

Søren cleared his throat. "You're going today, then?"

They knew she was leaving; she had told them last evening.

"Yes."

He nodded and turned his eyes back to his plate. "You have the map to Matthew's place in Emporia?"

He knew she did. They'd gone over it last evening. He'd written out detailed directions, too.

"Yes. Thank you."

"And his phone number?"

"Yes. I have it."

Ilsa interrupted the strained silence that followed. "May I help you finish packing?"

"I'm done. But thank you."

Kari kept her eyes on her own plate. Next to her Max sniffled and she knew tears were trickling down the cheek she'd stroked.

Lord, this is so hard.

Kari was desperate to change the subject. "I forgot to ask you something, a favor, actually."

Søren, Ilsa, and Max looked at her.

"I, um, I would like to hire someone, a professional, to come here and reproduce the portraits and family photos on the living room wall. So I can have my own copies. Would that be all right with you?"

Søren and Ilsa glanced at each other.

"That's actually a good idea," Ilsa answered.

Søren agreed. "Most of the old photos are one-of-a-kind images. Even our cousins down the road don't have some of the pictures we have."

"Wonderful. Thank you. I'll have the person I hire make more than one copy of each so that, God forbid, should anything happen to the originals, we'll still have the reproductions."

"I know of other family members who would be keen to have their own copies, Kari," Søren answered.

Max tapped Kari's arm. "Will you send me a picture of you, Kari? A nice, big one? I don't want to forget what you look like."

He looked so serious that Kari had to cough before she could answer. "Of course, Max. I'll take care of it as soon as I get home."

Ilsa began removing the breakfast things, and Kari and Max jumped up to help. After they had cleared the table, they settled back in their seats, each of them opening their Bibles. Kari opened the used black Bible Søren had loaned to her.

I will have to leave this here, she thought with regret.

As though he had read her mind, Søren said, "We know you can buy a study Bible of your own when you get home, Kari, but we would like you to keep this one. As a keepsake of your time with us."

Kari nodded. She couldn't reply.

"Let's read where we left off yesterday," Søren said. "1 Thessalonians, Chapter 2."

Kari found her way to the passage and smoothed the pages of the Bible with her fingers. She followed along as Søren read.

> *For this reason, we also thank God without ceasing,*
> *because when you received the word of God*
> *which you heard from us,*
> *you welcomed it not as the word of men,*
> *but as it is in truth, the word of God,*
> *which also effectively works in you who believe.*

Kari found it difficult to keep her attention on the passage. *When will I be back here with these precious people?* she wondered. *How long will it be? Will things be different? Will Max have grown into an incorrigible teenager? Will Søren have moved on with his life? O Lord, I cannot live with so many goodbyes!*

Kari's right hand clenched in her lap, and she stifled her own sniffs—until Max's hand found its way onto her lap and clasped her tense fingers. The sob jumped out then. Max slid closer to her and laid his head on her shoulder.

With merciful tact, Ilsa and Søren averted their eyes and Søren kept reading. As Kari listened, she felt as though she would always associate his mellow baritone with the reading of Scripture. She leaned her cheek upon Max's head and inhaled his scent, part boy, part barn.

Søren finished reading, but he did not ask questions or invite discussion as he usually did. Kari could tell he was struggling, too. To end the uncomfortable moment, she disentangled herself from Max, drew her legs over the bench seat, and stood.

"I'll be getting my things."

She fled to her room. She unbuttoned the plaid shirt she wore—one of Ilsa's—and shrugged it off. She tugged on a soft cotton top with spaghetti straps for the hot road ahead and, packing the Bible and a pair of sandals into the smaller of her two cases, she closed and latched it.

The last of her toiletries went into her overnight bag.

When she opened her bedroom door to bring her luggage out, Max and Søren were waiting. Søren took her two cases without a word. Max grabbed Kari's overnight bag. They strode through the kitchen and the screen door slammed behind them.

Kari sniffed and straightened. Then she marched into the kitchen and into Ilsa's arms.

"Goodbye," she whispered.

"No, in our ancestors' tongue we will just say, *Gud gå med deg*. Our God—and our love—will go with you."

Kari sniffed. "And with you."

"*Ja*." Ilsa squeezed her once more and let her go.

Kari stood at the top of the porch and stared out across the acres of Søren's farm, trying to hold it close while at the same time letting it go. Then, determined to be brave, she smiled at Max and Søren waiting for her by the Caddy.

She kept her voice low and light. "Everything squared away?"

"I think so." Søren rubbed his hand across his neck, up the back of his head, and over his close-cropped red-blonde hair, a sure sign of agitation.

I can't give in to these emotions, Kari told herself. *I can't—or I will never leave. And I must leave. I have work to do.* She placed her large handbag containing Rose's journal on the passenger seat and opened the driver's door. She kept her face slightly averted.

Then Max plowed into her. He threw both arms around her, sobbing, "Please don't go, Kari. We love you. We want you to stay."

Søren's arms joined Max's. "I know you have things you must do, but please promise to come back. We-we—"

He didn't finish, but his arms enfolded Kari and tugged her close. Kari leaned against him and could hear the strong, steady beat of his heart. She pulled back a little and looked up; he released her, took her face in his hands, and placed a soft, chaste kiss upon her forehead.

"Goodbye, Kari. May the Lord bless you and keep you until we meet again," he whispered.

Søren tore Max away from Kari, and she slid into the Caddy's front seat. As she glanced up, Søren's eyes caught and held her.

Blue. So blue! Like mine.

"Not goodbye," she managed. "Just *Gud gå med deg*."

The tanned lines around his eyes crinkled. "*Ja*, Kari Thoresen Michaels. *Ser deg snart*. We'll look for you soon."

∾ ✻ ∿

CHAPTER 2

The caddy raced down the open road, and Kari's view through the car's new windshield was flawless. Hot August sunlight poured down upon her head; miles of road blended together and sped by.

At first, Kari's thoughts insisted on revisiting those last moments before she left Søren and Max. The feel of their arms about her persisted and sparked a longing in her.

Lord, I left part of myself with them. Please help me to keep Søren and Max tucked safely in my heart until I can return. O God, bless them and keep them safe.

Kari wrenched her thoughts away from the image of Søren's blue eyes and focused her prayers on the tasks she would face when she returned to New Orleans. *I know I have responsibilities waiting for me, Lord, and I know you have spoken to me regarding Elaine and Samuel.*

Once she had remembered her siblings, the desire to find them had begun pressing her. Her need had grown stronger, more urgent, during her last week on Søren's farm—until yesterday.

Yesterday, they had attended the little church in RiverBend. The pastor had preached on the parable of the lost sheep from the Gospel of Luke— and the preaching of God's word had calmed her. Given her focus.

"Suppose one of you has a hundred sheep
and loses one of them.
Doesn't he leave the ninety-nine
in the open country
and go after the lost sheep until he finds it?
And when he finds it, he joyfully
puts it on his shoulders and goes home.
Then he calls his friends and neighbors together and says,
'Rejoice with me; I have found my lost sheep.'
I tell you that in the same way
there will be more rejoicing in heaven
over one sinner who repents
than over ninety-nine righteous persons
who do not need to repent."

The pastor's message had not focused upon the one sinner who repents but rather on the compassionate heart of God. "Love," he told the congregation, "involves risk. Love requires sacrifice.

"See how the shepherd risked his entire flock to retrieve one lost lamb? Every lamb is of value to the Lord who made us in his image. Every lamb is worth the life of the Savior. Every lost lamb is worthy of our diligent pursuit."

At that moment, the parable took on an added dimension for Kari.

O Lord, I have lost two little lambs—Elaine and Sammie. You did not restore my memories for nothing. Now I know that I must be willing to leave everything to seek for them. Thank you for speaking to me with such a clear word.

With that assurance before her, Kari's emotions had settled. With that assurance, she was able to leave Søren and Max and direct her efforts on the search before her.

Her first stop would be Emporia, Kansas, where she would visit with Matthew and Linda O'Dell. Matthew was Kari's uncle, the eldest of Joy and Edmund O'Dell's three sons—Matthew, Jacob, and Luke.

My father's younger half-brothers.

Matthew had offered Kari a gift she yearned to hold: He had offered Kari custodianship of the remainder of Rose Thoresen's journals.

Three more volumes!

Kari shivered with anticipation. She longed to soak up more of Rose's heart through her own words.

Matthew had brought the journals with him to the family reunion at Søren's farm to compare their handwriting to the handwriting in the journal Kari had found. However, when Matthew and his brothers had opened the old book, they had recognized Rose's distinctive hand on the spot. And after they determined that Kari was, indeed, their niece and had seen her love for Rose and her writings, they decided that she was the appropriate caretaker for the remainder of Rose's journals.

Unfortunately, with the emotional upheaval of that weekend, Matthew had forgotten to remove Rose's other journals from his RV and had unintentionally taken them back home. Kari was now on her way to Emporia to pick them up.

The stop was only a little out of her way. Besides, she was looking forward to seeing her uncle again. *I have uncles! And aunts, and cousins, and second cousins, and . . .* Her newfound wealth of relations and family friends was a continual wonder.

"I can't say I'm sorry that you must fetch Grandma's journals from our home, Kari," Matthew had said over the phone. "With meeting nearly one hundred new family members last week, you were a bit overwhelmed—and we had to share you with others. What we need is a nice, calm, quiet visit to get to know you better."

I completely agree, Kari thought as the Caddy ate up the miles.

In the late afternoon, Kari wound through the neighborhood where Matthew and Linda lived and found their modest home.

If ever an image epitomized the proverbial house with the white picket fence, this is it, Kari marveled. The cottage-style home was surrounded by a beautifully groomed lawn and lush, overflowing flowerbeds—and yes, an old-fashioned white wooden fence. The fence, with its pointed pickets, spanned the front of the yard and down both sides.

Kari pulled into the driveway. Almost immediately Matthew and Linda rushed out to greet her.

Their arms enveloped Kari and she melted into their welcoming embrace. Kari was again struck by Matthew's kind eyes as he pulled away to look at her.

"I can't get over how much you resemble Mother," Matthew whispered. "Every time I see you, it takes me back to when I was a little boy watching her in the kitchen baking or doing dishes."

He chuckled. "It refreshes my heart—makes me feel young again!"

Linda took Kari's overnight bag while Matthew pulled Kari's small bag from the trunk and lifted his chin toward the front door. "As soon as we knew you were coming, we pulled out every photo album containing pictures of Mother and Dad. We can't wait to show them to you."

Kari swallowed. "You have pictures?"

"Oh, yes. We have pictures!" Matthew said as Linda drew Kari toward the house. "Dad became quite the amateur photographer after we kids were born. He had a little darkroom in a shed in the back yard and always carried a camera with him. We also have pictures of Grandma Rose."

"What?" Kari stopped halfway up the walk. "You have photographs of Rose?"

"Come and see."

Kari followed them gladly.

Hours later, replete from a late dinner and filled to the brim with all the memories Matthew had shared with her, Kari still pored over the albums. Matthew had carried them into the guest room for her private perusal.

She studied the old black and white photographs pasted into the books, many of them cracking with age.

When I engage someone to replicate the family photos on Søren's wall, I will have him come here and photograph these, too, Kari decided. *They need to be reproduced before the originals fall to pieces.*

Kari scrutinized her favorite photograph of Rose. It was taken, Matthew said, when Rose was in her early eighties. Edmund O'Dell had captured Rose in a moment of reflection. The clarity of that black-and-white image spoke to Kari's heart.

I will have the copy of this one framed so I can place it near my bed, Kari decided.

Rose sat at a table in a straight-backed chair with her Bible open before her. Her hair, braided and pinned at the back of her head, was silver, streaked with even lighter strands. One hand rested on the Bible's open pages, but her face was turned slightly away, her eyes focused on some distant point.

Kari took in the old-fashioned organdy dress Rose wore. Although she could not tell the color of the flowing fabric, the pattern was lovely, the lace on the collar beautiful in its simplicity.

It was the expression on Rose's face that captivated Kari. She thought that some other woman caught in the same unguarded pose might have projected sadness or vulnerability, but Rose's photograph did not. Although Rose's head was turned a fraction from the camera, Kari could see and study Rose's countenance.

A strong chin.

Firm but sweet mouth.

Steady, calm eyes.

Soft gray, Matthew had told her.

It was a portrait of confident, patient hope.

Kari touched Rose's face with her fingertips.

Rose. My great-grandmother! What a legacy you and Jan left to us. I thank you from the bottom of my heart.

Matthew, Linda, and Kari lingered over breakfast the next morning. Kari had not yet told Matthew and Linda that she had recalled the memories of the night her parents died. As they sat down to eat in the morning, she had to first explain about her lifetime of panic attacks. About *The Black*.

"All my life," Kari began, "from as early as I could remember, I have had panic attacks. If I tried to think about Mommy and Daddy, I would grow anxious. If I tried to push the anxiety down and still think about them, the anxiety would turn into a panic attack. So, of course, I avoided thinking about them.

"The worst part, though, was this dream I had, this awful, recurring nightmare. In it I felt like I had forgotten something, something important. But the more I tried to remember what it was, the worse the nightmare grew. A horrid, dark mist, what I named *The Black*, would smother and swallow me. Sometimes a voice would say, *We don't want her. We don't want her!* As a kid, I woke up screaming more times than I can count."

Linda took Kari's hand. "I'm so sorry, Kari! Anxiety attacks are no laughing matter. I had a few after our son Richard had a serious accident. But I couldn't understand how they took over like that, why they overwhelmed me."

"I didn't understand them at first, either," Matthew confessed. "Linda is not a worrier. She is one of the calmest, most levelheaded individuals I know. And her faith is unshakable."

Linda nodded. "I was able, after a few episodes, to grasp the fact that the attacks were a physical response rather than a mental one. And after I figured out that I was not dying, that the symptoms would pass, I learned to wait them out. After a few months, the incidents eased and finally stopped."

She studied Kari with compassion. "I guess I got off easy. A six-year-old would have much more difficulty coping with an anxiety attack, especially a newly orphaned six-year-old. And to be oppressed like that your whole life? O my dear. I am so sorry."

Linda's loving empathy caused Kari to swallow. Hard. "Yes, well, I coped as best I could, mainly by avoiding the trigger, which was thinking about my parents. Then, after my divorce I started seeing a counselor, a therapist who deals with domestic violence. Anthony, the private investigator I hired for my divorce, recommended her. Her name is Ruth."

Kari chuckled a little as she remembered meeting Ruth. "I knew that Anthony was a Christian—he makes no bones about it—but Ruth was the first Christian I'd encountered to actually share Jesus and the Gospel with me—to challenge me, to confront me with my need for a savior, I guess."

Her chortle ended as a sardonic grin. "Let me say that her straightforward approach didn't go over well with me!"

She laughed and Matthew and Linda joined her. "Ruth brought Jesus into *every single conversation*, and I thought, *Good heavens, woman! Give it a rest already!*

"Then Ruth started digging around in my life, digging into places I didn't want to go. Ruth wanted to know about my childhood and, of course, because we were talking about Mommy and Daddy, I had a panic attack. Right there in her office."

Kari looked at her aunt and uncle. "As it was taking me over, Ruth did the most amazing thing. She wrapped her arms around me and said she would stay with me, that it would pass and she would stay right there with me until it did.

"Ruth is a very loving person. Her willingness to be with me—to share in my discomfort—affected me more deeply than I cared to admit.

"Well, after that, I told her everything about the panic attacks, about the nightmares, about *The Black*. Ruth suggested that I might be suppressing an early childhood memory. Of course, I had no idea what that memory might be. And, as much as I resented her preaching at me, because I had opened up to her I also started to trust her.

"Anyway, after I moved to New Orleans, found Rose's journal, and started reading it, the anxiety and nightmares eased. For the most part."

Caught up in Kari's tale, Matthew and Linda sat, with mouths slack, forks on their plates next to the unfinished remains of their breakfast.

Matthew's kind eyes sought Kari's. "I think we saw you have a panic attack in Søren and Ilsa's living room—after we told you that Joy and Grant's baby son Edmund had been kidnapped and that you were Edmund's daughter."

Kari nodded. "Yes. I guess you did."

"What has changed, Kari? You have a point to make here, yes?"

Kari loved her uncle more at that moment. "Well, something else happened after everyone had left the family reunion."

Matthew and Linda leaned toward her. "Will you tell us?" Linda asked.

Kari nodded. "It's what I've been working up to," she whispered.

Taking a deep breath, Kari plunged ahead. "That night the old, ugly nightmare came again, but it started differently. I was standing on the dirt road that runs by Søren's farm, the one that runs out onto the prairie. I saw people walking toward me. Happy people. Mommy and Daddy were with them, and they reached for me.

"It was so real, *they* were so real, that I could smell Daddy's cologne. But then the same old nightmare intruded. Before Daddy reached me, that dreadful curtain—*The Black*—came down to separate us. As always, I was struggling to hang on to something important, but I couldn't grasp it, couldn't find it.

"In this dream, for the first time *ever*, Daddy reached me. I put my head on his shoulder and he held me."

Kari wept for the exquisite joy of that moment, and Matthew placed his hand upon hers and stroked it.

"I felt safe. Loved! And, oh! I wanted to stay with him, but *The Black* was lurking close by. Then, without warning, I was standing—not on the road by Søren's farm, but by a highway in the dark. I was back from the road, standing in the weeds. I could see a very little by moonlight. Everything else, all around me, was dark. Shadowed."

"I could see the outline of our car closer to the highway. Daddy and Mommy had put me a distance from the road. The car had broken down and they were trying to fix it, I think."

Kari stared into Matthew and Linda's curious and concerned faces. "Daddy said, *Wait here where it's safe. Watch over them for us.* He hugged me and then he and Mommy went back to the car to try to fix it."

Matthew and Linda exchanged confused glances.

Kari rushed on. "I remembered then, seeing the lights rush toward our car, toward Mommy and Daddy. A truck. A big one. I remember the horrible, crashing, tearing sounds. Then silence."

Kari stared at the table. "I didn't want to look anymore, but Daddy's voice urged me to be brave. To look. To remember. So I kept dreaming, but in the dream, I remembered the accident. And more. You see, Uncle Matthew, I remembered everything *The Black* had been hiding from me all these years."

She shivered. "Mommy and Daddy had moved us away from the side of the highway because it didn't have much of a shoulder. I was supposed to watch Elaine and Sammie and keep them safe."

Matthew choked a little. "Who . . . who are Elaine and Sammie, Kari?"

"That's what I'm trying to tell you. I remembered them—my little sister. My baby brother."

"You are saying that you remember having a younger brother and sister?" Matthew was floored. Stunned. Linda's face expressed the same disbelief and alarm.

"Yes. Elaine and Samuel. Sammie." Kari sighed. "Elaine was three, I think. Sammie was an infant. Maybe six months? He was lying in a little car seat thing. Elaine was sitting on a blanket next to him."

She glanced up and saw their doubts. "I know. Believe, me, I know. I cannot believe that I forgot them for so many years. And there's more. Apparently we were taken somewhere, perhaps nearby or into Albuquerque.

"I don't know exactly where, but the room was very bright. A woman—a social worker?—was there. And a man and a woman. A couple. The man picked up Elaine. The woman had Sammie.

"The man said they would take Elaine and Sammie but *they didn't want me*. The social worker said it was all right—that I wouldn't remember or talk about them.

"The woman grabbed me and slapped me and said, *If you ever mention your sister or brother to anyone—if you ever say their names—well, very bad things will happen to them. Do you hear me? In fact, if you ever even **think** about your sister or brother again, I will know it, and I will have that man and woman throw your sister and brother in a river to drown*."

Linda recoiled in horror; Matthew's face turned dark red and he growled deep in his throat.

Kari didn't notice their reactions. "*The Black* surrounded me. That's when it started. The nightmares and panic attacks. Anyway, when I remembered the man and woman taking Elaine and Sammie, I must have started screaming in my sleep. The next thing I knew, Søren, Ilsa, and Max were in my room. I told them about the dream. I told them everything I remembered. Told them about Elaine and Sammie."

Kari dropped her face into her hands and sobbed. "But, still! I forgot my own sister and brother? How could I? I'm so ashamed!"

"Stuff and nonsense, Kari Thoresen Michaels. You stop that right now."

Shocked at the steel undergirding Matthew's words, Kari sat up and wiped her face.

He waved a finger over his plate of cold eggs. "The Accuser of the Brethren—Satan, if you are unfamiliar with this passage of Scripture—wants to condemn a six-year-old child for being unable to cope with an event that would have sent many an adult to the loony bin? You must begin to exercise discipline over your thoughts, Kari. Reject any blame for not remembering your siblings. Fix your faith and courage on what is ahead. Focus your mental and emotional energy on what you need to do. You're going to find them, aren't you?"

"Yes. At least I'm going to try."

"Try? Don't think for a minute that God brought these memories back to you so you could stew in defeat the rest of your days, Kari." The uncle Kari had considered merely kind and gentle was showing a very different side—a spine and a will of iron.

"This is a lot to take in," Linda murmured.

"Yes, but it is a call to action, not an invitation to a pity party," Matthew replied.

Kari ducked her head. "I'm sorry."

Matthew frowned. "Please reserve those two words for instances where they are appropriate. You have no cause to be sorry or to apologize, especially to us. Now—"

He gathered Linda's hand in one hand and reached for Kari's hand with the other; Linda clasped Kari's free hand, completing the circle. "Let's fight this battle where the war is being waged: In the spiritual realm."

He bowed his head. "Father God, you are the maker of heaven and earth. Your eyes roam to and fro across the earth and see everything. In you the lost are found. You found Kari, Lord God, and brought her back to her family. More importantly than that, you brought her to Jesus.

"Your plans span eternity, Lord God, and yet you are attentive to the very hairs on our heads. Now, Lord, you are revealing the next part of your plan for Kari. I am confident, Father, that you opened her memories 'in due season,' which means at the right time to accommodate your plans!

"Therefore we ask you, in the mighty name of Jesus, to lead her and guide her. Help her find Elaine and Sammie. According to your will let it be done, Lord, and may you receive the glory. Amen."

"Amen!" Kari repeated. Matthew's few simple words of prayer had galvanized her.

"What will you do first?" Linda asked, squeezing Kari's hand before letting it go.

"I will head to Albuquerque from here. I want to hire Anthony Esquibel, the investigator I used for my divorce. He has a lot of contacts in Albuquerque and Bernalillo County. He will know how to get started. And when I return to New Orleans, I will ask my attorney's investigator to join him."

"What does your friend Ruth say about all this, Kari?" Linda asked.

"I-I haven't told Ruth about Elaine and Samuel yet, but I will when I get to Albuquerque."

"Not to be indelicate, Kari, but these things take money. We—" Matthew looked to Linda for confirmation. "You are family. We can help a little. We will give what we can, and I am certain others will, too, when they hear about Elaine and Samuel."

Kari's mouth curved into a sweet smile and grew larger. "Those are about the most precious words I have ever heard, Uncle Matthew, but money won't be an issue."

The couple looked dubious. "Um, are you sure? Things have a way of costing more than we think."

Kari looked at both of them. "Please don't shout this from the rooftops, but Peter Granger left me a wealthy woman. That is to say, he left me and *my siblings* wealthy. Trust me when I say I have plenty of money. I am grateful to God that I can well afford whatever we need in the months ahead."

Linda blinked. Matthew muttered, "Well, then!"

Kari grinned more. "It is justice of sorts, don't you agree, that everything Peter Granger—or Dean Morgan, if you prefer—spent his lifetime acquiring should come to those he injured the most?"

Kari's head tipped to the side a bit. "In fact, shouldn't you and Jacob and Luke—who had to watch your mom grieve for her lost son—shouldn't you and your families share in my bounty?"

Matthew was already shaking his head. "No, no. There's no need, Kari. Don't give that another thought."

"If you say so, Uncle Matthew." But Kari tucked the idea away to think on more later.

Linda stood up. "Look at us! Look at the time! It's closer now to lunch than breakfast."

She started clearing the table and Kari jumped up to help. "Yes; I should probably get on the road again."

After Linda and Kari had cleared away the dishes, Matthew appeared with three volumes in his hand. The books were identical in size but their leather covers were differing colors.

"I don't want to forget to give these to you a second time."

Kari held the books in her hands with awe. "I cannot thank you enough for trusting me with Rose's other journals, Uncle Matthew."

"We pray they will be a blessing to you, Kari. In the same way the first one brought you to Jesus, we pray these will encourage you as you go forward."

Kari said nothing, but she caressed the cover of the top book.

As Kari pointed the caddy back onto the highway, she took courage from Matthew's prayer, and she prayed aloud for herself.

"Lord, my uncle and my cousins urge me to trust you. They say that you will help me through this difficult transition. And they say that *you* know where Elaine and Samuel are, that I can trust you—that in you the lost are found!

"I am so new to this faith thing, though. It is hard to believe you will find them after so many years.

"Nevertheless, I set my heart and mind on you. As Uncle Matthew said, I must fix my faith and courage upon the task ahead. I confess my trust in *you*, Lord—not in my own ideas, not in the abilities of my investigators, not in the money I can throw at this effort, but in *you*. Where you lead me, I will follow."

Kari took a deep breath and added, "I believe you work all things together for my good, so I will trust and rest in you. Amen."

CHAPTER 3

Kari reached Albuquerque the following afternoon and checked into the downtown Marriott. As soon as she reached her room, she dialed Ruth's number from memory.

"Ruth?"

"Kari? It's so good to hear your voice. Are you back in town?"

"Yes, I just got here. Can't wait to see you. I, er, a lot has happened in the last few weeks."

"You sound different, Kari."

No kidding! You thought my inheriting Peter Granger's estate was life-altering? Not even! Now my whole world has been turned upside down.

And Jesus! O my Jesus!

"Some interesting things have happened, Ruth. I can't wait to tell you."

They chatted for a few minutes before Kari asked, "May I treat you to dinner tonight? How about *El Pinto*? I could use a 'green chile fix.'"

"I'd love that," Ruth answered.

"Would you mind . . . I'd like to ask Anthony and Gloria to join us."

"Of course not. I would enjoy their company."

Ruth changed tack. "You were gone almost three weeks. Did you uncover any more about the woman who wrote the journal?"

"Um, yes, actually. That is part of what I want to tell you, but it will take a while to explain everything."

"Well, you have aroused my curiosity."

Kari laughed. "Shall we say six o'clock? And I warn you again that my tale will take time to tell. I will probably monopolize the conversation."

They hung up, and Kari looked for and dialed Anthony's office number. A receptionist answered on the first ring.

"Esquibel Investigations."

"Good afternoon. This is Kari, um, Hillyer. Kari Hillyer. Is Mr. Esquibel in the office?"

"One moment, please."

Good grief. I need to decide what my name is and have Clover get it fixed as soon as possible.

"Kari?"

"Hi, Anthony!"

"It *is* you! Are you in town?"

"Yes. For a day or so. Are you and Gloria free this evening? Would you allow me to take you to dinner? Ruth will be joining us, too."

"I'm sure we'd love to. Where and when?"

"El Pinto at six?"

"Thank you. We'll see you then. Looking forward to it, Kari."

As Kari replaced the phone's receiver, she decided to call Søren. Recalling how early Søren, Ilsa, and Max retired, she started dialing.

If I wait until after I get back from dinner, he will likely be in bed!

The phone rang twice before Kari heard Max's breathless voice on the other end.

"Hello?"

Kari's heart swelled at the sound of his voice. "Hey, Max!"

"Hay is for horses!" He giggled and Kari had to pull the receiver away from her ear as he shouted, "It's Kari!"

Then he said, "Where are you, Kari? Are you okay? I miss you sooo much!"

"I bet you only miss my help with your chores in the morning," Kari teased.

"It's awfully dull around here without you, and I sure miss your company in the barn."

The utter pathos in the boy's voice crushed Kari. "I'm sorry, Max. I miss you, too. I'm in Albuquerque."

"She's in Al-berkerkee," Max whispered to someone.

"Let me talk to her."

It was Søren's voice and Kari sighed and smiled at the same time.

"But I just started talkin' to her!"

"I'll let you say goodbye before we hang up," Søren insisted.

"Well, shoot." *Sigh.* "Here's Dad, Kari."

"I love you, Max." The words flowed out of Kari the way water gushed from the pump in the farm yard.

"I love you back, Kari!"

Then Søren's gravelly voice came on the line. "Kari?"

"Yes, it's me. How are you?"

"We're fine. We've been wondering about you."

It was a minor accusation.

"I've only been gone two nights!"

"*Three days* and two nights! We've been worried."

Then they were laughing until Søren whispered, "It's wonderful to hear your voice, Kari. We have missed you every one of those three days."

"I-I miss you, too."

She told him the short version of her visit with Matthew and Linda, told him she would be having dinner with Ruth and Anthony and his wife.

"I will get Anthony started on the search for Elaine and Samuel and head back to NOLA as soon as he has everything he needs from me."

"Call again when you get to New Orleans?"

"Yes. I promise."

"Well, *I* promised Max he could say good-bye."

Kari could have stayed on the phone with Søren longer, but she whispered, "All right."

"Kari?" Max launched into a long description of his pig, the one he hoped to enter in the state fair in September.

After a few minutes of replying, "Oh?" and "Hmm," and "Yes" to his excited gabble, Søren's voice in the background interrupted.

"Long distance is costly, Son, and she has a meeting she needs to get ready for."

"Oh, all right," Max grumbled. "Dad says I have t' let you go. Bye, Kari."

"Don't ever let me go, Max," Kari murmured, thinking he was hanging up.

Instead, Søren's voice came over the line. "I won't let you go, either, Kari."

Kari blushed and couldn't think of what to say.

"I'll talk to you soon," Søren whispered. "Until then, know that I am thinking of you."

The line went dead, but Kari kept the receiver to her ear, replaying Søren's last words over and over.

Kari had stayed on Søren and Ilsa's farm a bit more than two weeks and had been on the road for three days.

It's time for something dressier than jeans and boots.

Most of the nicer clothes she had brought on her journey had been unpacked and hung multiple times but never worn. Kari placed a sleeveless spring-green sheath on a hanger. She filled a small steamer, plugged it in, and spent five minutes working the wrinkles from the soft, nubby fabric.

Satisfied with the results, Kari laid a wide beige belt of woven natural fibers on the bed and a pair of complementary espadrilles with wedge heels on the floor. Kari matched the buckle with a long gold necklace, dangly earrings, and three bangles for her wrist. She placed the jewelry on the bed next to the belt and wandered into the bathroom to shower.

Much later, with her long hair freshly washed, dried, and hanging loose about her shoulders, Kari dressed for dinner. Then she called the front desk and asked for her car to be brought around.

The drive to El Pinto took close to thirty minutes as Kari battled rush hour traffic on I-25. She exited the freeway at Alameda, drove west toward the river, then turned right onto 4th Street. The road narrowed and wound through a rustic neighborhood shaded in old-growth cottonwoods until she turned into the adobe-walled compound.

More sprawling cottonwood trees shaded the gravel parking lot. Kari left her Caddy and made her way to the restaurant's portico. Ivy climbed upon the stucco walls, and large terracotta pots, overflowing with flowering geraniums and tall cannas, framed the entrance.

Ruth was waiting for her in the lobby. Kari reached for her and they embraced in a long hug.

"I'm so glad to see you, Ruth!"

"Me, too, Cookie," Ruth answered. "And I'm looking forward to hearing about your little adventure."

Kari's laugh came out in a snort. "Well, it will take most of the evening to tell you the abridged version of my 'little' adventure."

She had requested a table for four when Anthony and Gloria came through the entrance. After they had exchanged hugs all around, the hostess took them to their table.

The waiter took their beverage orders and left chips and salsa. Anthony, Gloria, and Ruth began nibbling on the chips, but Kari was too nervous to eat. She was grateful when the waiter returned with their drinks. She gulped half of her iced tea while the waiter took their dinner orders. As soon as he left the table, Kari began.

"I asked you here for dinner because I have so many things to tell you. What I have to say may take longer to tell than it takes us to eat—and, near the end, Anthony," Kari sipped on her tea, "I will be asking for your investigative help."

Kari's companions turned their collective stares on her, but she forged ahead. "There isn't any quick or easy way to tell you everything except to begin at the beginning. I apologize in advance for monopolizing the conversation. I came through Albuquerque only three weeks ago; however, in those three weeks everything in my life has changed. The most important thing that has changed . . ."

Kari's eyes began to smart and she glanced down. "The most important thing is that I have given my life to Jesus."

Ruth gasped. "Truly, Kari?"

Anthony and Gloria were murmuring, "Thank you, Jesus!" over and over. Tears leaked down Gloria's face. Kari found that she could not hold her own tears back.

"Truly, Ruth. He is my Savior now!" Kari's throat was clogged with emotion and her words were thick. "But that is not all. *How* he showed himself to me is the best part of the amazing, mind-boggling story I am about to tell you."

Without anyone saying a word, they joined hands around the table, and Ruth spontaneously prayed, "O God! Our awesome God! You are more wonderful than we can imagine. Thank you! Thank you for bringing Kari into your kingdom! Thank you for drawing her to yourself, Lord!"

Anthony continued where Ruth left off. "Yes, Lord. We are filled with joy, and we praise you. We worship you! We give you the glory. Lord, make our fellowship this night precious in your sight."

When they loosed hands, Ruth, Anthony, and Gloria stared at Kari as though mesmerized.

"Tell us what happened, Kari," Ruth demanded.

Kari wiped at her eyes. "I will. So, Anthony and Gloria, you already know that I inherited Peter Granger's house. His attorneys have maintained the house in perfect condition all these years, and I moved into it not long after I went to New Orleans. The house also has a garage, one of those old, detached kinds, behind the house."

Kari uttered a soft laugh and swiped at her drippy nose. "That's where it all began."

"In the garage?" Anthony's look was more quizzical than his question.

"Yup. In the garage."

"Okaaaay . . ."

They all laughed and Ruth spoke up.

"I know this part, but you need to hear it. Go ahead, Kari."

"Yes, well, I'll make this as 'bare bones' as I can. In the attic of the garage, you see, I found an antique trunk. It was filled with Alicia Granger's clothing. Alicia was, supposedly, my father's mother."

"Wait. *Supposedly?*" Ruth was the first of Kari's listeners to object.

"It will work better if you just let me tell it, Ruth," Kari suggested, wiggling one eyebrow.

"But . . ." Ruth blinked and, after a moment, shrugged. "All right."

"So you found a trunk." Anthony goaded Kari back to her tale.

"I did. And at the bottom of the trunk I found a journal."

"And a letter," Ruth put in.

Kari shook her head. "I'm trying to simplify. Otherwise we'll be here all night."

"Go on, Kari," Gloria urged. "Whose journal?"

"It belonged to a woman named Rose Thoresen. It was written between April 1909 and April 1911. I had no idea who this woman was or why or how her journal ended up in my great-uncle's garage."

"In a trunk. In the garage's attic," Gloria repeated. "And you didn't know who this Rose person was?"

"Right. No clue."

"Ooooh! I love a good mystery," Gloria chuckled.

Anthony squeezed his wife's hand. "Love, please let her get on with it."

Kari sipped her tea again. "Well, I read the journal more than once, and found out two things about Rose. The first was that she was a Christian. You probably know how I felt about *that*—but how she wrote about her walk with God? Even though I resisted, it captured my heart. She wrote about the events of each day and prayed right along as she wrote. What I mean is, it was all blended together. It was natural. Beautiful. I-I didn't know you could know God like that."

Three heads nodded.

"And the other thing?" came from Anthony.

"The other thing was how Rose described the work that she and her daughter, Joy, were doing. Someone gave them a big house in Denver, Colorado, one of those ornate, Queen Anne or Victorian houses with three floors and lots of personality? The house was pretty rundown, but Rose and Joy needed all that space. You see, they were engaged in rescuing young women out of, um, prostitution. They got them out and then led them to Jesus."

"Oh!" Gloria whispered.

"They called the place Palmer House—after the woman who had donated the house to their ministry. Anyway, I read her journal over and over, and I sort of fell in love with Rose. I wanted to find out more about her—what happened to her, to Joy, and to Palmer House."

"Interesting," Anthony commented. "So, this is why you drove to Denver?"

"Yes. Ruth knew this part of the story, but I'm about to get to the part she doesn't yet know."

At that moment, the waiter arrived with their dinners. No one at the table spoke until he left. Then her guests looked at Kari and waited for her to continue.

Kari stared at the plate in front of her. "I won't be able to eat and talk at the same time." She glanced up. "Why don't you go ahead and I'll keep telling you what happened. I will have this boxed up to take back to the hotel."

They joined hands again for a blessing, and then Ruth, Gloria, and Anthony began to eat. Kari picked up her tale.

"Rose's journal mentioned the name of the person who had built Palmer House—Martha Palmer's husband, Chester—and described the house's general location, so I went to the courthouse and searched their records. I looked through microfilm for hours, and I finally found the property listing and the address. I had a cab take me to the house.

"It was as Rose had described it—a beautiful old house with towers, turrets, peaks, and gables and, you know, *gingerbread*. It sat on a huge corner lot and looked like someone still lived there, so I sort of walked up the front porch steps to the door and scoped things out."

"Okay," Ruth said for the rest of them.

"I looked around the porch and at the door. The door had this huge brass door knocker. Very cool looking. Antique."

"What then?" Ruth asked.

"Well, then I used that old brass knocker. You should have heard it echo when I let it drop on that solid wood door!"

Gloria and Ruth giggled; Anthony was appalled.

"You knocked on the door of a stranger's house?" Anthony demanded.

Ruth defended Kari. "Well, of course she did. What else would she do?"

"But this Rose person—I mean, she has to be dead. And all the other people she talked about in her journal? They have to be dead, too, right?"

Kari's smile glowed. "As a matter of fact, one person mentioned in Rose's journal is still alive. And guess what? She lives at Palmer House."

Ruth's fork clanked on her plate. "No! Seriously? Who?"

"One of the women who lived at Palmer House, one of the ex-, er, prostitutes, a Chinese girl by the name of Mei-Xing Li, had a baby, a little girl she named Shan-Rose. Rose described Shan-Rose in her journal along with her daughter Joy, Joy's husband Grant, and their infant son, Edmund. Shan-Rose is in her eighties now, but she still lives at Palmer House!

"Of course, I couldn't believe my luck—which, of course wasn't *luck*, because *God*—well, I'll get to that. So I asked if Shan-Rose could tell me a little about Rose. As you can imagine, she knew who Rose was, but she was very surprised that I was inquiring about her. Anyhow, she invited me inside and asked how I knew about Rose."

Kari directed her next comment to Ruth. "You can't know how thrilled I was to be inside Palmer House! To see the great room Rose had described so vividly! To be where Rose had once been. I was almost overcome."

She looked from eye to eye around the table. "But that's when it got weird. Really, really weird."

"I knew it!" Anthony growled. "You should never have walked up to a stranger's door and knocked, let alone gone inside. What were you thinking?"

"No. I'm sorry, dear Anthony, but you are wrong." Kari's response was gentle but firm. "If I hadn't done exactly that, I would likely not be a Christian today."

Anthony's mouth opened a little. Gloria nudged her husband's ribs. "Let her finish, *Corazón*. She has more to tell us, I think." She turned to Kari. "So what do you mean by 'weird'?"

Kari nodded. "Not merely weird. *Really* weird. I showed Shan-Rose the journal and she *demanded* to know where I'd gotten it. I thought she or her great-niece, the snotty teenager who takes care of her, were going to snatch it right out of my hands! The minute they laid eyes on Rose's journal, they both acted like they'd seen a ghost.

"Well, I wasn't going to let anyone take Rose's journal, so I got up to leave. That's when Shan-Rose apologized. She was quite sincere, so I stayed. She asked if I would come back the next day. Promised she would tell me all about Rose, answer any questions I had. Mixxie—that's Shan-Rose's niece—said her aunt was overtired and would be at her best in the morning, so I agreed to come back the next day."

"And did you?" Ruth hadn't eaten another bite.

"Yes, of course. I came back around nine in the morning—and the situation got *weirder*. Instead of only Shan-Rose and her great-niece, a big crowd had gathered. I mean, they had a caterer setting up a breakfast bar in the dining room, for heaven's sake! And about twenty people, all Chinese except for one Anglo man and woman, were standing around, talking.

"When I walked in, every last one of them stared at me like I was an exotic bug. *Stared* at me. I won't go into all the details, but Shan-Rose's brother, Quan—Mixxie's grandfather—told me that the journal had gone missing a long time ago and they were curious as to how I'd come to have it in my possession.

"At first, I resisted their questions. When Quan assured me that they were not going to take Rose's journal away from me, I told them about inheriting Peter Granger's estate and how I'd found the book in the trunk in the garage.

"So then it got even stranger. As it turns out, all the Chinese in the room were descended from Mei-Xing, and the two Anglos were descended from Palmer House's housekeeper, Breona. That was interesting to me, because Rose had described Breona in her journal, too."

Kari shrugged. "Everything was *so* weird, but all the history of Rose's journal coming to life right there in front of me was riveting—and that's what kept me from running out the door.

"Then they asked me more questions—especially about my father. They wanted to know his name and his birthday, and then they wanted to know about my great-uncle, Peter Granger."

Anthony shifted uneasily and made a disgruntled sound in his throat.

Kari shook her head. "Please be patient. I'm getting there. Still a long way to go, though."

"Well, get on with it!" Ruth's impatience made Kari grin.

"All right, all right. As the morning went along, I felt more and more like Alice and that I'd fallen straight through the looking glass. Finally, the gathering started breaking up. Shan-Rose's brother, Quan, said that Shan-Rose needed to take a nap, but that the Anglo woman, Alannah Carmichael, would show me around the house."

Kari stilled. "It was while we were on the second floor of the house that Jesus spoke to me."

Ruth, Gloria, and Anthony stilled, too.

"Shan-Rose keeps the bottom floor of Palmer House in lovely condition, decorated with beautiful furnishings that fit the house's period and architecture. But when Alannah and I went upstairs? I was so disappointed. Of course, no one lives on the second or third floors now or had lived upstairs for a long while. The bedrooms smelled musty and felt abandoned. The furnishings had a dreary 'seventies' feel to them—not at all what I'd imagined.

"I was pretty let down. So when we came to Rose's room, I refused to open the door. I didn't want to be disillusioned further. I stood in the hall and told myself that I would imagine the room the way Rose had described it in her journal.

"I leaned against her door and sort of started talking to Rose—as if she were in the room on the other side of the door. I know that sounds odd, but I told her I wished she could have been there to tell me about her Jesus. I think it was the first time I had admitted to myself that I wanted to know Jesus like Rose knew him."

Kari's voice dropped to a whisper. "And that's when . . . Jesus spoke to me. He told me he was waiting for me to open the door between us. *Behold I stand at the door and knock*, he said. I didn't know that was actually a Scripture verse. I only knew that he was calling me to surrender my life to him.

"And I did."

❧ ✳ ❧

CHAPTER 4

No one at the table moved or spoke. The waiter approached, but Anthony waved him away. The moment was too holy to be disturbed.

Finally, Kari whispered, "That dim hallway in Palmer House filled up . . . with Jesus. I could not stand under the weight of his presence. Alannah felt him, too. We both sank to our knees, and wept for the beauty of it, the majesty of Jesus' . . . holiness, I guess. All I knew was that when I cried out to Rose that I wanted to know her Jesus, *he* answered me! He said, *I am here*. And when I surrendered, I could feel him working inside me. He was washing all the ugly, dirty parts of me away.

"After a while, Alannah and I got up and went downstairs, but I knew I would never be the same. Rose's Jesus was now my Jesus. He *is* my Jesus now."

Kari's tear-stained face turned toward Anthony. "So you see, dear Anthony, I don't regret knocking on the door of Palmer House—although things got stranger still."

Anthony nodded, but Kari's last words seemed to snap them out of their hush.

"What things, Kari?" Gloria asked. "Stranger how?"

Kari sighed and gathered her thoughts. "In order to keep my 'tale' manageable, I need to leave a lot of detail out. I'll skip ahead and say that, a few days later, Quan suggested I leave Denver to go visit Rose's homestead in Nebraska! I say 'suggested,' but it was a pretty strong suggestion."

"Homestead?" Anthony and Gloria were confused.

"Yes. Alannah and others told me more about Rose. Apparently, many years before she moved to Denver, Rose had bought an abandoned homestead in Nebraska. That's where she met her husband, Jan Thoresen, Joy's father."

"You pronounce 'Thoresen' differently now," Ruth observed.

Kari chuckled. "Oh, yes! Mixxie set me straight. Apparently the 'Th' is pronounced 'T' and 'Jan' is pronounced 'Yahn.' Mixxie was quick to point out my errors."

Ruth quirked one eyebrow. "She sounds charming."

"Our Mixxie is something else, believe me. Anyway, Quan gave me directions to RiverBend, the little town near Rose's homestead. He said that lots of Thoresens still lived nearby and would be delighted to tell me more about Rose.

"He went so far as to arrange for me to stay with the part of the family living on Jan Thoresen's old homestead. Said they were looking forward to meeting me."

Kari directed a look toward Ruth. "That struck me as odd, you know? Why would these complete strangers want to meet me?"

"Why, indeed," Ruth murmured.

Anthony's forehead creased in puzzlement and disquiet. "So you went? To stay with total strangers?"

Kari nodded.

"*Mija*," Gloria whispered, "Even I can understand Anthony's concern. You are a very wealthy woman now. Was that wise?"

Kari looked down. "Perhaps it wasn't wise, but I think if you had met Quan and Shan-Rose and Alannah and the others you might have felt differently, as I did. It may not have been wise, but it was *God*. This family, these people, they love the Lord with all their hearts. They . . . I felt safe with them. I felt welcome. Loved, even."

Ruth, Gloria, and Anthony looked at each other. Ruth responded, "So you felt safe taking Quan's 'suggestion' to visit Rose's homestead?"

"I did. I was confused as to why they were so insistent, of course, but never for a moment did I feel used or in danger."

"Go on," Anthony asked.

"So I went and I met a man named Søren—Jan Thoresen's great-great-grandson—and Søren's little boy, Max. Max's mother is dead, and Søren's sister, Ilsa, runs the home now. Søren and Ilsa showed me a wall of photographs of the Thoresen families. Jan and his brother, Karl, came from Norway to America in 1866—and their descendants number in the hundreds now.

"The best parts of the wall for me were the pictures of Rose and Joy. There were only a few, but to see Rose's face was priceless. As I looked in her eyes, it was like I knew her."

Anthony expelled a breath. "Well, no harm, no foul. It looks like you came through your adventure unscathed—and actually for the better! I'm so glad you know Jesus for yourself now, Kari."

Kari's mouth curved into a slow, mischievous grin. "Oh, I haven't finished my story yet, Anthony. Not by a long shot. Shall I go on?"

"Yes!" Ruth and Gloria said together.

"I stayed with Søren and Ilsa for the rest of the week. Actually, I couldn't leave because my Caddy had met with an accident. So I was 'stuck' on the farm until the neighborhood mechanic could get me on the road again."

Kari laughed. "I learned a lot about farming that week, let me tell you! I got up before dawn every morning and helped Max with all his chores, then I helped Ilsa can and cook.

"It was quite the learning experience. And I got to see Rose's old homestead, across the creek from Søren's farm. It was a pleasant time, actually. But that next Friday was when everything unfolded."

The waiter appeared again. He frowned at Kari's untouched meal "Was your meal unsatisfactory? May I get you something else?"

"Uh, no; I couldn't eat and talk at the same time. Would you box it up for me? And if you'll clear things away and bring us coffee, we would like to sit and talk a while longer."

"Of course." Taking Kari's hint, he said nothing further and went about his business while Kari continued her story.

"That Friday, after I'd been with Søren and Ilsa for a week, they announced that they were hosting a family reunion of sorts. With only that much warning, a horde of Thoresens and the families I mentioned in Denver descended upon us! Cars, RVs, trailers, and vans full of people. They set up a tent on the lawn like you'd expect to see at a big wedding. And food? Food, food, and more food—because as the day moved on, the crowd grew until a couple hundred people were milling around on the lawn—and they all wanted to meet me. *So strange!*

"That evening, Søren took me into their living room and introduced me to three old gents who were, as he explained, Joy Thoresen Michaels' sons from her second marriage. I knew from what I'd been told in Denver that her first husband, Grant, had died, and that Joy had remarried. These three men were her children."

Ruth, Anthony, and Gloria grew alarmed when Kari broke down.

"What is it, Kari?" Ruth whispered.

"I-I looked around, and my attorney, Clover, from New Orleans was there, too! So was his wife, Lorene. And Owen, Brunell & Brunell's investigator. I was so confused, but Søren asked me to trust them. Clover said everything would be all right."

Anthony muttered, "What in the world . . ."

"I know! I was *so* confused! Søren introduced me to Joy's sons, and they stared at me like I was an apparition and asked to see Rose's journal. Matthew, the oldest of the three, said they would not take her journal from me, so I brought it to them."

"That blamed journal!" Anthony was growling again.

"Yes. But the journal was the key to everything, the thread by which God led me and accomplished his purposes." Kari's voice was so low that the others strained toward her to catch her words.

"Matthew said that he and his brothers had some of Rose's family history to relate to me. He seemed sad, but when I looked in his eyes, they were so kind that I decided to trust him. I said all right, so Matthew told me."

Kari had to stop while the waiter placed steaming cups of coffee in front of the four of them.

"Told you what?" Ruth demanded as soon as the waiter left.

Kari massaged her temples. "First Matthew asked me if Rose's journal had said anything about the father of Mei-Xing's baby. I said, yes, that he had kidnapped Mei-Xing—and months later when she had been found, he was dead, and Mei-Xing was pregnant."

"My head is spinning," Anthony muttered.

"Mine, too," Gloria agreed.

"You think your head is spinning? How do you think I felt?"

Kari spent five minutes introducing them to Su-Chong Chen, his mother, Fang-Hua Chen, Pinkerton detective, Edmund O'Dell, and Mei-Xing's "backstory."

"Some of the details are still a muddle to me, but I think the gist of it is this: After Mr. O'Dell found Mei-Xing and brought her back to Palmer House, and after she had her baby, Mr. O'Dell worried that this nasty Fang-Hua woman might try to take Shan-Rose. Shan-Rose was, after all, Fang-Hua's granddaughter. So Mr. O'Dell took the precaution of assigning guards to Mei-Xing and Palmer House."

"But all this happened years ago, Kari! What does it *matter* at this point?" Ruth said what Anthony and Gloria had to be thinking.

Kari smiled through her tears. "As it turns out, it matters a lot. Matthew told me that on April 12, 1911, Rose put Shan-Rose and Edmund side-by-side in a baby buggy and took them for a walk in the park. She had two armed guards with her. Rose took her journal and her Bible with her. She wrote the last entry in her journal while at the park with the babies."

Kari sobbed and covered her mouth with her hand. She had to stop to gather herself. "As Rose was leaving the park, four men hired by Fang-Hua attacked Rose and her guards. In broad daylight! Fang-Hua's men shot and killed Rose's guards. They shot Rose."

"What? No!" Ruth's mouth hung open. "They shot Rose?"

"Matthew said Rose survived the shooting. But the men Fang-Hua hired kidnapped—" Kari stumbled to a stop, the words stuck in her throat.

Ruth, Gloria, and Anthony slid anxious looks toward each other, but it was Anthony who verbalized their questions. "They kidnapped Shan-Rose. But they recovered her, yes? I mean, you met her in Denver only days ago, right?"

"No, that's not what happened," Kari whispered. "This is the hard part. Those men made a terrible mistake. Apparently, the kidnappers thought Fang-Hua's grandchild was *a boy*. They didn't take Shan-Rose; *they took Edmund*. They took Joy's baby son, Rose's grandson."

"Oh! O Lord Jesus!" Ruth exclaimed.

"Yes, the men who took baby Edmund made a mistake, but their boss, Dean Morgan, the man Fang-Hua hired to oversee the job, hated Joy. I guess they had a history—I'm a little fuzzy on this part—but the upshot is that Morgan despised Joy.

"Anyway, when his men messed up, Morgan decided to take revenge on Joy. He took Edmund and drove away from Denver, never to be seen again. He drove from Denver . . . all the way to New Orleans."

Ruth's whisper was scarcely audible. "New Orleans? But . . ."

Kari lifted her eyes to her friend. "When he arrived in New Orleans, Morgan took on a new name and new identity, that of Peter Granger. He raised Edmund as his nephew, Michael Granger. *My father*."

Ruth grasped Kari's hand. Anthony muttered something to himself in Spanish. Gloria looked from face to face.

"What does it mean?" she asked. "I don't understand! What does it mean?"

Kari could not answer right away. Ruth handed her a tissue and Kari accepted it with a grimace. "The kidnappers inadvertently swept up Rose's journal in the baby's blanket. Peter Granger—the man also known as Dean Morgan—had to have found and kept it. He was the one who placed the journal in the trunk in the garage."

She dabbed at her eyes. "Can you understand why I couldn't tell you everything over the phone? Why I waited until I had you all together?"

Ruth bobbed her head. "Don't give it another thought, *Chica*. This is all quite a lot to take in. So many . . . implications."

"It has been twelve days since they told me," Kari agreed. "I am still trying to grasp all the 'implications.'"

"So Joy's son Edmund grew up as Michael Granger and is your father? You are certain?"

"Yes."

"His mother was Rose's daughter, Joy?"

Kari smiled through more tears. "Yes. Joy is my grandmother and Rose is my great-grandmother!"

Anthony interjected, "Wait a minute. How can you be sure? How can your attorneys be sure? How can they be certain this isn't some elaborate hoax, a plan to rob you of your inheritance?"

Kari sobered before she answered. "I have grown to trust my attorney, Clover Brunell, and he knew Peter Granger personally. When Clover was shown mug shots of Dean Morgan from his stint in jail in 1910, he positively identified him as Peter Granger. There is no doubt at all. But Anthony, there is more."

"More? I'm not sure I can handle 'more'—my head is about to explode as it is!"

Kari sat up straighter in her chair. "But this is where I will need you, Anthony, because as crazy as all this sounds, what I'm about to tell you is crazier."

Now Kari's pace quickened. "I have left out many of the details, but I spent that weekend meeting all of my family—my uncles, aunts, nieces, nephews, cousins galore. It was overwhelming, to say the least. Then, everyone left and it was just Søren, Ilsa, Max, and me again, on the farm. I felt like I would have the time to sort of think about and absorb all the ramifications, you know?"

Kari turned to Ruth. "You remember my recurring nightmare. The panic attacks."

Ruth tucked her chin, acknowledging Kari.

Kari addressed all of them, her intensity growing. "All my life I have had the same dream, a horrible dream from which I always awoke before it finished. In the nightmare a dark curtain came down between me and something that was hidden, something important. Well, I know what the dream was hiding now—what I had not been able to remember since I was a child. After everyone left the family reunion, I had the dream again— only this time the curtain was ripped away and I saw what it was hiding.

"The night my parents died, our car broke down on the side of Route 66 between Gallup and Grants. Before they tried to fix the car, Mommy and Daddy took me off the side of the road into a field. That's where I was when the truck hit my parents. I saw it, but when the police came, I was traumatized, I could not speak. *But now I remember what happened.* In that last dream, I saw it again and I remembered.

"I remembered that my parents set me on the side of the road with my little sister and baby brother. Mommy and Daddy told me to watch over them."

Ruth gasped, and Kari turned toward her.

"I have a sister and a brother, Ruth. They were with me, off the side of the road in the weeds, when the truck hit Mommy and Daddy. I remember now what happened. We believe they were taken away, adopted illegally—sold by a woman, a social worker, we think."

She stared across the table. "That's what I need you for, Anthony. I need you to find my sister and brother."

෨ ❁ ෬

CHAPTER 5

Kari spent the rest of the evening and the next morning at Anthony's office going over her story with him while he took exhaustive notes. By lunchtime, he recapped the only clues he had to go on.

"Your parents were missionaries who returned to the United States on sabbatical in October of 1958. They died October 8, 1958, only a week into their sabbatical. Your sister and brother were born on the mission field, which is why Owen Washington never found a record of their birth. Your sister, Elaine, is approximately three years younger than you, and your brother, Samuel, was an infant, making him about six years younger than you."

"Yes; and I recall part of the social worker's name tag," Kari reminded him. "First name, Marge, last name starting with an *S*."

"That really is the only usable bit of information we have," Anthony admitted, "If . . ."

"If?"

"If your memories can be trusted."

Kari flushed. "How many New Mexico social workers named Marge can there be on that exact date? Either there was one, or there wasn't."

"Calm down, Kari. If there was a Marge *S* working for a state or county agency, I promise I will find her—I will start today. And you wish me to work with Owen Washington from your attorney's office?"

Kari sighed. "I apologize, Anthony. Yes. I believe my attorneys will allow him to work exclusively for me when I tell them the situation. He has a large number of connections around the country who may help us. In any case, I will throw all my resources into this search—whatever the cost."

"Good to know. Searching records—particularly old ones—and finding the people who were working in the social services bureaucracy then, and conducting interviews with them will take time—and time equals money. May I have Mr. Washington's contact information?"

"Yes, but please wait for him to call you. He wouldn't know what you were talking about right now. If there's nothing more for me to do here, my car is already packed. I will leave for New Orleans today and meet with my attorneys and Owen as soon as I can arrange it."

"They don't know the rest of your tale? My brain still reeling from everything you told us at dinner last night!" Anthony rubbed the bridge of his nose between the thumb and forefinger of his left hand and grumbled, "I'll never be able to eat at El Pinto again without reliving that dinner!"

Kari was able to laugh with him. "I'm sorry, my dear friend. I knew it was too much, but I couldn't think of any other way to tell you and Ruth—and I certainly didn't want to tell you separately and have to go through the complete telling all over again."

"No, I don't suppose so! But you'll have to retell it when you meet with your attorneys and Mr. Washington."

"They already know that Peter Granger was Dean Morgan and that he kidnapped my father. They just don't know about my sister and brother."

"Well, that will make the retelling simpler. Er, sort of. Okay, Kari. I'll wait for Mr. Washington's call. In the meantime, I'll get on the records search."

Kari left Esquibel Investigations, skipped lunch, and headed east on I-40. *I am not going to waste three whole days on the drive back to NOLA,* she decided as she pushed the Caddy up to seventy-five miles per hour. Her route was the reverse of her drive from NOLA to Albuquerque a little more than one month before, but she intended to make the journey in two or two-and-a-half days, not three.

During the long stretches of open road, Kari had trouble focusing on her driving. Instead, her thoughts ran ahead, to the meeting she needed to have—as soon as possible—with Clover and Owen Washington.

And I know the right person to set up that meeting.

When Kari stopped to use the restroom, she placed a long-distance call to the offices of Brunell & Brunell.

"Miss Dawes, please. Kari Hillyer, er, Granger speaking."

She shook her head as the receptionist put her call through. *Kari Hillyer. Kari Granger. Kari Michaels. Sheesh. Pick one, for heaven's sake!*

Of course Clover, his law partners, and Owen knew the extraordinary circumstances surrounding Kari's family connections, but Kari had no idea if they had shared those revelations with the staff of Brunell & Brunell.

The refined tones of Miss Dawes flowed over the phone lines. "Good afternoon, Miss Kari."

Kari sighed with relief. *"Miss Kari" fits the bill no matter what my last name may be!*

"Hello, Miss Dawes. How are you today?"

"I am well; thank you for asking. It is lovely to hear from you. Are you on your way back now?"

"Yes; I'm on the road and should be home midday, day after tomorrow. That is why I am calling."

"Of course. How may I help you?"

Kari smiled. Miss Dawes was the consummate executive assistant: cultured, reliable, and unflappable.

"I would like to meet with Clover and Mr. Washington as soon after I arrive home as can be arranged."

"Of course, Miss Kari. Would Monday morning be soon enough?"

Kari realized she would be arriving home on a Saturday afternoon. "Oh, dear."

"If the need is urgent, I'm certain Clover will want to accommodate your schedule." It was "Miss Dawes' speak," her gracious way of saying that Kari's business at the firm was of the first order.

I could probably ask them to stand on their heads and they would do it! Kari didn't like the idea of wielding that kind of power.

"Let me think one second, Miss Dawes." Kari toyed with the idea of asking Clover and Owen to come to her house Saturday evening.

No; I'll be useless after driving so many hours, and Clover retires early.

Sunday morning?

No; we'll be at church Sunday morning.

That was it.

"Miss Dawes? If they have no previous plans and are amenable, I would like to take Clover and Lorene and Owen and Mercy to brunch after service Sunday."

"I am certain they will accept your invitation. Do you have a restaurant preference, Miss Kari?"

"Um, no."

"It would be my pleasure to make the reservation, Miss Kari."

"That would be super, Miss Dawes. Thank you."

"May I do anything further for you?"

"No, but thank you for asking. Good bye."

Next Kari dialed her housekeeper, Azalea Bodeen, and listened to the line ring on the other end. Kari could only imagine Azalea's consternation if Kari were to arrive home unannounced. Not that Kari believed Azalea would be found wanting in any respect! No, it was the housekeeper's sense of propriety, how things 'should' be done, that was Kari's concern.

Kari's brow creased. *And how did I end up with a housekeeper, anyway? Oh, yes. I have Oskar Brunell to thank for that.*

Kari recalled her first morning in Peter Granger's quasi-mansion. She had awoken to the smell of freshly ground and perked coffee wafting up the back stairs from the kitchen. And something else. Something delicious.

Her first thought had been, *If this is a cooking and coffee-making burglar, I wonder if we can come to a mutually satisfying arrangement: He pilfers a priceless antique and leaves me with food and liquid treasure.*

Kari had followed her nose down the back staircase and found Azalea pulling from-scratch popovers from the oven.

"Good morning." Kari's silent approach had frightened the woman more than the woman's presence in the house had surprised Kari.

The woman had shrieked and dropped the tin into the sink. "There! Ya skeered th' wits outta me!"

She had turned, holding her hand over her heart.

"I was thinking something similar when I woke up and realized someone was in the house with me," Kari had answered evenly.

"What? Mr. Oskar din't tell ya he hired me t' do fer ya?"

Kari chuckled at the memory—and then someone picked up her call.

"Mrs. Bodeen? This is, er, Miss Kari. I am on my way home and thought I should let you know that I intend to arrive early Saturday afternoon."

She listened for a moment, smiling at the soft accents coming through the line. "Yes, but please do not interrupt your weekend off. Surely whatever needs to be done can be done tomorrow or Monday?"

She listened again. "Dinner? Um, I will probably make a sandwich or something."

And listened again. "No, no, please don't put an entire pot roast in the refrigerator for me! I insist. Heavens. It would take me a week to eat it. Some cold cuts and greens will be fine. Yes. Thank you, Mrs. Bodeen. You are quite good to me."

Kari disconnected and returned to her car.

Heavens! In the month I was away from New Orleans, I forgot how gracious NOLA people are.

And how stinking rich you *are,* sneered an inner voice.

Kari drove until her eyes were bleary. She pulled into the first reputable-looking hotel she saw alongside the road. It had been dark for some time; all Kari wanted was to sleep a few hours and then get back on the road.

Before retiring for the night, Kari called the front desk and set up a five a.m. wakeup call. Then she did something she had been holding back on: She opened the first of Rose's three additional journals. It wasn't that Kari lacked the eagerness to dive into the journals. No; it was that she felt the sacredness of doing so.

I want to take my time and savor them.

In the back of her mind she wondered what Rose's first entry would be, her first entry after Edmund was taken. What would Rose's deepest thoughts reveal about the events of April 12, 1911? How would she respond?

Kari's faith was so new that she harbored a tiny fear, a fear that those events might have, at least initially, shaken Rose's faith.

The binding of the first of the three journals was a deep blue. With gentle hands, Kari folded the cover back and turned the first page. The inscription on the next page, like the inscription in Rose's first journal, read

Rose Thoresen
My Journal

Kari blinked. No, that wasn't what was written. The last word was not "journal"; it was "journey."

Rose Thoresen
My Journey

"My journey," Kari breathed. Her heart pounded, and she devoured the first words penned in Rose's fine script.

Journal Entry, July 13, 1911

Lord, it has been a while since I made an entry. I suppose for many "good" reasons it is understandable: I was hoping my journal would be found—and Edmund with it—but they have not come back to us as yet. I had hoped, too, that Grant's health would improve, but you have taken him home. I even told myself that I was "simple waiting for my arm to heal"— and yet, while it healed, I did not shirk my duties to my daughter in her grief or to Palmer House.

I know you see everything, even my many reasons for procrastinating, and I am grateful that you have never been far from me. I have felt your presence daily. In the interim between my last entry and this one, my voice, if not my pen, has been raised continually to your throne, O God.

And so for three months I have delayed purchasing another volume to replace the lost one. I insisted to myself that I would wait until my old journal was found before I continued to record my thoughts. However, Mr. O'Dell's visit two days past has made me adjust the focus of my resolve.

You already know what Mr. O'Dell had to tell us, Lord. He said that they have no leads to follow at present, that the trail has gone cold. Oh, he was quick to assure Joy that he will not give up, but what will he do without a lead of any kind?

My mind was quick to inform my heart that the situation was hopeless. I know better than to let my mind rule my emotions—or the other way around. You, Lord, are my King. I will be ruled by you, and you alone, not by my thoughts or feelings.

Accordingly, I went out straightway yesterday morning and purchased this little book. I did so as an act of faith. However, I no longer consider it merely a journal, but rather a record of my journey. Is not our walk with you a journey? And over time when the faith of many might wither or wane, I am determined to express my trust in you in some tangible, ongoing manner. Let me adhere to your exhortation found in Psalm 12,

> *But I have trusted in thy mercy;*
> *My heart shall rejoice in thy salvation.*

So, Lord, let me say this: I love you. I trust you. I know you have heard our prayers and that you are already working on our behalf. I await your answer, O God, my King, with patience and hope.

Yes, I love you, Lord. Thank you for loving me.

Kari gently touched the last words of the entry. *Yes, I love you, too, Lord. Thank you for loving me.*

"Thank you for loving me, Lord," Kari repeated to herself. "And thank you for Rose's example of unflinching perseverance."

Kari fell into an exhausted, dreamless sleep until—much too soon—the phone in her room rang. It was her wakeup call. She pulled herself out of bed, dressed, grabbed coffee and a donut from the hotel's hospitality area, and pointed her car down the road.

The rest of her drive was uneventful, but the humidity increased with every mile. Long before she drove across the lake into the city, the August temperatures and matching ambient moisture had convinced her to put the top up and use the air conditioning.

Then the drive became easier, more familiar, and when she turned into her neighborhood, she marked the known streets and houses along the way. When Kari pulled into the driveway of her house she realized how much she was looking forward to being home.

Home.

The house on Marlow Avenue felt like home?

She eased the Caddy down the drive toward the garage door. Every aspect of the grounds and the house's exterior called to her: the pale pink stone, the slate roof, the freshly edged grass.

Why, even the windows are gleaming! she noted with a grin.

She got out to unlock the garage and was not surprised to spot Toller Bodeen jogging across the grass toward her. Azalea would have alerted her son to Kari's imminent return.

"Hi, Toller."

Her groundskeeper smiled in return. "Aft'noon, Miss Kari. Can I get your bags and put th' car away for ya?"

Kari didn't argue. She was beat. "Yes. Thank you."

He carried her luggage around to the front door, waited while Kari unlocked and opened the door, then wordlessly (and with little apparent effort) hauled her bags up the staircase to Kari's room.

With a nod, Toller bid her goodbye. "I'll hang th' keys in th' kitchen when I'm done, Miss Kari."

"Thank you, Toller."

"M' pleasure. Welcome home, Miss Kari."

Kari wandered through the house, a soft smile on her lips. She touched her favorite knick-knacks and stroked the top of an end table she particularly liked. The house was immaculate, of course, and all was as she had left it.

I'm home.

Those words seemed incongruous to Kari since she had spent only a few months in the house—uneasy ones at that—before leaving on her trip. When Kari had left for Albuquerque and Denver, she had still felt like she was living in Peter Granger's house, not her own.

But something had changed.

No, many things had changed.

Lord, I confess I'm a little confused. I am grateful and glad to be here— but I felt so "at home" with Søren, Ilsa, and Max. And I bought Rose's land! I intend to build a house on it. Now I feel a sense of belonging to this *house of all places. I hope you will straighten me out.*

Kari climbed the beautiful staircase to her room on the second floor. Toller had left her bags against one wall.

Hot shower! her weary brain telegraphed to stiff muscles.

"Yes."

Kari grabbed one suitcase, opened it on her bed, and rooted around in it, tossing dirty things into a pile on the floor until she found something clean and comfortable to wear. She left the contents of her suitcase strewn across her bed and fled to the bathroom.

She scrubbed herself and washed her hair. Then she stood in the shower until the hot water was exhausted and her skin tingled. When she climbed out, she felt for the towels and wrapped one around her steaming body and another around her wet hair. Then she headed for her room.

What?

The jumbled mess she had made was gone. So was her luggage.

Kari scanned the room: Her toiletries were stacked neatly on her vanity; her clean clothes were either hung or folded into her dresser drawers; her dirty clothes were missing.

Kari glanced again into her closet and spotted her suitcases. They were nested into one another and placed on the shelf above the rod. Where they belonged.

Kari stepped out into the hallway and, from far down the back stairs, heard the faint sound of the washing machine. Shaking her head, Kari dressed and set about drying her hair.

Before she finished, she smelled something cooking. Something that set her insides rumbling.

Kari sighed and felt a contentment that was unfamiliar to her.

Lord, please bless Azalea Bodeen. Again, I'm glad to be home.

CHAPTER 6

K ari slid into the pew next to Lorene and touched her arm. She was a bit late; the singing was in full swing. Lorene turned and hugged her. Clover glanced over, smiled, and would have hugged her, too, but it wasn't the right time. Clover's son, Oskar, and his wife Melanie, nodded from the next pew over.

The service was exactly what Kari needed: The worship sent her heart soaring to Jesus, the pastor's message convicted and challenged her to apply—not merely assent to—what the Bible taught, and the community of believers enfolded her.

Lord, thank you. I have longed for this all my life and didn't know it, Kari prayed. *I always wanted and needed a family—because I have always longed to belong to* you.

After the service, Owen and Mercy Washington found them.

"Honey, it's so good to see you home." Mercy smiled and hugged Kari. "And thank you for your kind invitation to Sunday brunch. It's a real treat."

Kari arched one eyebrow. "You may rethink your thanks before we are done today. It's something of 'a working lunch.'"

"Ooooh, Chile! You be mysterious!" Mercy laughed back.

True to her word, Miss Dawes had made reservations for five at a large hotel that touted an extravagant and traditional New Orleans Sunday brunch. Kari and her guests met in the lobby and were shown to a round table nestled into a semiprivate window nook.

"This is perfect," Kari told the maître d' as he seated her. "Thank you."

"Our pleasure. Would Madam and her guests care for coffee?"

"I know I would," Kari replied. She looked at the others. Owen and Mercy nodded, but Clover and Lorene declined.

After they had received their coffees and ordered from the brunch menu, Clover patted Kari's hand. "Miss Kari, we are so glad to see you safely home. You left on a little jaunt a month ago that turned into an adventure and something quite unexpected."

Lorene and Owen nodded and Mercy said, "Owen told me how you found that woman's journal and it led you to your real family. What an amazin', astonishin' story! How you adjustin', girl?"

Kari thought for a moment. "To be truthful, pretty much everything about the last four months has been unexpected. Unexpected, life-altering, and ongoing! I feel as though I am living in a blender, a whirlwind of continual upheaval."

Her guests' heads bobbed sympathetically.

Kari smiled at Mercy. "You asked me how I am adjusting? Without Jesus I think I would be an absolute hot mess—like I was when I first came to NOLA. But with him? With Jesus? It is as though something calm and stable has settled and taken root on my insides. And I-I don't feel broken like I used to feel."

Kari thought a moment longer. "For all my life I have had a deep longing for family—to belong somewhere, to someone. To be completely loved and accepted. To be a part of something greater and enduring. Now I have almost *too* much family! I certainly feel pulled in diverse directions, but . . . but that calm, that peace down deep in me doesn't budge. It doesn't shift."

She looked around. "Does that make any sense? I mean, I wanted to find Rose so badly and, in a way, I did. I found Palmer House and scads of family to whom, quite literally, I was the answer to eighty-plus years of prayer! I even bought Rose's land, her homestead, to keep it from passing out of the family. And when I was staying with Søren, Ilsa, and Max on the Thoresen homestead, I fit right in."

Kari smirked. "Would you believe it? I mucked out stalls, fed chickens, and milked goats! *Me!* I wanted to stay forever."

She sobered. "Except, of course, I knew I couldn't. I-I have responsibilities here! So when I left those dear people, it nearly broke my heart—but when I got home, here to New Orleans, it *was* home, although I still long to return to the land I bought and the family I left in Nebraska."

She laughed again but wrinkled her forehead. "It's a little confusing. To feel at home in two different places."

Owen pulled a pocket New Testament from his suit coat. "I think I know what you are describing, Kari. The Apostle Paul said it like this: *For I have learned in whatever state I am, to be content.* He didn't mean 'state' as in Nebraska or Louisiana, He meant 'condition' or 'circumstances.'"

"I agree." Lorene spoke, and Kari leaned toward her to catch her soft drawl. "As Christians, we can be 'at home' wherever Jesus is. Since he lives in us and has promised never to leave us or forsake us, we can weather whatever is going on around us and remain at peace in our hearts. Is that what you are describing, Kari?"

"I think that must be it." Kari rested her elbows on the table and her chin on her folded hands. "I've never had such peace! It's a bit unnerving, actually. It feels . . . unnatural."

"Ah! Yes, unnatural." Clover bent toward Kari. "A moment ago you said that you no longer feel broken. 'Broken' is a very telling word. We are all broken in one way or another because of sin and what this sinful world does to us, but—and thank the Lord!—Jesus came to heal the brokenhearted."

A jolt ran through Kari. "That's exactly what Rose wrote in her journal! She wrote, *Lord Jesus, I am so glad that you came to heal the brokenhearted.* And my friend Ruth said something about it, too. She said that God will heal every wound we have, even a broken heart."

Those around Kari nodded, and Clover patted Kari's hand in the way she had come to love. "If we have been broken our entire lives, then brokenness feels normal. When we aren't broken any longer, we have to adjust to our new normal: Peace, deep joy, a sense of wholeness. Welcome to your new normal, Kari."

"Wow," Kari breathed.

Mercy grinned at Kari. "So let me ask you again, Hon. How you adjustin'?"

Kari grinned back. "I'm living in peace, Mercy. Peace and contentment."

They laughed together and then Mercy asked, "So which part of this lunch is bein' the 'working' part, Kari?"

"Oh! I had almost forgotten, and it is important, too. It will take a few minutes to explain . . ."

For the next half hour, Kari described the nightmares of her childhood, how all her life *The Black* had hidden an important event from her, and the night Kari's memories came flooding back.

When she told them about her parents leaving her in the dark night off the side of the road—to watch over a sister and baby brother—her friends broke out in excited or unbelieving exclamations. But when she described how Elaine and Sammie had been taken away, how the social worker had slapped and threatened her, Owen pushed his chair back from the table and stood up. He shifted from foot to foot, clearly agitated.

"Excuse me. I need a little air." He stalked away without another word.

Kari looked from his retreating back to Mercy. "What just happened?"

Mercy dabbed away tears. "You don't know this, Chile, but somethin' like that happened to Owen when he was only five. He an' his big brother, Lincoln, got sent to foster care.

"They split them boys up 'cause they couldn't get a family to take the two of 'em. The foster family they put Owen in was horrible—abusive and neglectful. The worst part was that he never saw his brother again. Lincoln died in a gang shooting jest walkin' home from school. That boy was but thirteen. Owen never knew his daddy. Lincoln was all he had in th' world."

Clover struggled to his feet. "Don't you fret, Miss Kari. Owen's filled with righteous grief and anger at the moment. I'll go bring him back when he's ready."

As Clover ambled away, Lorene murmured, "It is amazing that you have not thought of your siblings all these years."

"I know. I have beat myself up over it quite a bit. My friend Ruth tells me that the trauma I experienced that night, plus the threats of the social worker, likely sent me into a psychotic episode. In order to protect Elaine and Sammie from what the social worker threatened to do to them, my subconscious found a way to keep me from remembering and saying anything about them."

"Gracious heavens!" Mercy muttered.

The waiter offered dessert, so Kari ordered brownies with praline ice cream for everyone. The man had set the dessert plates on the table and was refreshing the coffee cups when Owen and Clover returned.

"I apologize, Miss Kari." Owen took his seat and squeezed Mercy's hand. "You told Mercy this was a working lunch. Is it about your sister and brother, then?"

"Yes," Kari answered. She looked to Clover. "I have hired Anthony Esquibel in Albuquerque to begin the search. I would like to hire Owen to join him. Is that possible?"

Clover pulled on his chin. "Yes, of course." He glanced at Owen. "Please hand whatever work that cannot wait off to that investigative firm you got an offer from. Consider yourself assigned full time to Kari's case."

"Got an offer from? What? Are you leaving Brunell & Brunell?"

"Not enough in-house work for a full-time investigator, Miss Kari, once I found you."

"But—"

"Don't you worry about Owen, Miss Kari. If he accepts that offer, Brunell & Brunell will hire him *and* his firm for any work we need done." Clover turned to Owen. "You can tell your new firm that this is your first case for Brunell & Brunell."

"Yes, sir." Owen's ebony face gleamed like polished flint when he addressed Kari. "I promise I will do my best."

"Thank you," Kari whispered.

"Does Mr. Esquibel have a place to start?" Mercy asked and then she murmured, "I mean, it's been a long time. Thirty-some years?"

"Thirty-three years. My sister, Elaine will be thirty-six. Samuel will be between thirty-three and thirty-four. But we do have one solid clue with which to begin the search: When the social worker leaned over me and shook me, her name tag was right in front of my face. Her first name was Marge. Last name began with an *S*."

"I will call Mr. Esquibel first thing in the morning, Kari," Owen promised.

"And I will call a meeting of the senior partners tomorrow," Clover announced, "to inform them of Miss Kari's revelations. We will discuss how they impact the Granger estate's probate."

Kari returned home and wandered aimlessly around her house. Finally, she picked up the phone and called Søren. *I need to hear his voice*, she realized.

Once again, Max answered the phone.

"Hey you," Kari greeted him.

"Kari! Guess what? My pig made weight! Dad says I can enter him in the state fair!"

With those few words, Kari was back in RiverBend.

Thank you for long distance, Lord!

Miss Dawes called Kari the following day after lunch. "Good afternoon, Miss Kari. Mr. Clover Brunell held a meeting this morning to apprise the senior partners and executive staff of the information you provided during brunch yesterday. Afterwards, Mr. Washington asked me to call you. He is leaving for Albuquerque this evening and will make his first report as soon as he and Mr. Esquibel have completed their initial records search."

"Thank you, Miss Dawes. I appreciate your phone call."

"Hmm. And may I say, Miss Kari, that I wish you the very best. I, um, was astonished by the facts that have come to light. I-I quite sympathize with you and, um, will be praying for Mr. Washington and Mr. Esquibel's success in locating your siblings."

Kari had never heard Miss Dawes stumble in speech. "Thank you, Miss Dawes. Your concern touches my heart, and I appreciate your prayers."

She thought for a moment. "Miss Dawes, is Mr. Oskar in the office?"

"Yes, Miss Kari. May I connect you?"

"Please." Kari listened to the on-hold music piped through the phone until Oskar's voice came on the line.

"Good afternoon, Miss Kari. What may I do for you today?"

"Hello, Oskar. I wanted to check in with you regarding the probate." Clover and his son Oskar had warned Kari that the probate of Peter Granger's will would take months.

"It was progressing nicely but, of course, with the information you have provided regarding your siblings, we will need to amend the court documents to include them. These actions—while we include the proper language to confirm their rights and communicate to the court how, when your siblings are located, they will share in the estate—will extend the probate period."

"Of course. That was exactly my purpose in asking to speak with you. I want to ensure that my sister and brother receive their fair share of the estate."

Kari thought for a moment. "Oskar, my uncle and my cousins have quite a number of old photographs that I would like copies of. Can you recommend someone who would be willing to travel to Kansas and Nebraska and make reproductions of them for me?"

"I cannot suggest anyone off the top of my head, Miss Kari, but I will ask my assistant, Miss Fletcher, to investigate and make a recommendation."

"Thank you, Oskar. And, um, I don't have a lot to do at present, so I suppose I am ready to begin the education you hinted at earlier."

"Earlier" referred to the several days in April over which Brunell & Brunell's attorneys had revealed the details of Peter Granger's estate to Kari. At their first meeting, Clover had introduced Kari to Brunell & Brunell's other senior partners, Clover's brother, Jeffers Brunell, and their cousin, Clive.

However, *The Seniors*, as they were referred to, were semiretired and primarily provided oversight to the firm. And while Clover still devoted his time to the administration of Peter Granger's estate, it was his son Oskar who, aided by a team of accountants and financial consultants, provided the day-to-day management of Peter Granger's considerable assets.

Now Kari needed to become better acquainted with those assets so she could steward them responsibly.

"Very good, Miss Kari. Suppose we ease into the process by a series of two-hour orientations? Perhaps twice a week to begin with. And I suggest that we personally visit some of the estate holdings so that you see them as more than a line item on a balance sheet."

"Whatever you feel is best, Oskar. I want to learn and begin to feel useful."

"Very good, Miss Kari."

After they said goodbye, Kari wandered through the house again looking at it with fresh eyes. *Yes, my father grew up here, but the woman who raised him was not his mother and Peter Granger was not his uncle. That man's name was not even 'Peter Granger.' It was another false identity for the evil man Rose and Joy knew as Dean Morgan.*

As she rehearsed the facts, angry thoughts and feelings started to roil around in her belly. She pulled herself up with a sharp rebuke.

I'm not going to fall into that trap a second time!

"No!" she said aloud. "I forgave Dean Morgan. I will not allow myself to slip into bitterness again. Lord, you forgave him at the end of his life. You saved him the same way you saved me. I will speak forgiveness over him every time I think on him. Thank you for helping me. Thank you for grace!"

Kari found herself at the top of the stairs in the doorway of Peter Granger's bedroom. "But forgiveness doesn't mean I need to treat this house as though it still belongs to him."

She breathed a small laugh. *I still find it ironic—a paradox of justice?—how everything he worked for and valued is now mine.*

Ours, she amended. *Mine, Elaine's, and Sammie's.*

She had a realization. *And some day, in his timing, God will bring them here, if only to visit.*

She stepped through the doorway and surveyed the large master bedroom and its attached bathroom.

The first time Kari had visited the house had been in Clover's company. He had shown her Peter Granger's bedroom and said, "Mr. Peter had a bathroom installed *ensuite* in his last years. I confess it is in need of modernizing. That is something I wager you will enjoy doing yourself."

Kari considered his suggestion again. "Time to remove Peter Granger's imprint from this house," she muttered. "Time for a makeover!"

She tripped back downstairs to call Lorene Brunell.

Lorene was delighted with the prospect of remodeling and redecorating the master bedroom and bath. When the phone call ended, Kari look around the living room with fresh eyes. "If I am going to live here and make this a real home, I need it to reflect me and not Peter or Alicia Granger."

She identified a few things that she did not particularly care for and went in search of a piece of paper and a pen to jot them down. Her search led her into Peter Granger's ground-floor office. The office opened from the house's spacious foyer and shared a wall with the living room. Kari had not really spent any time in the room.

Because it kind of creeps me out, she admitted.

She looked around, studying the thoroughly masculine décor and furniture, particularly the large desk in the center of the room. Kari could imagine Peter Granger sitting at that desk—gloating over his escape from Denver. Plotting the deceptions that Kari's father would grow up believing. She shivered.

My house. I will make this my house. All of it.

Kari pulled the chair out from the desk and, after hesitating a moment, sat down.

She opened desk drawers, searching for pen and paper. The drawers were all empty, and Kari recalled one of the senior partners—or was it Oskar?—saying that Brunell & Brunell had gathered all of Peter Granger's papers into their files for safekeeping.

Still, when she pulled the bottom desk drawer out, she thought she heard something shift in the drawer.

Aha! Maybe they missed something.

Kari pulled the drawer out as far as the stops would allow and ran her hand to the back of its deep recesses.

Nothing.

Oh, well.

Kari leaned back in the expansive leather chair—obviously intended as an "important" man's chair—and surveyed the office with a more subjective eye. One wall was lined with built-in bookshelves filled with expensive volumes.

All these books were stored in the attic until I arrived, Kari reminded herself. As she studied the titles and their ornate bindings, she confessed to admiring the collection.

Two other walls were paneled in costly woods. The carved chair rails and engraved panels were most certainly fashioned by an artisan.

Kari shook her head. *Beautiful!*

She ambled around the desk, examining the paintings on the walls, deciding what would stay and what would not. *After I clear that wall, it would be a perfect palette to display the family pictures I want to have framed.*

She sat at the desk again and studied the room. She frowned. *It's too dark in here.*

She swiveled the chair and faced the window behind the desk. Heavy damask drapes hid the glass, contributing mightily to the room's depressing atmosphere. Kari stood and swept them aside.

"Oh!"

The window hidden behind the curtains was tall; the lower two-thirds of it was paned; the upper third was rounded and formed a sunburst. Kari loved the window and the view of the grounds through it—the sweeping lawn and a mounded swath of flowering rhododendrons and hydrangeas. And a single, gnarled live oak with broad branches almost sweeping the ground, branches that practically begged the child in anyone to clamber up their thick arms and onto the trunk.

Kari looked at the edges of the drapes in her fisted hand. "Well, *you* have to go."

She knew where to find a stepladder and went off to fetch it. Within minutes she was slipping drapery hooks off the rods and dropping the thick fabric to the floor.

Soft light flooded the room, and the window framed the sprawling oak perfectly.

"This," Kari whispered in delight. "This is splendid."

Getting her teeth into the task, she pointed at the oversized desk chair. "That monstrosity must go, too," she murmured, "and probably the desk. I will ask Lorene where to look for new, lighter furnishings."

But in the natural light streaming from the window, the wood in the room was coming to life. Kari realized that the sculpted trim on the walls was a match to the ornate carvings on the desk's drawer fronts.

"The same person who carved the paneling also built this desk," she realized.

She studied the desk more objectively, admiring its craftsmanship and glowing wood grain. "I doubt I could find a desk as beautiful as this one," she admitted, "and it certainly belongs with this room. Okay, get rid of the chair, but maybe not the desk."

She stopped again in front of the window and sighed. "Whatever new window treatments I select, they must preserve this view."

As she considered keeping the desk, she imagined it turned toward the window rather than away from it. "Yes. With the desk facing that way and a more feminine chair . . ." She pushed against the desk only to realize how heavy it was.

Well, and I don't want to scratch the floor.

Kari went out the back door and shielded her eyes against the hot August sun. "Toller? Are you out there?"

"Yes, Miss Kari!" He walked out from behind some shrubs and trod across the lawn toward her. "What do you need?"

"Could you come in the house with me? I could use some muscle."

Miss Fletcher called Kari with the name and number of a respected photographer. "He is quite cutting edge, Miss Kari. He has a new kind of camera that puts the pictures on computer disks. He claims he can make reproductions of old photographs and fix things like cracks and fading in the copies."

"Really!" Kari took his number and went the same day to visit his studio. She was impressed by the man's computer setup and knowledge.

"I can bring the photographs onto my computer," he explained, "make corrections to them, and then print them in the size you request."

"This would be something of a project," she told him. "It would require that you travel to Nebraska and Kansas to, er, shoot all the photographs I have in mind."

"If you are willing to pay my expenses and fee, I am willing to take on the project," he replied. "This is actually a good time of year for me to do this. Not as many weddings and graduations to photograph."

"I, um, would also like you to make a family portrait of my cousin and his son for me—and take a photograph of me for them."

"I'd be delighted to do so."

Kari hired him on the spot.

CHAPTER 7

As August gave way to September, Kari immersed herself in her New Orleans life: twice-weekly meetings with Oskar Brunell, the renovation of the office and master suite, Rose's journals, her Bible, her church.

Clover had his staff begin the legal work to change her last name to Michaels. "It will only take three weeks, Kari. If you would like to begin using it now, I don't see the harm." He wheezed out a guffaw. "Might cut down on the confusion."

"I agree!" Kari replied.

Kari Thoresen Michaels. My father's real name was Edmund Thoresen Michaels. Kari loved the sound of it, loved that her name would be the same as his.

Kari purchased an office chair more her size and style, one that would complement the desk she was growing to appreciate. She visited an office supply store and came away with a desk pad and three bags of supplies to fill her desk's sizable drawers. She had the phone company install and place a vintage French-styled telephone on her desk.

When she stood back to view the results, Kari was satisfied— particularly with the tied-back curtains that opened the room to light and the view Kari wanted. A shade covered in ivory watermarked silk, that she could raise or pull down as she desired, completed the window treatment.

Then Kari began to use her office in earnest. She started each morning with coffee and fifteen minutes of Bible study and prayer. She finished each morning's devotions by reading a single entry from Rose's blue journal.

I don't want to read them all at once. I want to savor them, she told herself. *I'm no longer desperate to know everything about Rose and her Jesus, because her Jesus is my Jesus, now. I can enjoy her journals slowly.*

Kari opened to her marked place in the blue journal.

Journal Entry, November 4, 1911

Today our beloved Mei-Xing was married to her sweetheart, Minister Liáng. She is the first of our "girls" to be married from Palmer House, but I know she will not be the last. We work and pray for our girls to be healed in their souls and to become strong, whole, and independent women, but we also pray they will find love and happiness.

And so, Lord, we give you great praise for Mei-Xing's happiness, and thank you for a man of Minister Liáng's abiding character. He will be a good husband to Mei-Xing and a good father to Shan-Rose, and Mei-Xing will be a strength and a help to him in his ministry.

I shall miss Shan-Rose. We all shall. Tonight I realize that the absence of her little voice has left a void in this house.

But I shall not dwell upon our loss. Rather, I shall rejoice in her future. I sense your call upon this child, Lord God, even at an early age.

And I lift up our Tabitha to you, Father. She was unable to leave school and come to us for this important occasion. I ask you to sustain her, Holy Spirit, for you are the Comforter and our Helper.

Kari gave Lorene free rein to remodel the master bedroom and bathroom, and Clover's wife dove in with gusto. At the same time, Kari made sure her elderly friend did not overwork herself.

As the decorators and contractors came and went, Lorene asked Kari for her input, but Kari acquiesced to Lorene's impeccable taste.

"All I ask is that the suite be thoroughly modernized and lovely," she told Lorene. "If I ever have guests I would like them to be comfortable."

Lorene smiled. "My dear, your guests will think they have died and gone to heaven when I finish—but I do hope you will move into the suite when we are done. I am redecorating with you in mind."

She tapped her finger on her chin, thinking. "And while we're making a mess of your upstairs, why not let me redo the other two bedrooms at the same time? We can get all the muss and fuss done with in a single dustup."

"What a super idea! Thank you, Lorene. You don't know how much I appreciate you. How much I love you."

The older woman drew Kari into her arms and Kari inhaled the powdery scent that was uniquely Lorene's. "I think I do know, Kari. I think Clover and I have the dear privilege of loving you and being part of your family."

Within a few weeks, contractors, painters, and wallpaper hangers were moving up and down the staircase hauling tools and materials. Either the decorator or crew boss was always on site to manage the workers; still, Kari fled to the kitchen to avoid the sense of upheaval she was so sensitive to. The few hours each day Azalea was in the kitchen, Kari worked alongside of her.

While she peeled carrots or chopped salad fixings, Kari's thoughts turned continually to Owen and Anthony and their search for Elaine and Samuel. The phrase "illegal adoption" circled in her mind, too.

Early one afternoon, Kari left the house with directions to one of New Orleans' main library branches. *I was a librarian. I know how to research a topic. I want to find out more about illegal adoption*, she told herself.

Kari spent hours reading on the subject. She stayed until evening when the overhead lights blinked off and on, signaling closing time.

She left the library horrified by what she'd read. Pieces of Rose's journal, hinting at the age some of Palmer House's girls had been when sold into the brothels, came back to her. So did entries where Rose described how false newspaper employment ads had ensnared young mothers and their children together.

Lord, what if a family did not adopt Elaine and Sammie? What if—

She couldn't voice the concerns her research had raised, but her heart trembled.

Father! I am calling on you! she prayed.

Four weeks after taking Kari's commission, the photographer called. "Miss Michaels? Bill Blair here. I have your photographs ready. Would you care to come see them?"

"Would I? I'll be there within the hour."

The display the photographer had arranged for Kari stole her breath away.

"I took the liberty of framing those reproductions you wanted to hang," he said quietly. "When I saw the wall of photographs at your cousins' home in Nebraska, I knew you thought to do the same thing. I located a few vintage frames and found others that are vintage reproductions."

He had assembled the framed photographs in chronological order, oldest to newest, in a row upon a table, and leaned them against some draped blocks so she could see how they would look when hung upon a wall.

At the end of the row, in a burnished frame, was the family portrait of Søren and Max she had requested. Søren's hand rested on Max's shoulder, and his expression was sober, but Kari thought she detected a tiny smirk of humor behind his eyes. Max's grin, on the other hand, was wide, displaying a complete assortment of missing or half-grown-in teeth.

Kari lifted the photograph and smiled back at Max.

I'd like to plant a kiss on your forehead, young man.

"They are wonderful, Mr. Blair. So, so wonderful!" Kari already visualized how the framed images would look on the wall in her home office. She could not wait to get home and hang them.

"And here is your photograph."

Kari blinked at the confident woman staring back at her. *Is that really me? Is that the person Max sees? And Søren?*

"It's perfect. Thank you."

The photographer opened a photo album on the table. "The remainder of the photographs are in this album."

Kari turned the album's pages slowly, relishing the treasure within its covers. "And you made the other copies I asked for?

"Yes. Three additional sets. I will ship your picture and two albums to your cousin and the other album to your uncle. I must say that I usually take longer to complete a project this detailed, but I became quite caught up in the work."

He coughed, a little self-conscious. "It was a privilege to do this work. You are lucky to have such a family heritage."

"Thank you. Yes, I am certainly blessed," Kari whispered. She closed the album and turned back to the framed display.

The image that most captured Kari's heart was the picture of Rose taken by O'Dell. The photographer had enlarged it and removed all signs of cracks, yet the new imaged retained the clarity of the original.

Rose's soft gray eyes, looking with hope into the future, brought a lump to Kari's throat.

"Ah. That one is my favorite, too," the photographer added. "What a lovely woman."

"My great-grandmother," Kari answered.

She wiped a tear from the corner of her eye before it could wend its way down her cheek.

Kari called ahead and Toller was waiting when she arrived home.

"Want me t' carry these boxes int' the house?"

"Yes, one at a time, please. There are two of them, and they aren't heavy, but what is inside is precious. I'll carry the album."

Mr. Blair had swaddled each framed photograph in a piece of soft flannel and then enfolded the bundle in a wide strip of bubble wrap that he taped so each bundle was a snug package. Kari helped him place the twenty bundles into two boxes.

She led the way to her office and directed Toller to place the boxes on her desk.

"Tomorrow, when I've unwrapped them all, could you help me hang them? I want them to go on that wall there."

She grinned. "And of course I'd like them to be straight—without putting a bazillion holes in the paneling, so I'll need your help for sure!"

"A'course. I'll bring a level and ever'thing else we need t' do the job."

Kari spent the evening unwrapping each photograph with care and staging them as she wanted them hung.

Being surrounded by photographs of my family's faces will make this office truly mine—but Rose's photograph? It goes right here on my desk.

Kari sighed in satisfaction.

***

ANTHONY POURED OWEN A CUP OF STOUT COFFEE as they prepared to begin another day. So far, their tedious records search had been unfruitful. Owen reached for the mug and sank into the cushions of the chair he'd come to think of as "his" chair in Anthony's office.

"I'm not prepared to say we've come up empty yet," he muttered, "so I'm hoping you have another avenue we haven't yet explored."

Anthony gave his head a minute shake. "If it were someone else, someone other than Kari, I might be tempted to call it quits."

Over the past three weeks, with Brunell & Brunell providing legal intervention and assistance, Owen and Anthony had backtracked every state employment record they could lay hands on and had searched the ranks of State retirees.

They had done the same with county records. Since the accident in which Kari's parents died occurred between Gallup and Grants on their way to Albuquerque, they had included the counties of McKinley and Cibola.

When McKinley and Cibolo turned up nothing, they branched out into the surrounding counties: Bernalillo, Sandoval, San Juan, Valencia—and the more distant counties of Catron, Socorro, Rio Arriba, Torrance, and Santa Fe. They cast their net wide and far . . . and caught absolutely nothing.

The two investigators had interviewed many a retired social worker who may (or may not) have had remembrance of the accident. Still, they had turned up no hint of the mysterious *Marge S.*

They *had* located the accident report filed by the New Mexico State Police. Although NMSP records back that far were stored in boxes in a warehouse, turning up the report in question had been fairly straightforward. The two men spent the better part of an afternoon flipping through paper until Anthony's fingers fell upon the right one.

Unfortunately, the report listed two adults, both deceased at the scene, and a six-year-old child as the lone survivor of the accident. And when Anthony and Owen had tried to track down the trooper who had filed the report, one Gary Showman, they found that he had passed away—as had the other two troopers listed as "on scene."

"Because I take Kari seriously, I'm not ready to call it quits," Anthony concluded.

Owen frowned as he nodded his agreement. "I believe Kari, too. I believe she witnessed the abduction of her siblings and I believe she was threatened, abused, and traumatized, but maybe we're missing something? Maybe we're making a wrong assumption somewhere?

"I mean, we've driven the highway out to where the accident took place, and the area is pretty unpopulated. Could some other department or agency have responded or been involved? What proof do we have that *Marge S* was a social worker at all? We have assumed she was, but what if she wasn't?"

Anthony heard him out and then slipped into deep concentration as he sipped his coffee. Owen didn't disturb him. He had his own troubled thoughts.

Lord, Kari is counting on us to uncover a secret that has been buried for decades. We can't possibly do this on our own. We need your help your miraculous help. You are the God of the impossible, Lord, and nothing is too difficult for you. Please show us the way forward.

Anthony sat up, two lines between his eyes creased in thought. He stared in Owen's direction, but Owen could tell he was still immersed in whatever idea had taken hold, so he waited.

"Hang on one blessed minute," Anthony mumbled.

Owen waited. And watched.

Anthony fumbled in a drawer and pulled out a worn New Mexico map. He unfolded it on his desk and stood over it, tracing it with his finger. When his finger came to rest, he hmmed to himself and then looked at Owen.

"What if . . ." He didn't finish his question. Instead, he pawed at a well-used rolodex until he found the number he was looking for.

"What's going on?" Owen couldn't keep quiet any longer.

"Have an old friend—emphasis on *old*—lives in an assisted living facility in Crownpoint. He must be in his late eighties now, but I'm pretty sure . . ." Again, he trailed off.

"What?" Owen insisted.

"Used to be a boys' ranch out there, somewhere along that stretch of road. I only remember because my friend regaled me with some of the outlandish problems those boys caused over the years . . ."

Anthony was still thinking, but Owen couldn't wait. "Wouldn't a kids' ranch like that be registered with the State?"

"Not necessarily. Not if it were privately funded. Or federally funded. And things like licensing had to have been a lot different in the fifties. Seems to me . . ."

And he was off in his thoughts again, but his finger was dialing the number on a rolodex card. "Morning. Anthony Esquibel speaking. Yes. Is Nathan Running Bull still a resident? He is?"

Anthony listened. "I see. So, um, is there a certain time of day when he is more apt to have the energy for visitors?"

He tapped a pencil on his blotter and nodded. "He is a friend. We go way back. Yeah. I would like to drive up and visit Nathan. Tomorrow. We can be there by eight. Yes. Please let him know? Thank you."

He put the receiver back into the phone's cradle. "Up for a road trip?"

"Sure. Who is this Nathan Running Bull and why are we going to visit him?"

"He was the stock manager on the boys' ranch I mentioned."

"And this ranch?"

"If I remember right, it was about five miles off the highway, maybe another five miles from where the accident took place."

"What does this have to do with Kari?"

"The ranch had staff there to deal with the issues many of the boys had. Counseling staff. Administrative staff. House parents. That sort of thing."

"But why would any of them have been called out to the scene of a vehicular accident?"

"I don't know, but when you asked if another department or agency could have responded, I started asking myself the same question—and Nathan's name popped into my head. We don't have any other leads, so I want to trace this one down.

"B'sides. I need to see my old friend. Been too long."

Early in the morning, Anthony and Owen climbed into Anthony's pickup and beat the I-40 morning traffic west out of Albuquerque.

"Tell me about Crownpoint," Owen asked. "How long is our drive?"

"'Bout ninety-five miles, so less than two hours. Crownpoint itself is small—not even three thousand residents—and most of them are Native people. The town is close to the border of the Navajo reservation."

"And this man we're going to see?"

"Nathan Running Bull was, as a young man, a cop on the reservation, but he didn't care for it. He wanted something more natural, closer to his roots. Went back to handling livestock.

He still had lots of connections on the res, though, and helped me on a particularly troubling investigation about twenty-five years ago. Been friends ever since, although we've sort of lost touch over the last few years."

They entered the tiny town and located the assisted living center where Nathan Running Bull lived. The aides were still clearing away breakfast trays when Anthony found the room toward which the receptionist pointed them.

The door was standing open, but Anthony knocked anyway.

"Nathan?"

"Yeah, I'm here, you ornery old greaser."

They walked into the room and Anthony stuck out his hand to an elderly gent sitting in a recliner. The man was thin, fragile looking and, although sitting upright, was somewhat stooped over anyway. His hair was long and white; his face was a mass of burnt sienna creases set in a perpetual scowl.

"I see you haven't lost your charming disposition, Red Chief," Anthony observed.

Nathan grinned and the two old friends shook hands. Owen watched and said nothing as the friends exchanged animated insults.

Finally, Nathan raised his eyes to study Owen. "Who's your companion?" he demanded.

"This is Owen Washington. Hails from New Orleans."

Owen reached for Nathan's hand and was surprised at the man's grip. Nathan's dark, deep-set eyes studied Owen.

"You mustn't think badly of us for our mutually degrading remarks. It's how we old friends love on each other." Nathan turned a glare on Anthony. "Took ya long enough to come and visit, you old beaner. I been in this place three years now!"

Anthony shrugged. "I didn't need anything from you before, *Cochise*. Now I do, and I figured I'd better get it before you kicked the can."

Nathan started wheezing, and Owen realized he was laughing. Still shaking with breathless humor, Nathan gestured for Anthony and Owen to pull up two chairs.

When Nathan could speak again, he gasped, "It does my heart good to see you, old friend. Thank you for taking the time to come see me."

"You are a sight for sore eyes, Running Bull. Brings back a lot of memories."

Anthony and Nathan exchanged news and ran up and down many a memory lane before Nathan glanced at Owen and said, "I thank you for your patience while Anthony and I caught up, young man. However, I think *Antonio* was not all in jest when he said he needed something."

Nathan looked at Anthony. "And what can this decrepit old Indian do for this fat, lazy Mexican, huh?"

"Fat? I'm not fat!" Anthony protested. "I *may* be ten pounds overweight—and I'm sure not lazy!"

"All those homemade tortillas Gloria serves," Nathan added, as though Anthony hadn't spoken. "Warm, lard-filled *tortillas*. And carne adovada. Chicharrones. Red chile. Sour cream. Guacamole."

His drawn out sigh was tinged with drama. "Anthony, the people in this place are slowly starving me to death."

Anthony cracked up. When he stopped and caught his breath he said, "You cantankerous old red man—you always were jealous of my wife's cooking."

The two men grinned at each other again and Owen found himself grinning along.

In a conspiracy-laced whisper, Anthony said, "Tell you what, *Raging Bull*, if you are able to help us today, I will convince Gloria to cook you lunch—a hot meal with all the things you love—and I will bring it here myself, and we will eat it together. What do you say?"

"What is it you want, *Zapata*? I will say anything," Nathan mumbled. "Anything! Whatever it takes."

They shared another affectionate laugh. Then Anthony got down to business.

"Thing is, *mi hermano*, I have a client who is also a good friend. Back in 1958, her folks were killed in a car crash south of here, on what was Route 66 back then. The highway was pretty primitive by today's standards. Road had no shoulder to speak of."

"That was a long time ago," Nathan remarked, "and yes; that was a lonely stretch of road."

"Yeah, it was. And this woman—her name is Kari—was six years old when it happened. Her folks' car broke down alongside the road. They set her and her little sister and baby brother back from the road to keep them safe."

Anthony cleared his throat. "Thing is, a semi came barreling down the road and struck her parents and their car. Killed both of them."

Nathan shook his head. "Very sad. I'm sorry to hear this."

Anthony nodded. "Yes, it was tragic. And it was made worse by something else that happened."

"Yeah?"

Owen, who was watching and listening, thought he detected a dreamy quality to the old man's response. He glanced at Anthony and saw he was frowning a little.

"Nathan, are we tiring you?"

"What? Sure. Probably. I usually wake up early and take a nap—after they feed the animals." He chortled and then lapsed into silence.

"Should we go and come back in a couple of hours?"

Nathan eased his head up and cracked one eye. "No. Slap me if I doze off, eh, *Generalissimo*?"

"Um, right. I'll try to keep this brief then. Where was I? Yeah, so after the truck killed Kari's parents, she doesn't remember much until she was in a bright room. A man and woman, a married couple, she thinks, were holding her sister and brother. Another woman in the room, a woman who seemed to be in charge, was giving Kari's sister and brother to this couple.

"Kari started screaming for them not to take her siblings. That's when the woman in charge grabbed Kari's arm, slapped her, and told her to never speak of her sister and brother again. Said if she did, that they would drown her sister and brother."

Nathan seemed to wake up. "Stole those kids, did they?"

Owen broke his silence. "You don't seem too surprised."

"Happened lots on the res back in the day, young man. Seen too many bad things and heard the weeping of too many mothers to be surprised at what Anthony says happened. I'm sorry though."

Owen was shocked and didn't know how to respond. He glanced at Anthony, who pressed ahead. "When that woman leaned over to slap Kari, Kari saw that she was wearing a name tag. She says the tag was practically in her face. What she remembers is the name *Marge*. She believes the woman's last name started with an *S*."

"What can I help you with?" Nathan asked.

Owen thought he seemed confused.

"Well, at first we thought this Marge *S* was a social worker. That did not pan out, so we started thinking of other agencies that might have intervened. For some reason, I thought of that boys' ranch you worked at. Do you remember it? You told me a lot of tall tales about the fun you had with those boys and all the mischief they got into."

"Boys' ranch?"

Owen and Anthony exchanged looks.

"You used to tend the horses at that ranch, remember? You taught the boys to ride and how to care for the horses, took them on trail rides? I can't remember the name of the place. Gabaldon Boys Ranch? Garcia? No, that's not it."

"Gabron." Nathan's voice sounded sharp again. "Gabron Boys' Ranch. Of course, I remember it. Few miles northeast of Thoreau."

Anthony blew out a relieved sigh. "That's right—Gabron Boy's Ranch. What we want to know is, did a woman by the name of Marge work there?"

"Work where?" Nathan had slipped back into that sleepy, dreamlike state.

"You want I should slap you, old man?"

Owen knew Anthony didn't mean his threat. He was frustrated and trying to jog his friend out of his stupor.

"What? I'm awake. And who you calling old?"

"*Marge*. Did a woman named Marge work at Gabron Boy's Ranch?"

"Well, a'course she did."

A chill jittered down Owen's back and along his arms until it reached his fingertips.

Anthony's hands were clenched in fists on his thighs. "She did? Can you tell us her last name?"

"She was one mean Anglo, that old battle axe. Mean as a snake. You didn't want t' get crosswise of that one."

"You're talking about Marge? Marge from the boys' ranch?"

"A'course I am. I'm not senile, *Pancho Villa*."

"Well, spit out her last name, *Geronimo*, or you won't be sharing chicharrones and carne adovada with me anytime soon."

Owen could tell Anthony's excitement was as taut as his own was, but the shock of Nathan's next words blew him away.

"Her name was Marge Showman. That brother of hers was one mean State bull. I didn't want t' get crosswise with him, neither."

Showman. The State trooper who had filed the accident. His name had been Gary Showman.

Owen breathed a silent plea. *Lord! Is this your hand at work? Are we finally going to catch a break?*

CHAPTER 8

Anthony pushed his truck down the state road as hard as he could in good conscience. "Marge Showman! Her brother, Gary Showman, was first on scene at the accident. Sounds like they may have had an illegal adoption thing already going on for him to have called her to the scene of the accident. Or maybe he took the kids to her. And the other two officers? Must have already been on the take."

Owen grunted his agreement. "We'll figure it out. Now that we have all their names and their connection to Kari, it's straightforward digging."

"Gary Showman is dead. His sister is likely to be. Nathan Running Bull said she was an 'old' battle axe."

"Yeah." Owen didn't say more. That they had gotten this far was nothing short of miraculous.

O God, we're trusting in you. He was surprised to hear his heart add, *because, Lord, in you the lost are found.*

They grabbed lunch from a Blake's Lotaburger drive-through on their way in to Anthony's office. Once there, they brainstormed their next steps while they plowed through burgers and fries.

Owen stopped chewing and spoke around a mouthful of burger. "What's this green stuff on my burger?"

Anthony lifted an eyebrow. "Green chile, of course. Grown only in Hatch, New Mexico."

"On a hamburger?"

"You're in New Mexico, bud. Eat up. It's good for you."

Owen's taste buds decided the chile wasn't bad. He chewed, swallowed, and took another bite.

Green chile might grow on me.

Maybe.

That afternoon, the two men went to a library and began delving through the telephone books of every town near and between Grants and Gallup. They searched for the name "Showman." Listings for most of the tiny villages around the larger towns were lumped into a larger town's book.

Such was the city of Grants phone book. Owen finished with the Grants listings and opened to the little section in the back for Thoreau. He ran his finger through the *S* section.

"Found something."

Anthony peered over his shoulder. "Huh! Another Gary Showman?"

"Has to be his son, right?"

"Write that down."

They tore back to Esquibel Investigations. Anthony glanced at the clock as he dialed the number Owen handed him.

"Yes, hello. My name is Anthony Esquibel. I'm looking for Gary Showman?"

He listened for a moment. "When will he be home from work?"

Anthony slanted a look at Owen as he listened to the response. "I don't want to interrupt your dinner. What would be a convenient time to call back? Well, if you don't eat until 6:30, may I call back in twenty minutes? Yes. Thank you."

"Twenty minutes?"

"Yup. Coffee while we wait?"

When Anthony called back in exactly twenty minutes, Gary Showman answered and demanded, "You selling something?"

"No, sir, I am not. My name is Anthony Esquibel of Esquibel Investigations in Albuquerque. If I may ask, are you related to the Gary Showman who was a New Mexico State Police trooper and who passed away in 1982?"

Anthony listened to silence on the other end for a few seconds before Showman asked, "Who did you say you were again? And why do you want to know?"

"Mr. Showman, I assure you that you are not in any trouble, but I am looking for relatives of Gary Showman and his sister Marge Showman. Are you a relation?"

The man, still wary, answered, "Gary Showman was my dad. Marge was my aunt."

"Mr. Showman, tomorrow is Saturday. Would you allow me and my associate to take you to lunch? We have some questions for you and would compensate you in some way for your time."

"Could I have your number? I would like my sister to call you. She's an attorney."

Anthony hesitated, wondering at the man's defensive posture. "Sure. Ask her to please call me today."

They hung up and Anthony looked at Owen. "He knows something and is scared."

"Is kidnapping a first-degree felony in New Mexico?" Owen asked.

"Yep. No statute of limitations."

"But the guilty parties are dead."

Anthony shrugged. "Could be the family knew enough to blow the whistle and chose not to. That would be obstruction. And dirty little secrets aren't pleasant when made public."

Some thirty minutes later the phone rang. Anthony picked it up on the second ring.

"Esquibel Investigations."

Owen could hear only one side of the conversation, but Anthony gave him some verbal cues as to what was going on.

"Ms. Sanchez, we are only looking for information. We would like to meet with you and Gary. In fact, please feel free to invite anyone who might have information about either Gary or Marge. Especially Marge.

"Yes, especially Marge. She has a daughter? Yes, please bring her. And we are more than willing to pay you for your time. Say, fifty dollars an hour, per person?

"Well, shall we say only the immediate relations of Gary and Marge? No, no kids, please. Yes. Lunch and fifty dollars an hour. That's right.

"Where and when?"

They made the arrangements and Anthony hung up. "Sounds like we'll meet at least three descendants of Gary and Marge tomorrow."

"Marge had a daughter? But her last name was still Showman?"

Anthony lifted one shoulder. "Lots of unmarried pregnancies in New Mexico."

They met at the agreed-upon restaurant in Thoreau at 11:30. Gary was large and intimidating, even for a man nearing retirement. Owen wondered if his father had been as formidable, made more so by the uniform he'd worn.

Gary's sister, Judy Sanchez, wasn't nearly as physically intimidating, but her attitude was professional and cool. She, too, looked to be in her sixties, with short, iron-gray hair.

The oldest of the three, Marge's daughter Dot, reminded Anthony of the aging hippies who lived in the Jemez Mountains. She seemed more curious than anything else.

They shook hands all around and sat at a corner booth that provided a modicum of privacy. No one said much until the waitress had taken their orders.

Judy spoke first. "What's this all about? And until we understand what it is you want, I will do all of the talking. Consider me their lawyer." She poked her chin in Gary and Dot's direction.

Owen let Anthony talk. "Ms. Sanchez, as I said on the phone, we are only interested in information. We are willing to stipulate that nothing you might reveal to us would be used in any legal setting. That said, the defensive posture you have presented tells me you must have an inkling as to why we are here."

Anthony stared at the woman, but she did not flinch or look away.

"Our 'posture,' as you call it, tells you nothing. Please ask your questions and I will determine what our answers will be—if we answer at all."

Anthony shrugged. "Very well, then. Before I ask anything specific, let me tell you about our client."

Anthony outlined the accident and Kari's remembrance of what happened afterwards. He presented a copy of the accident report filed by Gary Showman and spoke of Marge Showman's employment at Gabron Boy's Ranch.

The waitress returned to serve their food. Those seated at the table remained silent until the waitress, with curious glances, finished setting down plates and walked away.

"Go ahead and enjoy your lunch," Anthony instructed. "I'll talk and you listen while you eat."

He finished recounting Kari's description of the accident and what followed. He described the results of his and Owen's research.

"Here's what we think happened," Anthony concluded, looking at Gary and Judy. "Your father, Gary Showman, and his sister"—he nodded at Dot—"your mother, Marge, had an illegal adoption racket going on. They took Kari's three-year-old sister, Elaine, and her six-month-old brother, Samuel, and sold them."

He looked directly at Dot, whose eyes were large in a white, bloodless face. "Marge threatened Kari. Marge told a six-year-old little girl that if she ever mentioned her sister or brother again, that she, Marge, would call their adoptive parents and have them drown those kids. Kari was so traumatized by her parents' death and Marge's threats, that she blocked those memories for thirty-three years.

"Now that she remembers what happened, the only thing she wants is to find her siblings. She doesn't care about prosecution—and, after all, Gary and Marge are both deceased, right? So no prosecution. And Kari doesn't care about publicity, doesn't care about making what happened public. All she cares about is locating her sister and brother. So what's it gonna be? Are you willing to help us?"

"Don't say anything, Dot," Judy cautioned. "Let me handle this."

Judy toyed with her fork and half-eaten lunch. "Suppose we might have some information. What assurances will you give us that you won't destroy our family's privacy?"

"Whatever assurances you ask for," Anthony answered. "You're an attorney. Draw something up. We'll sign it. We only care about those two kids."

In response, Judy Sanchez pulled a small cassette recorder from her purse and switched it on. "This is Judy Sanchez, New Mexico State licensed attorney, speaking with Anthony Esquibel and Owen Washington, September 5, 1991. Also present are Mr. Gary Showman and Miss Dorothy Showman.

"Mr. Esquibel and Mr. Washington will identify themselves and attest to the confidentiality of this meeting. No information provided here today can or will be used in a court of law or be made public in any fashion or venue. Information provided here today may be disclosed to their client and her legal counsel only and may be used exclusively pursuant to locating their client's siblings."

She nodded to Anthony and Owen.

"Anthony Esquibel of Esquibel Investigations, Albuquerque. I stipulate to the conditions of this meeting as laid out by Ms. Sanchez."

"I am Owen Washington, in-house investigator for Brunell & Brunell, Attorneys at Law, New Orleans, Louisiana. I agree to the conditions of this meeting as laid out by Ms. Sanchez."

Judy Sanchez nodded as she turned off the recorder and replaced it in her purse. "Mr. Esquibel and Mr. Washington, Gary and I knew what kind of man our father was. We may not have known the depths of his depravity, but we had our suspicions and our own experiences with him.

"Let's say that we grew up in a pretty abusive family, but our mother got the worst of it. Aunt Marge told us that Dad was the spitting image of *their* dad, which explained a lot to us."

She shifted, clearly uncomfortable with what she was revealing. "After Dad passed away, we found a few curiosities—a separate bank account in his name, for one, and records of substantial cash deposits over the years. These things confused and concerned us. We asked Aunt Marge about them, but she put us off."

The woman cleared her throat. "We actually threatened Aunt Marge, told her we would bring the police in to sort things out, but Marge was ready for our threats. She fired back, 'If you get the police involved, your mother will lose everything: She will lose your dad's pension, all that money in the bank, and her reputation. What will she have then? What will she live on?'"

Judy Sanchez looked from Owen to Anthony. "To tell you the truth, our mom only started living after our dad died. For the first time that we could remember, she was happy. She had enough money to travel a little, fix up the house the way she wanted, buy nice clothes. We knew she would have enough for her old age. And what exactly did we actually know about Dad's suspected illegal activities? Nothing."

Judy sighed. "Then Aunt Marge died two years later. I'll let Dot tell you what she found."

Dot stared at the two investigators. "My mother got pregnant with me when she was fifteen. As you can imagine, life after that was not easy for her. Somehow, she provided for me and managed to leave me a nest egg and a home that was paid off. I couldn't figure out how she'd done it, but Gary and Judy and I knew that whatever Mother and Uncle Gary were involved in, they were in it together and it had to have been illegal.

"I am so sorry. So sorry for the pain they caused Kari? Kari is her name?" Dot sniffed into a napkin. "A while after Mother died, maybe a year? I found a notebook. I couldn't make heads or tails of it, but I knew it was important, because every entry had a dollar amount beside it. I-I made a copy of its contents."

Owen and Anthony exchanged a glance.

"We'd like to have that copy," Anthony said.

"Its contents are covered by this meeting's privacy agreement," Judy added.

"Of course. Only to be used to locate Kari's missing siblings."

Judy nodded, and Dot removed a sheaf of papers from her bag. She handed the stapled papers to Owen.

"I hope this will help you find her sister and brother."

***

MISS DAWES' RICH, DULCET TONES wafted through the phone line. "Good morning, Miss Kari."

"Good morning, Miss Dawes! How are you today?"

"I am fine. I thank you for asking. Miss Kari, if you are available tomorrow morning, Mr. Washington and Mr. Esquibel request a meeting to brief you on the results of their inquiries."

Kari's heart thudded into her shoes. "Brief you on the results" had the ring of finality. Unsuccessful finality.

She stuttered her response. "I-I, of course. W-what time?"

"Nine o'clock, if that is convenient for you?"

"Yes. I will be there. Is-is Mr. Washington home then? Has he returned from New Mexico?"

"He and Mr. Esquibel are flying in this evening, Miss Kari."

Drat. So no genteel way of preempting the meeting, of getting the "skinny" from Owen in advance.

Kari sighed. "Thank you, Miss Dawes."

Kari arrived early the following morning. She was not surprised to find Clover seated at the conference room table with Owen and Anthony.

Seems like I have sat at this table a thousand times, Kari thought. She looked for good news in their faces, but did not find it.

"Can you give me the bottom line, Owen? Anthony? I can't bear the suspense."

Owen's eyes filled with sympathy. "The bottom line, Miss Kari, is not what we hoped for. We have reached a dead end."

Kari stared at the table. She willed herself not to cry.

I'm done crying at this table, in front of these fine men, she told herself. *I am more mature than I was six months ago. I need to act my age.*

Taking a firm grip on her emotions, she cleared her throat. "Thank you for your candor, Owen. I'm ready now to hear your report."

"We found your 'Marge S,' Kari. The woman whose name tag you remembered was Marge Showman. She was not a social worker, as it turns out. She was the business administrator of a boys' ranch not far from the scene of your parents' accident. The name tag had to have been from the ranch."

Kari nodded her understanding.

"She lived her last years in Thoreau, New Mexico, and passed away in 1984. We interviewed her daughter. She had kept a footlocker of her mother's things. In that footlocker she found a notebook, a kind of coded ledger."

Anthony looked up from his notes. "Apparently, Marge Showman had a longtime relationship with a pregnancy center located in Grants. She was, herself, an unmarried mother in her early teens and the center had helped her. In return, Marge had volunteered at the center during summer breaks, first while finishing high school and later while going to college.

"After she graduated with a degree in social work, Marge began to work with the center to arrange private adoptions for the center's clients. Back then private adoption was more common than not and quite without restriction. We think Marge's work with the pregnancy center may have begun with the best of intentions, but Marge's intentions look to have changed as time went on."

Anthony picked up the thread. "We don't know how or when Marge 'branched out' and began arranging her own private adoptions. Raising a child alone had to have been difficult financially.

"What we think is that she figured out how to use the center's name and resources but cut them out of the loop. Once she managed to put herself solely in charge of an adoption, she upped the price for healthy infants, and gave the birth mother only a small portion of the payment for expenses.

"We think that occasionally the birth mother may have asked questions or demanded more money. Marge had a brother who was a state policeman, and we believe that when Marge needed a little muscle to bring the birth mother into line, she paid him to provide it.

"We believe Gary Showman grew bolder over time. He referred young pregnant women directly to Marge, who represented herself as being employed by the pregnancy center. Many of their new 'clients' came from the Navajo or Pueblo reservations and were desperate for secrecy.

"Apparently, the people at the center never had suspicions about Marge—and why would they? They never saw the children she brokered on the side."

Anthony took a sip of water. "As we mentioned, Marge kept a ledger of all the adoptions she brokered. Her daughter gave us that ledger."

Kari fidgeted.

"According to the ledger, shortly after the date of your parent's accident, Marge noted the transfer of two children, a girl, approximately age three, and a boy, six months, to a J.B. Cole. The only other notation under the same date was the word 'Portland,' which we think must refer to a city."

Excitement bubbled up in Kari and she stirred. Owen's expression quelled her.

"Kari, we found 'J.B. Cole' in Marge's ledger five times and a total of three other sets of initials with no last name. "We did more digging and we *think* 'J.B. Cole' refers to a married couple, a Joseph and Belinda Cole. However, this man and his wife could not have been the adoptive parents—they never had any children.

"We believe Joseph Cole acted as a cutout. A middleman. His role was to put distance between adoptive parents and Marge Showman, so that the children could not be traced back to her. As far as we can tell, Marge never entered the names of adoptive parents in the ledger—only the initials of the go-betweens. Yes, we found J.B. Cole, but we have been unable to find names for other three sets of initials in the ledger."

Kari stilled as implications began to come clear.

Anthony continued. "Marge retired in 1965 and she stopped volunteering at the pregnancy center at the same time. Entries in the ledger spanned a period of fifteen years but ceased when she retired.

"When we tracked down the Coles, Belinda had passed away in 1969. When we finally located Joseph Cole, he, too, was deceased. No one where he had lived out his last years remembered him. We could not locate any family or friends. Like I said, he and his wife had no children.

"In short, we believe Joseph and Belinda Cole passed Elaine and Samuel to an adoptive family that paid well for them. Unfortunately, we have no record of that family and no way to trace them."

Every fear Kari's research had raised in her heart grew larger. "What if . . . what if a family did not adopt them?" she whispered. "What if instead . . ."

Clover looked confused, but Owen and Anthony did not.

"Kari, we have no way of knowing if they were brokered other than to a family," Owen said, keeping his voice steady, "You can't let your fears rule you on this. And please remind yourself that Elaine and Samuel are both grown now."

Clover muttered, "I am not following," and looked from face to face.

Anthony chimed in. "Kari, the one thing that gives me hope over that kind of thinking is the dollar amount Marge Showman applied to her ledger."

"What do you mean?"

"She logged four thousand dollars for Elaine and Samuel. For herself. The Coles had to have received as much. Eight thousand dollars. That was a *lot* of money in 1956. A wealthy adoptive couple— a couple who could not have children, who longed for a family, and who had the means—they would have paid that for two beautiful children. Uh, we think other buyers . . . would not have paid as much."

"How-how-how does that amount compare to other entries?" Kari's stomach clenched as they discussed with dispassion *the cost of buying children.*

"It was pretty high, actually," Owen admitted. "I had noticed that but hadn't come to any conclusions. However, Anthony is right. And, most, er, traffickers don't want infants because of the care they require."

"Traffickers?" Clover frowned and then reddened. "No!"

"But there's nothing to say they wouldn't pay and then resell them!" Kari's heart was breaking. "You have to keep looking. You have to!"

Owen and Anthony exchanged disconcerted glances.

"What would you have us do next, Kari?" Owen asked as gently as he could. "Where would you have us look?"

"Well, how many Portlands can there be in the U.S.? Portland, Oregon? Portland, Maine? How many families in these cities have two children with the first names of Elaine and Samuel?" Kari demanded. "Can't you look at school records? Maybe census records?"

"Between twenty-five and thirty towns and cities in the United States are named Portland or have the word 'Portland' in their names. We would have to visit every Portland in the country and every school in every city—with no guarantee that the adoptive parents retained the children's given names. In fact, it is likely that they changed their names."

"Well, what about newspaper ads in those cities? And I don't care what it costs!"

Anthony answered. "That's not a bad idea. We can do that. It will cost a lot, but since you are willing and able to pay, we can arrange them and target Portland towns and cities."

"Well, do it! And what about those milk cartons?" With every moment, Kari's tone grew harsher. She was angry, angrier than she had been in a long time.

If she did not restrain herself, she would soon be throwing a major fit in front of people she loved, whose respect she valued.

"Kari," Owen's voice was patient, but Kari heard the caution in his tone. "Do you remember when we went to brunch together—you, Clover and Lorene, Mercy and myself—the Sunday you told us all about your recovered memories?"

Kari nodded, but like mercury in a thermometer, the rage coursing through her veins was rising higher.

"Do you remember we talked about God's peace? His contentment?"

"Yes." Kari grated the word through clenched teeth.

"Peace acts like the Holy Spirit's umpire," Owen said, his words soft. "Peace helps us to determine if we are working in God's will or under our own power, our old, uncrucified flesh.

"Right now, you are disappointed and upset. Understandably so. But you don't want to go off and do or say things while you are upset. That is not how our Lord leads us. He leads us in peace—not in frustration."

Kari bit back the hot words that fought to flood her mouth. She made herself recount how dear Owen was to her, how kind and gentle his manner was, and how consistently steady and stable his behaviors were. He was a godly man, filled with the fruit of the Holy Spirit.

Lord, please help me! These feelings are not leading me in "paths of righteousness." Please help me to calm down. Please help me to surrender my disappointment to you.

She took a deep breath and blew it out. And again.

"But what do we do now? What can *I* do?" Kari felt like her heart was crumbling.

Anthony looked away. Owen did not. "We can pray for Elaine and Samuel, Kari. We can pray for them. As your family prayed for your father, even after he had had been gone decades."

"But I—" The words choked her. "*But I want them!* I have already waited my entire life for them and I want them! I—"

Kari broke.

She laid her head on the table and sobbed.

CHAPTER 9

The next month dragged by, and Kari struggled each day to find and keep her emotional footing. Her activities became tasteless chores; she lost interest in many things. She grew short-tempered and surly with those around her.

Kari was depressed and, somewhere inside, she knew it.

She hadn't realized how emotionally dependent she'd become on finding Elaine and Samuel—not until Owen and Anthony had reached a dead end. She hadn't recognized that she'd hung all her hopes on finding them—not until Owen and Anthony told her that every avenue had been exhausted.

With mulish determination, she pushed ahead and refused to give up the search. Underneath her stubborn persistence was a growing resentment.

***

KARI'S FORTIETH BIRTHDAY ARRIVED, and with it more depression. She had planned to ignore the day, but Søren, Max, and Ilsa called to wish her a happy birthday. Kari thanked them for the flowers they sent, and made an effort to express her appreciation—even if she was faking it.

They shouldn't have bothered. They can't afford luxuries like florists! And for what?

When Clover and Lorene asked to take her to lunch, Kari pretended she had a cold and asked for a raincheck.

I can't fake a whole lunch. Besides, I need to keep Anthony and Owen on task.

Then, over her protests, Anthony returned to New Mexico, saying Owen could handle any follow-on tasks she assigned.

Fine!

Kari had not spoken with him since.

She labored for days to script the newspaper ads, but was outspokenly disgusted when Owen told her that dairy farmers no longer ran missing children's faces and stories on the backs of milk cartons. The milk carton project had died when a number of prominent child psychologists proclaimed that children "might be traumatized" if they read about kidnapped or missing children at the breakfast table.

Idiots.

Against Owen's advice, Kari reached out to the host of a popular television program whose son had been abducted and murdered in 1981.

92

"Look, Kari, we have a legally binding agreement with the Showman family not to publicize their parents' part in the abduction," Owen warned her. "Going on national television will lead to questions that you cannot, ethically or legally, answer."

"I'll keep them out of it," Kari insisted.

But the television host declined to document her case for his program. "I'm sorry I won't be able to help you," he said, "but you have no pictures of your sister or brother, you won't provide any of the background information about their abduction and, frankly, too much time has passed. I can't base an entire program on two names and an event that occurred thirty-some years ago. Perhaps I can do a small spotlight on the newspaper ads at the end of the show."

The quarter-page ads ran in twenty papers for four weeks and cost Kari several hundred thousand dollars.

Owen set up a call center and staffed it with a half-dozen people.

More money.

Owen and two investigators from his new firm reviewed and followed up on the calls.

Much more money.

The call center received hundreds of calls in response to the newspaper advertisements—and opportunists and charlatans galore came crawling out of the woodwork.

Not one lead panned out.

"You've re-created a scene from that movie *Annie*," Owen grumbled. "I expect Lily St. Regis and Rooster Hannigan to show up any day now. You know—with half of a locket."

Kari's face blazed red. "That's not funny, Owen. I don't appreciate your making light of something so serious."

Owen straightened and smoothed his ebony features into stiff, dignified lines. "No, it's not funny. I apologize, Miss Kari."

As he walked away, Kari knew she was the one who should have apologized.

Kari called Ruth that afternoon and spoke of her mounting disappointments. She sat at the desk in her redone office. Her desk faced the window now instead of away from it. She stared out the window at her favorite view as they talked.

"I cannot believe Owen has become so indifferent about the search! It's like he has given up and is merely going through the motions. I wonder if I should hire someone else to take over the investigation."

"But I thought he said there wasn't much more they could do without the name of the adopting family?"

Kari practically growled at Ruth. "I'm paying him a lot of money. He needs to do the job and put his whole heart into it!"

"I want to be honest with you, Kari," her friend answered. "I am less concerned about the condition of Owen's heart than I am about yours."

Kari's response was immediate. And heated. "What do you mean by that?"

"Listen, Cookie. I understand how important finding Elaine and Samuel is to you. I truly do, but it sounds—it *feels*—like you have shut God out of the equation. Are you are doing this all in your own strength? Are you insisting on doing it your own way? Or are you praying over everything and trusting God to direct you?"

"I figured God would be in whatever I did," Kari mumbled. "He's the one who let me remember them, right? So I assume he wants me to find them, and I'm working as hard as I can."

She added with a derisive sniff, "I wish other people were working as hard."

"Um, yes, but the Bible talks a lot about *how* we work to follow the Lord, how we pursue him, Kari. He is always to be first in our lives—not the work he has given us. We must be careful, watching for anything that seeks to usurp that first place and being quick to tear down whatever tries to exalt itself over Jesus as the only King in our hearts.

"I'm describing something of a paradox, an ongoing battle that every believer experiences. The Bible tells us that we have a spirit that longs to do what God desires, that patiently waits for him to speak and guide us. The Bible also tells us we have 'a flesh,' our 'old' sinful nature, the part of us that demands its own way.

"Our flesh opposes the things of God, Kari. And frustration is one of the key indicators that we are operating out of our flesh rather than our spirit. Tell me, Kari, are you frustrated?"

"Well, of course I am! Why wouldn't I be?"

"Because, Kari, I'm saying that frustration is a symptom that you are doing things under your own steam instead of letting the Lord be your helper and your guide.

"Without realizing it is happening, our hearts can wander or become preoccupied with things other than our relationship with God. How is your heart right now, Kari? Is it fully committed to the Lord? Or is it distracted? Distant from God? Resentful?"

Kari was silent and her jaw clenched. She didn't like what Ruth was dishing out. Didn't know how to answer.

"Kari? Are you still there?"

Kari stared out her window. "Yes."

New Orleans' weather in late October was still quite warm. Flowers bloomed, died, and bloomed again. Frequent rains kept the lawns lush and green. And the sprawling tree dominating Kari's view from her office seemed never to change. It was full of years yet ageless.

Not so in RiverBend. According to Søren's last phone call, he and his neighbors had experienced an early harvest and they anticipated a harsh winter. Nights were cold, and their trees had already shed their leaves.

RiverBend.

Kari's heart strained toward Søren, toward Max, toward Søren's farm and the peace she had found in their simple life.

Toward Rose's homestead.

Rose.

"Kari? Your family waited a long time to find you. Perhaps . . . perhaps you could take a lesson from Rose's journals about trusting God instead of trusting in your own ideas and that mammoth pot of gold you're sitting on?"

Kari smarted under Ruth's last words. She mumbled out a reply. "Yes. Perhaps you're right. Thanks, Ruth. I'll talk to you later."

She sat unmoving for a long while after she hung up, rehashing Ruth's words and lost in her thoughts, some confusing, others convicting. When she roused herself, she reached inside her pencil drawer for the key to the deep bottom drawer of her desk—the drawer where she kept her Bible and Rose's journals.

Kari had not read her Bible as faithfully as she had her first month home. As for Rose's journals? She had not finished reading the first one yet. The harder Kari drove herself and the more invested she became in the search for her siblings, the less time she spent in her Bible and the less interest she had in Rose's journals.

Is Ruth right? Has my heart . . . gone astray?

She placed Rose's journals in a stack to one side and opened her Bible. She let it fall open and started reading at the first chapter heading she found: Isaiah 46.

> *Bel bows down, Nebo stoops low;*
> *their idols are borne by beasts of burden*

Kari frowned and closed her eyes. *Bel? Nebo? Who were they? What do they have to do with me?*

She struggled through the next verses. Verse 5 began to arouse her interest.

> *With whom will you compare me or count me equal?*
> *To whom will you liken me that we may be compared?*

"Who is asking this question?" Kari wondered. "Is it God?" She read on.

> *Some pour out gold from their bags*
> *and weigh out silver on the scales;*
> *they hire a goldsmith to make it into a god,*
> *and they bow down and worship it.*
> *They lift it to their shoulders and carry it;*
> *they set it up in its place, and there it stands.*
> *From that spot it cannot move.*
> *Even though someone cries out to it, it cannot answer;*
> *it cannot save them from their troubles.*

"Isaiah is talking about idols," Kari realized. "Idols made from gold and silver—idols that cannot answer. That cannot save these people from their troubles."

Ruth's last words thundered in her ears: *Perhaps you could take a lesson from Rose's journals about trusting God instead of trusting in your own ideas and that mammoth pot of gold you're sitting on?*

Kari did not like where her heart and mind directed her next. "Am I, am I like these people? Have I poured out my money to make an idol? To circumvent God's place in my life?"

With growing dismay, she continued reading.

> *Remember this, keep it in mind,*
> *take it to heart, you rebels.*
> *Remember the former things, those of long ago;*
> *I am God, and there is no other;*
> *I am God, and there is none like me.*
> *I make known the end from the beginning,*
> *from ancient times, what is still to come.*
> *I say, 'My purpose will stand,*
> *and I will do all that I please.'*

"Oh, no! Am I a rebel against God?"

Thoroughly convicted, Kari slipped from her chair onto her knees. "Lord! Please forgive my rebellion! I have poured out gold and silver and fashioned an idol from my 'good ideas' and my desire to find Elaine and Sammie. But, O God! You already know where they are."

She reached for her Bible and laid it open upon the chair in front of her. "You are God, Lord. There is no other," she whispered aloud. "You are God, and there is none like you. You know the end from the beginning. Your purposes will stand, Lord, despite all my trying and struggling. You will do all that *you* please.

"Lord, please forgive me." She reread the last verse.

> *What I have said, that I will bring about;*
> *what I have planned, that I will do.*

Kari wept then, utterly broken before God. "Lord, I'm sorry, so very sorry! Do what you have planned, Lord. I surrender to you."

She reread the thirteen short verses of the chapter and then read them again. She spoke them aloud. Each time she read, "They pour out gold from their bags," she remembered the hundreds of thousands of dollars she had spent on the newspaper ads and call center against the counsel of her friends—friends more mature in their faith than she was—and she wept anew.

"Father, I promised you I would use this money for your kingdom. I have wasted it. I am so sorry! Please forgive me."

Later, when Kari got up from the floor, she saw the stack of journals on her desk. She sat down, picked up the blue one, opened it to where she had left off weeks ago, and began reading.

Journal Entry, October 27, 1911

Dear Lord, thank you for the work you are doing in my daughter's heart. Father! How hard it is for us to allow you to nail our flesh to the cross. But how precious the outcome of such a crucifixion.

Joy shared with me this evening that she has been reading in Isaiah, one of her favorite books of the Bible. I recall how you spoke to her from Isaiah when you called her to Corinth, to the work she would undertake, only three short years ago.

Many good things have happened in those three years, Lord. Many hearts have surrendered to you in that time, and I am grateful, despite the cost.

And now you have spoken to her again through this same book, Lord. As we talked, Joy shared with me a passage from Isaiah, Chapter 46.

Remember the former things of old:
for I am God, and there is none else;
I am God, and there is none like me,
Declaring the end from the beginning,
and from ancient times
the things that are not yet done, saying,
My counsel shall stand, and I will do all my pleasure:
Calling a ravenous bird from the east,
the man that executeth my counsel
from a far country: yea, I have spoken it,
I will also bring it to pass;
I have purposed it, I will also do it.

Kari was stunned. "That is the same passage I read a bit ago, but in a different translation!" She devoured the journal's next paragraphs.

Joy understands now that she must allow you to be God, to have the preeminence in her heart. "I have been very hard on Mr. O'Dell, Mama, very hard, indeed. However, I shall put undue pressure upon him no longer," she told me.

"I know he, too, is grieving for Grant and is doing all that can be done without my adding to his burden. We will do all we can and, when we have done all we ought to do, it is God himself who will accomplish his purposes, for he alone must receive the glory and honor.

"I must trust more deeply in the Lord rather than my own or Mr. O'Dell's efforts. I should never relent in prayer, but I must relinquish control of the outcome."

Kari stood and paced the room. She could not stand or sit for the adrenaline coursing through her veins.

"O God! O God!" she prayed. "You have surely spoken to me—and I must not fail to heed what you have said."

Kari reached for the telephone and dialed Owen's number. When he answered, she struggled to make certain her words were gracious, her tone sweet. "Good afternoon, Owen. Would you mind meeting with me? Yes, please. At your earliest convenience."

She did not miss the reluctance in his response even as they set a time and place for breakfast the following morning. *He's thinking I have come up with another harebrained scheme*, Kari thought.

She shook her head. "I am truly sorry, Lord," she whispered again.

***

"OWEN, THANK YOU FOR MEETING WITH ME," Kari said when the waitress seated them. She had asked for a small table, and now she reached her hand across the short distance and placed it on top of his. "I have something I need to tell you."

Owen's dark eyes met hers. "Okay."

"I have been a complete fool for weeks, maybe months. The Lord spoke to me yesterday. He showed me that I—" Kari choked a little as she forced the words out, "that I have made an idol of my sister and brother, that I have placed finding them above Jesus, above his lordship in my life. He reminded me that Jesus is the only Lord I should have."

Owen nodded and his hand tightened a little in hers.

"And Owen, I have treated you terribly. I've disrespected you as a friend and as a brother in Christ, and I have slighted your wise counsel. I am so very sorry. I-I ask for your forgiveness. Will you forgive me? Please."

She saw a little glistening in his eyes before he looked away, but he did not pull his hand back.

Then he cleared his throat and met her imploring gaze. "Yes, I forgive you, Kari. I'm happy the Lord spoke to you."

"I-I'm glad, too. But it means I . . . I need to stop now. Stop chasing after Elaine and Sammie."

Tears welled in Kari's eyes. "I don't know how to stop, Owen. I don't know how to give up the search. I don't know how to let them go."

Owen's brow wrinkled in sympathy. "I may know something of your difficulty, Kari."

She remembered then, Owen standing and leaving the table the Sunday when she had shared the news of her recovered memories. She remembered he had lost his older brother when he was still a child himself.

"Yes, I think you must."

He placed his other hand atop their joined fingers. "May I pray for you, Kari?"

Kari bowed her head in response. Owen spoke quietly but with firm conviction and firmer faith. "Lord God, you are the Almighty God. You know our hearts, our weaknesses, our frailties, our failures. O Lord, I pray you look down upon this child of yours, Kari. Give her a heart to seek you first and foremost and to always keep you as her greatest desire.

"And you are the Father of compassion, Lord—you understand loss. For you so loved the world, the whole world, O God! You so loved the world that you gave up your Son for us. You sacrificed your Son to gain us, though we often fail you.

"I pray you give Kari the spiritual strength to surrender another piece of her heart into your care—the place in her heart where she holds Elaine and Samuel. I know you will keep that piece safely, Lord, for you understand and love us. We can surrender anything to you, Lord, for you will hold it for us. You will hold it safely and tenderly. Amen."

Kari clutched Owen's hand and whispered, "Lord, I give you Elaine and Sammie. I trust them to you."

Her voice caught. "Please. Please heal my broken heart."

CHAPTER 10

In spite of Kari's prayer of surrender regarding her sister and brother, the next days were only marginally better. She returned to her morning habit of Bible study, prayer, and reading a single entry from one of Rose's journals—she then kept to her routine with a tenacity born out of desperation.

Lord, please help me. Sunday our pastor preached on hope being the anchor to our souls, but I feel like I am without that anchor in my emotions. With all you have given me, I have this sense of longing, and it all goes back to Elaine and Sammie. Please help me to find hope again, even if it is without them.

Kari's Bible study this day started in the book of 2 Corinthians. She pushed through the first chapter's greeting and stopped to soak in the verses that read,

> *Praise be to the God and Father*
> *of our Lord Jesus Christ,*
> *the Father of compassion*
> *and the God of all comfort,*
> *who comforts us in all our troubles*

"Owen said you were the Father of compassion when he prayed for me, Lord. And I am grateful that you are the God of all comfort," Kari prayed. "I need me some of that, please."

She kept reading, but toward the end of the first chapter, she stumbled to a stop.

"What in the world does this mean?" She read the verses aloud to herself, hoping they would make more sense if she heard them.

> *For no matter how many promises*
> *God has made, they are "Yes" in Christ.*
> *And so through him the "Amen"*
> *is spoken by us to the glory of God.*

Kari pondered the passage. "For no matter how many promises God has made, they are *yes* in Christ?" Although her mind struggled to grasp the passage's significance, her heart leapt in hopeful response.

"No matter how many promises God has made, they are 'yes'? But what does this mean?" Her fingers thrummed a frustrated cadence on the open page of her Bible.

I guess I'll ask someone at Bible study this morning to help me.

She parked at the church a few hours later, hoping her early arrival would allow her to spend a few minutes with someone more versed in the Bible. The first person she ran into was Julie Cairns, a woman a few years younger than Kari was. She was checking her youngest, a boy of two, into the nursery.

"Hey, Kari!"

"Hi, Julie."

Kari waited while Julie disentangled herself from her clingy toddler and his diaper bag. The two women walked together toward the fellowship hall where the Bible study would be held.

"Say, Julie, I'm wondering if you could help me with a passage I read this morning. It's kind of puzzling me."

"I'd love to, Kari, but I promised the leaders I would make the coffee and set up the serving cart and I'm a little late doing so as it is."

Julie looked around and brightened. "Say, see that tiny old woman sitting there? That's Miss Em. She's practically a fixture in the church, and she really knows her Bible. I'm sure she would love to help you."

Kari's eyes followed Julie's finger and lit upon an imposing elderly woman with a ramrod-straight back already seated at one of the study tables. Her wiry gray hair was pulled into an impossibly tight bun on the top of her head. Her solemn, watchful expression was formidable.

"Um, *that* woman? The one who looks like she eats small children for breakfast?"

Julie guffawed. "Yes! That's our Miss Em."

"Sheesh. She's kind of scary looking. Sort of reminds me of the actress Margaret Hamilton."

Julie nodded. "She is a bit intimidating, isn't she? However, don't let her face fool you—she has a heart of pure gold."

Julie hugged Kari. As she turned away, she threw over her shoulder, "By the way, I don't know who Margaret Hamilton is, but Miss Em has always reminded *me* of the Wicked Witch of the West."

Kari stared after Julie and then hooted in laughter.

Julie stopped. "What? What did I say?"

Kari, laughing so hard that she had trouble breathing, waved her on her way. "Go," she managed, and Julie, clearly confused, sped off to the church kitchen.

Kari calmed, took a deep breath, and walked over to the elderly woman to introduce herself. "Miss Em? Good morning. My name is Kari Michaels. Julie said you might, that is, I was hoping I could ask you a Bible question before Bible study started this morning."

Up close, Kari could see how paper-thin Miss Em's dark aged skin was, how fragile her bones; that the old woman's erect posture was an illusion, a leftover from younger years.

She was surprised but relieved when Miss Em's crinkled eyes lit up.

"A'course, a'course. Sit down, young lady, and we'll talk."

Frail physically, perhaps, but sharp as a tack, Kari thought.

She moved a chair so that she could face Miss Em. "Thank you. I've only been a Christian a few months and I'm reading the New Testament through for the first time."

"Good for you." Miss Em smiled in approval, and Kari liked how her "scary" expression relaxed into well-used laugh lines.

So not the Wicked Witch at all, Kari admitted.

"What is your question, dear?"

"Oh!" Kari came to herself. She opened her Bible and pointed to the passage. "This passage really spoke to my heart, but I don't understand what it is saying about God's promises."

Miss Em read the passage and then found the same chapter and verse in her well-worn Bible. "Let me read it to you in the King James, child. I find that reading Scripture in various translations helps to clarify the meaning. Let's see, in the King James, the first part reads,

> *For all the promises of God*
> *in Christ are yea, and in him Amen,*
> *unto the glory of God by us.*

"So the first thing we see is that the Apostle Paul says, 'Look, God has made certain promises to us.' That is a wonderful thought, isn't it? The second point Paul makes is that all God's promises, 'in Christ are yea and amen.' D' you know what 'yea and amen' mean?"

"Um, not really."

"Well, 'yea' means 'yes,' and 'amen' means 'so be it,' or 'I agree with God.'"

Kari's brow furrowed. "So all God's promises are yes?"

"All God's promises are 'yes' *in Christ*. Christ is the one who fulfills God's promises. And the Bible tell us in many, many place that we who belong to God, are 'in Christ.' Whatever promises Christ has fulfilled or made available, are available to us because we are *in him*. Our part is to say 'amen' or 'so be it' to those promises."

"What about . . . what if you think God has promised you something but it is impossible?"

Em studied Kari and became thoughtful. "As you are a new Christian, I would first say that God is not a wishing well. He is not our fairy godmother or one of those fancy cash machines. On the other hand, I would also say that God is not troubled by the impossible. Scripture tells us that nothing, not one thing, is impossible with God."

She leaned toward Kari. "Why don't you tell me what is troubling you and, perhaps, with the Lord's help, we can sort it out?"

Kari's mouth opened a little and she thought about what to say next. "All right, but it's sort of long and messy. Um, I should tell you that my parents died in a car crash when I was six."

She gulped a little. "Right afterwards, my little sister and brother were taken. Illegally. We think they were adopted out. That happened a long time ago, but recently I have been looking for them. What is troubling me is that I have been told that they cannot be found. That it is impossible."

Miss Em gazed into Kari's eyes with compassion. "I am very sorry, young miss. You must feel that part of your heart has been cut away."

Kari blinked back the tears. "Yes, that's true. And I-I guess that ever since the investigators hit a wall and could go no further, I have been engulfed by this sense of-of hopelessness. I believe the Lord spoke to me to surrender the situation to him, but even though I have prayed and given the search for Elaine and Sammie to him, I'm still a bit depressed about it all.

"You see, I had forgotten about my siblings for years. I knew I had forgotten something, something important, but I could never remember. Then, when I became a Christian, it was like God ripped the blindness from my mind and I remembered everything—everything about the accident and the people who took my sister and baby brother."

Kari looked at Miss Em through misty eyes. "This passage talks about God's promises. The thing is . . . I believed that the Lord caused me to remember Elaine and Samuel for a reason—so I could find them. And a few days later, I was sure—no, *I was certain*—that the Lord spoke to me to go after them. And I heard him speak the same thing through godly individuals whose walk with God I trust.

"It felt like a promise from God, so when my investigators told me it couldn't be done, that Elaine and Samuel could not be found, it was like God's promise had failed or that I had failed? I don't know which. I only know that now I feel very let down. Defeated.

"This morning I read this verse for the first time, and it touched me. It was like these words were written for me, like God was, again, speaking directly to me."

Kari searched Miss Em's lined face. "But am I imagining it? Am I being weird?"

"No, you are not being weird, my dear girl. I think what you felt was a 'quickening' of the Scripture to your heart. 'To quicken' means 'to make alive.' They's many times the Lord will make his word alive to us—it is his way of planting himself deep down in our souls and making himself known to us in a personal way. Yes, the Holy Spirit uses God's word to speak his promises to us, and no, missy, you are not bein' weird."

"But what if . . ." Kari didn't know how to frame another worrisome question. "I mean, I'm a new Christian and all. What if God *didn't* promise me that he would find Elaine and Samuel? What if I misunderstood or presumed?"

The older woman nodded, again thoughtful before she answered. "Well, what if you did? Let us say you utterly misheard him. Does that change God or his character? No, he is good and faithful. He never changes. And so it should not change our faith in him. He is well able to redirect us if we get a little off course. They's no shame in that.

"Frankly, Kari, it takes time and 'sperience to learn to hear God's voice, to become confident when he speaks to us. But we only learn by taking to prayer what we *believe* he has spoken to us and, after prayer, followin' his guidance—as you are doing."

Miss Em smiled and her rheumy black eyes glowed. "Again, let us suppose we misunderstand his direction and continue to do what we believe he has spoken to us. The Lord values our *obedience* to him very much—even if we miss his intentions. He desires for us to have a heart that responds to him. He is looking for a perfect heart toward him, rather than perfect accomplishment. And if we miss him? He will find us and redirect our steps.

"But let us address what is at the core of your question. You want to know if God *is able* find your sister and brother—you want to know if he can do what you have been told is impossible."

Kari nodded. "Yes. That's it."

"Because you have already done all *you* can to find them."

"Yes. We have, literally, exhausted every possibility money can buy."

"Just so! Scripture tells us that when we have done all, we are to *stand*. A'course he does not intend for us to stand passively or casually or in defeat; we are to stand firm in faith.

"What is faith's attitude? Faith expects. Faith waits in hope. Faith is patient. Faith watches and prays. And so the Lord wants us to stand in hopeful, patient, watchful, prayerful expectation.

"The Bible tells us that Abraham is the father of faith. He is our example of how to remain in faith when things not only *look* impossible but also truly *are* impossible. After all, God promised Abraham a son, but Abraham and his wife were old—far too old to have children.

"That *fact*, however—the fact that both Abraham and his wife were beyond bearing children—did not weaken Abraham's faith. Romans 4 reads:

> *Without weakening in his faith,*
> *he faced the fact that his body*
> *was as good as dead . . .*
> *Yet he did not waver through unbelief*
> *regarding the promise of God,*
> *but was strengthened in his faith*
> *and gave glory to God,*
> *being fully persuaded that God*
> *had power to do what he had promised.*

Miss Em leaned toward Kari. "Our God has the power to do what he promises. They's times we think of him with human limitations, think he has to work in a logical way, a way we can understand or a way we can help make happen."

"But let me tell you a little secret: *God doesn't need our help.* If we have done all he asks us to do, what remains is for us *to stand.* He is perfectly able to keep his promises without our help."

Miss Em lifted a bent, gnarled finger. "What that means is that God can answer your prayers in a completely unanticipated, unprecedented, illogical manner. So don't close off an avenue for him to work simply because you cannot see how he could do it.

"He is the God who made the universe. He can do whatever he wants to—and nothing is too difficult for him. When he does the impossible, it is he who receives the glory."

She stared at Kari for a long moment. "I don't know your story, dear, but I can tell it is a difficult one—and yet look what Father God has done already. Would you say that the manner by which he brought you to Christ was less than miraculous?"

"No," Kari mumbled.

"Hey?"

Kari lifted her chin and repeated herself in a stronger voice. "No! It *was* miraculous. It truly was."

"And how long did that miracle take?"

Kari snorted. "How long? Um, if I were to be honest, it took eighty-two years—but when the Lord began to move, he moved quickly. In a matter of months."

Miss Em leveled an appraising look upon Kari. "All right, then. You need to leave room *and time* in your heart and mind for God to work a miracle. He already brought you a mighty long way. He brought you to Jesus by way of a miracle. He caused you to remember your lost memories by way of a miracle. So while you wait with 'spectation for him to work another miracle, you keep doing good."

Kari perked up. "Good?"

"Oh, yes. While we wait, we do the good God has given us to do.

> *"Let us not become weary in doing good,*
> *for at the proper time we will*
> *reap a harvest if we do not give up.*
> *Therefore, as we have opportunity,*
> *let us do good to all people,*
> *especially to those who belong*
> *to the family of believers.*

"It don't matter if God answers today, tomorrow, or eighty-two years from now, you set your heart to follow him, say 'amen' to his promises, and keep doing the good God leads you to do."

Kari blinked. "Say 'amen' to God's promises and keep doing good. All right. I think I can do that."

"And don't forget to give God the glory when the miraculous occurs."

"I won't. Thank you, Miss Em."

The woman's face creased into another smile and she patted Kari's arm. "There now. You're welcome, Kari. The Lord bless you."

She slanted her eyes toward Kari. "Now don't go tellin' people I resemble that mean ol' Miss Gulch, hear?"

Kari's brow shot up. "Um, yes, ma'am! I mean, *no*, ma'am. I won't."

That night Kari was restless. She turned Miss Em's words over and over, testing them for validity.

Coming to a settled conclusion, she prayed, *Lord, you are certainly more powerful than I ever gave you credit for. Nothing is too difficult for you—finding Elaine and Samuel is not too difficult for you. Just as you knew where Daddy was all the years he was missing, you know where Elaine and Samuel are right now.*

Father, my job is not to figure out how you're going to bring them back to me or spend my time and effort to make it happen. My job is to stand firm and trust you, say amen to your promises, and do the good work you've placed before me.

Kari slept deeply that night and awoke the following morning lighter of heart. As she sipped her morning coffee, she realized her heart was, finally, at rest.

Thank you, Lord, for showing me how to live in peace.

CHAPTER 11

Kari finished her dinner, cleared the little dining nook in the kitchen, and washed up the few dishes she had dirtied. She usually ate dinner around seven and tidied up afterwards so that Azalea would find the kitchen clean when she came in the morning.

As Kari hung the damp dishtowel, the phone rang.

Right on time, she smiled to herself. She went into her office and settled into her chair before she picked up the phone.

"Hey there!"

"Max says hay is for horses, ma'am."

"Søren, how I love that boy. I miss him, too."

She and Søren spoke most evenings. He would call before 7:30 and they would talk for ten minutes or so, sharing the news of the day. Afterwards, Max would come to the phone and Søren would allow him exactly five minutes to bend Kari's ear.

Then, after he told Max to scoot off to bed, Søren would pick up the phone, read a short Scripture passage, and they would pray together and say goodnight. The calls were never long because his day began earlier than hers did, and he retired for the night soon after.

It wasn't much when taken one call at a time, but over weeks, it added up to something significant. Søren and Kari grew to know each other better. They began to know real fellowship.

If this is courtship, it is the strangest form I've witnessed or experienced, Kari reflected, *but I have to admit that it is effective. Søren and I are growing in the Lord together, and we are getting to know each other—the "real" us—rather than the superficial us.*

As the days passed, Kari's respect for Søren increased. She appreciated how he used every minute of his day and what he accomplished with his time. She admired his discipline and purpose.

Søren's example forced Kari to reevaluate how she employed her time. After some thought and prayer, she modified her daily routine.

A mere fifteen minutes with God each morning is not enough. I need more. More time, more discipline, more Jesus.

She made herself rise earlier than she'd been accustomed to so that she could run while the outside air was still cool. First thing each morning, she ran two miles. She followed her run with an hour of personal time with God.

She spent much of that hour reading Scripture and thinking on it, trying to understand it and apply it. Then she prayed for direction for her day and prayed over needs that came her way.

After a few days, she was amazed to find that the hour she'd set aside for the Lord went by so quickly. In one respect, an hour felt as though it was not enough; on the other hand, she found herself filled with new strength and assurance.

These morning activities became daily constants, but after that, her weekly schedule varied: On Tuesday mornings she attended a women's Bible study at their church. It was in this group of twelve to fifteen women that she really began to "fit in" and feel like part of her church.

On Thursday mornings, she volunteered with her Bible study group at a local shelter for women fleeing—and often hiding—from situations of domestic abuse. "Domestic abuse" was a new term for Kari, but when she met the women at the shelter, she recognized herself in them.

Her group held a short Bible study with the women in the shelter and brought lunch for them. While they ate, the women from Kari's church would listen and, if the opportunity arose naturally, share Jesus. On one occasion, Kari and a woman from the shelter entered into what Kari felt was meaningful conversation. Kari was able to let the other woman know that she, too, had experienced violence at the hands of her husband.

"Even after I got out of the marriage, the hurt was still there," she explained. "I was lucky—no, not lucky, but blessed, I believe—to have a counselor who knows Jesus. She told me that Jesus came to heal even these kinds of hurts. I am certain he can heal your heart, too."

The questions the woman put to Kari were difficult ones, beyond what Kari felt prepared to answer. The encounter only fueled Kari's desire to know her Bible better.

The other three mornings each week, she met with Oskar to read reports, analyze accounts, and make minor business decisions under his tutelage. He introduced her to the team of accountants, tax specialists, and financial planners who assisted him. He showed her the reams of fanfold printouts that had to be studied daily.

And at least two afternoons a week, she and Oskar set out on what Oskar called "field trips," visits to businesses and properties Kari owned. They toured manufacturing plants, oil and gas wells, and her real estate holdings—commercial properties, rentals, and hotels scattered throughout New Orleans. She met with managers, employees, tenants, and boards of directors—all to put places and faces to the wealth she owned.

They traveled in Oskar's black town car, driven by his chauffeur, and often accompanied by his assistant, Bettina Fletcher. Oskar's car was equipped with a writing tray for his use and a mobile phone on which Oskar and Miss Fletcher took and made calls during the drive. In between, Oskar reviewed correspondence and prepped Kari for the meetings or visits ahead.

"Most of your businesses and other operating assets are solely owned by you, meaning they are not publicly traded," he told her. "Depending upon the entity's size and needs, the day-to-day administration is by a management staff or, for the large concerns, by a board of directors. I hold the title of Chairman on all boards and management teams; however, I primarily provide oversight and auditing authority. A CEO or VP leads the board or team and runs the business."

The breadth and depth of Peter Granger's estate boggled Kari's mind. And, as the reality of what Kari owned became clearer, so grew the terrifying and heavy weight of it.

So, too, grew the conviction that she should not bow to the temptation to relegate the management of the estate entirely to someone else—merely so she could live a carefree life. At the very least, she needed to be familiar with the scope of her holdings and participate, even marginally, in its management.

"I don't want the life of the *nouveau riche*," Kari confided to Oskar one morning in the car. Miss Fletcher was not with them on this occasion, and Kari felt able to speak more openly.

"I don't want a lazy, unproductive, unfruitful life. I want my life—and my money—to count for something, something for God. I hope you will help me learn to be a good steward of what God has given me."

Oskar had studied her, not certain she really wanted to hear his advice.

"Please, Oskar. I need direction. Guidance."

"Then I will tell you what my father told me," Oskar said at last. "If you truly want your life to be fruitful, you must discipline and prepare yourself for hard work and service to others. You must pray and develop a good plan—a plan under the Lord's guidance. Then you must give yourself to that plan. Wholeheartedly.

"If you apply yourself, you may, someday, feel confident enough to manage many of these holdings yourself and make decisions as the Lord directs you."

He paused before adding, "You are in a unique position, Kari. Yes, you, a woman living in what is mostly a man's world, are the owner of all these businesses and properties.

"But if, *as a woman*, you wish to be taken seriously by the many men who, essentially, work for you, then you must strive to become a woman they will respect, a woman of understated authority and decorum."

He hesitated a moment more. "I have two daughters, you know, Scarlett and Suzanne. Suzanne, the older of the two, is happily married. She has given us two beautiful grandchildren and is happy with the life she has chosen.

"But Scarlett? She earned a B.A. and has completed her last year of law school. She's different from Suzanne. She is ambitious—in a good way—and has a steady head on her shoulders."

He sighed. "Times are changing. The fact that I don't have a son to carry on in the family business . . ."

Kari stared at the older man. "Then why can't she?"

"Twenty years ago, that suggestion would not have held water, but now? And in the coming years? I'm happy that Scarlett has opportunities no women in our family have ever had. The world is full of opportunities for her, but I hope she will choose to come back here. We'll see."

When Kari first met Oskar, she had thought of him as only a younger version of Clover. Now Kari was coming to know and understand Oskar as his own person—an intelligent, wise, and people-savvy individual. She was beginning to acknowledge that it was Oskar who was the real genius behind the good condition of her many holdings. Wherever they went, his quiet and judicious manner influenced the outcomes of many board meetings and management decisions.

Kari was starting to recognize, too, that Oskar was the single individual she trusted to oversee her holdings.

While I am available, it would behoove me to learn all I can from him and his example.

So Kari determined to apply herself and follow Oskar's lead. She bought a briefcase and took home work she could do from her office. She studied prospectuses and account holdings, and reviewed recent earnings and market trends. She went to the university library and researched her own companies, looking at their past performance, but also looking at their public face.

If I own these companies, I want to be sure that they are projecting integrity, she told herself.

By herself, she revisited an apartment complex she owned. She walked the grounds and studied the complex's eight buildings, looking for practical and cosmetic improvements, and jotting them down to suggest to Oskar.

Lord, I wish for these tenants to be pleased with and proud of where they live.

After a few weeks, she knew that she *was* beginning to learn. When Oskar would refer to a specific holding, she had a good picture in her mind of the business or property.

She was gratified when Oskar commented on her progress.

"You have an aptitude for business, Miss Kari, and you have natural instincts. Instincts are vital and they cannot be taught—which makes them an especially valuable commodity. You still have much to learn, particularly about the politics of business, but I'm pleased at the speed with which you are picking things up."

They had spoken for quite some time after that, and Kari began to pray about the glimmer of an idea that was forming in her mind.

I hope Oskar will advise me when the time is right, when I have a well-thought-out plan to present to him.

That evening Kari cleaned up after herself and waited in her office for Søren to call. When he did, Kari was surprised when he asked, "What are you doing for Thanksgiving?"

Kari's eyes darted to her desk calendar. "Thanksgiving?"

"It's two weeks from tomorrow. Do you have plans?"

"Um, no. Nope."

"Well, why don't you come here? Spend a week with us."

Kari fell back against her chair, first astonished and then excited. "Really?"

"Of course, really." He added, under his breath, "If you're a little cash-strapped, I'm sure Ilsa and I can scrape together enough for a ticket."

"Søren! Don't be ridiculous." Kari paused a beat. "Although I'm not sure if I have enough in my piggy bank. I'll have to break it and see what's in there."

They laughed at that, and Kari was glad that she and Søren always found something humorous in their nightly conversations.

"Well, listen, Kari. If you fly into the nearest city, we will pick you up. And if you come early, say the Sunday or Monday before Thanksgiving, you'll miss the worst of the airport craziness—and we'll have you for more than a long weekend."

"Well, I . . ." Kari stopped herself. Family! She could think of nowhere in the world she would rather be on Thanksgiving than with family.

"Yes. Yes, I'll come!" Kari heard a war whoop in the background and giggled. Max had obviously been listening for her answer.

A week in RiverBend? The grin on her face grew larger. "I love it," she added. "I love everything about it! I'd better get reservations first thing tomorrow. I hope it's not too late."

Kari called Miss Dawes soon after the offices of Brunell & Brunell opened in the morning.

"Good morning, Miss Dawes."

"Good morning, Miss Kari. How are you this morning?"

"Well, actually, I'm looking forward to Thanksgiving. My cousins in Nebraska have asked me to spend the week with them. Of course I need to learn how to do this myself, but would you be so kind as to book a flight for me this one time?"

"Certainly. And in the future, if you wish to make your own travel arrangements, I can give you the name and number of our agency."

They discussed the timeframe and Kari hung up knowing Miss Dawes would handle the details in her own inimitable manner.

A week with Søren, Ilsa, and Max! She was bursting with the news, so she called Ruth.

"Hey, Ruth! Are you with a client?"

"Not at the moment, Cookie. What's up?"

"Søren and Ilsa invited me to spend Thanksgiving with them!"

"How wonderful, Kari. I'm so happy for you."

"What will you be doing that weekend?"

"Oh, goodness! No lack of what to do, I assure you. I have three kids and their families here in Albuquerque. It means a house bursting at the seams on Thanksgiving—not to mention days of preparations beforehand."

"Well, I am leaving early so I can help Ilsa get ready. I imagine we'll have a horde of cousins over while I'm there."

"And will you go there for Christmas, too?"

Kari hadn't thought that far ahead. "Wow. I don't know. I hadn't even thought about it. What will you do for Christmas?"

"I usually go to my daughter's in upstate New York. It's the one time of year when I can put work aside for two weeks and spend quality time with the grandkids who don't live nearby."

Ruth has such a full life with her children and grandchildren, Kari thought. *I am so grateful to have anyone—even distant cousins—to call my own.*

Christmas? Hmmm . . .

After they hung up, Kari wandered through the foyer and living room, visualizing how she might decorate her home for Christmas.

The tree could go there—or there! I could twine garlands around the bannisters all the way up to and across the mezzanine. And I would want poinsettias—lots of them! And—

She stopped, struck with a tantalizing thought.

Why not?

***

KARI STEPPED THROUGH THE AIRPLANE'S DOOR and gasped. The wind that buffeted her had a sharp, penetrating bite to it.

"Welcome to fall in Nebraska!" she muttered.

She pulled her coat close and hurried down the flight of steps to the tarmac. She heard Max before she saw him.

"Kari! Kari! Over here!"

Kari looked for and found Max's waving hand in the small crowd waiting for the passengers to deplane. The hardy souls were bunched together against the chilling wind.

Then Kari caught sight of Søren behind Max. Max's grin was huge—and Søren's grin matched his son's. Kari half-ran to them and was swept into their open arms.

Kari laughed aloud. "You are both smiling like Cheshire cats!"

"What's a Cheshire cat?" Max demanded.

"She can tell you later. Let's get out of the cold first." Søren, ever practical, pulled them toward the little terminal.

Max chattered nonstop on the drive to the farm, and Kari loved it. Søren, for his part, smiled and occasionally put in a word or two.

I'm home! Kari's heart sang as they raced down the highway. *Well, my Nebraska home, that is.*

She recognized the turnoff to RiverBend and rubbernecked as they motored down the single street and under the lone blinking light. Then they were in the country, surrounded by the stubble of harvested fields. The occasional patch of snow reminded her that RiverBend had already experienced a taste of the coming winter.

She sat forward when Søren's car drove along the edge overlooking the river. A mile later, they crested the bluff, and he drove slowly down the sloping road bordering Rose's homestead.

Kari had eyes only for the tiny house nestled in the hollow of the bluff—not the creek alongside it, or Søren's farm beyond. Only Rose and Jan's little house.

The wind was particularly harsh as they descended and its icy fingers buffeted the car and found its way inside through every crack.

Rose's house looks so alone. So cold and fragile.

Kari craned her neck to keep the listing house in view as they mounted the wooden bridge spanning the creek.

I can't let it fall to pieces. I need to do something to keep it standing, she decided.

Her week on the farm was all Kari could have asked for. Lars and Dalia Thoresen, cousins from the farm next door, would be joining them, as would their entire brood and a handful of friends and relations from the neighborhood.

Dalia, Ilsa, and Kari baked and cooked days in advance. When they weren't in the kitchen, Ilsa and Kari were cleaning house and pulling out the silver, linens, and best dishes to give them a good cleaning.

"I hate to put you out, Kari, but the guest room bathroom is the only downstairs toilet we have—the upshot of this house originally being built before indoor bathrooms. And believe me when I say we will need both bathrooms on Thursday," Ilsa informed Kari.

"It's not a problem. I will pack all my things away and make sure the bathroom is tidy."

Thanksgiving morning Søren and Max moved sofa and easy chairs to the corners of the long living room/dining room and hauled in three long folding tables from the barn. Then they brought in a dozen folding chairs to add to their six dining chairs.

"Will this be enough?" Kari asked as she wiped down the folding chairs.

"Lars is bringing over another dozen and we have a card table the teens will sit at."

Thanksgiving dinner was both riotous and holy. Kari could not stop smiling although she spent more time watching and listening than talking.

After she helped Ilsa serve dessert, Søren sidled up to her. "You seem to be having a good time even if you are a bit quiet."

"I'm soaking it all in, Søren. It is charming, all of it—even the kids' squabbles and the noise of six different conversations going on at the same time."

He snorted. "Charming? I'd call it chaos myself."

"Yes, but it's *glorious* chaos, isn't it? You don't know how belonging to all this fills a deep hole in my heart. I've never known such contentment."

Søren studied her for a moment and then, as though making up his mind, took her hand and tugged her toward the back door. "C'mon. I want to talk to you."

He pulled their coats, hats, and gloves off the hooks next to the door. When they were bundled up, they walked down toward the barn.

"Let's go inside. It's warmer."

It was, as he said, warmer in the barn. The twenty stamping milk cows and Søren's two bays generated their own heat.

Søren pulled some carrot tops from his pocket and fed them to the horses. Kari leaned over the Dutch door and rubbed one bay's soft nose. He snuffled her hand, but when he found nothing to eat, he swung his head back to Søren.

"So you wanted to talk?" For some reason, Kari's heart was pounding.

"I do, Kari." He brushed off his hands and faced her. "The truth is, I want to know if you feel differently now than you did in July."

"About what?" Kari wasn't going to make it easy for him.

He huffed. "You know about *what*. About us, Kari. You and I. We are so suited for each other, and Max already loves you. He has 'suggested' on numerous occasions that you would make a good mom."

"He has, has he?" Then Kari stalled. "Wouldn't people talk about us being cousins and all?"

Søren's snort made Kari smile in spite of herself. "Like I told you before, we're half cousins—and cousins so far removed that I haven't figured out if we're third, fourth, or fifth cousins."

He looked sideways at her and waggled an eyebrow. "We might make some cute kids, though."

"That's an alluring thought, Søren, but I'm pushing forty. It's a little late to start making babies."

Søren took Kari's arm and gently turned her toward him. "Look at me. I love you, Kari. You and I love the Lord in the same way—we would be equally yoked. You and I and Max could have a good life together. What do you say? Will you marry me?"

He wanted to kiss her—she could see it in his eyes. He was leaning, just a little, toward her, waiting for her permission, and she was starting to think how inviting his lips looked, starting to wonder how they would feel on hers.

But it still hasn't been that long since I was married to David. And as Christians, we can't indulge in flirting. I must be honest: Am I ready for marriage? A real, holy marriage before the Lord? Am I ready to make that kind of commitment?

She hadn't realized she was frowning until Søren released her arm and backed up a step.

"It doesn't look like you feel the same way I do."

Kari sighed. "Søren, if I went with how I *feel*, I would throw my arms around your neck and kiss you right now. However, how I *feel* is not quite in sync with what I believe is right or prudent at this time—what I believe God is speaking to me.

"Nothing would make me happier than to become Kari Thoresen in name and fact, to become Max's mother and your wife. You are both so dear to me, but . . ."

Søren was watching her closely. "But?"

"But I'm not sure. I am hesitant, as though the timing is not right. If it were God's will and his timing, wouldn't I feel more confident?"

He nodded. "Yes, you would. And I would not want either of us to make another mistake. We should both be sure and certain about entering into marriage. So, you will think about it? Pray about it?"

"Yes. I will think about it, of course, but mostly I will pray about it."

He smiled. "That's fine then, and I guess you must be right about the timing. However, I wanted to be up-front with you about my feelings and intentions: I love you. When the time is right, when God says it is right and you are confident in his direction, I hope you will return my affection."

He drew her into a soft embrace. "I want you to know my heart, Kari. I don't want you to be in any doubt of my love for you."

Kari leaned her cheek on his shoulder and breathed in the scent of him—hay, strong soap, shaving cream, and something else, something distinctively Søren.

"I want you here with us, Kari. Always," he whispered into her hair.

A little jolt ran through her. *Here? Always? But . . .*

She had, for a few days, left the weight of Peter Granger's estate back in New Orleans. Now that weight returned, pressing on her, reminding her of her responsibilities.

But I can't . . .

She said nothing of what she was feeling. Instead, she murmured back, "I promise to pray until I know God's will, Søren. That is what I promise."

After the work and fun of Thanksgiving, life on the farm returned to a slower pace, and Kari again helped Max with his chores each morning.

I do love it here, Lord, she prayed as they fed the chickens and gathered eggs. *I love the peace and the simple, uncluttered routine. And I love our time in your word as a family! But I also love my life in NOLA—my house, my work, my friends there.*

Søren says he wants me here. Always. But when I think about leaving NOLA forever, when I imagine pulling apart from those other things and people I love, I feel grieved. Confused.

You must show me the way, Lord. You must show me how a marriage to Søren could work. Because right now I don't see it, Lord.

I don't see it.

She prayed as she awoke each morning, she prayed as she worked, she prayed as she climbed into bed in the evening. She heard only a single word.

Christmas.

When family devotions ended on her last full day in Nebraska, Kari asked everyone to wait. "I have something to ask the three of you," she announced.

"What is it?" Max, who had been given permission to stay home from school on Kari's last day, leaned against her arm and stared up at her. "Shucks, Kari, you know we'll do it, whatever it is."

His adoring gaze almost undid Kari. She laughed aloud. "Well, then its settled. You are all going to spend Christmas with me."

"What?" The word burst from three mouths simultaneously.

Søren was the first to add on, "You mean go to New Orleans?" even while he shook his head "no."

"Yes, silly. Come to New Orleans. Why, when was the last time you or Ilsa had a vacation? Come stay with me over the holidays. I'm thinking ten days or two weeks? We'll have a perfect, wonderful time."

"Say yes, Papa! Please?"

But Søren shrugged and still shook his head "no." "We can't pick up and go like you can, Kari. We don't have anyone to take care of the farm while we're gone. And, frankly, I couldn't afford to pay someone if we did."

Kari nodded and tapped a finger on her cheek, thinking. "What if you did have the money to pay someone, someone to house sit for you and manage the day-to-day chores? Say, a young unmarried farmer from church? Someone you know and trust."

Ilsa, her face shining in anticipation, looked from Kari to Søren. "What about Seth Norquist? We've known him all his life. We know his parents. He is engaged to Jenny Frisk and he is looking to make extra money before they get married in the spring. He would jump at the chance."

"Yes, he is a fine, responsible young man, but again, I cannot afford to pay him to care for our farm."

"It would be part of my Christmas gift to all of you," Kari said softly. "I would pay his wages and buy your plane tickets, and you would stay at my house. I want you to see my world, Søren, and I don't want to be alone for Christmas. I want my family to be with me."

Kari watched him fold his arms in that stubborn Norwegian/Irish manner she knew well.

"I don't take money from a woman. And that's the end of it."

But it wasn't the end of it for Kari—and she was prepared to do battle. "Søren, look at me."

From under glowering brows, his intense blue eye lifted to hers. "You won't change my mind, Kari."

"Well, then I guess there is no future for us, is there?"

Ilsa and Max stilled. Søren's brows bunched closer together and his gaze shifted away.

"You listen to me, Søren Thoresen. You spoke to me from your heart the other day, and I said I would pray on and *think* about what you said.

"Well, guess what? I am a wealthy woman. No, I am a stinking, *filthy* rich woman. That isn't going to change. And *I think* that if you can't take me as I am, then you can't take me at all.

"Consider this Christmas trip as an experiment of sorts, Søren, because if we are to have any future together, we have many, many details to sort out. And as I have thought and prayed—as I promised you I would—I have realized that I can't commit to be the kind of wife who only stays in the kitchen—or one who only lives on this farm year round.

"I have big responsibilities back in New Orleans, and I will not shirk them. If we are to have a future, you need to know my life firsthand and accept from the get-go that ours would not be a conventional marriage.

"So what will it be? Will you accept my Christmas gift and come dip your toes into my world? Or will you and I remain as we are—'cousins in Christ' and nothing more?"

Max was staring so intently at his father that Kari was certain the man's shirt was going to spontaneously combust. Ilsa, mouth pursed, slid her eyes from her brother and back to Kari, uncertain whose argument would prevail.

Finally, Søren muttered, "Is that how it would be then, Kari? A part-time marriage? Only half of a commitment?"

Kari chose her answer with care. "Of course it would be an entire commitment—on both our parts. We would be wholly committed to each other, which in my estimation means we would also commit to supporting each other's work and sharing our responsibilities."

She softened her tone further. "What is so wrong with my sharing my money with you and Max and Ilsa, Søren? Can you not consider it a blessing from God rather than an affront to your manhood?"

She smiled and cocked her head a little. "And I was really looking forward to having the three of you with me for Christmas, to spoiling all of you a little. All right, spoiling you *a lot*. Can't you imagine the fun we could have? Can't you loosen up and enjoy yourself a bit?"

Max wriggled in his seat. "Please, Papa?"

Søren chewed his lip and hesitated.

Tired of waiting for him to answer, Ilsa slapped her hand on the old wood planks of the table. "For heaven's sake, Søren! I want to go. I haven't had a real vacation in five years."

She grinned at Kari. "On behalf of the three of us, I accept. With pleasure! Thank you for such a thoughtful Christmas gift."

Max jumped up and hugged Ilsa, then Kari. Then he ran to his father. "Gosh, Papa! Just think! We get to spend Christmas at Kari's house in New Orleans! And fly on a real airplane!"

Søren huffed and shook his head. "All right. You win."

He put his hands on Max's shoulders. The boy was positively vibrating with eagerness. "Settle down now, Son. You need to be calm when you are around our animals."

When Max bounced out the door, Søren sighed and studied Kari. "You should understand, Kari. What you propose is . . . a lot different from what I'd had in mind. A lot different. It is hard for me to consider it."

"Yes. Change is hard, I know. But if you meant what you told me in the barn, then shouldn't we approach, er, *things* realistically?

"Not having money is a problem you are accustomed to, Søren. Well, *having* money is a different kind of problem—but it is still a problem. The money won't go away if we ignore it, and I am still charged by God to steward it well. That requires time and effort on my part."

He ran his hand up his neck and across the top of his close-cropped hair. "I'm beginning to see that. . . but I don't particularly like it."

CHAPTER 12

K ari finished her morning devotions and glanced at the calendar. *December 12. They will be here in exactly seven days! It will be so wonderful to have them here for two whole weeks.*

Kari was both excited and nervous for Søren, Max, and Ilsa to arrive. She stacked her Bible and Rose's journals to place them in the bottom desk drawer. However, when she grabbed the drawer's pull, the drawer was stuck. It would not move.

With more effort, Kari yanked on the handle and the slides gave. As the drawer flew outwards, Kari heard something inside shift.

Again.

She felt around in its deep recesses but found nothing.

Again.

I keep hearing something sliding about in this drawer, but there's nothing in it!

Kari pushed away from her desk and got on her knees. By lifting the front end of the drawer, she was able to free the drawer from the wooden slide stops and remove it from the desk. She set it on its end—and heard the movement of something as it slid and thudded against the end of the drawer.

There's definitely something . . .

Kari tipped the drawer over so she could examine its underside, but it looked normal—securely tacked in place. It did not budge. She set the drawer on one side, then placed a hand on the drawer's bottom side and the other inside the drawer.

"What? That can't be right." Rather than the quarter- to half-inch breadth she anticipated, two inches or more separated her hands.

"This drawer has a false bottom," Kari whispered. "It has a secret compartment—and that compartment is not empty!"

Excited and a little nervous, Kari placed the drawer right side up on her desk's blotter and swiveled her desk lamp over the drawer to give her better light. She examined the inside of the drawer from one end to the other.

At the back, she found a small metal piece protruding from the end of the drawer. She pressed down on it, but nothing happened. However, when she pressed it *in*, the bottom popped up. Kari slid the thin board a tiny bit toward the back, which released the front end from the groove that held it in place.

More eager than ever, Kari lifted the false bottom out. There, in the space between the two bottoms, lay a thin album. With nervous fingers, Kari picked it up.

She moved the drawer and false bottom to the floor and then laid the volume on her desk. Standing over it, she opened it.

It was a scrapbook, filled with newspaper clippings.

Kari's breath caught in her throat. She thumbed slowly through the pages. Every clipping was meticulously trimmed and glued to a page. And every clipping had to do with the one topic: The kidnapping of Edmund Thoresen Michaels.

"Oh! O dear Jesus!" Kari whispered. She sat hard in her chair and turned back to the front of the book.

Headlines from the Denver Post screamed the story, but the book contained excerpts from other newspapers, too—papers in Boulder, Cheyenne, Lincoln and Omaha, and even farther away in Billings, Spokane, Seattle, and Portland.

Kari read intently, seeing for the first time the facts of her father's abduction laid out in cold black on white. As Joy and Grant had experienced their loss. As Rose had.

The clippings went on for months.

Dean Morgan—Peter Granger—kept track of the investigation this way, Kari realized. *It is how he knew he was safe here in New Orleans.*

Kari devoured the articles but stopped when she came across clippings from two Seattle papers—articles covering a related topic: The arrest of Fang-Hua Chen.

Shan-Rose's grandmother!

Not many days later the same papers reported Fang-Hua's untimely death: She had been beaten to death in her jail cell.

No one had been arrested in her death. The men who had beaten her were never identified.

Kari felt not one ounce of compassion for the woman.

"If this woman had been dealt with earlier, I might have grown up in the bosom of my family, my real family."

She sighed. "I know, Lord. I can't go there. I can't live on fruitless 'what-ifs' and futile 'what-might-have-beens.' Lord, please show me how to live for today?"

She recalled only one allusion to Fang-Hua's death in Rose's blue journal, what had been, as Kari had read it, an oblique and passing reference to the event.

She picked up the cracked blue book and searched for the right page to reread the entry with new eyes.

Journal Entry, January 16, 1912
I found myself thinking today of the woman responsible for Edmund's abduction: Fang-Hua Chen. When I am tempted to anger and hatred, Lord, you remind me that she has already faced your judgment. She has faced you in all of your power, glory, and righteousness without the saving blood of Jesus to cover her sins. What could be more punishment than that?

No, when I am tempted to dwell upon her actions and the recriminations that rise up with those thoughts, I lay claim to the Scripture found in Romans 12:21, and I purpose again to spend my heart and energy on what you have given me to do.

Be not overcome with evil,
but overcome evil with good.

Lord, I have laid my hand to the plow; I have counted the cost of my complete commitment. I will not turn back, Father. I will not falter to do all the good I can in the time you allot me.

Electrified, Kari sat back. *Overcome evil with good. I will not falter to do all the good I can in the time you allot me.*

Miss Em said 'and keep doing the good God leads you to do.'

"Lord, you know I have been tinkering with an idea, an idea I think is from you. I will place it before Oskar and ask for his counsel and help. If it is of you, would you please speak to both of us about it? I want to do what you ask of me."

As she prayed and her idea started to clarify, she pulled paper from another drawer and started to outline a business plan to support it.

"Yes, Lord! Thank you for helping me to put my thoughts into practical terms. Now to broach the idea with Oskar."

Kari met with Oskar the next morning on her regularly scheduled day with him. They perused reports together, examined stock and bond prices, and read letters from managers and boards.

Recently, he had begun asking her to state her opinions and make suggestions. He played the devil's advocate to get her to think and justify her position. Through these exchanges, Kari learned to articulate herself in clear, succinct statements. She even started emulating Oskar's judicious tone.

"I'd like you to dictate the responses to these letters," Oskar said. "I'll look them over and suggest changes or improvements. They will go out under my signature, but I wish you to have the experience of writing business correspondence from a manager's perspective."

Kari took the letters and walked down the hall to Miss Fletcher's office. As she left, Clover slipped into Oskar's office.

"Good morning, Son."

"Hello, Father! I didn't know you were in today."

Clover sat down in one of the armchairs in front of Oskar's desk. "Miss Dawes tells me that Kari has been working with you regularly. I thought I'd drop in and see how she's doing."

"She's doing well, actually. Has an excellent head for business—despite what she's been led to believe about herself."

Clover nodded his agreement. "That ex-husband did some damage."

Oskar's face reddened a bit, but he kept his temper in check. "Well, we'll undo that damage, if I have anything to say about it."

He looked across his desk to his father. "You want to know how Kari is doing? She is a natural analytic. She sees the heart of an issue within seconds or minutes of taking in the relevant facts. And she's good with people—open and transparent, frank but not overbearing. So far the money hasn't affected her, hasn't engendered an attitude of entitlement or privilege."

Clover smiled at his son. "I agree. My hope is that it never does."

Half an hour later, while Miss Fletcher typed the responses she had dictated, Kari returned to Oskar's office. "Miss Fletcher will bring the letters as soon as they are ready. If . . ." Kari fidgeted a little, "if we have a few minutes, may I talk to you about something else?"

"Certainly. What did you have in mind?"

Kari took a file folder from her briefcase. "You might not know this, but my Bible study group spends one afternoon a week at a women's shelter. These are women who have been threatened or abused, some beaten, by their spouses or boyfriends. By their pimps. Some of them are in fear for their lives. Most of them have children with them.

"It is horrid to see the emotional damage on their faces, in their eyes, in how they talk. It will take time for that damage to ease, for them to find a way forward with their lives.

"It is true that many of them are in this predicament because of wrong choices or wrong behaviors. We can even call it sin. But all I see are women who don't know Jesus, women whose lives will never change until they have *him*.

"You see, I was in a similar situation . . . in my last marriage. David abused and controlled me until Anthony helped me throw him out. But when he was gone from my life, I still had no job, no money, and no hope.

"I was damaged—that's why I have compassion for these women. And I cannot imagine the plight of abused women who also have children to care for."

Kari cleared her throat. "Of course, I see needs at the shelter—repairs and upgrades to the house, food, immediate necessities I can help with.

"One of the shelter's greatest needs is for additional space. More women flee domestic violence each day than the shelter can house. Yes, I could add on to the existing house or buy a second home, but none of those improvements addresses the spiritual needs of the women.

"I would like to do something more overarching, something with Jesus at its core. My Bible study group can only speak of the Lord the few hours we are there. I feel he should be the essence of the shelter's mission.

"And so I have been noodling on an idea. You know of my grandmother and great-grandmother's work in Denver—I've told you about Palmer House. I would like to start a foundation to carry on their work. I want to fund domestic violence shelters that operate from a Christian perspective."

She laid her business plan before Oskar. "This is a rough outline of what I have in mind."

Oskar read the plan from start to finish and then read it again. "You are suggesting an endowment?"

"Yes, that's the word I was looking for." She wet her lips. "Er, what do you think?"

"The cost aside, I think it is a noble plan but easier to conceive on paper than in reality."

Kari exhaled. "You mean because people aren't things that you can fix by throwing money at them? That people can't be ordered into neat little roles?"

"Precisely. Working with people, particularly damaged people, is an immense challenge. You are, in essence, suggesting a ministry to wounded, damaged women. The success of such a venture would depend more on spiritually mature leadership than on financing. The leader and his or her staff would need to be seasoned, able to withstand terrific spiritual pressure, already experienced in ministry to abused women.

"And the leader must have an acknowledged, uncompromising call upon their life to minister in this area. It is not a role for a new Christian."

Oskar turned serious eyes upon Kari. "When God gifts and calls a person to such a role, it is generally a life's vocation, not a passing thing. Do you have such an individual or individuals in mind?"

Kari turned inward, considering the ring of truth in Oskar's words.

What he is suggesting is that I could not lead this venture, that I am not mature enough in the Lord, that I do not have such a call upon my life.

Kari pondered Oskar's wise words and arrived at a strange, disconcerting realization. *I believe the idea for a Christian women's shelter came from the Lord, but however he chooses to bring it to pass, I am not the one to lead it. I am more the "Martha Palmer" in this equation than the "Rose." Or am I more the "Joy"? You gave her the vision to rescue the girls, but it was Rose and her spiritual maturity that made it possible.*

I have something else for you.

"Oh!" The thought jumped into Kari's head with such clarity that she started.

"Kari?"

"Oh. I, um, I believe the Lord spoke something to me just now. I'll need to consider it. Pray over it."

"Yes. Let's do pray. I don't want to discourage you from pursuing your idea, Kari. So, let's pray about it and continue to flesh out the plan. In the meantime, I'll look into where the startup funds might come from should you decide to go ahead."

Kari nodded. "Thank you."

"And now I have some news for you, Kari."

"You do?"

"Yes. The probate on Peter Granger's estate is complete. This means a couple of things for you, and I want you to be clear on them."

"All right . . ."

Oskar smiled, but his smile was tinged with sadness. "The first item, as ordered by the court, concerns ownership of the estate."

"You mean Elaine and Samuel's shares."

"Yes, and I'm sorry if this part wounds you, but because your siblings have been missing so long and because there is no way to locate them, the court cannot grant them a share of the estate. To do so would prove too difficult to apportion and manage—in laypersons' terms, it would hamstring your ownership.

"So the court has chosen to award all of the estate to you—with the stipulation that, should anyone step forward with a claim, the court will review that claim and make a determination at that time."

Kari stared across the room. "I see."

"In your heart and actions, Kari, I know you will make sure that the estate is well managed. If Elaine and Samuel are ever located, their portions will not be found lacking."

"Thank you, Oskar. I appreciate that."

"The other relevant point is this: Now that you have inherited, the estate is no longer Brunell & Brunell's responsibility to manage. You are free to choose how to manage the entirety of it yourself."

"I see no need to make any changes," Kari murmured. "The estate has obviously thrived in your care."

"If you are certain, I will draw up papers for you to sign."

"I'm certain."

"Then, whatever large decisions you make—for example, to establish and fund the foundation you've outlined—can go forward. As we've discussed, let's pray about how to proceed. Does that meet with your approval?"

"Yes. Thank you."

On her way home, Kari prayed for guidance and wisdom.

I believe you gave me the idea for a Christian women's shelter, Lord, but it seems as though you must have someone other than me to lead it?

She heard the voice in her heart repeat itself.

I have something else for you.

She sighed. *Well, if you have something else for me, Lord, I'd sure like to know what it is.*

That evening, Kari called Ruth. They hadn't spoken in a few weeks, so it took them the better part of an hour to catch up.

"It's so good to hear your voice, Ruth," Kari sighed when they'd exhausted all the news, "and I miss your face!"

"Me, too, Cookie. Any chance you could jet over here for a weekend?"

Kari started to shake her head when she had a different idea. She sat up. "Wait. Why don't you come here? Could you come this Friday? I could use your advice on a scheme I'm cooking up."

"Uh, not unless you have a magic carpet. I've already blown my budget on a ticket to visit my daughter's family in New York for Christmas."

"Well, let me buy you a ticket to NOLA!"

Ruth hesitated. "Are you sure?"

"I would love to have you. Say yes?"

"Only if you're certain."

"Of course I am."

***

KARI IDLED THE CADDY alongside the Arrivals area and scanned the curb for Ruth. When she saw her friend waving, she pulled forward.

Ruth dropped her weekender onto the back seat and climbed into the passenger seat. She and Kari embraced briefly and then Kari put the car in gear and merged into the traffic exiting the airport.

Ruth beamed at Kari. "This is such fun! I never do anything so spontaneous. And the weather here is a bit balmier than Albuquerque's right now."

"We might get some rain, but otherwise, the weekend temps should be perfect."

After Azalea fed them a wonderful dinner and left for the day, Kari and Ruth poured themselves coffee and settled in the living room to talk.

"So you said you were cooking up a new scheme," Ruth reminded Kari.

"Oh, yes." For the next quarter hour, Kari outlined her idea for a foundation that would establish a Christian women's shelter in New Orleans and train staff and community leaders to minister to victims of domestic violence.

"The aim would not be only for helping battered women and their children, Ruth. It would point to the root of the problem: that broken families beget more broken families. We would establish Christian study groups and mentorships for the men in these relationships, too—if they were willing to change.

"If the family can be salvaged, we will work toward that. If it cannot, we will help the women recover and raise their children," Kari explained,

"The first shelter would be the prototype, and we would use it to present the Gospel to every woman and child who crosses its threshold. I want to bring Jesus to as many as the Lord allows. Additionally, the women would receive godly counseling and be enrolled in vocational training and a job placement program. We'll help them get a decent job and then transition them to their own apartment. Then we'll follow them for a year or longer.

"After we've gotten the NOLA program off the ground, I would like to replicate it in other cities." Kari smiled at her friend. "I want to name it 'Palmer Foundation.' Every shelter would be a Palmer House."

Ruth nodded. "That's perfect. Fitting. Named for Rose and Joy's work in Denver."

"Yes. In a way, it would be the continuation of their work. The details are still rough, and the main need, of course, is leadership—experienced *spiritual* leadership, leadership that relies upon God's word and his power.

"When I was in Denver, I asked my cousin Alannah why the ministry of Palmer House had ended. She said that the new leadership had no idea what the power of God could do, that they relied more upon programs and methods than upon God. For that reason, I don't think what I have in mind will be effective unless the leader and staff of the program know Jesus really well and depend upon the transforming power of the Holy Spirit and God's word to accomplish the work."

Ruth, deep in thought, nodded her agreement.

Kari continued. "I would head the foundation, but I'm not in a position to be the leader. My role would be primarily financial oversight. I will need the Lord to help me find the right person to actually lead the program. What do you think?"

Ruth rested her chin upon her hand and studied Kari for a long moment. "Does, um, I mean, is it imperative that the pilot program be in New Orleans?"

Kari blinked as what Ruth asked sank in. "Are you suggesting . . . are you suggesting Albuquerque?"

"It's a smaller city than New Orleans, but the need there is as dire. And I, well—"

"*You!* You have the experience and the spiritual maturity! Oh, Ruth— why didn't I think of it? You would be perfect!"

Ruth held up her hands. "Let's not jump the gun. What you're describing is wonderful, but I won't commit myself to it until we've fleshed out the details and prayed long and hard over them. It would mean big changes for me—a lot more work and a *lot* more responsibility. I would need to have assurance of the Lord's direction."

"All right," Kari agreed. "So let's spend the weekend working out those details and praying over them."

"Well not the *entire* weekend, right?" Under her breath Ruth muttered, "I should have known that free airplane ticket was too good to be true!"

They laughed together and Kari placed her hand on Ruth's. "I'm sorry—there's no rush. Tomorrow I'll show you the city. When we're tired of walking, beignets, and *café au lait*, we can talk some more."

"Okay, but now let's talk about your Christmas guests." Ruth waggled her eyebrows suggestively, and Kari blushed.

"You mean you want to talk about Søren . . . and me."

"Yup. Spill it!"

Kari giggled and then sighed. "Well, when I was there for Thanksgiving, he did ask me again . . . about us."

"What did you say?"

"I said I still wasn't ready, that I wasn't at peace with the idea yet. That I wasn't confident about the Lord's will. He understood and said he could wait, but then he said something about wanting me to be there, on the farm with him and Max, *always*—and that really threw me for a loop."

Ruth frowned. "Hmmm."

"Exactly! Later, after I'd thought about it, I told him I couldn't see myself living there year-round. I-I have a life here, too. And duties."

"And this new ministry?"

"Heavens! I haven't even mentioned that to him yet."

"I don't know, Cookie. Doesn't seem like you're in a position to become a farmer's wife."

Kari's brows lifted. "It's not whether I am or am not 'in a position.' It's also not what I want or need right now.

"It's been on my mind a lot, and if we were to marry, I think Søren and I should be able to shift back and forth from Louisiana to Nebraska—perhaps spring and summer there, winters here—with me flying into NOLA once or twice a month to manage my responsibilities."

She shook her head. "And another thing. Søren is scared of my money. I really hope he can come to accept it as a blessing and not continue to treat it as an inconvenience to be shoved into a closet. Part of my inviting them to spend Christmas with me is to show them my life here. Show them how they could fit in."

Ruth shrugged. "Well, times are changing. Many women work outside the home now."

She leveled a cautioning glance on Kari. "God himself put you in this unique position. He made you steward over a pretty vast fortune, meaning he has plans for you to use that fortune for his glory. Søren could be a powerful strength to you in that effort—or he could be a real roadblock.

"I hope Søren is mature and flexible enough to accept you as you are, Kari—and accept the position where God has placed you. If he isn't, then I hope you are wise enough not to sacrifice yourself. Again."

As usual, Ruth was able to put her finger on Kari's concerns before she herself was able to.

"Thank you, Ruth, for helping me to clarify my concerns."

"No problem. I love you, *Chica*. Now, I think I'm ready for bed. It's been a long day."

They climbed the stairs and said goodnight, but Ruth's warning lingered long in Kari's mind as she tried to drift off to sleep.

By the time Ruth left early Monday morning, her input had added important components to Kari's plan.

"We should meet again, right after Christmas," Kari enthused. "I'll fly into Albuquerque and we can noodle on this more."

"Good grief. Give me a week or two to recover from the grandkids, please! After two weeks with them, I'll be frazzled."

"All right, all right! Mid-January then."

"Perhaps I can arrange for you to meet with some of my peers," Ruth suggested, "other Christians who could be allies. I'd like you to share your vison with them—and I know they would have valuable input."

"Yes, that would be a good step in the right direction."

Kari went from the airport directly to the Brunell & Brunell offices and spent the morning with Oskar. When she returned home, she glanced at the calendar.

"This Friday," she rejoiced. "Søren, Max, and Ilsa will be here this Friday!"

CHAPTER 13

Kari hired a limo to take her to the New Orleans airport. As the driver dropped her at the curb, she left him with instructions to circle the arrivals pick-up zone until she waved him down.

She scanned incoming flights, hurried toward the gate, and got there as the flight was deplaning.

There they are!

Kari walked as fast as she could toward them—and then Max (despite his father's instructions) came flying toward her. He barreled into Kari, hugging her about her waist.

"Kari! Kari! Guess what? We flew in over a big ol' lake an' almost landed right in it!"

"Had to have been Lake Pontchartrain. There's a bridge that goes across that lake. We'll have to drive over it. It's the longest bridge in the world."

"Wow! This is the best trip ever!" He looked up and grinned. "Gosh, Kari! I'm so glad to see you! Hey! You sure are pretty t'day."

"Hay is for horses!"

Kari and Max giggled, and they hugged again.

Kari had taken pains with her clothes, hair, and makeup. She admitted to herself that she wanted to look her best for Søren.

She apparently looked good enough, because as soon as he and Ilsa reached her, Søren pressed a warm kiss upon her cheek and held her tighter than he usually did.

"You take my breath away," he whispered.

Kari blushed and turned toward Ilsa. "I'm glad you're here. All of you."

Ilsa smiled. "I'm glad we are, too. Søren has been a bear for days. Maybe he'll calm down now that we're officially on vacation!"

While Søren and Max collected the luggage, Ilsa and Kari chatted. Kari couldn't stop smiling.

"I'm so excited for you to see my house," Kari confessed. "It's too big for one person, especially during the holidays. You guys are going to make this Christmas a happy one for me."

"Well, I'd be more than delighted to help you clean and get ready for Christmas. Perhaps do some baking?"

Kari snorted. "You can help me finalize the decorations, but you'll have to fight Azalea for the 'privilege' of cleaning and baking."

"Who?"

"My housekeeper, Azalea Bodeen."

Ilsa's eyes widened a little. "You have a housekeeper?"

"And a groundskeeper. His name is Toller Bodeen. He's Azalea's son. The Bodeen family has been caretakers of my house for decades."

Ilsa looked uneasy. "I won't know what to do with myself. Neither will Søren."

Kari nodded. "Well, you are on vacation, remember? I have lots of fun activities I can suggest for us over the holiday. And in case you *need* some work, I will be giving Azalea and Toller a week off, starting Christmas Eve. We'll have to fend for ourselves for a week."

"But still, a housekeeper?"

"Yeah. Welcome to my world, Ilsa," Kari whispered.

Søren, Max, and Ilsa chatted with Kari until she flagged down the limo and it pulled up to the airport's Arrivals curb. They gawked in silence when the liveried driver stepped out and touched his hat.

"May I get your bags, sir?" he asked Søren.

"No, I'll get them," was his automatic response.

Kari placed a soft hand on his arm. "It's his job, Søren," she whispered.

The driver popped the trunk and loaded the bags into it before Søren could recover. Then the driver opened the back door of the long vehicle.

"Madam?"

Kari gestured Ilsa toward the door. "There's plenty of room."

Ilsa stepped in, followed by Max. Kari heard Max exclaiming before she followed them. Søren climbed in last and the driver closed the door behind him.

"Golly, Kari! This is a rich person's car! Is it yours?" He ran his hand over the leather of the seat that spanned the back and curved to run down one side of the vehicle.

"No, Max. I hired the car specially to pick you-all up so I wouldn't have to park and walk to the terminal to fetch you."

His eyes were busy exploring the limo's interior. "What's that?"

Kari popped open the refrigerator. "Would you like a soda?"

Max looked at Søren. "May I, Papa?

Søren was staring out the window, watching the unfamiliar city fly by. He turned and swept his gaze around the car's interior, taking in the long, curving seat, the television, the phone, the stemware, the refrigerator.

"Sure, Son." He looked out the window again. Kari could feel distress bleeding from him.

He's completely out of his element, Lord. Please help him.

When they arrived at the house, Kari waited for the driver to open their door. When he did, again touching the brim of his hat, Kari followed Søren out of the limo. She saw Søren, and then Ilsa and Max, stare at her house; she watched them take in its size, the chiseled pink stone, the slate roof, the pale gold pillars and the decorative wrought iron surrounding the wide front porch.

"Is this your house, Kari?" Max asked, his eyes wide.

"Yes. This is it."

Kari directed the driver to take the bags in and leave them in the foyer. She led the way up the porch and unlocked the front door. When the driver finished bringing in the luggage, Kari stepped outside and gave him a generous tip.

When she returned, Max was still standing in the foyer, his head all the way back, gaping at the ornate ceiling and chandelier high above him.

I did the same thing, Kari remembered.

Søren and Ilsa had moved into the living room, so Kari left Max and followed them. Ilsa had one hand to her mouth. Her eyes were open wide. Søren, hands stuffed in the pockets of his jeans, stared around.

Kari tried to see the room with fresh eyes—the large living and dining rooms and their high ceilings, the tall paned windows and expensive drapes, the polished wood floors and carpets, the furnishings including many antiques. The nine-foot Christmas tree in the corner and the other decorations only added to the elegant charm of the house.

"I was overwhelmed the first time I saw it," Kari whispered.

Ilsa nodded. Søren's glance passed right over Kari. His eyes were shuttered.

Kari prayed, growing a little desperate, *Lord, I'm going to need your help here.*

Kari grabbed Ilsa's overnight case and started up the stairs. "Let's take your bags upstairs, shall we?"

Max grabbed his suitcase and followed on her heels.

"Your Christmas decorations are exquisite," Ilsa murmured as she and Søren trailed behind. She paused on the first landing and considered the stained glass window. With one finger she traced the glowing panes of brilliant blues, purples, and greens that formed a peacock looking over his shoulder and down upon his fully fanned plumes.

"This is exquisite."

"Thank you. I think so, too." Kari climbed higher, made the turn at the second landing, went up three more steps and walked out upon the mezzanine overlooking the foyer. Max followed closely behind her.

He leaned over the rail and studied the parquet floor far below and the intricate coved and corniced ceiling above. "This is sure somethin'."

"I love the view from here, Max. The first time I saw it, I wondered if my father had stood right here, looking down like we are. It made all of this," she gestured with her free hand, "a little easier to accept."

Kari walked on and stopped in front of the newly remodeled master suite. "This will be your room, Søren and Max. There's a bathroom through there. Please make yourselves at home."

Max went exploring without further urging. "Wow! This is super!" He ducked into the bathroom and shot back out. "Papa! Look at this! There's a tub *and* a shower! An' I've never seen a bathtub like this! It's like a little swimming pool."

Søren and Ilsa stepped into the bedroom, so Kari followed them. She patted the new king-sized bed. "I hope you and Max don't mind sharing. This is actually the master suite. I recently had it remodeled. I guess I'll eventually move in here, but I thought it would be easier for Ilsa and me to share the hall bathroom than for all of you to share it."

"Not that we don't at home," Søren muttered.

"I think it's wonderful, Kari," Ilsa whispered. She put her head into the bathroom and Kari heard her muffled, "Oh, my! I officially have bathroom envy."

"You'll have to thank Lorene for the décor. She managed the remodel for me. She has superb taste."

"It's so fancy, Kari!" Max gushed. "Really, really cool."

"Yes, well . . ."

Søren said nothing. He stood silent with his hands jammed into his pockets, so Kari tipped her head and added, "Ilsa, your room is down this way."

She and Ilsa went down the wide hallway, past Kari's room on the left and another bedroom on the right. Kari gestured to the next bedroom as they came to it. "This will be your room, Ilsa. The bath is right here at the end."

Ilsa stepped into her room and sighed. "Oh, Kari. This . . . this is so lovely."

Lorene's fingerprints were upon this room also, and Kari admired the new paint, paper, curtains, and linens and how they enhanced the beautiful old furniture.

For the first time since her guests had arrived at the house, Kari relaxed and smiled. "I'm glad you like it. I really hope you'll enjoy your stay."

Ilsa placed her bag on the bed and moved to the window to look out. "Enjoy our stay? You might have trouble getting me to leave, Kari. I might play the 'poor shirttail relative' card—and then you'll be hard-pressed to get rid of me!"

Ilsa laughed and Kari relaxed a little more.

"Cousin, you are welcome to come as often as you like and stay as long as you want!"

"Get thee behind me," Ilsa joked.

They snickered in tandem.

"Well, I'll leave you to unpack, then. You should find hangers in the closet and all the drawers are empty."

"Thank you, Kari."

Kari went back down the hall to the master suite. Søren was sitting on the bed listening to his son's exuberant chatter. He glanced up when Kari stopped in the doorway.

"Azalea is serving dinner at six. Until then, feel free to unpack and come see the rest of the house. Maybe you'd like to walk around the grounds with me?"

"Sure, Kari. We'll be down shortly." Søren didn't seem quite as shell shocked as he had been a few moments ago.

Kari attempted a smile. "See you then."

"And this is Azalea Bodeen, my friend and housekeeper," Kari said as she introduced her guests. "What's on the menu for dinner tonight, Azalea?"

"Blackened catfish, steamed crayfish, red beans and rice, and a spinach salad, Miss Kari. For dessert, I've whipped up a chocolate-pecan king cake."

"Chocolate cake with pecans? Yum!"

Kari hugged Max around the shoulders. "Not merely a chocolate-pecan cake, but a *king* cake, a New Orleans' specialty. And wait until you taste Azalea's breakfast beignets or popovers, young man."

"Baynays? What are those?"

"It's a French word pronounced more like 'bain-yays.' Think of them as hot, fresh doughnuts sprinkled with powdered sugar." Kari turned to Ilsa and Søren. "Shall we go outside?"

With Max appropriating her hand, Kari led the way out the back door and down the steps. Ilsa called from behind her.

"Is that the infamous garage?"

"Yup. That's where I found the Caddy and then discovered Rose's journal. In the attic."

"Can we go up there, Kari?" Max asked. "Into the attic?"

"Of course. But first let me show Ilsa and your dad around the yard."

She saw Toller striding across the lawn and waited for him to come close. "Søren, Ilsa, this is Toller Bodeen. He's my groundskeeper."

"Pleasure t' meet y'all," Toller said. As he shook Søren's hand, he added, "Would you like a tour? I understand you own a farm. I'd like t' hear 'bout it. Got t' be different than Louisiana farming."

Quite naturally, he and Søren began talking and, within minutes, they had moved off together, leaving Kari, Ilsa, and Max to wander the grounds. Kari was a bit relieved.

"What I really want to show you, Max, is on the other side of the house. You see, I own a tree that is begging to be climbed."

Over dinner, Kari kept an eye on Søren and was glad to see him start to unwind. As for Ilsa and Max, they had no difficulties falling into "vacation mode."

"This is the best catfish I've ever tasted," Ilsa raved.

"Yes, Azalea has pulled out all the stops. I think she has made it her mission to spoil us rotten. You'll get to sample some very good Louisiana cooking while you're here—right up till Christmas Eve. Why, she's even filling the fridge and freezer with good things we can delve into after she leaves for her own Christmas celebrations."

"I can cook for us, too," Ilsa offered.

"I'm sure we will fend for ourselves just fine, but after Christmas, while Azalea is still on vacation, I'd like to take us out to eat a few times. I want you to savor some NOLA ambience from the French and Garden Districts."

Azalea brought in the king cake then and served everyone a slice.

"This is yum!" Max proclaimed. He slid another—sizable—bite of cake and pecan filling into his mouth.

"Fabulous," Ilsa agreed.

"Quite goo—" Søren's brows bunched together and he fished something from his mouth. "What in the world is this?" It clinked as he dropped it onto his plate. It was a tiny plastic baby.

Kari hooted and couldn't stop. "Søren! If you could see your face!"

Azalea came back with the coffee pot. "I see ya got the baby king," she observed.

"The what?" Søren was busy forking the rest of his cake, suspicious of another surprise. "I about broke a tooth on it."

"That's why it's called a king cake, Mr. Sør'n. Has a little baby Jesus inside it. We bake king cakes for Christmas and special occasions, but it's really for Epiphany, January 6, the traditional date for celebrating the three kings' visit t' the stable and their bringing gifts t' the real King."

"That's so cool!" Max picked the plastic toy from Søren's plate and wiped it off. "Baby Jesus even has a little crown!"

"'Cause he's th' King, o'course."

After Azalea finished serving dessert, Kari insisted her housekeeper go home. "We'll clean up, Azalea. I'll see you tomorrow."

"Good night, then, miss."

"Wow. Azalea's a treasure," Ilsa whispered as soon as the back door closed.

"Don't I know! And wait until you taste her coffee in the morning."

They awoke the next few days to the tantalizing smells of Azalea's coffee—along with sausages, fried potatoes, fruit, juices, and pastries. Every dinner was an exploration of another facet of Southern cuisine. Their days were spent sightseeing all over the city, their evenings playing board games in front of a crackling fire.

One afternoon, as Kari had promised, she drove them over Lake Pontchartrain. She played the tour guide as she paid their toll and they drove onto the causeway.

"You can see the causeway is actually two bridges—one in each direction, both with two lanes of traffic."

The unobstructed view from the Caddy was spectacular—the causeway so long and the lake so vast, that the bridge appeared to stretch into infinity. The sun shone down from a sky filled with fluffy, swift-moving clouds. The sun-kissed, white-capped waves sparkled from far below.

Max was in awe. Even Søren, gawking from the passenger seat, grinned his pleasure to Kari.

"What a wonderful day!" Ilsa sighed. "And such pleasant weather you have here."

"Yes, but you know it's not always this nice, right? We have tropical storms. Downpours. Floods. Hail. Hurricanes. Even tornadoes."

"You have tornadoes here?" Søren was surprised.

Kari's smile was wicked. "Oh, yes. Woe to the driver caught on this bridge when a tornado decides to dance with Lake Pontchartrain!"

Søren glanced into the back seat and snorted a laugh. Max's eyes were darting about as though a funnel cloud might drop down on them out of the blue. Then he followed Max's gaze and frowned. "So where would you go if you were out here and a tornado struck?"

The bridge had no shoulders, and he spied precious few places to pull off in case of an emergency.

Kari arched her brows. "Where, indeed?"

On Sunday, Kari's guests accompanied her to church. Afterwards, they joined others from the service for brunch.

"I haven't had this much fun in a decade," Ilsa declared on Monday evening, "and I've never been pampered like this!"

"Well, tomorrow is Christmas Eve. We'll be on our own after that until New Year's."

"I've looked in your freezer, Kari. You won't have to cook for a month."

"Are you having a good time, Søren?" Kari needed to hear from him.

He shrugged. "Sure. It's different, but a nice change."

"Well, I'm having an awesome time," Max assured her. "This is the best vacation ever!"

The morning of Christmas Eve, Kari got up early and made the coffee. Not long after, Søren and Ilsa wandered down the back stairs and joined her at the small kitchen table built into the bay window.

"I like this little nook," Ilsa commented over their first cup. "It is cozy, and the view is delightful—not the awe-inspiring wide-open spaces of the prairie, but lush and green and intimate."

"Mmm." Kari nodded in agreement. "I agree. To be truthful, I have come to love this house and its beauty. At first, it overwhelmed me—and I was absolutely creeped out because it had Peter Granger's fingerprints all over it. Well, I've made enough changes that now it feels like it is mine.

"Whenever some aspect of the house does remind me of him, I try to recall that my father grew up here, and I replace Granger's image with Daddy's. For example, I can picture him right where we are, eating his breakfast before school, milk and cookies afterwards."

Kari caught Søren watching her. "What is it?"

His smile was one-sided. "You haven't been here long. I hadn't imagined you having real ties to New Orleans, to this house."

Kari met his gaze. "Yes, it has grown dear to me."

He kept studying her, and Kari hoped Søren understood what she meant.

Before bed, Kari helped Max hang his stocking from the fireplace mantel. She pointed to the underside of the mantel. "Look, Max. There's only one hook here. It had to have been where my father hung his stocking."

"That's pretty special, Kari." Max put his stocking's loop over the hook and stood back to view it.

Later they left for the Christmas Eve service. Kari loved every part of the candlelit evening: The reverence of the traditional hymns, the message, the fellowship of other believers.

As they sang *Silent Night*, Max leaned into her and snuggled under her arm. Søren slid closer and slipped his arm behind Max and around Kari. The three of them joined their voices with the rest of the congregation and sang the timeless words.

Silent night, holy night!
Son of God, love's pure light.
Radiant beams from Thy holy face
With the dawn of redeeming grace,
Jesus Lord, at Thy birth
Jesus Lord, at Thy birth

Kari yearned to belong to Søren and Max. *Lord*, she prayed, *if ever I needed your guidance, it is now. I trust you. Please show me which way to go.*

Christmas was spent slowly savoring the morning and playing wild, competitive board and card games in the afternoon and evening. They ate whenever and whatever they liked, praised Max's silly jokes and riddles, and generally kept to themselves.

I'm so glad they came, Lord, Kari rejoiced.

The days after Christmas were much like the days after Thanksgiving. Time slowed and they made the most of those languid hours. Kari, Søren, and Max took long, wandering walks together and talked for hours, Kari and Ilsa cooked, and together they all kept the house tidy.

***

NEW YEAR'S DAY 1992 DAWNED BRIGHT AND CLEAR. Kari teased Max into running with her early in the morning. They returned to the house, breathless and laughing.

Ilsa met them. "Kari? You have a phone call. It's your attorney."

Kari took the call on the living room phone. "Happy New Year, Clover!"

At his first words, she paled. "Oh, no! But is he all right?"

Søren and Ilsa turned to watch her. She listened, asked questions, and ended the call with, "We will be praying, Clover."

When she hung up, she sat down, stunned. Søren sat beside her and took her hand.

"What is it, Kari?"

"It's Oskar. He's had a heart attack."

Ilsa exclaimed, "What? But he's too young . . ."

"He is fifty-five. Clover said that Oskar got up this morning and had been up only an hour when he began to complain of being dizzy, of pain in his jaw and shoulder."

Søren asked what they all wanted to know. "Is he going to be all right?"

"They don't know yet. He's in the hospital and they are running tests."

Late in the afternoon, Kari and Søren left Ilsa and Max at the house and drove to the hospital. They sat with Clover and Lorene, Oskar's wife, Melanie, and Oskar and Melanie's daughter, Suzanne, and waited for Oskar to come out of surgery.

Hours later, the doctor came out to speak to Melanie and Suzanne.

"Mr. Brunell came through the surgery and is in recovery."

Kari exhaled. *I didn't realize I was holding my breath.*

"He is resting now. We did a bypass on two arteries. His recovery period from the open-heart surgery should last approximately six weeks; however, I need to tell you that his heart muscle itself has suffered some damage.

"We will not know the extent to which he will be restricted until he has healed from the surgery but, based on the damage I observed, he may require oxygen for daily activities—and I do not include work in his daily activities. Oskar will not be able to resume the rigorous schedule I understand he is accustomed to."

"He won't be able to work again?" Clover repeated. Kari could see how dazed her old friend was.

"Certainly not for months and, after that, certainly not full time. The damage to his heart will leave him weak."

Lorene stared at Kari, and Kari had never seen her look as frail as she did now. She placed a fiercely protective hand upon her husband's shoulder. "Clover cannot take on Oskar's schedule. I will not allow him to even try."

Kari well remembered part of her first conversation with Clover and Lorene. She had arrived in New Orleans that day, and they had invited her to their home for dinner. Clover had described the firm of Brunell & Brunell, and his role as one of the senior partners.

I'm eighty-one years old and semiretired now, Clover had mentioned.

We just cannot seem to grasp that we can't do any longer all we used to do with such ease. So we mind each other's blind spots—he mine, and I his, Lorene had added.

Kari met Lorene's gaze and nodded her acknowledgment.

Lorene will not allow Clover to overextend himself. We must find someone else to fill Oskar's shoes.

"I understand, Lorene. Don't worry—we'll figure it out."

It was a sour note on which to end Søren, Ilsa, and Max's visit. The same driver arrived the following morning to take them to the airport.

"We had a wonderful time, Kari," Ilsa assured her, "but we know how dear, how important Oskar is to you. We'll keep him in our prayers."

Søren squeezed her hand. "Yes, we will pray. I'll call you from home to let you know we've arrived safely. And," Søren added, "we'll pray for the right person to take over from Oskar to manage your little empire."

The three adults chuckled, but Kari's heart could not join in. It felt the weight of those words.

Life would be easier without my "little empire," Lord. I would have a life with Søren and Max. A simple, uncomplicated life.

At the airport, Kari hugged Ilsa. When she hugged Max, he clung to her. "I love you, Kari," he mumbled. "Wish you were coming home with us."

Kari's eyes smarted. *Lord? Do you have a way in mind for me to become this boy's mother? I know nothing is impossible for you, but it seems like life just got a lot more complex.*

Søren reached for her and she went to his arms. He didn't say anything, but when he bent to kiss her, she did not hesitate. Their lips met—and in the sweetness of that kiss, Kari's heart ached for more.

O God! Please show us the way.

CHAPTER 14

Seven days into the new year, Oskar called Kari. "They've released me from the hospital, but I will have a nurse helping me here at home for at least a week."

"I'm so glad, Oskar! Mellie must be relieved."

"Yes, she is. Me, too. I guess I dodged a bullet. I can only believe it was God's grace." He paused, and Kari could hear, in the background, the hiss and flow of an oxygen tank.

Then Oskar spoke again. "Listen, I need to talk to you. Can you come visit me?"

Kari was a bit taken aback at Oskar's getting straight to the point. Next to Clover, Oskar was the most 'old-school' Southern gentleman she knew. He never brought up business until he'd made personal conversation first.

Whatever he needed to talk to her about, it was important.

"Of course," she answered. "Today?"

"Yes, if you will."

When Kari rang the bell at Oskar and Melanie's house, Melanie herself let Kari in.

"Hi, Melanie. How are you holding up?"

"Much better, now that Oskar is home, but . . ." Oskar's wife, a tiny brunette with large hazel eyes, looked exhausted, despite her assurances to the contrary.

Kari touched her arm. "What can I do, Melanie? Tell me."

"Well, I'll be frank, Kari. I do need you to do something."

Kari nodded. "Tell me."

"I need you to keep Oskar from diving back into his work. He is so weak, Kari, and it terrifies me that he is already pushing himself. I-I was against him asking you to come over so soon, but he was insistent."

Melanie Brunell took a deep breath. "The nurse has Oskar on a strict schedule, but he's not exactly in a . . . cooperative frame of mind."

"I see." Kari chewed her bottom lip, wondering how she could help keep Oskar contained when his own wife could not. "I will do my best, Melanie."

The older woman nodded her gratitude. "Come this way."

Oskar was ensconced in a comfortable recliner in a room at the back of the house that could only be described as a "rec room." Kari noted a television, a tiny children's table and chairs, a shelf of games and puzzles along one wall, a comfortable sofa, and a second recliner.

144

"This must be where you entertain your grandchildren, Oskar," Kari said by way of greeting. "I can envision many a happy hour of them playing in here."

Oskar smiled, and Kari was glad to see that he had good color. She took in the cannula providing oxygen to him and the nurse sitting at a small side table in the corner, writing notes in a ledger of some kind.

"Thank you for coming so promptly, Miss Kari." He nodded to the nurse. "Please help me to the table, Mrs. Talbot."

The nurse stood in front of Oskar and allowed him to place his hands on her arms so she could pull him to standing. She steadied him and dragged the oxygen tank as they walked to the table.

Once Oskar was seated and comfortable, he said, "Thank you. That will be all for now."

"Very good, Mr. Brunell, but you may sit up like this for no more than thirty minutes."

Kari had never seen Oskar shoot a dirty look at anyone—until this moment. She glanced between Oskar and his nurse and saw that his response had not fazed Mrs. Talbot an iota.

"I'll be in the kitchen if you need me," the nurse replied, "and will return in thirty minutes to help you take your walk." She gave Kari a glance of finality. "Thirty minutes, miss," and closed the door behind her, leaving Kari and Oskar alone.

Oskar glared after her and grumbled, "Bully."

Kari slapped a hand to her mouth, but a snort of laughter found its way out between her fingers.

Oskar glowered at her. "Think this is funny?"

Kari shook her head. "No, the state of your health is quite serious. However, *you*, my friend, are a tad humorous."

"Only a tad?"

Kari grinned. "Well, maybe more than a tad." She was gratified when Oskar grinned back, more like himself.

She placed her hand on Oskar's. "Honestly, I am so grateful that you are still with us, Oskar. You gave us all a fright. I'm so grateful to the Lord for keeping you here."

"Yes, me, too," Oskar sighed. "I'm starting to understand how bad it was. And I am forced to start coming to terms with the changes to which I must adjust."

They were both quiet for a moment; then Kari broached the topic they were both avoiding. "Your dictator has allowed us thirty minutes, Oskar, and I also promised Melanie I would not overtire you. What was it that you wished to tell me?"

"Yes. All right." Oskar stared at his hands briefly and then dove in. "I must inform you that I will not be able to manage your estate any longer, Miss Kari." His words were tinged with regret.

Kari's eyes misted. "I know, Oskar. Please don't worry. We'll figure it out."

"I've already figured it out."

"Well, that's wonderful, then, isn't it? Who do you have in mind?"

Oskar said nothing at first and, as he focused on his breathing, Kari realized how dependent upon the oxygen he was.

"I have you in mind, Miss Kari."

"What?" Kari sat back in shock. "You've got to be joking!"

Oskar wagged his head. "No. No, I'm not joking. For the time being, it needs to be you."

"But-but I'm not ready! I'm not qualified!"

He dogged ahead. "You've already come a long way, and it's either you or someone new I'd have to train. I don't have the time or energy to start someone from scratch and, honestly, I'd rather it be you."

He stared at his hands. "I don't want you to be dependent upon someone else. I want to see *you* take control of your holdings. You are a strong woman, Kari, and you are in a position to become stronger. I recognize that not many women have such an opportunity, and I guess I want to see you do this."

He now stared at her. "It's your choice, of course, but if you were to give yourself wholly to growing into this role, to learning every aspect of it, then in a few years you would be fully versed and capable. At that point, you would be in a position to hire someone to assist you and take the day-to-day management responsibilities from your shoulders—but you would be able to judge for yourself how your businesses are doing under that new management.

"I don't want you to ever again be completely dependent upon someone, Miss Kari. I don't want you to live in the dark when I know you are capable of doing this job yourself."

Kari's eyes dropped to the tabletop, and she could not form a response. Her thoughts were reeling. At the same time, she was experiencing a tiny thrill at the idea.

Oskar took her hand. "Listen to me, Kari."

She looked up, met his gaze.

"You need not be completely on your own—for a time you would function as my surrogate. During that time, I would continue to groom you and you would consult with me. I would be available to review your decisions and advise you.

"This is a once-in-a-lifetime opportunity for you, Kari. Even if you feel it is not working out and you decide to bring in someone to replace me, you will have attempted it and had the experience of trying—and that experience will be invaluable. And Palmer Foundation? You will be better prepared to manage it as it gets on its feet."

Oskar squeezed her hands and paused to catch his breath. "I was already praying about you taking on a more active role in the management of your holdings, Kari, because I saw that you have what it takes. And the Lord knew that this . . . this situation with my health was coming. I can't help but believe that our work together was preparation for your next step."

When he'd gathered himself again, he said, "What do you say, Kari? Will you at least give it a try?"

Kari rubbed her hands over her face. *O Lord! I'm in total shock. Is this what you wish me to do? I must admit that the idea holds some allure, and Oskar seems to think I could succeed.*

"I suppose that I could try, at least for a few weeks," she murmured. "Everything is in good shape at present. How badly could things slip in a matter of weeks?"

She fixed him with a stern look. "But I'm not you, Oskar. If you weren't going to be available to advise me, as you said, I would refuse outright."

"So you'll do it?"

Kari took a deep breath. "I'll do it for a month or two. We can reevaluate then."

"You'll need help—a good assistant. Take mine. Bettina Fletcher is a remarkable woman and already knows your estate inside and out. You'll need a car and driver. Again, take mine."

He pressed a set of keys into her hand. "Office keys. This will not be easy and you'll need every advantage. I've told you that you have good instincts. Trust them. Don't be afraid to make hard calls. And should you make a mistake, I will let you know and we'll fix it.

"In fact, nothing you do cannot be undone except in the case of relationships. If you ruin a valuable relationship, that might not be mended as simply as reversing a decision. Remember to put people first, people above money, and you'll be fine."

"It is time for your walk, Mr. Brunell."

Neither Kari nor Oskar had noticed that the thirty minutes had flown by. The nurse's entrance was Kari's signal to leave.

Kari stood. "What should I do first, Oskar?"

"Call me this evening. I will have a list for you."

He held up his hand, forestalling the nurse. "One more thing—and this is important. I would like to give you a key piece of advice, Kari, if I may."

"Of course!"

Oskar gathered his thoughts before he spoke. "The thing is, you will always encounter a number of unscrupulous individuals during your travels. I'm certain a few have even slipped in under my radar and are lurking in your companies.

"Greedy, insecure persons, those in love with money and power? You *will* encounter them. People like that press and push. They intimidate. They diminish others to lift up themselves.

"What I want to say is this: Don't let anyone intimidate you. Stand up for what you know is right—right for your businesses and right for the many people they employ. Use the power of ownership—the power God has given you—to maintain the integrity of your businesses."

He squeezed her hand. "You are the face of Granger Capital, Granger Limited, and Granger Holdings now."

Oskar waved Mrs. Talbot over and allowed her to help him to his feet.

Kari—well and truly terrified—embraced Oskar with care. "I'll show myself out, then, and call you tonight."

But when Oskar and his nurse left the room, Kari sat back down and did not get up right away. Instead, she bowed her head over her hands, hiding her face in her open palms.

Lord, I hope you know what you're doing. I would never have seen this coming.

On her way to the front door, Kari encountered Melanie. "He seems in good spirits, Melanie."

"Did you accept his proposal?"

Kari was surprised at the question. "You mean after I got over the shock? I agreed to try. For a few weeks or months anyway."

"I'm so relieved. Oskar seems to have a great deal of confidence in you. I think it will take the pressure off of him to have you leading in his place."

The caddy must have navigated the route home by itself, because Kari had no memory of the drive. She went straight to her office and sprawled face down upon the carpet.

"Father, I don't know if I can do this! I need you to speak to me—so I know that you approve and will help me."

A sudden, distressing thought interrupted her. *Søren! Søren will not be happy that I'm committing myself to running my own businesses . . . my "little empire." My multi-million-dollar empire.*

But isn't this what I've been afraid to daydream about?

***

KARI ROSE EARLY THE FOLLOWING MORNING while it was still dark. She read her Bible and prayed and then showered and applied her makeup. With Miss Dawes' impeccable standards in mind, Kari donned an elegant but business-appropriate suit—tailored skirt, jacket, and blouse—and pulled her hair into a sleek French braid.

When the expected knock sounded on her front door, Kari gathered her handbag and briefcase. She opened the door to Oskar's driver.

"Good morning, Miss Michaels."

"Thank you for picking me up, Mr. Branson."

"It will be my pleasure to drive you, miss. And Mr. Oskar asked me to give you this." Branson handed Kari a sealed envelope.

"Thank you."

Kari slid into the back seat of Oskar's black town car, opened her briefcase, and tucked the envelope inside. She removed her leather-bound organizer from the case and reviewed the notes Oskar had dictated to her over the phone last evening. Satisfied, she returned the organizer to her briefcase and snapped it shut.

As the car traversed the city, Kari prayed. *Father, I will fall flat on my face if you do not hold me up—and that is a fact. So I commit this day to you, Lord. Please speak to me as I go about my work. I trust in your direction. I know you will uphold me with your strong right hand.*

Branson opened the rear door. "We've arrived, Miss Michaels."

Kari gathered her things and stepped out. "Thank you, Branson."

"I'll await your call, miss."

Kari nodded and walked up the stone steps to Brunell & Brunell. It was past dawn now, but far earlier than the offices opened to its clients. The worker bees of the firm, who began their days no later than 8 a.m. but often before, were admitted by a security guard while the doors were still locked.

Kari rapped on the tall glass doors, and the guard opened for her. He blinked, clearly confused.

"I beg your pardon, miss, but the offices do not open until nine."

Kari smiled and extended her hand. "It's Miss Michaels. As of this morning I work here. I will be filling in for Mr. Oskar Brunell."

"Very good, miss." He stepped back and Kari walked through.

The receptionist was typing furiously. When Kari nodded to her and began walking by, she jumped to her feet, also confused.

"Miss Michaels? I'm afraid no one is in the office at this time to see you. Um, may I call Miss Dawes for you?"

"Thank you, but that won't be necessary. I'll be working from Mr. Oskar's desk today."

"Oh." The receptionist's eyes widened a little, but Kari kept walking.

She passed through the large rotunda that housed the cubicles of Brunell & Brunell's attorneys, legal aides, and secretaries. On the other side, she turned down a hallway and arrived at the door to Oskar's private office. With a deep breath, she inserted the key. She swung the door wide and left it open.

"Good morning, Miss Michaels."

Miss Fletcher, her stance uncertain, stood in the hall outside Oskar's office.

"Good morning, Miss Fletcher. I'm glad you are here."

She offered the envelope Oskar had sent via his driver to Miss Fletcher. "Please fax this to every holding Oskar oversees on my behalf and then file it."

The woman pulled a single sheet of paper from the envelope and unfolded it. It took only moments to read its short contents.

January 7, 1992.
To all whom it may concern:
Effective immediately

> *Due to health considerations and at my physician's advice, I hereby transfer all authority and duties performed by myself on behalf of the former Peter Granger Estate to Ms. Kari T. Michaels. At Ms. Michael's request, I will act in an advisory capacity and continue to monitor the health of the estate and its holdings on her behalf.*

> *Ms. Michaels will work out of my office at Brunell & Brunell. You may contact her through the same channels to which you are accustomed to communicate with me.*
Cordially,
Oskar G. Brunell

Miss Fletcher lifted her eyes to Kari. "I'll take care of this right away."

"Thank you. We have a busy day ahead. Shall we get to work?"

"Yes, ma'am."

Branson dropped Kari home that evening after seven. She was hungry and mentally exhausted. She dropped her briefcase and handbag in her office and set off for the kitchen.

Azalea, per the instructions Kari had left in a scrawled note, had made Kari's dinner and placed it in the refrigerator with heating instructions. Kari had started the microwave when the phone rang.

She glanced at the clock and sighed. *Søren.*

She deliberated for a moment about letting the call ring through to her machine, but shook her head. She retraced her steps to the office and picked it up.

"Hi, there! How was your day?"

Søren's voice was full of energy, and Kari sighed again, weary and over-hungry.

"Hi, Søren. Today was . . . different. I actually just got home."

"Really? What did you do all day?"

Kari flinched. *Here it comes.*

"I spent the day in Oskar's office. I will be, that is, I am taking his place for a while."

There was silence on the other end of the line.

"Søren?"

"I'm here. I'm . . . well, I'm surprised. No, I'm a bit shocked. What do you mean by 'taking his place for a while?'"

"You know I was working with Oskar, learning the ropes of how he manages my holdings, so to speak. Now that he is incapacitated, we have decided that I should pick up the reins. I will oversee my own businesses, at least for the time being. He will continue to advise me, and I have a good staff to support me, but it will require my full-time attention."

Kari had determined not to sugarcoat the situation.

I must be frank and unapologetic.

"You. *You* are replacing Oskar and are managing in his stead?" Søren spoke the words as though he was sampling them—and finding their taste to be unpleasant.

"Yes, I am."

"Oskar worked a punishing schedule, Kari."

"Um, yes. I know."

Yeah. I finished my first ten-hour day, she added silently.

"And how long will you be doing this?" A touch of accusation rang in Søren's tone—and a point between Kari's eyes began to throb.

Kari placed a finger to her forehead and rubbed. "I don't know. It could be weeks or months. It could be longer, but certainly as long as it would take to find and train a suitable replacement. And that will not be a simple undertaking."

Silence hung on the line between them, but Kari could visualize Søren running his hand up the back of his neck and over the top of his short hair. She could plainly see his clouded expression.

When he did speak again, his voice was rough. "What does this mean for us, Kari?"

She swallowed. "In the immediate, I don't see that it changes anything except that I will be busier than I was. I have a lot of work to do to come up to Oskar's speed."

"In the immediate? What about the future? Our future?"

"I'm focusing on what needs to be done right now, not six months from now."

"Well, it seems to me that you are digging in, creating more entanglements in New Orleans rather than freeing yourself from the existing ones."

"I-I didn't promise anything, Søren. I didn't promise to disentangle myself from my obligations. And I did tell you that if we married I couldn't be a full-time farmer's wife."

His response was abrupt. Angry. "Right. And where have I heard that before?"

Kari recalled then that Søren's first wife, Max's mother, had hated living on the farm. She had left her husband and son so she could "find herself."

What she had found was death at the needle-end of a syringe filled with heroin.

"Don't do that, Søren. I'm not like Max's mother. I love your farm. I love being there. But I like living here, too. And in the same way you have your responsibilities, I have mine. Can't we have both? Can't we split our time and efforts between the farm and here?"

Kari swiveled her chair so that she could see the wall with all the family photos on it. She got up and touched the picture of Søren and Max.

Lord, you know that someday I want this picture to include me.

She made herself answer softly. "Right now I need to be here to learn how to take care of my businesses, but eventually we could figure out how to balance our lives, couldn't we? It might take a little while, but couldn't you see yourself living here part-time? Probably in the winter?"

"Me live in New Orleans? In your house?" Those few words were laced with amazement. Incredulity. Near derision.

I don't want to argue with him, Lord. Please help us!

"Søren, it has been a long day for both of us. I'm tired and I'm sure you are, too. Perhaps we could think about this and have a conversation when we're both rested. If we are going to share each other's lives, we need to find our common interests and figure out how it would work—"

"Common *interests*? My life is here on my land, Kari. We have nothing in common in New Orleans. And every time I turn around, you are changing. I hardly know who you are anymore! Frankly, I have more in common with your groundskeeper than I do with you, Kari."

It stung, the way he tossed her conciliatory efforts aside, but she persisted.

"We are merely talking logistics, Søren—my place or yours, when and where. I told you I couldn't live on the farm year round. And right now, I have responsibilities to tend to. So I need to work. So what? A lot of women work these days. Why can't you accept that? I know we can figure out the details if we try."

Søren's next words were flat. "You are set on this? You, who can afford to hire a brigade of managers, you are set on doing it all yourself?"

"It's not that simple, Søren, and I'm not by myself. I have a good staff, lots of help. I . . ."

Yes, Kari's heart responded to the core of Søren's question. *Yes, it is the right thing. And I* want *to do this.*

"Yes, Søren. I'm set on this. For the present. I feel it is important to have my own hands on the wheel. Can you please try to understand?"

She could hear Søren's ragged breathing over the line, but he said nothing for a long moment.

Then he said, "I'm willing to wait for you, Kari, but it sounds like you will be fully occupied for the foreseeable future."

His answer wasn't angry. It was resigned.

"Until you come to a place where you can begin to move toward marriage with me, I think we should take a break."

"A break?" Kari couldn't breathe.

"Yeah. Some time away from each other. Time to think."

"And pray?"

He snorted a little. "Yes, and to pray. Because until the Lord shows you that what you're doing is wrong, this—us—isn't going to work."

Until the Lord shows me? Kari felt her calm give way to anger.

"You know, Søren, the word 'us' implies *two* people, two individuals. I don't think you have really considered what 'us' means. I don't think you've prayed about my circumstances at all except to *wish it all away.*"

She drew a deep breath. "I'm willing to share everything I have with you. Think about it! Think about your farm. We could modernize it—and isn't that what you've longed to do for years? I'm willing to compromise and live there with you part of the time. In fact, shuttling back and forth doesn't present a problem. I could buy my own plane if needed, for heaven's sake!

"Søren, I'm willing to make any reasonable adjustment to make this work—but I don't hear anything on *your* part about sharing, compromise, or adjustment. It's as though you expect me to show up in RiverBend with nothing and merge into your nice, neat, simple life without a ripple.

"Do you want me to give up all I am and all I have, even though it is only partially mine? Well, that isn't going to happen. I have to protect the part that belongs to Elaine and Samuel. I—"

Søren cut in, and his retort was cold.

Biting.

"Elaine and Samuel are not 'coming home,' Kari. And they are not the children you remember them as. They are grown and have their own lives. You aren't going to find them in this lifetime. These are *facts*. You need to accept the truth and, once and for all, *let them go*."

Let them go? Nothing Søren said could have hurt her more. Stung, Kari sank into her desk chair. His words echoed a dark refrain she could not shut out.

Elaine and Samuel are not coming home, Kari.

Elaine and Samuel are not coming home, Kari.

Elaine and Samuel are not coming home, Kari.

For the first time since her last nightmare in July, anxiety bubbled up in her chest and squeezed her throat. Kari blinked and swallowed, pushing back on the rising panic.

No! No, I won't have a panic attack! Not now!

"I-I need to go, Søren," she whispered.

"Wait! I'm sorry. That was overly harsh. Uncalled f—"

"I need to go. Please. Please don't call me . . . for a while."

She managed to fumble the handset back into its cradle but didn't get it on right. The handset rolled out onto the desk and Kari heard the dial tone, a faint humming in the distance.

Or was that the sound of her own blood rushing in her ears?

She was hyperventilating. The edges of her vision were graying, darkening.

Kari stumbled to her feet. "Jesus, please help me!"

But *The Black* crashed down upon her and threw her to her knees. The mist surrounded and engulfed her, and Kari knew she would soon lose consciousness. Even as her limbs lost sensation and she crumbled facedown on the carpet, she prayed with desperate abandon.

Lord, I don't care what Søren said! Just as Abraham faced the fact that his body was dead, I face the impossibility of finding Elaine and Sammie, and I choose to trust you anyway.

I choose to trust you anyway.

I choose to trus—

❧ ❈ ☙

PART 2

By his divine power,
God has given us everything
we need for living a godly life.
We have received all of this
by coming to know him,
the one who called us
to himself by means of his
marvelous glory and excellence.
And because of his glory and excellence,
he has given us
great and precious promises.
(2 Peter 1:3 & 4a, NLT)

CHAPTER 15

MAY 1992

Kari dressed with her usual care for another long day at the office. Under her breath she hummed the lines of an old hymn, one that had come to mean a lot to her through the last five months.

I need thee, O I need thee
Every hour I need thee.
O bless me now, my Savior
I come to thee

"Every hour, Lord, every hour," she whispered. "Not once a day or once a week, but every hour."

In her Bible study time this morning, she'd taken heart from a passage in Philippians 4. Now she was turning those lines over in her mind, examining them from all sides. Deciding how to put them into practice.

Finally, brothers and sisters,
whatever is true, whatever is noble,
whatever is right, whatever is pure,
whatever is lovely, whatever is admirable
—if anything is excellent or praiseworthy—
think about such things.
Whatever you have learned or received
or heard from me, or seen in me
—put it into practice.
And the God of peace will be with you.

"True. Noble. Right. Pure. Lovely. Admirable. Excellent or praiseworthy. Lord, every hour please help me to think on these things. Help me to facilitate and increase good things wherever I go. Help me not to be mired down in the morass of problems I face every day."

She sighed over her last words. "Ha! Morass of problems? You know I have no shortage of those."

She closed her eyes. "Lord, please teach me how to build others up and draw them to Jesus. I have such influence! Show me how to wield my authority wisely."

Branson knocked at her front door and Kari caught up her handbag and briefcase.

"Good morning, Mr. Branson."

"A fine morning, Miss Michaels."

"Yes. Yes, it is!"

"What does my day look like?" Kari asked Bettina.

"You have a meeting first thing with your tax advisor regarding next year's changes to the tax code. You also have two conference calls, one at 10:15, the other at 3 p.m. Sandwiched in between you have a meeting with one of your hotel managers regarding upcoming renovations. I believe he will be showing you the architectural drawings. I have scheduled an hour with him."

"Taxes first thing, you say?" Kari shuddered in faux horror. "And what about lunch, Bettina?"

"You have a working lunch with Mr. Oskar."

"Oh! He's coming in?"

"Yes, Miss Michaels."

"Excellent!"

Kari smiled. She would enjoy having lunch with Oskar, even if it was a working lunch.

She settled into her day and lost track of time until Miss Fletcher mentioned that Oskar was waiting in the rotunda.

Kari got up and checked her appearance in the mirror behind her door. "Why the rotunda? Why didn't he come to my office?"

Bettina looked aside but her lips twitched. Then she frowned and pursed her mouth.

Kari had only a second to shoot her assistant a quizzical look. She grabbed her handbag and headed toward the rotunda at a brisk pace. As she cleared the hallway and stepped into the open space, she was greeted by a cacophony of shouts and whistles.

"Surprise! Happy birthday!"

Amidst a wealth of balloons and crepe paper streamers, every Brunell & Brunell employee called their birthday greetings. Clover and Lorene; the other senior partners, Jeffers and Clive Brunell; Oskar and Melanie; and Miss Dawes grinned near a long table upon which was laid a generous lunch and a very prominent, very large birthday cake.

Someone started singing "Happy Birthday," and the smiling employees joined in.

Stunned, Kari asked Miss Fletcher. "Is today my birthday?"

"It most certainly is." She giggled at Kari's chagrin.

Kari swiveled back, still in shock, to receive handshakes and hugs from the well-wishers.

"All right. All right, everyone," Clover called. "Miss Dawes and Miss Fletcher have arranged a wonderful lunch for you. Please enjoy it. When everyone has had a chance to eat, we'll cut and serve the cake."

He motioned to Kari. "Miss Kari? Would you like to go first?"

"Yes, but before I do . . ." She addressed the little crowd. "Thank you. Thank you all for wishing me a very happy birthday. Did you surprise me? You did indeed. I had completely forgotten what day it was."

She lifted her shoulders in a helpless shrug. "You could knock me over with a feather about now!"

The employees laughed, and then Kari joined Clover at the buffet table. She helped herself to a sampling of the assorted sandwiches and salads, sat down at the table Miss Fletcher indicated, and waited for Oskar and Melanie to join her.

As they took their seats, a young brunette woman followed and wheeled Oskar's oxygen tank to his side. She sat down next to Melanie.

"Miss Kari, this is our daughter, Scarlett Brunell. I know we've talked about her, but the two of you have not actually met."

"Scarlett! Yes. I'm so glad to meet you."

"I'm pleased to make your acquaintance also, Miss Michaels. Mom and Dad have told me much about you."

Kari nodded and studied the woman. What she noticed was the same self-composure Oskar possessed—and she liked what she saw.

"You graduated law school last spring, I believe?"

"Yes, ma'am, I did."

"Where are you working at present?"

"I'm clerking for Sutton, Brown, and Darling, in Charleston. I will finish my year with them next month, after which I intend to return to New Orleans and find a position here. I'm in town this week to sit for my state bar exams."

"And did you inherit your father's business savvy, Scarlett?"

Scarlett met Kari's questioning gaze. "I hope someday to be half as wise as he is, but, yes, I believe I possess some business acumen. I earned dual bachelor's degrees in accounting and business with an emphasis in global economics."

Kari tipped her head and considered her. "How long will you be in town, Scarlett? Do you have time to come see me before you leave?"

Scarlett's eyes widened a fraction. "I will make time, Miss Michaels."

Kari nodded. "I'll have Bettina set it up."

Kari returned home that evening around six. She sat at her desk and read reports while she ate the meal left by Azalea.

Azalea. I never see her anymore. I appreciate the clean, organized home she provides and enjoy the wonderful meals she fixes, but I don't wake up to her coffee and beignets—I'm gone when she arrives in the morning, not back until after she leaves.

I miss her smiling face.

Kari sighed and returned to the printout she was studying. The phone rang around eight. When Kari picked it up and heard the young voice on the other end, her heart did flip-flops.

"Hey, Kari!"

"Hay is for horses, Max." Kari grinned and discovered that her eyes were watering. "I'm so happy to hear your voice, Max!"

"Well it's your birthday, so I had to call. Happy birthday, Kari! Did you have a party? A cake?"

"I sure did. My office threw a big party at lunchtime. You should have seen that cake—three layers of vanilla cake with raspberry filling between one layer and chocolate fudge between the other. Iced in real whipped cream—not that greasy, shortening kind of frosting."

Max's shudder came through the phone. "That kinda frosting is slimy and sticks to the roof of my mouth. But your cake sounds real yummy.

"Hey," he switched topics in the same breath. "When are you going to come visit again? Not until Thanksgiving? It's feels like a long, long time since I've seen you, you know. I'm nine now."

"Yes, I know, but I can hardly believe it." Kari wondered what Søren had told Max about their break up.

She wondered if Søren still thought of her.

In the week following their disastrous argument over the phone, Søren had called several times and left messages. When she had finally called him back, their conversation had been cautious, each of them careful not to broach the topic of dispute.

After that, Søren had phoned once every two weeks, and they had exchanged news—or what little news Kari felt comfortable sharing with him.

I can hardly talk to him about my workday if it sets him off, she had rationalized.

Kari blinked, suddenly realizing that Søren had not called for more than a month.

Time flies when you're not paying attention.

"Is your dad there?"

"Yup. You wanna talk to him?"

"Yes, please."

"Hello?" Søren's greeting was gruff. Guarded.

"Hi. We haven't talked in a while. How are you doing?"

"I'm okay. Happy birthday, by the way."

"Thank you. I had forgotten it was my birthday, until they threw me a party at work."

"So you're still doing Oskar's job?"

Kari didn't hesitate. "Yes, I am—and doing well, according to Oskar. I have also gotten my foundation off the ground. My friend Ruth is leading the pilot program in Albuquerque. When we've worked the bugs out of it, we hope to expand it to other cities."

"Your life seems very full." Søren sounded resigned.

"It is, but not so full that I don't have room for you and Max. I miss you. Both of you."

He sighed. "Do you ever intend to hire anyone to handle all that work for you?"

"Yes, I still hope to." She hesitated a second and then plunged in, "Even when I do, I will need to maintain an oversight role, need to keep my eyes on things. And I'll want to stay involved in my foundation. Or do you expect me to give up my house in New Orleans and never come back here? You've had time to think about my suggestions. Could you ever see your way to a compromise? A way of splitting our time between here and there, between your responsibilities and my responsibilities?"

It was a minute before he answered. "To be honest, I've wondered a lot about it, Kari, and I kind of swing back and forth. One minute I think that if you were here—even two weeks out of every month—those would be two weeks of heaven on earth. Then I think . . . I think you must love what you do more than you love us. That Max and I would always hold second place. And that's no way to enter marriage."

Now Kari huffed. "Søren, do you love your farm?"

"Is that a trick question?"

"No. I'm truly asking: Do you love your farm?"

"Well, of course I do. You know that."

"What would you say if I asked you to give it up?"

"I'd have to say 'no,' Kari—but that's a silly question, isn't it?"

"Why is it silly? Because God gave that land to your great-grandfather, and then your grandfather, and then your father, and then you? Because to abandon it would be wrong—even if it were easier than staying?"

"Well, yes."

"It's no different for me, Søren. God gave me this estate. It's mine to use, *to employ* for his glory. To abandon the responsibility of it, when he's made it clear that I am to understand and administer it, would be wrong."

"But you're a *woman*, Kari!"

And there it was.

Kari could feel how conflicted he was: His words were heavy with competing frustration and longing. Kari's voice dropped to a whisper.

"God knew I was a woman when he gave Peter Granger's estate to me, Søren. Did he make a mistake?"

Søren didn't answer.

Into the silence, Kari breathed, "This-this . . . this 'little empire' of mine, as you call it, would be much less of a burden if you were my husband, Søren. I would draw strength from you and our Lord—because *a cord of three strands is not quickly broken.*"

The line crackled, but Kari had to believe Søren was listening, perhaps even considering.

"How is your farm doing, Søren?"

A sigh wafted across the miles.

Finally, "It's . . . not good, Kari."

"But it is your family's heritage—*our* family's heritage. I could help you. We could modernize, like you told me you needed to. Get things back on an even keel."

The silence resumed and went on far too long.

Did I push too hard, Lord?

Kari coughed a tiny cough. "Well, thank you for letting Max call. It was the high point of my birthday. Please . . . please tell him I love him."

"Kari . . ."

"Yes?"

"Um . . . I will tell him."

"Thank you, Søren. I hope to talk with you again."

But I doubt it will be any time soon.

***

SCARLETT BRUNELL SAT ACROSS from Kari, a calm but expectant expression on her face, as Kari considered her.

It was their second meeting. After exchanging pleasantries during their first meeting, Kari had changed the tenor of their meeting. It became a job interview.

Now Kari was ready to act. "Your recommendation from Sutton, Brown, and Darling is outstanding. I would like to hire you as an associate, Scarlett, to begin a week after you complete your year with them.

"The position would be part business consultant, part legal advisor. You would shadow me and take on some of the more mundane tasks I've been saddled with. You would assume more responsibility as you learn the ropes."

Kari glanced at the recommendation letter on her blotter. "Of course the position would be on a trial basis at first."

"Of course," Scarlett murmured.

Kari smiled. "However, if you show the potential to become half the businesswoman your father is, I'd be happy for you to stay on with me."

"Thank you."

"So are you interested?"

"Very much so, Miss Michaels."

"Good. Here is my offer."

Kari handed Scarlett an envelope. The young brunette unfolded the single sheet of paper and scanned the letter. A smile played across her mouth as she read it again.

"I accept."

Now Kari smiled. "I'm so glad. Welcome aboard, Scarlett."

CHAPTER 16

Linnéa Olander checked her appearance before leaving her apartment. Her dark blonde, shoulder-length hair was upswept and pinned in a soft, sophisticated French twist; her navy dress and short matching jacket hung in simple, elegant lines. Small burnished earrings and a complementary broach on the jacket's wide lapel were her only pieces of jewelry. Sensible but stylish navy pumps completed her ensemble.

She wore minimal makeup: A light foundation to conceal the dark circles under her eyes.

With briefcase in one hand, purse clutched under her arm, and her distinctly Scandinavian features and coloring, Linnéa looked every bit the Stockholm businesswoman—affluent but conservative. Perhaps even demure.

Quite the contrast to my appearance and behavior while clubbing in St. Petersburg the last two weeks.

Linnéa stifled a yawn. Her monthly trips into Russia took their toll.

She had dropped into a deep sleep while her train steamed from St. Petersburg to Tallinn, Estonia. Then, when she boarded the ferry to Stockholm, she had been too rested to sleep again. She had endured the hours-long voyage by staring at the moon glimmering on the black water as the ferry clipped the neck of the Gulf of Finland, surged through the tumultuous Baltic, and threaded its way among the islands surrounding Stockholm until it reached port last evening. Two hours later, finally home in her apartment, she had collapsed into bed, exhausted.

Now it was time to go into the office and report.

No rest for the wicked.

She studied her reflection, closely examined her face. Fine lines were chiseling themselves around the corners of her mouth and eyes, lines that hinted at the encroaching years—lines that bespoke the stress of her work. Linnéa would be thirty-eight years old in a few months, but her features were beginning to manifest the strain of her occupation.

Yes, her trips into Russia took their toll. Physically. Mentally. Emotionally.

A triple life will do that to you.

She smoothed her expression into placid lines and turned from the mirror. She locked her apartment door on the way out and stepped into the third-floor lift.

When the lift opened on her apartment's lobby, the stout doorman, Gustav, smiled his welcome.

"Good morning, miss. It is good to see you back."

Linnéa's mouth curved in affection. "Gustav, you are a welcome sight."

His smile widened. "Will you be home for a bit now?"

"Yes, I believe so, but you know how my bosses are—no languishing about for me! I must go straight in and report on my sales."

Linnéa's Swedish was flawless, not even hinting at an American accent. She doubted Gustav—or anyone else, for that matter—suspected that she was of American origins.

Gustav swung the building's heavy door open with a flourish and held it as Linnéa stepped outside.

"Have a pleasant day, Miss Olander. We are glad you are home."

Gustav used "we" in the royal sense. He took his position as doorman and general guardian of the apartment tenants quite seriously, and his consideration for the residents of "his" building was genuine.

"Genuine" is a trait sorely lacking in my life, Linnéa reflected.

"Thank you, Gustav. I am glad to be home, too."

Linnéa grinned as she headed toward the bus stop at a brisk pace. Once seated, she soaked in the views as the bus navigated the route from her apartment into Stockholm's downtown business area. The city, a mix of old and new, sprawled over a series of islands—and rarely did a bus route not cross one or more of the bridges spanning the waters that separated those islands.

Much of Stockholm's old architecture had been preserved and integrated into newer structures as the city grew. Linnéa loved the stately stone or brick buildings lining the waterways, the spires of churches peeking over gabled rooftops, the rolling streets and wide pedestrian walkways and plazas.

It is good to see the people of Stockholm again, she reflected. *Whatever beauty the city of St. Petersburg itself possesses, the Russian people do not.*

They are so drab.

So dreary.

So hopeless.

She shook her head.

Too much like me.

Thirty minutes later, she stepped into the vestibule of a tall commerce building and clipped her company's identification badge to her jacket's lapel. She nodded at the security guard and went directly to the elevator where she pressed the button for the fourth floor.

Linnéa was dressed for her position as an account executive for Marstead International, a Stockholm-based aeronautics and technology firm. Marstead occupied the entirety of the third and fourth floors of the building. Four smaller businesses leased suites on the first and second floors.

In actuality, but not widely acknowledged, Marstead owned all of the building—including basement and sub-basement levels, levels that did not appear in any architectural drawings, particularly those filed with the city.

Marstead was a respected and flourishing enterprise with a global reach, but unknown to a large slice of its employees, it was also a well-developed front for a branch of a clandestine joint American and NATO alliance intelligence agency.

The elevator "pinged" to a stop and opened to a foyer on the fourth floor. Linnéa stepped out. A receptionist sat to the left of the lift, not far from the wood-paneled wall where the foyer dead-ended. A wide hallway opened in the other direction and led to a pair of closed double doors. Beyond those doors lay the public face of Marstead, a warren of clerical cubicles and, lining the windows, the executive offices.

A large and priceless oil painting hung on the wall over the receptionist's shoulder. The landscape seemed to point the way toward the office area. First-time visitors to Marstead were so taken by the painting's vivid colors and its celebrated artist that they rarely spared a glance for the bare, paneled wall that dead-ended on the left.

That wall had a door, but it was not visible to the naked eye. The door's seams disappeared into the grain of the wood overlaying the wall.

Linnéa greeted the receptionist. "*Hei*, Ingrid. Good morning."

They spoke mostly English inside the Marstead enclave.

"Welcome back, Miss Olander. Can I get you a *kaffe*?"

Flaxen-haired Ingrid, like Linnéa—but unlike seventy percent of Marstead workers—held Alpha designation: an agency employee. The question about coffee, which she asked of certain Marstead workers when they entered the offices, was code for *Are you under duress or is everything secure?*

"Thank you. Perhaps later." *All is fine.*

Ingrid pressed a button under her desk. With the softest click, the undetectable door in the paneled wall slid open.

"Go right in. The director is waiting for you."

Linnéa nodded and went through. She sighed as the door slid closed behind her.

Not even a moment to put down my briefcase.

She walked at a brisk pace down a hall past three offices until she reached the director of the agency's corner headquarters. She knocked and opened the door.

Daniel Alvarsson closed the folder he was perusing and folded his hands upon it. "Ah. Olander. Good to see you. Sit, please."

Linnéa took a seat in the straight-backed chair in front of the director's desk.

"I'll want your report by the end of the day, of course, but give me the gist of your take first."

It was always the same when Linnéa returned to Marstead, so she was neither surprised nor unprepared: Alvarsson wanted the bottom line first.

"I have photographs. Phase one of the new design."

"Indeed! Well done. Have Vinck develop them and include them with your report."

"Of course, sir. Will you need anything else?"

"Not at this time. Carry on, Olander."

Linnéa paused at the hidden door into the foyer and pressed a call button. Ingrid, on her side of the door, pressed the button under her desk and Linnéa stepped out. The area was engineered so that neither the elevator nor the double doors into the main area could open while the door on the paneled wall was in operation.

"Thank you, Ingrid." Linnéa walked down the hallway, through the double doors into the public Marstead offices. Her own office was on the far side of the open area.

She smiled and replied to the many greetings called to her as she made her way to her office. When she reached it, she unlocked the door, closed it behind her, and collapsed behind her desk.

Her telephone rang almost immediately.

Linnéa swore under her breath, but answered with a relaxed, "Linnéa Olander."

It was Christor Vinck, the young head of Marstead's in-house technology department. "*Hei*, Linnéa. Alvarsson says you have film? I would be happy to come get it."

The chipper voice coming through the receiver set Linnéa's teeth on edge. "Christor, I have been sitting at my desk for all of five seconds."

"I'm sorry, Miss Olander. I'll call back later."

Linnéa sighed to herself. Christor—a socially immature twenty-seven years old—had a huge crush on her. One appreciative word from Linnéa made his day; one perceived slight devastated him. Linnéa did all she could not to encourage his hopes, but she also tried not to crush his fragile ego.

"It's all right, Christor. Give me ten minutes to unpack my briefcase. I'll bring the camera to you as soon as I can."

"Really?" Christor loved it when Linnéa visited his domain deep in the Marstead sub-basement.

"*Ja*, really. But first I need coffee, okay?"

"I have a new IKEA espresso maker in my office. Top of the line!"

"Um. Is that so?"

Drat.

The kid knew exactly which buttons to push. Linnéa pictured a small, white, porcelain cup sitting in the hollow of her hand, a frothy head steaming under her nose. She closed her eyes and mentally leaned toward the fragrance of dark-roasted heaven—

"Call me before you leave your office. I'll have a fresh cup waiting for you."

Linnéa cleared her throat. "Um, all right. Thank you."

She placed her leather briefcase on her desk, unlatched it, and lifted the lid. Inside the front corners of the case's lid she felt for two springs bulging ever so slightly under the lining. She pressed them simultaneously. The tiny hidden camera, mounted in the case's left locking mechanism, popped out into her hand. Six tiny rolls of film followed the camera. No one noticed the pinhole on the briefcase's side or noticed when, with a two-fingered touch to the lock, Linnéa snapped photographs.

The same camera fit into a similar mechanism on the clasp of two of Linnéa's evening handbags. The bags were small and glitzy, the kind a party girl carried when she went out on the town. One bag was black, the other a glimmering red. Linnéa carried lipstick, powder, and her hotel key in one of the bags when she was out partying, but she could hold either bag in one hand and shoot an entire roll of film with the touch of two fingers. If she needed to photograph documents from above, the camera popped out easily for Linnéa to hold it directly over the papers.

She skimmed through the stack of messages left while she was gone, gave Christor the "heads up" he requested, and grabbed the rolls of film before she headed for the lift. Inside the elevator car, she placed her fingers on the embossed words "Marstead International" above the lift menu and pressed twice: Push-push. And again: Push-push. The hidden buttons would send the lift to the sub-basement.

She stepped out into the chilly concrete hallway that led away to Christor's lab. "Lab" was the right word for his work area. From the five spacious rooms he occupied, Christor kept Marstead and its agents moving forward as new technologies emerged, while his team of technicians managed Marstead's computer and internal security systems.

As part of his role, Christor developed and printed photographs, analyzed their data, and delivered concisely worded reports to the appropriate parties.

Linnéa glanced up at the camera mounted above his door. Even if someone managed to accidentally (or intentionally) reach the sub-basement, Christor's lab was nearly impenetrable. Only a finger on the inside of the lab could open the solid steel door once it was under lockdown.

When the door slid open, Christor was waiting, a steaming cup in hand. He handed the cup to Linnéa with a flourish. "Freshly brewed!"

"Thank you, my friend," Linnéa murmured. She exchanged film for coffee and followed Christor as he led toward his workspace.

"We won't be using film much longer," Christor threw over his shoulder.

"No? What then?"

"Photography is moving into the digital age. Before you go out again, I will fit new hardware to your case and handbags, smaller hardware that will hold the tiniest camera you have ever used."

"And the photographs? What will capture them if not film?"

"A small computer chip the size of a fingernail. You'll get clearer pictures with the new camera and will be able to fit more photos on a single chip than you could on six rolls of film."

"Really? Interesting."

"Yes, quite. And no development needed. I will download the photographs from the chip to my terminal and print them from there. But until then? Into the gaping maw we go."

Christor's "gaping maw" was his euphemism for the large machine into which he loaded the film and printed both negatives and large, glossy photographs. The negatives went directly into a safe larger than the developing machine. The photographs went into Linnéa's report to the director—and, at the end of the day, into *his* safe.

An hour later Linnéa left the sub-basement with a sealed envelope. She returned to her office, locked the door, and booted up the terminal on her desk. While it whirred and came to life, Linnéa opened the envelope, took up a magnifying glass, and studied the photographs she'd removed.

Satisfied with what she'd seen, she began to type her report. It took her four hours to adequately document her "take" from the two weeks in St. Petersburg. Then she typed a synopsis that she would attach to the front of the report.

When she finished, she printed the report, placed the photographs and report in a fresh envelope. Before she turned off her machine, she copied the files to a floppy disk and added it to the envelope. Then she deleted the files from her machine.

Ever security conscious, Christor's computer team remotely scrubbed her machine's contents each evening. The only existing files of Linnéa's work resided on disks in the director's safe.

Linnéa sealed the envelope. Then she hand-delivered the materials to the director for his perusal and disposition.

Marstead was, after all, engaged in the development and acquisition of the world's most cutting-edge technologies. Marstead workers—even Beta staff—were tightly screened. And Marstead management drilled all employees on the pervasive dangers of technology theft.

As a result, Marstead operational security was tight: Unauthorized personnel and cameras were forbidden on the premises; all employees signed strict confidentiality agreements and adhered to austere rules against "loose lips." They were accustomed to the strict handling of documents.

That Linnéa prepared and hand-delivered sealed documents to her boss was not only common knowledge, it was standard operating procedure.

After a late lunch, Linnéa returned to her office and faced the tasks that had built up during her foray into Russia.

It was dark when Linnéa returned to her apartment. She had put in a long day and the evening stretched out before her.

Empty.

Like me.

She shied from the question that seemed to face her at the end of every day: *What does it matter?*

What does all this matter?

And the question she did not dare look full in the face: *What does my life matter?*

In her core, in the deepest part of her being, Linnéa found only one abiding certainty: *I am worthless.*

As a child, long before Linnéa could articulate such a word, that emotional conviction had found a residence.

My life has no worth. No value. No purpose.

Because I am worthless.

This, without doubt, was why she had given her life to Marstead.

❧ ✳ ☙

CHAPTER 17

K ari patted the hood of her Caddy. "I've been neglecting you, my old friend. But not today. Today I'll take you for a fine, long drive." She backed out of the garage and pressed the button to lower the door.

God bless Toller, she thought. *I must remember to thank him for having the opener installed.*

I'll leave a note, since I so rarely see him.

Kari shrugged away the nagging guilt that she rarely communicated with Azalea or Toller in person anymore. Rarely saw them.

In typical NOLA fashion, a steady, soaking rain had fallen during the night. Now, as midday approached, the moist air was warm and pleasant on this fourth Thursday of November. Kari put down the Caddy's top before backing down the driveway to the street.

It had been months since she had taken anything other than a Sunday off. The relative unfamiliarity of time on her hands bothered her—but not as much as the cold fact that Søren had not invited her to fly to Nebraska for the holiday.

In actuality, months had gone by since Søren had last called.

What did you expect? Your lives have nothing in common except Jesus and a distant familial relationship.

Kari turned a corner and sniffed at the air. *Fall. Not quite the fall I'm used to, but still . . .*

Not the fall of Nebraska, you mean.

She turned on the radio to drown out her thoughts.

Thanksgiving dinner at Clover and Lorene's was the next best thing to spending the holiday with Søren, Max, and Ilsa. Oskar and Melanie would be there along with Scarlett and their other daughter Suzanne and her family. Owen and Mercy Washington would be there, too. Lorene had promised that after dinner they would play games, stuff themselves on desserts, and visit far into the evening.

Good. That way I won't be sitting home wondering what Søren and Max are doing.

For heaven's sake! Stop thinking about them!

Perhaps Clover and Lorene will even invite me to spend Christmas with them.

***

LINNÉA APPRECIATED THE FACT that Swedes did not celebrate Thanksgiving. The U.S. holiday was just another workday at Marstead.

That did not keep Linnéa from wondering what her family back home would be doing or wishing she might be with them—but she was allowed only one trip into the U.S. per year. Why? Because the logistics of transitioning Linnéa to her American identity and slipping her into the States for a visit were complicated and fraught with security concerns.

It had been drilled into her for years: *The work is paramount. Nothing must jeopardize the work. All—every desire or attachment—must be sublimated to the work.*

The work? Linnéa's account executive position with Marstead was deep cover for her real work: Russian technology acquisition and information gathering.

Put more plainly, Linnéa's work was stealing emerging technology and other classified information from America's strongest Cold-War rival.

For that reason, every part of Linnéa's Marstead cover was strictly controlled. Nothing—not love, not family, not choice—was allowed to compromise her Swedish identity.

How many Thanksgivings and Christmases have I spent alone? Away from Mama and Dad. Away from Sammie and his family? All to ensure that American and Allied interests win the Cold War.

But the Cold War is over, she reminded herself. *The Soviet Union is no more.*

This was true, but the Russian Federation and a number of its former satellite countries still possessed nuclear devices and nuclear material. Who knew what would become of them or who might obtain them and use them against America and its allies?

Since the 1991 dissolution of the Soviet Union, Russia was a nation whose political, economic, and military structures were in tremendous flux. The old order and ways were devolving into chaos while new power brokers and agendas were rising.

The very real concern was that *no one was minding the store.* Who was actually holding the reins of power during Russia's struggle to reinvent itself? Who would emerge victorious from the battle? What weapons or nuclear materials might fall through the cracks while the warring political, military, and intelligence factions struggled to assert their authority?

Meanwhile, Russian scientists were still hard at work, designing and testing new weapons systems and prototypes, inventing fresh technologies, and refurbishing and advancing older ones. In Russia's budding new economy, information and technology enterprises were booming, and St. Petersburg was Russia's hub for global economic initiatives.

Marstead had a branch office in St. Petersburg—a vital foothold on Russia's flank. Marstead was always on the hunt for prospective partnerships and capital investment opportunities, and Linnéa spent two weeks out of every month in that city, ostensibly networking with Marstead's Russian counterparts.

In reality?

Linnéa was a spy.

The Cold War might officially be over, but the United States would never surrender her role as the world's scientific leader. America and her allies needed to ensure that former Soviet Union arms and materials remained intact and tightly controlled. The U.S. government needed eyes and ears in sensitive places. What better means to an end than for one of their agents to form attachments with those 'in the know'?

Linnéa was that agent, and her role was to form such "attachments" with highly placed men—military or scientific—and, over time, ferret out the information Marstead wanted.

It was Seduction 101.

It was Linnéa's job.

It was her patriotic duty to safeguard America's freedom and security.

She had surrendered her body, heart, and soul to the effort—with emphasis on "her body."

Why not? I have no value, and the information I gather does.

Although Linnéa knew with her mind that her work was important, the role she played was repugnant and depressing: The dangerous, flirtatious dance to attract and snare the right mark. The initial, innocent conversations over drinks leading to long dinners and whispered confidences. Her eventual surrender to the mark and her "enjoyment" of it.

It was all part of her job—guiding the man through the phases of infatuation, romance, affection, love, and trust.

Followed by the betrayal.

She had spent a full year stringing one middle-aged mark along. He was unhappy and underappreciated at home and at work. Linnéa made him feel young and virile again; she listened to him talk. She flattered him. Appreciated him. Her soft, milky blue eyes assured him that he was interesting, intelligent, and charming.

She adored him, she said; he worshipped her in return.

They had planned a life together, she and Ludya. For a month, they doodled out the details, first on cocktail napkins, then in long weekends of detailed discussions. They dreamed and talked and planned until there was nothing more to do but take the leap.

Linnéa had produced fake travel documents and they booked separate travel arrangements to Buenos Aires where they would meet. They planned to rent a secluded house, miles from the city, and go to ground for six months. Eventually they would purchase new papers and a car and drive to Venezuela. From Caracas, they would fly to Barbados and a life of long, golden days on the beach.

Ludya had left his wife, his grown children, and his grandchildren for a life with Linnéa—a lush life to be financed by the files he agreed to pass to her. She, in turn, told him she would trade the technology to a prospective buyer for more money than they would ever need.

Ludya had turned the information over to Linnéa. He had, perhaps, at that last moment, perceived the truth about them—about her—but she had wept tears of joy as they parted, swearing to meet him in two short days. He had stared into her eyes and vowed to always love her.

Two days later, Ludya had arrived in Buenos Aries with little to his name. He waited where they had agreed to meet.

Linnéa had not appeared.

She had not asked her handlers what became of him—that would have been unprofessional. Her revulsion with herself was only marginally improved when she imagined that Marstead had picked him up. Ludya, having nowhere else to turn, would have chosen to give up every secret he possessed rather than fall into the hands of the hands of the FSK—the FSK, Russia's Federal Counterintelligence Service, the successor to the KGB.

This was how she preferred to think of him spending the remainder of his ruined life. At least he would not have perished in the FSK's "care."

Yes, her job was seduction, but there was nothing pure or simple about it.

It was treachery. Emotional treachery.

And I am very good at my job.

That thought collided in her mind with its companion belief: *Because it is all I am suited for.*

With every liaison, Linnéa had surrendered more of herself. Every betrayal had chipped off a piece of her heart, a chunk of her soul.

At first Linnéa had assured herself that, when the time was right, she could leave Marstead, start over, reassert her "real" self, and recover what had been stripped away.

But now, as the end of her thirties loomed near, Linnéa made the dispassionate observation that the course of her life was set. There would be no "recovery."

Her real self—*Laynie Portland*—stared back in the mirror.

Linnéa Olander was not her real name.

Ironic that Linnéa means "twin flower," isn't it? It was a question she'd posed more times than she could tally.

She had been raised as Helena Portland. Laynie, for short.

Linnéa, Laynie. Laynie, Linnéa. Another facet in her complicated life. *But then again, Laynie Portland isn't my real name either.*

Don't go there, Laynie.

She made herself look in the mirror again, at the woman she was, not the woman she could have been.

That ship has sailed, Laynie. Or Linnéa. Whoever you are. She swallowed and frowned. *I could have chosen differently, couldn't I?*

But she was no longer certain, no longer sure she could have chosen differently. She was too good at what she did. Too good at playing the seductress to see herself in any other role.

Why? Why did I start down this road?

It was the question that she would not—could not—delve deeply enough into the shadows of her own heart to answer.

Linnéa did what she usually did when her spirits sank this low. She removed a cushion from her divan. Built into the recesses of the sofa frame was a safe. Linnéa dialed the combination and removed a bulky Marstead-issued cellular telephone. She switched it on and checked the battery as the phone powered on.

Then she dialed a number she knew by heart. This was the only phone she was allowed to use for these calls and only infrequently. Linnéa glanced at the clock. It was midmorning in Washington State, nine hours earlier than Sweden's time zone. They would be gathering, cooking and baking for the festive dinner.

"Hello, Mama?"

Her mother's distinctive Southern accent—marking her as a transplant to the Evergreen State—flowed over the lines and over Linnéa's soul. "Laynie, Sugar! I been missing you somethin' fierce. You must of heard me wishin' and prayin' for you to call."

"How are you and Daddy?"

"We're fine, darlin' girl. We're fine. Ever'one's here. We're jus' wishin' you were here, too."

They talked for twenty minutes and then Linnéa asked to speak to her father.

"Laynie? I'm so glad you called."

"Mama sounds good, Daddy. Is everything really okay?"

Her father didn't answer until he'd moved around the corner, out of the kitchen and into the dining room, to answer. "Not as good as we could hope. She's relapsed a little and cannot walk right now.

175

"The doctor has started her on another new medicine. He hopes the MS will go into remission again and she'll regain the strength in her legs."

Laynie shivered. Multiple Sclerosis. It was the boogie man in their family's life, particularly for Laynie's father. MS was stealing his beloved wife away, piece by precious piece. Stealing the only mother Laynie had known.

"I'll call again next week to hear how it is working."

"It would be nice if we could call you, Laynie, instead of waiting for your calls. What if we really needed to get ahold of you? What if we had an emergency?"

The precautions Marstead demanded were stringent: Her family knew she worked for Marstead and had the number to the Marstead switchboard. However, her family believed *Laynie Portland* was a Marstead employee. They had never heard of a Linnéa Olander.

"If you call during business hours, the Marstead switchboard can reach me, Daddy. You have the number."

"Still. Seems strange that we can't call you direct or at home."

The rationale she'd been told to give her family was that the cost of calling from the U.S. was too expensive, so they should call her at work. Marstead gave her unlimited long distance—from her office.

In reality, it was about maintaining her cover by controlling access to her. During office hours Laynie's parents or brother could call and leave a call-back request with the switchboard operator. After hours, they could leave a recorded message. If the message were urgent and after hours, they could send a wire to an address they believed was Laynie's apartment in Stockholm.

In reality, the address was a Marstead operations center. The wire would be screened and forwarded by courier appropriately, including to Laynie's apartment.

Linnéa's training snapped into place. "It's about cost control and my weird schedule, Daddy. Don't worry. And if it's after hours and there's a real emergency, you know a telegram will reach me fastest."

The relay Marstead had in place would deliver a wire within the hour.

"Yes. Well, I'm glad you called, Little Duck. We love you. We are praying for you."

The "we are praying for you" part grated against Laynie's nerves.

I have no value to a holy God, Daddy. Don't you understand? God has never wanted me and he never will.

But Laynie simply answered, "And I love you and Mama, too, Daddy."

❧ ✳ ❧

176

CHAPTER 18

APRIL 1993

I n the eleven months she had been with Kari, Scarlett had proven to be a hard worker, unafraid to take on new tasks. Scarlett's actual business experience might have been thin, but her education and instincts were first-rate. The quality Kari appreciated more was loyalty: Scarlett was loyal to a fault.

Scarlett worked out of a small office not far from Kari's office. They shared Bettina Fletcher's services, and began each day with a short meeting.

"I received a curious email this morning, from an anonymous individual concerning your plant in Houston," Bettina informed Kari during their Monday meeting.

"Oh?" Email messages from within Brunell & Brunell were common enough but were less so from without—although Kari believed the trend could only increase.

"The email is from a Houston Internet provider, but we do not recognize the sender. Since it concerns Granger Mills, I can only assume that it is from a Granger Mills employee."

She handed Kari a printout.

Kari read aloud: *Please inform Miss Michaels that the Granger Mills management team will be meeting next Tuesday to vote on significant changes to the plant and its staffing.*

"I'm not familiar with Granger Mills," Scarlett said.

Kari's brow creased. "Granger Mills is a textile mill and sewing factory, Scarlett, but I don't recall receiving notice of 'significant changes.'"

"More concerning, you did not receive an invitation to the meeting in which those changes will be discussed and decided," Scarlett murmured.

"Hmm. Apparently someone at Granger Mills decided I should be put in the know. How many employees at Granger Mills, Bettina?"

Bettina consulted the sheet she'd printed along with the email. "Three hundred fifteen, at the most recent count."

Kari tilted her head, thinking. "Oskar expressed some concern when we visited Granger Mills last. His 'inside man' was retiring and he was not altogether confident in Mr. Hancock."

Kari tipped her head, and considered an idea. "Bettina, do you know an administrative assistant at Granger Mills who can be trusted?"

Bettina glanced up. "I am acquainted with a Mrs. Jensen. She provides administrative support to the management team, but not directly to Mr. Hancock."

"How long has she been there?"

"Fifteen years. Perhaps longer?"

Kari sat back, lost in thought. When she sat forward again, she said, "I'll be frank with you: This anonymous email provokes some concern in me regarding Mr. Hancock. It may be that I came away with an unfavorable first impression, but I think it is more. Certainly my instincts were twitching when we were in the same room."

Kari glanced up at Bettina. "Please book a flight for us into Houston a week from tomorrow, back out the same evening."

Bettina cleared her throat. "Unfortunately, I will not be able to accompany you. If you recall, my mother is having out-patient surgery that day."

"Yes, that's right. Hmm. We'll have to muddle along without you. And please tell her I'll be praying for her." Kari's brows bunched together. "As for that meeting? What a bother. Walt Hancock gives me the creeps."

"What is his position?" Scarlett asked, making notes in her own organizer.

"He's the plant manager and V.P.," Kari replied.

"What, in particular, bothers you?" Scarlett asked.

Kari thought another moment. "When Oskar introduced me to the management team, Hancock was mildly deferential at that moment but dismissive within the actual meeting."

Kari corrected herself. "No, dismissive isn't the right word. 'Excluding' is perhaps more accurate. I sat next to Oskar at the conference table with Hancock and his four-member team, but I may as well not have been there.

"He rarely made eye contact with me, and when Oskar asked my opinion it was like Hancock never heard me."

"Did he not realize that you are the outright owner of the company he manages?" Scarlett asked.

Kari shrugged. "I think my disquiet may run deeper than that. I sensed that Hancock places little value on females in the workplace. His manner is condescending. I don't believe any women hold management positions either, yet I recall a woman sitting against the wall whom two managers consulted regularly.

"She seemed very astute—had the facts and numbers Oskar asked for at her fingertips—yet was not invited to sit at the table or address the management team directly. The only other woman in the meeting was Hancock's admin, Mrs. Blake, who took notes and said nothing."

Kari sighed. "I confess this email is raising more than one red flag. I would like to know who sent it."

She tapped her pen on her notebook a few times. "Bettina, I've changed my mind. I want to fly into Houston Sunday afternoon—unannounced. I'd like you to have Mrs. Jensen meet us for dinner that evening. And see if she knows who the other woman in the last meeting I attended was."

"Her name should be in the meeting minutes, shouldn't it?" Scarlett inquired. "And we have a copy of those minutes, don't we?"

"Right you are. Have that woman join us for dinner, too. And again, I don't want anyone else knowing that we're coming to town early or that they are having dinner with us."

Bettina nodded. "I'll take care of it."

Near the end of the day, Bettina knocked on Kari's door.

"Miss Michaels?"

"Come in."

Bettina sat down in front of Kari's desk. "Your flight and hotel reservations for Houston are confirmed for Sunday. I also made a dinner reservation for four at DouPre's."

"Ah. You located the mystery woman?"

"Yes. One Cadie Bryant. As it turns out, her name was not in the meeting minutes, but Mrs. Jensen knew who she was as soon as I mentioned her."

"Oh?"

Bettina nodded. "Miss Bryant is regarded as the in-house whiz. She's only been with Granger Mills for a year or so. Her mind is a steel trap for facts and figures but . . ."

"Let me guess: She is underpaid and underappreciated."

"Exactly." Bettina hesitated a moment. "Mrs. Jensen told me . . ."

"Yes?"

Bettina frowned. "Perhaps it would be better for her to tell you herself. She says that she is, and I quote, 'looking forward to an opportunity to speak candidly with you.' End quote."

"Hmm. I think I am looking forward to our conversation, too."

***

KARI AND SCARLETT ARRIVED IN HOUSTON around two Sunday afternoon. A driver waited for them; he held up a sign that read "K. Michaels."

He smiled pleasantly. "Afternoon, ladies. Welcome to Houston. I'm Maurice; I'll be your driver while you're in town." He collected their luggage and saw them to the car.

The city was warmer than New Orleans that day, but the humidity was as high.

"I'm going to shower and dress for dinner," Kari murmured as she and Scarlett parted to their separate rooms. "Meet you downstairs at a quarter to six?"

"I'll be there."

At exactly 5:45, Kari and Scarlett met in the hotel lobby. Maurice picked them up and whisked them downtown. He pulled up in front of a tall tower.

"The restaurant is located on the top floor," he told them. He handed Scarlett a card. "Please call me when you are ready to return to the hotel."

Kari and Scarlett walked into the building's lobby and found the elevator to the restaurant. When they stepped out, two women looked at them with expectant expressions.

"Miss Michaels? I'm Emma Jensen. This is Cadie Bryant."

"Thank you for meeting with us this evening," Kari replied. "This is my associate, Scarlett Brunell."

Kari studied the two serious-faced women. Mrs. Jensen was petite and pleasant looking, perhaps fifty years of age. Miss Bryant was a tall, stately African American. She appeared to be Kari's age. Kari did not miss the thick briefcase Miss Bryant carried.

"Shall we find our table before we talk?" Kari suggested.

The women agreed and followed Kari and Scarlett to the hostess. As they were being seated, Kari wondered how she would broach the subject of the factory's state, but as it turned out, she had little to do but listen and ask clarifying questions.

"Miss Michaels, no doubt you received our email?" Mrs. Jensen began.

"Yes. So you sent it?"

"I sent the actual email, but it was from the two of us," Miss Bryant answered. "We are both in positions to see and hear things at the plant that concern and perhaps alarm us. I believe that some, er, *issues* have gone undetected for years. However, a specific management decision finally prompted us to reach out to you."

Miss Bryant spoke extemporaneously before, during, and after dinner. Whenever Kari asked a question, she had answers at the ready. Mrs. Jensen frequently expanded on Miss Bryant's narration.

Two hours later Kari could scarcely remember what she'd eaten for dinner.

But I'm pretty certain what I'll be having for a midmorning snack Tuesday.

"Miss Bryant, how long have you worked at Granger Mills?"

"Two years in the fall, ma'am."

"What position do you hold?"

"My position is "Accounting Analyst," ma'am."

"And your education?"

"I hold a master's in business administration."

Kari considered the woman. She was placid, transparent, and utterly in command of the fiscal state of Granger Mills.

"Miss Bryant, you seem to pull exact facts and figures right out of your hat. Do you happen to have what they call an eidetic memory?"

A light blush rose on the woman's cheeks. "True eidetic memory is something of a myth, Miss Michaels. I am, however, adept with figures. I can recall exact numbers and make calculations in my head with ease. I-I don't think that my manager, Ted French, the Granger Mills comptroller, realizes how much I have, er, figured out. He doesn't give me much credence, but as an analyst, I've learned how to 'backdoor' systems with tougher security than Granger Mills' system."

"Surely with your education and talents you could work somewhere more prestigious than a textile mill and sewing factory?"

She blushed again. "Actually, for a number of years I was a forensic accountant for a large CPA firm in downtown Houston."

Kari looked her question and Miss Bryant appeared pained. "So why am I at Granger Mills? It's a matter of priorities, I guess. My sister and I were raised by an aunt who became homebound two years ago. My aunt requires continual care that she cannot afford, so we, my sister and I, live in our aunt's home and provide it ourselves.

"My sister carries most of the caregiver load while I provide the finances. My aunt's home is only two miles from Granger Mills. The quick commute makes it possible for me to go home during lunch and give my sister a needed break."

"In other words, you and your sister have put your lives and careers on hold to love and care for your aunt." Kari wanted the woman to know that she esteemed her selflessness.

"Yes, ma'am." Miss Bryant's response was a hoarse whisper.

"God bless you, Miss Bryant."

The woman blinked back sudden tears.

Kari changed the subject. "Since you are obviously overqualified for your present position, have you applied for promotions at Granger Mills?"

"Of course. However, 'upward mobility' doesn't seem common within Granger Mills."

Kari turned to Mrs. Jensen. "Are there *any* women in management at Granger Mills?"

"No, ma'am."

Kari lapsed into silence, thinking over the information they had provided her. When the waiter appeared with the check, she roused herself. "Thank you, Mrs. Jensen, Miss Bryant, for your time and, er, *candid conversation* this evening. I appreciate you both. I particularly thank you for your service to Granger Mills."

While Kari signed the credit card receipt, she added, "Mrs. Jensen, my administrative assistant could not come with us on this trip. Would you kindly attend the meeting Tuesday to take minutes for me?"

Emma Jensen swallowed. "Mr. Hancock's assistant, Mrs. Blake, usually takes the minutes," she said. "And I hardly think Mr. Hancock would be pleased to see me in the room."

"Hmm. I take your point. However, I wish for my own set of minutes, and I desire them to be accurate and complete."

She looked at both women. "You need not fear repercussions; I will ensure that your positions are secure. So, Mrs. Jensen, are you up to the task?"

"Yes, ma'am."

"Very good. Now, Miss Bryant. You've brought along supporting documentation, I presume?"

"Yes, Miss Michaels. Months of reports and an executive summary to guide you through the salient pages. I've also highlighted the particulars as I've described them."

"Thank you. Scarlett will take them from you. I'd like you to be in attendance Tuesday also."

"Of course, Miss Michaels."

"Tomorrow I plan to visit my factory. I wish to be free to go wherever I decide to go and speak to whomever I choose to speak. Mrs. Jensen, can you arrange for visitor passes to be waiting for us, say, around ten in the morning?"

"Certainly. Would you care for a tour?"

Kari chewed the end of her thumb for a moment. "Who is the sewing factory shift supervisor?"

"Um, Jeff Baines supervises the mill; he is on the management team. Eric Thompson supervises the cutting and sewing floors. He is not on the management team."

Scarlett jotted down the two names and their office numbers, and Kari said, "I will ask for Thompson when we arrive. You understand that I do not wish for any advance notice of our visit tomorrow?"

The two women cut glances at each other and nodded.

"Thank you again for your time."

Scarlett had spoken little during dinner, but she had listened intently. During the drive back to their hotel, they were silent until Scarlett's soft chuckle roused Kari from her reflections.

"What is it?"

Scarlett shook her head, still giggling. "It's just . . . I am looking forward to tomorrow and Tuesday." She turned her head toward Kari. "I'm learning a lot from you."

"From me?" Kari was nonplussed.

"Oh, yes." Scarlett laughed again and then they lapsed into their own thoughts.

***

MAURICE DROPPED THEM at the front entrance to the plant a few minutes after ten the following morning. Scarlett was equipped with notebook, pen, and a binder of selected reports.

Kari was armed with several hours of prayer.

Lord, I've never been in a position like this! I certainly have never faced such a situation before, she continued to pray as they walked to the front entrance.

Oh, how I need your discernment! I need your help, your guidance, and most of all your peace. I realize, Father, that it is not enough for me to 'do' the right thing here; I must also behave in a manner that demonstrates the fruit of your Holy Spirit—regardless of how difficult that might be.

Lord, I can only be the woman you desire me to be if you help me. And so I am leaning upon you.

Scarlett stepped up to the security desk. "I believe two visitor passes are waiting for us? The names are Scarlett Brunell and Kari Michaels."

"Yes, ma'am. Please wear them at all times. But who will be escorting you today?"

A tall, harried-looking man pushed through the door into the lobby. "Miss Michaels? Miss Brunell? I'm Eric Thompson."

They shook hands and Thompson gestured toward the door into the plant proper. In the hallway on the other side, he stopped and stared at Kari. She could see worry in the creases around his mouth and eyes.

"I was pretty surprised to receive your call this morning, ma'am. As you requested, I have not mentioned your visit to anyone, but . . ."

"But nothing, Mr. Thompson. I own this mill lock, stock, and barrel," Kari replied evenly. "I appreciate your willingness to follow my orders."

Somewhat relieved, Thompson released a deep breath. "Yes, ma'am. Right this way."

In the hallway outside the sewing floor stood long lines of employee lockers and a cabinet containing disposable ear protection. Thompson handed Kari and Scarlett spongy earplugs.

"It's noisy in there with all the machines running at the same time."

They entered the sewing floor then and Kari experienced what he meant. Perhaps one hundred sewing and serger machines were spaced upon the floor and busy workers ran them. Other employees wheeled bins of bundled fabric pieces to the sewers and shuttled finished pieces to the next sewing station. A few curious eyes noticed them.

Thompson started to lead Kari down one of the rows, but she placed a hand upon his arm.

"Mr. Thompson, I wish you to remain here while I tour the sewing floor."

He hesitated and then said, "I have some work in my office. Perhaps I could leave you here for a quarter hour?"

"Actually, I would like you to remain here, Mr. Thompson."

Where I can keep one eye on you, Kari added silently, *despite Mrs. Jensen and Miss Bryant's confidence in you.*

He stopped on the edge of the sewing floor per Kari's request. With arms folded across his chest, he observed as Kari, followed by Scarlett, began a slow navigation of the machines. The workers glanced at them as they passed but did not stop what they were doing.

Kari paused to watch a dark-haired seamstress. Kari was impressed at how quick and fluid her motions were. When the woman noticed Kari, she paused in her work.

"May I help you?" she shouted.

Kari extended her hand. "I'm Kari Michaels, the owner of Granger Mills."

The woman squinted at Kari, but she offered her hand in return. "Yolanda Martinez."

"It's a pleasure to meet you, Ms. Martinez."

Yolanda eyed Scarlett as she jotted something in her notebook and opened the binder, her finger looking for something.

Kari pointed to a box next to Yolanda's machine. "May I sit here a moment?"

The woman shrugged, so Kari sat down and leaned toward her. "Ms. Martinez, do you mind my asking how much you make as a seamstress?"

Yolanda cut her eyes toward Thompson. He remained on the edge of the sewing floor as Kari had requested, but his presence was causing Yolanda some distress.

She moved her head in a tiny "no" motion, her eyes still on Thompson.

Kari glanced at Thompson, too. "I hope you will trust me when I say that I will allow no one in this plant to threaten your job or your wage."

The woman stared down, hands in her lap. Silent.

"Perhaps you could verify the information I already have? Scarlett will read your piece rate and, if it is correct, simply lift your hand. No one will see you do so."

Kari looked at Scarlett who read from the binder. Almost imperceptibly, Yolanda's hand twitched.

Kari stood up. "Thank you, Ms. Martinez. And thank you for your service to Granger Mills. Have a good day."

Kari and Scarlett moved on, greeting workers in what appeared to be a random fashion. However, Kari made certain to introduce herself to both male and female sewers of differing ethnicities. In all, Kari and Scarlett spent two hours on the floor and collected information from thirty-two workers.

"Enough?" Kari asked Scarlett.

"Yes. Every rate matches the printout Miss Bryant provided."

"Let's see the rest of the plant, then, shall we?"

They approached Thompson, who unfolded his arms and wordlessly led them out into the hallway.

"Thank you, Mr. Thompson. Would you be so kind as to show us to your office and dial Mr. Baines' extension?"

Still silent, he showed them into a small office cluttered with stacks of papers. He dialed the extension and handed Kari the receiver.

"Mr. Baines? Kari Michaels here. Yes, 'the' Kari Michaels. I'm in Mr. Thompson's office. Right. Here in the plant. Would you kindly join us? Yes, now. And please do not call anyone or mention that we are here."

She paused and listened, then added, "That is an order, Mr. Baines, and I assure you that I expect my instructions to be followed."

Baines showed up minutes later, out of breath and perspiring. Kari shook his hand and introduced herself and Scarlett.

"I would like to visit the textile mill, Mr. Baines, if you would be so kind as to escort us?"

"Of course, Miss Michaels." He led the way into the hall.

Kari thanked Thompson a final time. As she turned to leave, he whispered, "Watch your back, Miss Michaels."

It was softly spoken.

Kari did not look back but nodded her acknowledgment.

Baines led them down the long hallway and out of the building. They crossed a span of asphalt and entered a larger, taller building. Baines handed Kari and Scarlett hardhats and ear protection before opening the heavy door to the factory.

The mill was a vastly different world, dominated by larger machines, all roaring at differing pitches. Forklifts conveyed packed boxes to pallets and pallets to an adjoining warehouse.

"Stay close to me, please," Baines instructed. Kari and Scarlett did as they were told. Baines pointed to various machines and called out their functions.

"Here we blend cotton, wool, mohair and, sometimes, synthetic fibers," Baines shouted. "Our customers range from hotels and hospitality to airlines and the medical field. And of course, for the time being, we mill for our own sewing factory."

As though he had let something slip, Baines frowned and clamped his mouth shut. Kari nodded and said nothing. It was an effort on her part not to react to the slip. She was relieved when they left the mill floor and entered the relative quiet of the hallway.

Scarlett removed her ear protection. "Whew."

"Yes," Kari said.

A voice boomed behind her. Kari had been half expecting it, but it still made her jump.

"Miss Michaels! You really should have let me know you were coming. I would have escorted you myself." Wade Hancock's words were jovial, but his expression was not.

"Good morning, Mr. Hancock. This is my associate, Scarlett Brunell."

"Any relation to good old Oskar?"

Kari answered before Scarlett could. "Yes; *Mr.* Brunell is her father."

"I see. Well, you can imagine my chagrin when I heard you were here."

"And I'm a little surprised at your 'chagrin,' Mr. Hancock. Surely you know that I enjoy visiting the plants and factories I own? By the way, how did you hear of our visit?"

Hancock's gaze shifted involuntarily to Baines and back. "Uh, of course, word travels fast in a large factory like this, Miss Michaels. And please call me Wade."

"No, thank you. I prefer Mr. Hancock."

She turned to Baines. "Well, thank you for the insightful tour, Mr. Baines. I believe your job is finished here today."

She locked eyes with him until he dropped his startled gaze.

"And good day to you also, Mr. Hancock. Thank you for taking the time to greet us." Kari nodded and started down the hallway toward the exit, Scarlett at her side.

"But Miss Michaels! Shouldn't we talk?" Hancock's booming voice resounded in the hallway.

Kari kept walking.

Only Scarlett knew how furious she was.

They returned to the hotel in silence. As they strode across the lobby, Scarlett spotted a poster and offered a suggestion. "Perhaps now would be the perfect time for a massage and a half hour in the sauna?"

Kari groaned. "What a marvelous idea. My neck and shoulders are tied in knots. Even my knots have knots. Does the hotel have a hot tub? Whirlpool?"

"Yup. Do you have a suit with you?"

Kari sighed. "No."

"Then, right this way!" Scarlett took Kari's arm and steered her into the hotel's boutique.

An hour later Kari and Scarlett, coated with scented oil and wrapped in hot towels, lay on side-by-side masseuse tables. Kari groaned as the masseuse revisited her neck, stretching the tense scalene muscles that ran up the side of her neck into her scalp.

"You know what, Scarlett?"

"Mmm?"

"You deserve a big bonus."

"Ohhh! And I'll happily accept!"

They laughed, and Kari sighed under the strong, capable fingers of the masseuse.

～ ✳ ～

$\mathcal{C}$HAPTER 19

Kari set her hotel room alarm for 6:30—sufficient time to rise in the morning, dress, pray, and make the ten o'clock management meeting. She was startled awake at six by the ring of her room's telephone. She fumbled in the dark for the receiver.

"Hello?"

"Miss Michaels? This is Emma Jensen. You need to know that Hancock has moved the management meeting up to 8 a.m. I only know because one of the managers called me a minute ago to come in early and print out some reports."

Kari glanced at the clock. "It's going to be tight, but we can make it, Mrs. Jensen. Anything else?"

"Just that Hancock is furious. He raged around the executive suite yesterday afternoon pointing fingers and breathing fire."

"Did you escape unscorched?"

"So far."

"Thank you for your call, Mrs. Jensen. I owe you."

Kari threw on her robe and padded two doors down the hall to Scarlett's room. Scarlett answered the door as bleary-eyed as Kari had been, but she roused when Kari delivered the news.

"Shall I reschedule Maurice and meet you downstairs at 7:30?"

"Refresh my mind—the car has a phone in it, doesn't it?"

"Yes; that's how we reach Maurice when he's waiting for us."

"All right, but make it seven o'clock. We have a stop to make before the meeting. And could you have room service prepare coffee and muffins to go?"

Kari made quick work of her toilet and pulled out her most business-like suit. When she had dressed, applied her makeup, and done her hair, she opened her Bible. There, within the passage in Isaiah she'd opened to, was the confidence she sought.

> *Do not fear, for I have redeemed you;*
> *I have summoned you by name;*
> *you are mine.*
> *When you pass through the waters,*
> *I will be with you;*
> *and when you pass through the rivers,*
> *they will not sweep over you.*

When you walk through the fire,
you will not be burned;
the flames will not set you ablaze.

"Thank you, Lord! So much for fire-breathing, plant-managing V.P.s," Kari muttered. She left her room with a determined stride.

Kari gave Scarlett a moment to sip half of her coffee. "I need to be fully prepared for that meeting this morning. Now that we've pried our eyes open, I need you to make some calls."

Scarlett asked for and received the phone from Maurice.

"The cord is a mite short," he apologized.

"We'll make do," Kari answered.

She spoke to Scarlett. "I would like you to call our Mrs. Jensen and get the number for the HR manager."

Scarlett hung up a minute later. "I have it."

"Get him on the phone for me?"

Scarlett dialed and handed Kari the bulky phone.

"Mr. Crane? Kari Michaels here. I apologize for calling so early, but I'm pleased that you are in the office. My associate and I will be arriving at the plant shortly. I need you to meet us at the front entrance. Yes, say, 7:25.

"I won't mince words, Mr. Crane. You are not to mention my call or my arrival to anyone on pain of immediate dismissal."

Kari listened a moment. "I see. Let me put you on with my attorney, Miss Brunell."

Kari handed the phone to Scarlett. "Mr. Crane is of the opinion that I don't have the authority to terminate him."

Scarlett snorted and took the phone. "Mr. Crane? This is Scarlett Brunell. I wish to remind you that Granger Mills is a wholly owned subsidiary of Granger Limited and that Granger Limited is wholly owned by Kari Thoresen Michaels. Yes, the woman to whom you were speaking."

Scarlett listened a moment. "Miss Michaels does not require the plant manager or the plant's management team in order to act, Mr. Crane. She *allows* a management team to run Granger Mills. I must point out that she is not in any manner subject to the V.P. or management team; rather, they serve at her pleasure.

"As she has given you a direct order, any deviance from her instructions would be deemed gross insubordination and grounds for immediate dismissal."

She listened again. "Yes, 7:25 at the front entrance. Thank you."

Scarlett disconnected and took another sip of coffee. "I think Mr. Crane has altered his opinion."

She handed the phone to a wide-eyed Maurice, who watched them via the rearview mirror. "I apologize for listening in on your conversations, but *wow*. Guess I'd like t' be a fly on the wall in that meeting with you, Miss Michaels!"

Kari addressed the dark eyes in the mirror. "The wall may be the only safe place in that meeting, Maurice."

Mr. Crane was waiting at the front entrance as asked. He showed them to his office where Kari gave him instructions and waited for him to complete them.

At exactly 7:58 a.m., Kari strode into the plant's executive suite with Scarlett and Miss Bryant on her heels. A tense Mrs. Jensen jumped to her feet and walked them down the hall to the conference room.

Kari entered the room and went to the head of the table, Scarlett close to her side; Mrs. Jensen and Miss Bryant waited by the door.

Hancock's face flushed crimson when he saw Kari, but he managed to stand and sputter, "Good morning, Miss Michaels! Why, we weren't expecting you, but, of course, we're delighted you are here. I assure you that this is an informal management meeting; we are merely visiting some options and procedures—"

"Good morning, Mr. Hancock. Please give me your seat."

"What?"

"Your seat, please. Take the one at the foot of the table." She waited for him to move, then stood in front of the chair.

Kari looked around. "Good morning, gentlemen."

She remained standing. Waiting.

The four managers—comptroller, facilities, quality assurance, and Baines, the mill supervisor, shifted uncomfortably until one of them stood. The other three immediately joined him.

"Good morning, Miss Michaels."

They cut surreptitious glances in Hancock's direction. He waved them away and sputtered, "Why are you looking at me?"

Kari acted as though she hadn't noticed their discomfort. "Gentlemen, this is my associate, Miss Brunell. Please sit to my right, Scarlett."

Kari took her seat. Scarlett sat also and began unpacking her briefcase and placing papers in front of Kari. Hancock and the managers looked at each other and slowly resumed their seats.

Kari turned to Mrs. Blake on her left. "Mrs. Blake, do you have copies of today's agenda?"

The woman turned to Hancock, who flushed again.

"No," he said. "There's no agenda for today's meeting."

"Is that true, Mr. Hancock?" Kari glanced at Mrs. Blake again. "Please hand me the papers in front of you."

"Mrs. Blake," Hancock interrupted in a rush, "You are excused. We won't be needing you today."

"That's correct, Mrs. Blake," Kari agreed. "We do not require your services this morning. However, if you value your job, you will leave that stack of papers as you return to your desk."

Mrs. Blake blanched and hurried to gather her notebook and pen. She placed one hand on the papers and then swallowed and left them where they were.

"Mrs. Jensen, please assume Mrs. Blake's chair and take notes for this meeting. Miss Bryant, take the chair next to Mrs. Jensen."

"These women are not invited to this meeting!" Hancock was as close to shouting as Kari would tolerate.

"I. Invited. Them." She waited for him to go silent.

"Please pass out the agendas, Mrs. Jensen," Kari ordered.

Hancock was on his feet again. "Now, see here, Miss Michaels! This is my meeting!"

"No, Mr. Hancock." Kari stood and faced him. "Let me be explicit. This is not your meeting. This is not your management team. Not your conference room, not your building, not your plant, not your factory."

She placed her hands on the table and met the eyes of each man, ending with Hancock. *"This is my meeting."*

Utter silence ticked away.

"Do I make myself clear?" Kari asked softly.

While Hancock stewed, variations of "Yes, ma'am" and "Yes, Miss Michaels" fluttered in the air.

Kari took her seat. "I see the agenda has but two items, finalization of a contract and board bonuses. Very well, let's take them in order. Item one: Final edits to the contract with Montoya Textiles."

She looked around. "Montoya Textiles. Where is that company located, please?"

No one answered, but all the managers cut their eyes toward Hancock.

Kari repeated herself. "I asked where Montoya Textiles is located."

Hancock shrugged and lifted his chin. "You are likely unaware, but the cost of American worker wages has skyrocketed. In order to keep the plant solvent, we decided to run a pilot program, a limited test. We intend to outsource a portion of the plant's sewing to workers who are able to provide a more economical product. I'm sure you don't wish—"

"I asked where Montoya Textiles is located."

Ted French, the comptroller stuttered, "It-it is in Mexico, ma'am."

"I see. And how much of the plant's sewing would this 'pilot program' outsource to Mexico?"

No one answered, so Kari looked to her left. "Miss Bryant?"

"Fifty percent, Miss Michaels."

"The proposed contract would put fifty percent of this plant's sewing employees out of work?"

No one responded.

"Mr. Hancock, as *you* are, no doubt, aware, your position description states that no contract of this scope is to be entered into without my consideration and approval." Kari shrugged. "Very well, I have considered it. I do not give my approval."

"Now see here! You can't do that!" Hancock shouted. "We have already made a significant investm—"

"Excuse me, Mr. Hancock. My meeting. Any investment you made without my authority came out of *my* pocket. Any further questions? Anyone? Next item."

Kari read aloud. "Item two: Proposal for management bonuses based on cost savings realized in quarter three from pilot program contract."

She smiled. "Well, that's a simple one, isn't it? Since there isn't going to be a contract with a factory in Mexico, there will be no bonuses. Not for you gentlemen, anyway. The proposal is overturned."

At the end of the table, Hancock seethed. Baine and the other managers stared anywhere but in Kari's direction.

Mrs. Jensen scribbled furiously, a tiny smile twitching on her lips.

"Item three."

"There is no item three," Hancock snarled.

"I added it. See?" Kari held up her agenda where she'd penned a sentence.

"Item three: Report on Granger Mills wage discrepancies. Miss Bryant, will you please address the board with your findings?"

"Yes, Miss Michaels."

"Wait! She has no standing in this meeting!" Hancock shouted again.

Kari decided she'd had enough. "Mr. Hancock, *sit down*. I am chairing this meeting. You are speaking out of turn and shouting into the bargain. If I hear another unsolicited word from you, I will have you ejected from the room."

Hancock's jaw went slack.

One of the managers actually snickered. He coughed and muttered in Kari's direction, "I beg your pardon."

Kari smiled a tight smile. "No apology needed. Please continue, Miss Bryant."

"Thank you. I have before me a report that documents discrepancies in wages paid over the past twelve months."

She handed a sheaf of stapled papers to the comptroller—her boss—who was seated on her left. "Please pass these reports around—although," she added in a quiet aside, "you should already be familiar with these numbers."

French, the comptroller glared, snatched the reports from her hand, took one, and passed the remainder to his left.

Miss Bryant began. "Page one. Wages are paid by piece rate and level of sewing difficulty. You will see that the report is broken down on gender and racial lines in comparable categories. The upshot of the report shows that a) men are paid more per piece than women and b) Caucasians are paid more than Hispanics who are paid more than African Americans."

She looked at Kari. "The twelve-month period reported here is not an anomaly. I have analyzed wage data for the past five years, and the same discrepancies are evident. Now, if you turn to page two, I will cover wage discrepancies among exempt workers."

Miss Bryant, with thorough and concise points, made her way through the report and concluded, "The data demonstrate a clear, persistent, and illegal pattern of discriminatory practices, both in wages and promotion opportunities."

"Thank you, Miss Bryant. Questions, anyone?"

Then Kari said nothing. She waited for reaction from any of the managers present but saw only pursed lips or grimaces. The movement of Emma Jensen's pen came to a halt, and she glanced at Kari.

When no one spoke, Kari nodded to herself. "Very well." She removed five envelopes from a folder Scarlett had placed in front of her and handed the envelopes to Scarlett. Kari nodded to Miss Bryant, who stood up and left the room.

When the door closed behind her, Kari remained silent only a moment. Then she sighed.

"I don't know how deeply the corruption runs in this company, but the end of it begins today. The envelope Miss Brunell is delivering to you is your termination of employment. Every manager in this room is fired for insubordination, gross misconduct, and illegal wage discrimination."

As pandemonium erupted, Miss Bryant reentered the room. Five security guards followed her.

Kari held up her hand to stem the shouts of an angry Hancock and the other managers. "You will be escorted to your desks and given thirty minutes to clear them out. Security will then escort you from the premises."

She stood. "I will gladly pay back every nickel out of which we have cheated these workers rather than allow my company to prosper in sin. And do not expect me to shelter you from personal legal culpability. Rather, expect me to assist the law in prosecuting you with whatever means are at my disposal. Furthermore, I will consult my own legal counsel as to whether it behooves me to initiate legal proceedings against you myself over the damage you have caused this plant."

She nodded to the security guards. "Take them out of here."

Hancock shook off the arm that reached for him. "You have not heard the last of me, Miss Michaels. You'll pay through the nose for this. My attorneys will sue you for breach of contract and unlawful termination."

"I look forward to it," Kari answered. "If the courts rule in your favor, so be it. But you will not regain your position here and the resulting publicity will ensure that you are finished in this industry."

One guard said in a loud voice, "Come with us. Your thirty-minute clock starts now."

The five stunned men, corralled by the guards, left the room.

Kari turned to Scarlett. "As soon as they are gone, have the guards accompany you to Mr. Crane to deliver his termination letter."

Emma Jensen gaped. "Mr. Crane, too?"

Kari shrugged again. "HR knew the wages being paid. That makes Crane complicit and Cadie over there can prove it. She has unearthed a very interesting pattern of bonuses collected by Mr. Crane. But before we disperse—"

A knock sounded on the boardroom door. Eric Thompson poked his head into the room.

"You asked for me, Miss Michaels?"

"Come in, Mr. Thompson. Thank you for waiting. Have a seat, please."

Kari looked around the table from Mrs. Jensen to Cadie Bryant and Eric Thompson. "Granger Mills is in a world of hurt. I have begun a shakeup that is nowhere near done, and I need people I can trust to steer this plant through the firestorm ahead."

All three chins bobbed at her, but their expressions were uncertain. Kari's gaze strayed toward the clock on the wall.

Only 9:15?

She rubbed at the spot on her forehead that had been throbbing for an hour. "Mrs. Jensen, I would like you to call a mandatory all-hands meeting before lunchtime for the day shift. What time do you propose?"

"Ah, well, the machines shut down at 11:50 for forty-five minutes."

"Let's have them shut down at 11:30. And no matter how long the meeting takes, afterwards I still want the employees to receive their full lunch period."

"Yes, ma'am."

"Before you leave to make those arrangements, I need to speak to the three of you."

Kari sighed. "I don't know many people here, but you have shown yourself to be loyal to me. In my book, that means everything. Effective immediately, the three of you comprise the plant's management team. Mr. Thompson, I am appointing you the interim plant manager. Miss Bryant, you are the interim comptroller. Mrs. Jensen, you are the interim HR manager.

"We will talk at length later, but I wish you to stand with me during the employee meeting so the workers can see the new face of Granger Mills. Miss Brunell and I will stay on in Houston through the week to help you get on your feet.

"I realize, Mrs. Jensen, that you will be up to your neck in alligators at first, so we will advertise for a new HR manager and an assistant immediately. However, after we've filled those positions, if you desire a place on the management team, it will be yours. Also, once Miss Brunell and I return to New Orleans, I expect weekly—daily, if needed—phone conferences. I also intend to dispatch Miss Brunell to visit you every other week as things progress.

Maurice arrived at the plant's front entrance close to nine that evening, summoned, at long last, by Scarlett's call. As he opened the rear door for them, he hesitantly said, "Been wondering all day what that fly on the wall mighta seen."

One side of Scarlett's mouth curved up. "He would have seen Miss Michaels taking names and cleaning house, Maurice. And it was a sight to behold."

Unseen by Kari, Maurice pumped his fist. "Yes!" he whispered.

Kari and Scarlett were both exhausted. They exchanged few words during the drive until a short distance from the hotel.

"You did such a wonderful job today, Miss Michaels," Scarlett said softly. "I confess that I'm a little in awe."

A long moment passed before Kari responded. "It wasn't me, you know. The email alerting us to the problem? Mrs. Jensen and Miss Bryant's fidelity and possession of the facts? Those weren't me. I will be forever in their debt for the risks they took. Even my composure through this day's difficulties wasn't me. It was God's grace."

Kari's sigh was heavy. "It's hard enough for people to find decent jobs these days. Harder for women and minorities. And it hasn't been that long since I was without a job, very nearly hopeless. Very nearly homeless.

"So, taken all together? It was God's grace that enabled us to save those jobs before it was too late."

She thought for a moment. "Hancock will, no doubt, sue me. Perhaps the other managers will, too. Given how difficult it is to remove upper management these days without supplying a 'golden parachute,' they may even win large settlements from me. *I don't care*. I refuse to reward bad behavior—and I wish my employees and the public to know this about me and about my companies.

"In addition, while it is within my power, I will not allow jobs to move across the border or offshore merely to increase my bottom line. As long as we break even with enough over to keep facilities up-to-date—and perhaps beyond that—I will keep the jobs here."

They turned into the hotel parking lot and, in the dimness of the car, Scarlett acknowledged Kari's words with a reflective nod.

As an afterthought, Kari added, "Hmm. Granger Mills. Granger Limited. You know, with the bad press coming at us, I'm sort of relieved that my name isn't on that plant."

CHAPTER 20

"*H ei*, Ingrid."

"Good morning, Linnéa. Can I get you a *kaffe*?"

"Not this morning. Thank you."

Linnéa went directly to her office. She would be leaving for St. Petersburg the day after tomorrow and had much to do first.

She turned on her computer and looked through her leather-bound organizer for the day's appointments and tasks. At the top of her list was a mandatory briefing with the director and his top analysts to prepare her for her next objective.

Petroff—*Vassili Aleksandrovich Petroff*—was Linnéa's next mark. He was the 'big fish,' the exotic catch for which Marstead was angling. Petroff breathed rarified air and lived in an exalted position—high enough to sustain Marstead's emerging technology needs for years—if Marstead could hook him.

It was time to dangle a line, and Linnéa was to be the bait at the end of the hook.

She had a tentative date with the man when her work returned her to St. Petersburg. Marstead's long-term hopes hinged on her.

Linnéa shivered. *I dread going back to Russia.*

Yes, Petroff was a brilliant scientist, but the risk of entering into a long-term relationship with him had more than one dangerous facet.

First, the man was brilliant in every way.

I must be more careful than I have ever been.

Second, Petroff was rumored to be possessive. Nothing he considered "his" was ever outside his watchful control.

If Linnéa succeeded in attaching herself to Petroff, such a 'relationship' could become restrictive. Oppressive.

And, third, Linnéa worried that her meticulous backstory might not stand up under *this* man's scrutiny—because in addition to being a brilliant, obsessive scientist, Petroff was political.

He was connected.

He is KGB, she fretted.

Marstead might not have proof, but after her few encounters with Petroff, Linnéa was convinced.

He may not be active FSK at the moment, but he has all the markers and instincts of a former KGB agent. And if he is former KGB, he has the means to sniff out and dissect my other life.

It was for such an opportunity—and against such jeopardy—that she lived in deep cover, unknown to her stateside family as "Linnéa Olander." Linnéa shuddered to consider what Petroff could do—would do—to her parents or her brother's family should he trust her and find his trust betrayed.

My family is my only vulnerability.

When it came to her family, Linnéa was grateful for Marstead's stringent security constraints.

Another danger Petroff presented had been a surprise, a shock, especially to Laynie. *Why? Why this man? Why do I feel such attraction for him? Such untapped emotion when I'm with him?*

It was a new and disturbing experience for Laynie to find herself pulled toward a mark. She might be tempted to give more than her body to this man—and such a temptation might prove fatal.

Why? she asked herself again. *Why am I like this? So cold and unfeeling toward a decent man but attracted to someone who would snap my neck should the circumstance dictate?*

A familiar voice answered. *Because you are worthless. You don't deserve a good man.*

Yes, that was it. *Worthless.* It was why she resisted fully giving herself even to her parents, why she had resisted their faith . . . and why, ultimately, she had chosen the life she now lived.

Her mind wandered back to that day, the day Marstead came calling for her.

***

IT WAS A FEW WEEKS BEFORE LAYNIE GRADUATED with a bachelor's degree in political science and a minor in modern languages from the University of Washington. Two Marstead agents had approached her. They identified themselves as recruiters for a global technology firm looking for bright, new, entry-level employees.

Flattered and curious, Laynie had allowed them to buy her dinner.

The recruiters introduced themselves as Angela Stewart and Bert Norwood. They were seasoned recruiters, former agents themselves, now tasked with seeking out fresh talent.

"We have offices around the world, Miss Portland, and we actively seek college graduates with the right mix of aptitude and skills to work and grow in the worldwide market. Actually, we have been observing you for some time," Stewart, the woman agent, offered after their entrees were served.

"Hmm?" Laynie showed no surprise, even though she *was* surprised. Very. But then she had always been good at masking what few feelings she had.

Stewart glanced at Norwood, who nodded. "Yes, indeed. Your academic record is outstanding and you have a gift for languages, technology, and analysis. We feel that you have the potential to serve . . . the interests of your country."

Laynie snapped to the twist in the conversation. The fact that she said nothing, did not question the abrupt turn, did not even flick an eyebrow, but only glanced with indifference at the woman, confirmed what the two agents had come to believe about Laynie: She was unflappable, born with a natural poker face.

Unknown to Laynie, the agents saw something else, too.

Something in Laynie's soft blue eyes shifted. The change was so subtle that an untrained observer would not have caught it. However, neither Stewart nor Norwood were untrained; in point of fact, they had a combined thirty-two years of active field experience, and yet they almost missed it.

"She's young and inexperienced," Norwood said as he described the encounter to their superior later, "but she's intelligent and savvy beyond her years. When Stewart dropped our opener on her, *click!* Something shifted and came down over those baby blues. It was like she dropped 50 IQ points without blinking. Instant stupidity. I tell you, if she had started giggling, neither of us would have been the least bit surprised."

Their superior was skeptical. "Tell me more."

"Well, sir, I'm saying she switched personalities on us."

"Interesting. Describe the rest of the interview."

Norwood shrugged. "Always, at this point in the interview, the prospect is fully engaged, either breathless with excitement—in which case we proceed—or angry over the subterfuge, which signals the end of the interview. Since she gave us nothing by way of reaction, we were not sure which way to go. Eventually we forged ahead."

He looked to Stewart, who added, "Sir, we could have been discussing the color of grass for all the interest or notice she paid us. And that's not all."

"Yeah. Tell him the rest, Stewart. The fun part."

Angela Stewart's mouth twisted into a half smile. "Let's see: After her little personality shift, she ate her dinner with gusto, flirted with the attractive waiter, asked us what we thought of him, and wondered aloud if the lemon meringue pie on the menu was fresh—because, and I quote, *You know, if lemon pie isn't fresh, the fluffy white part gets all chewy and gross,* end quote. Then she allowed *us* to ramble on until we sputtered to a close."

Their superior frowned. "You're saying her behavior was an act?"

"Yeah; that's exactly what we're saying," Stewart confirmed. "When we finished, she sat back in the booth and, *click!* the real Laynie Portland—the intelligent, savvy young woman—was back.

"She looked us in the eye and said, 'Let me see if I understand you correctly. You are representatives of a U.S. intelligence agency, unnamed so far, and you are trying to recruit me. Do I have it right?'"

The man across the desk from the agents leaned forward and folded his hands under his chin. "Interesting. So, a natural?"

"A natural," Norwood echoed.

"Sociopath, you think?" In the intelligence business, the same traits that made for successful agents—cleverness, glibness, and the ability to charm, lie, and remain unflustered—were shared by people with deeply flawed psyches.

Norwood and Stewart glanced at each other and both shook their heads. "The shrinks will have to sort it out, of course, but we don't think so. Miss Portland exhibited true empathy, particularly when we turned our conversation toward her family. And she seems genuinely proud of America and interested in keeping her safe."

Their boss shuffled some papers on his desk. "All right. Let's get her on board and see how she works out."

***

AFTER GRADUATION, LAYNIE SUBMITTED to a battery of tests and entered a rigorous training program. Six months later, she told her family she had been offered a job, a marvelous opportunity—in Europe.

"I will get to travel. See the world," she told her parents.

Polly had been tearful; Gene stoic. Laynie, who had always been protective of her brother, was more concerned about his reaction. He, however, was in the throes of his sophomore year at college and doing well without her.

Shortly after, Laynie left the States and was sent to Sweden. Marstead—not the US intelligence agency Laynie had originally thought it to be but rather a joint U.S./NATO agency—embedded Laynie in Swedish culture. Her papers identified her as Linnéa Olander, an American ex-pat of Swedish descent with family living in Upsala. Supposedly, Linnéa had returned to her roots and never looked back.

She lived "in country," learning the languages and tradecraft she needed. After three years of intense language and culture training under Marstead's supervision, she applied to the Master of Science in Economics program at The Stockholm School of Economics—in Swedish, *Handelshögskolan i Stockholm.*

Her entrance into the master's program had been seamless, and she excelled. The program was beneficial in many respects. One important aspect had been the nationally diverse student population and the friendships and acquaintances she had formed while there. Some of her fellow students were from Russian or Soviet Bloc countries, and she was instructed to spend time with them, gain their friendship and trust.

When she graduated, she was offered a position at Marstead—one that required her to spend two weeks out of every month in their St. Petersburg office.

And, of course, under Marstead's tutelage, Laynie perfected her "other" skill: Seduction.

"I chose this life," Laynie whispered when she came to herself. "I have no one but myself to blame. I chose this life because it suits me and because I deserve nothing more."

Laynie was exhausted when she returned home that evening. She locked her apartment door behind her, checked that none of her "tells" had been disturbed, and poured herself a stiff drink. And then added another splash.

She drank a lot during her forays to St. Petersburg—it was part of her cover, after all—but she hated the drunken parties, the meaningless flirtations, the overtures and pawing that went part and parcel with her masquerade.

But, oh! Oh, how thin the duplicity was wearing.

Laynie stared with surprise at her glass. She had downed its entire contents.

When did I start drinking at home?

A little drunk and melancholic, her thoughts turned toward home. Toward her family.

***

LAYNIE'S FATHER, Gene Portland, was a third generation Swedish immigrant. Gene's grandparents had settled in Seattle, and their Swedish family name had been Olander.

Gene's father, Harold, an ambitious man, had loved everything about America, but to his parent's dismay, Harold thought their Nordic surname too "different." After some deliberation, he decided to change the family name to something "more American." Something suggestive of Olander, but not as foreign sounding.

He settled on Portland.

Gene Portland met Polly Whitney in North Carolina while Gene was in the military. It was an uphill battle for them. Neither set of parents approved of their union. They did not care. They married anyway and were happy.

Gene made money in the Seattle real estate market and he and Polly were modestly well off—but they were childless. After ten years of trying for a baby, they decided to adopt—only to be told that they were unlikely to be approved by any adoption agency.

White children, they were advised, would not be given to a mixed-race couple. Undeterred, they advertised for a private adoption, for a child of any color and, without much notice, had been offered a sister and a brother.

The cost was outrageous; it would suck their savings dry. Gene figured the private agency was gouging them, but Gene and Polly paid the money willingly. And they were overjoyed.

Gene and Polly had always been open with Laynie and her brother about their adoption, which was wise on their part, because Laynie came to them wounded, her earliest memories clouded by a sense of loss.

Laynie remembered Polly rocking her for hours as she wept and wailed. She couldn't recall what she was weeping *for*, but Polly had recounted their first weeks in the Portland home so many times that Laynie couldn't tell her mother's voice from her own memories anymore.

"In a private, closed 'doption, you aren't given much t' go on," Mama's *rich, mellow voice echoed in Laynie's head.* "The only paperwork we were given said that your birth parents were killed in a car crash. Well, our hearts ached for you and Stephen, but we were so grateful to have you, to give you all the love we had stored up."

"Tell me about our names," Laynie would ask. She always asked, because the tale her mother told her was what made Laynie feel closest to her oldest memories, closest to the longing she felt.

"Well, you wouldn't stop crying, baby girl," Mama would whisper. *"Our poor Little Duck! So confused and distressed! What a fuss you made! I held you and rocked you every night till you wore yourself out. You cried ever' night for weeks, you did.*

"You cried until your voice was gone and you could only croak. Daddy said you quacked like a little baby duck, and that seemed to tickle you. You liked it when he called you Little Duck."

Laynie remembered, too, stroking the dark, sleek skin of Polly's arm as they rocked, remembered holding her own arm next to Polly's and wondering at the many differences between them.

Chocolate.

Laynie smiled at those memories. *Mama's skin is like beautiful, sweet chocolate . . .*

"But what about our names, Mama? Our real names?"

"You always in such a hurry at this part, baby girl! Well, a'course the agency would not give us your names, your birth names, since ever'thing 'bout the 'doption was sealed. They told us you were both so young that we should give you the names we chose, so we named your brother 'Stephen' after Daddy's grandfather."

Laynie would always argue at this point of the story. "But that was wrong."

"So you told us! 'No; he's Sammie,' you insisted. We called him Stephen and his 'doption papers read 'Stephen Theodor Portland,' but you refused to call him anything but 'Sammie.'"

"That's right. Now me," Laynie would demand.

"Yes, you, Little Duck," Mama would laugh. "We tried to name you Grace after my mother and, my word! How you pitched a fit. 'I Laynie!' you screamed again and again. 'Laynie! I Laynie!'

Laynie, Laynie, Laynie!

The next part of the story was where Laynie's memories sharpened and where her sense of loss was the greatest.

"What else did I say?"

Polly would dither, but she knew that Laynie would insist.

"Well, honey, you talked about Care. You would stomp your little foot and shout, 'Care say I Laynie! Care say I am! I not stupid Grace! I Laynie!'"

Polly would sigh and add, "You sure were a handful, honey, let me tell you."

Laynie's mama liked to move past that part of the story in a hurry, but Laynie wouldn't let her. That one word, Care, *invoked such deep anguish in her that the tears would gush, seemingly from her very being.*

Care. Something about Care sparked a voice Laynie clung to, a voice that, to Laynie, meant everything . . . and yet nothing:

No! You can't take them away! You can't take them!

Laynie would weep as though her heart would break, and Laynie's mama would pull her onto her lap and rock her, knowing she could not heal a wound that Laynie herself could not even identify, let alone articulate.

Polly could only hold and love on Laynie until the storm subsided.

"Well, we named you Helena Grace, after Papa's grandmother. Helena was close enough to Laynie that it didn't send you into a tizzy," Polly would conclude.

"But you called me Laynie anyway."

"Yes, Sugar. We called you Laynie anyway. We still do," Polly would agree, agonizing over the shapeless, faceless pain her daughter suffered.

Afterwards, Laynie would go in search of Sammie. When she found him, she would tug his roly-poly toddler's body into her lap or, as he got older, close to her side, and tell him a story.

Polly would watch from around the doorway as Laynie, sometime during the story, would pat Sammie's hand and murmur, "You are Sammie. I am Laynie.

"Care said so."

Laynie woke with a start. Her apartment was dark, and she was chilled to the bone. She shivered; the inside of her mouth was sticky. Gummy.

You're a mess, Linnéa—inside and out.

It was more than that, though, and she knew it.

I am Laynie. You are Sammie.

Sammie, not Stephen.

Care said so.

Laynie, not Helena.

Care said so.

Laynie, not Linnéa.

O Care, where are you? Why did you leave me?

Laynie leaned her forehead on her hands.

"I am so close to cracking up."

CHAPTER 21

K ari had been home from the ordeal in Houston less than three hours when the peal of the doorbell roused her from muddled thoughts. She heaved a sigh and went to answer the door.

"Oskar? Melanie?" She took in Oskar's serious expression and opened the door all the way. "Please. Come in."

She showed them into the living room and sat down across from Oskar. "What is it, Oskar?"

"I want to apologize to you, Kari. Scarlett filled me in on everything—including that scoundrel Hancock's plan to outsource half of the sewing workers' jobs."

"Actually, he planned to outsource them all," Kari drawled. "He was getting ready to test his little plan when we intervened."

Oskar looked old. Worn.

"It's my fault. I never trusted Hancock. Once my trusted source retired, I should have provided more oversight. Should have looked in personally—"

"Oskar, it's all right. In fact, a trial by fire was what I needed. I learned a lot and proved a few things to myself, things I needed to find out. The ordeal showed me changes I need to consider. All in all, the experience caused me to grow."

Oskar could see with his own eyes that Kari was fine, and it struck him that she was right. She radiated a new maturity and confidence.

"Yes, I see. And our girl? How did she do?"

"Scarlett and I work together as effortlessly as a hand in a glove. She is everything I hoped she would be."

Melanie glowed at Kari's praise. "She's coming into her own, then."

"She has you two to thank for her sterling character."

Oskar sat taller, a measure of stress bleeding away. "Well, then, since you think everything is all right . . ."

"It is. But thank you for coming to visit me. And since you're here? How about we sit outside on this pleasant spring day and enjoy a coffee and some of Azalea's fresh popovers?"

"I love Azalea's popovers!" Melanie replied.

Kari mulled over Oskar and Melanie's visit until she, grateful to be home and in her own bed, fell into a deep sleep. When she awoke, she was still preoccupied with her reflections of the night before.

Yes, Scarlett is proving to be as clever and competent as I had hoped, Kari thought. *And, with her support, it is time for me to initiate some changes—changes necessary for the future health of my holdings.*

Later that week, Kari invited Scarlett to lunch and began to open up to the younger woman.

"I like you, Scarlett, and you have a future with me, should you choose."

"Thank you, Kari. I enjoy working for you and look forward to the future, to new experiences and opportunities."

Kari smiled. "Ah, the future! The future has everything to do with why I asked you to lunch today. I've been giving a lot of thought to how I want to structure the management of my holdings going forward.

"My relationship with Brunell & Brunell has been more than satisfactory; it has been perfect. However, the arrangement has become rather convoluted from a business perspective. Since Brunell & Brunell no longer has a fiduciary responsibility toward Peter Granger's estate and Oskar is no longer managing for me, the fees I pay to Brunell & Brunell to use their offices and in-house staff do not make sense—especially since I am managing my own holdings. To be candid, I see no reason for us to be working out of the offices of Brunell & Brunell any longer."

Kari smiled again. "And so, I plan to remove myself from Brunell & Brunell, and form my own management company. I'd like to make the move soon, and I've been looking at office space.

"You know I own Decatur Towers? I have decided not to lease out the top floor of Building One when it comes available October 1. Instead, I will move into the suite December 1, and I would like you and Miss Fletcher to come with me."

Scarlett was already nodding, and her eyes gleamed with anticipation.

Kari grinned at Scarlett's enthusiasm. "How does *Michaels Enterprises* sound for a company name?"

"I like it! Memorable. Classy, not ostentatious."

"Thank you. We'll need to staff up, of course: HR, accounting, financial planning, additional administrative assistants, computer techs, a security service. I intend to ask Clover if Brunell & Brunell will need the personnel we've been using, if he will continue to employ them. However, if Clover will release them, I will make them offers. They know my businesses inside and out, after all.

"And I asked you to lunch today to offer you the position of in-house legal counsel, Scarlett. The work over the next six months will be intense as we move and restructure. Are you interested?"

"Absolutely, Miss Michaels." Scarlett looked ready to jump out of her skin. "I love working for you, and I look forward to the challenge of establishing Michaels Enterprises. I-I know you will be very successful."

Kari extended her hand to Scarlett. "Well, then. Let's enjoy our celebratory lunch, shall we?"

Kari met with Clover and Oskar on Friday that week and, to her surprised delight, found them supportive of her transition.

"This is a perfectly understandable and wise move," Clover told her. "At this juncture, the role of Brunell & Brunell is redundant."

"Yes, I agree," Oskar declared. "With the right-sized organization, your overhead will make more sense, and you will have the undivided loyalty of the staff of your own choosing. I also believe you will find that your standing in the business community will flourish when you are operating under your own name."

Kari was disconcerted when her eyes misted. "I cannot thank you enough," she whispered, afraid her voice would fail her. "You have been the best of friends and the best of advisors. I-I love you both."

Clover laid his hand upon Kari's. "We have loved you from that first day you sat in our conference room and Mr. Jeffers read Peter Granger's will to you. Through all these changes, you have handled yourself admirably, Miss Kari. We are proud, both as your attorneys and as your friends, to see you come into your own."

Kari saw the same approval reflected in Oskar's expression. "You had this in mind all along, didn't you, Oskar? When you had me start meeting with you to become 'acquainted' with what I owned?"

He nodded. "Yes, I confess! I saw in you the potential that, given the right guidance and your own inclinations, would grow you into a capable businesswoman. I wanted to give you the opportunity to see, for yourself, what you could do." He cleared his throat. "I hoped you would rise to meet the challenge, Kari, and you have."

"Thank you," Kari whispered again. "Thank you for seeing in me what I could not."

***

IN A MEETING WITH THE Brunell & Brunell personnel who supported the management of Peter Granger's estate, Kari announced her intentions. At her request, Oskar and Clover sat in on the meeting.

"All of you, as employees of Brunell & Brunell, have labored on behalf of Peter Granger's estate for years. A few have faithfully cared for my holdings," she nodded at two accountants, "for decades.

"I will be leaving these offices December 1 to establish my own management organization. Since the estate has been the primary purpose for your positions at Brunell & Brunell, my leaving could put your continued employment with this firm at risk. Therefore, in the next few days you will receive offers to come work for me.

"I'm happy to report that Scarlett Brunell has accepted the position of in-house counsel for Michaels Enterprises. She will be handling employment offers and questions until a human resources position is filled."

Kari then deferred to Clover.

"Thank you, Miss Michaels. Miss Michaels' move to her new offices is a good five months away, giving each of you time to consider your options and responses. Certainly every one of you is essential to Brunell & Brunell as long as Miss Michaels' offices are here and she utilizes Brunell resources.

"Once you receive your offer, please take the time you need to make the decision that will be best for you and your families. I believe you will have thirty days to accept or decline her offer?"

Kari nodded to Scarlett, who spoke next. "Yes, that is correct. If you accept our employment offer, the transition from Brunell & Brunell to Michaels Enterprises would be seamless and occur on December 1. If you decline the offer, Mr. Clover will address your future employment options at Brunell & Brunell."

Kari and Scarlett fielded questions before the meeting broke up. For the most part, Kari thought the news was received well.

"Do you think they will all accept?" she asked Scarlett.

"I do. I see no reason for any of them to refuse."

Miss Fletcher appeared at Kari's elbow. "Miss Kari? Might I have a word?"

"Of course." They stepped into Kari's office, and she closed the door to give them privacy. "What can I do for you, Bettina?"

"I was wondering if you intended to take me with you? That is, I very much would like to go with you."

Kari grinned and hugged Bettina. "Of course I do! I would be mad to do otherwise. Hmm. I can let you in on a little secret, I suppose. Your offer will be for the position of Chief Executive Assistant. You will still work directly for me but you will also supervise the secretary pool. Does that appeal to you?"

"Yes! Thank you."

Kari sobered and made sure the woman understood her. "I wasn't kidding a moment ago, Bettina. I value you. I need you. I hope my offer reflects my esteem."

Bettina flushed with pleasure. "Thank you, Miss Michaels."

***

WITH THE NEWS NOW PUBLIC, Kari pushed ahead with her agenda. She and Scarlett interviewed for a human resources manager, and selected a sweet but no-nonsense woman by the name of Laurel Nance. Scarlett made room in her office for a desk for Laurel, and they set her to work establishing employee guidelines and obtaining health insurance bids. Each day they found more tasks to add to Laurel's list and more reasons to be grateful for hiring her.

"Scarlett, do you think Oskar would be willing to suggest contractors to renovate and furnish the office suite? We should plan the layout and ask for bids. Whomever we select will have a bare two months to make the offices ready for us."

Oskar did more than that. He offered to help Scarlett and Kari determine the staffing numbers Kari would need and he recommended an architect to draw up the office layout. He pored over the drawings, making suggestions and corrections.

However, when he began showing up at Brunell & Brunell daily, acting more as Kari's partner than part-time advisor, Kari cautioned him.

"I won't have you overtaxing yourself on my account, Oskar," she warned. "Melanie tells me that four hours a day is your limit—doctor's orders. If you are here one minute more than that, I will have security escort you out."

Oscar turned a petulant glare on her. "Overtaxing myself, my foot! This is the most fun I've had in eighteen months!"

Kari glared back. "And as long as your 'fun' lasts no more than four hours a day, you may remain."

She had to pinch her leg to quell a twitching smile.

***

AS SUMMER HURRIED TOWARD FALL, Kari's schedule grew heavier, but she had never felt more satisfaction. Staffing was nearly complete. Kari, Scarlett, and Oskar approved the layout of the offices. They took bids from three contractors and selected one.

Oskar—within the confines of a strict four-hour day—would approve the project plan for the construction and oversee the work when it began in October.

He, Laurel Nance, and Bettina—aided by Lorene Brunell—would select the color scheme, paint, carpets, window treatments, and office furnishings. In the meantime, Kari and Scarlett kept busy with the day-to-day tasks of managing Kari's holdings.

***

KARI RUBBED HER EYES. She and her team had been working steadily toward the move. It was August now, and they were all tired, but Kari was possibly more fatigued than anyone else.

She was single-minded, utterly focused on the tasks at hand and ahead, so it was with some surprise that she found her thoughts turning toward the prairie property she owned—Rose's homestead.

During the few breaks she allowed herself, a picture of the little house came to mind more and more frequently.

Why am I thinking of Rose's house now?

The last time she had seen it, the old house was listing precariously. Was it still standing? Could it survive the buffeting winds of another Nebraska winter?

I must take steps to ensure that Rose's house does not fall down—and I need to do so soon.

The more Rose's house intruded on her thoughts, the more she itched to return to RiverBend.

I would like to oversee the project myself. Make sure it is done right.

And didn't I promise myself I would build a house there? But that will mean spending time—perhaps a week or so—not far from Søren.

Kari was stunned to realize how far from her thoughts Søren and Max had been. For months.

No, it's been longer. We've not spoken in nearly a year.

Kari felt a sharp pang in her heart, an aching for what might have been.

I guess it wasn't meant to be.

She sighed and pressed the intercom button on her phone. "Bettina? Could you come in here, please?"

Miss Fletcher showed up on Kari's door a moment later. "Yes, Miss Michaels?"

"This might sound strange, but would you please find me a reputable contractor who specializes in preserving old buildings?"

"Certainly."

Miss Fletcher's smile and instant response made Kari wince. "I'm sorry; finding a contractor won't be the hard part. The hard part will be finding one who is licensed and located in the vicinity of RiverBend, Nebraska."

"Um, Nebraska. Hmm. I see." Then she smiled again. "I'm certain I can find someone, Miss Michaels."

"Thank you. Oh, and I also need an architect. A local is fine. Someone who designs homes."

Curiosity crossed Miss Fletcher's face, but she merely replied, "Of course, Miss Michaels," and turned on her heel to get started on Kari's requests.

Kari opened her organizer and looked at the months ahead where, hopefully, her calendar was not as packed as it was for the next foreseeable weeks.

The view was not encouraging.

The rest of August is out of the question of course, and September will not work, either. What? October is no better? Wait—the last week of October.

Kari wasted no time penciling out the last week of October. "There."

She picked up her phone and pressed the intercom to Miss Fletcher. "Bettina? Please mark me out of office October 25 through 29. And book me a flight into the airport nearest RiverBend for Sunday, October 24. And a rental car, please."

Oskar and Lorene will handle any problems with the office renovations, and I'm certain Scarlett and Laurel can manage the day-to-day without me for a week.

Because I need to see Rose's house again.

ℭHAPTER 22

K ari shivered as a fresh shaft of wind buffeted her. She drew her jacket closer and pulled the hood over her head, tucking wayward strands of hair inside.

Even the little creek down the incline from where she stood could have been shivering, as cold as the morning had dawned. The creek's clear water rushed by, gamboling over rocks on its way south toward the river. The banks of the creek were rimed by frosty spray; fronds and weeds alike sparkled with ice crystals.

On the opposite bank, where Kari had spent many summer mornings looking from Søren's side toward Rose's house, the poppies were gone, killed by fall's first freeze.

Kari shrugged. *The poppies probably died weeks ago*, she rationalized, but the creek bank's forlorn appearance saddened her.

How can that summer have been more than two years ago?

She placed a hand to her eyes against the morning light and searched farther east, beyond the creek, up the long pasture, toward the imposing barn and comfortable old farmhouse.

Søren's pastures. Søren's barn. Søren's home.

This was the second day her contractors had been on site, and she'd seen no signs of him. No sign of Max or Ilsa.

Surely, he's noticed all the activity by now?

Won't he come to investigate?

Behind Kari, the whine of heavy machinery intruded upon her reverie. Yesterday, a backhoe-mounted jackhammer had broken up the cement slab that had been the foundation of the previous house. Now an excavator, its long, jointed arm ending in a massive claw, picked up broken chunks of concrete and piled them into a dump truck.

The air rang with the crashing sound of a load being dumped into the bed of the waiting truck. Yards away, Kari's contractor and the construction foreman had their heads together in close conversation.

At Oskar's recommendation, Kari's architect had drawn up plans for a four-bedroom, two-bath ranch house. "No sense going smaller than that, Kari, even if you think you have no need. People never regret having too much space, but they sure bemoan not having enough."

Kari glanced from the heavy machinery toward the aging homestead house. Before the crew began work on the new house, she had insisted that they ensure the old house would not fall into further disrepair, that it would remain standing as a testament to Rose's life.

The contractor, at Kari's request, had assigned half the crew yesterday to shoring up the back corners of the house, undergirding its floors, patching the roof, replacing broken or missing window glass. It hadn't taken more than the one day. To their surprise, the porch that spanned the front of the old place and wrapped around one side—the porch Rose's husband Jan Thoresen had built with his own hands—needed little work.

In fact, the porch had been sturdy enough to keep the front of the house square, had likely been what kept the house standing through the years. It was sturdy enough for Kari to stand upon and stare through the windows into the old house.

Kari had, a few times yesterday, climbed the porch steps and gazed with longing into the four simple rooms. Kari felt Rose's nearness as she studied the house's interior. The old structure, impossibly tiny by today's standards, had been ample enough to house a loving marriage and a small family for more than twenty-five years. More than large enough to birth the legacy that had touched and changed Kari forever.

The house would never be lived in again, but Kari had asked the workmen to build a fence around the house . . . to set it apart. To mark its significance.

Kari looked back across the creek toward Søren and Ilsa's fields and barn and house. Although her life in New Orleans was full and satisfying, she felt a strong, urgent desire for more.

For love.

For a family of her own.

Kari's thoughts turned toward Albuquerque and the new Palmer House Ruth was overseeing for women escaping domestic abuse.

When it became clear that I wasn't the leader you had in mind for this ministry, you spoke to me. You said you had "something else" for me. Is my business all you have for me, Lord?

A future of only work didn't feel like the "something else" that the Lord had spoken to her.

O Lord! I have followed what I believed to be your guidance, and you have blessed and blessed me. When I'm in New Orleans, I am content. It is only when I'm here that I begin to wish for more.

Perhaps spending time here isn't as good for me as I thought it was?

A truck Kari instantly recognized crested the bluff to her far right and headed down the slope toward the bridge over the creek. Even on a frosty morning the truck left a trail of dust in its wake.

Søren was driving the truck. Kari knew it, and her heart's rhythm picked up.

She watched as the truck trundled over the bridge and onto the road that bordered his farm. And then it screeched to a stop. Sat unmoving for several deafening beats of Kari's heart.

With a grinding of gears, the truck reversed. Backed in a wide swath. Headed back toward the bridge. Picked up speed.

He's coming.

Her insides turned to gelatin.

When the truck drove onto Kari's land, one of the contractors waved it down and gestured to a parking spot away from the machinery. Kari did not move from the creek bank.

She saw the truck stop where directed—and then Max burst from the passenger seat and sped toward her. And Søren. Søren followed, his eyes fixed on Kari.

"Kari! Kari!" Max plowed into her and hugged her. Hard. Then burst into tears.

"Dear Max! Please don't cry!"

"But I'm s-so g-glad to s-see you," he blubbered. "And we didn't know you were coming! Why didn't you tell us?"

"I-I . . ." How could Kari explain to him without involving his young heart in the kind of pain and difficulties even adults found difficult to navigate?

And yet when Søren's long strides reached her, he opened wide his arms and Kari went to them. He enfolded her in a fierce embrace that assured her that nothing had changed—that after two years his feelings were unaltered.

Kari burrowed into the warmth inside his unbuttoned jacket. "Søren! I thought you'd never come."

As though cued by the same maestro, Kari lifted her face and Søren bent to place a kiss upon her lips. The intensity of that kiss, as long as it lasted, was not long enough, and it was all Kari could bear when it ended.

Søren pulled back a fraction. Far enough to see Kari's face. "We've been gone since before dawn yesterday. Took Ilsa to the airport to go visit friends. We stayed overnight with a cousin. We didn't know you were here."

Max jammed himself into a crack between them. "Yeah, we didn't *know* you were here, Kari!"

Kari stroked his head. "I arrived Sunday evening and met the contractor at eight yesterday morning. I must have just missed you."

"Not as much as we've missed you!"

Kari sniggered at the double meaning. "I've missed you, too."

Søren, still holding her against the chill wind, murmured, "What are you doing here, Kari?"

Max broke away and stared at the excavator and then the new fence around Rose's house. "Yeah. And what're you doing to that old house?" Max pointed.

Kari shrugged and Søren let her go. "I had the contractors shore up the back so it wouldn't fall down. Fix the roof." She slanted her eyes at Søren. "I couldn't bear the thought of it blowing down this winter."

He nodded. "It looks good. Chuck Haroldson is your contractor?"

"Yes."

"He's a reliable man. What about the other? Where they're tearing up concrete?"

Kari hesitated. "Remember I told you I wanted to build a house on Rose's land?"

Søren nodded again. "I remember."

He looked sad, suddenly, but asked, "So where are you staying?"

"Um, a hotel. Down the road."

"The closest hotel 'down the road' is thirty miles. That one?"

"Uh. Yes."

Kari turned her attention to Max. "You've grown so tall, Max!"

And not only in height. Kari saw that Max, at going on eleven years of age, was beginning to think his own thoughts, form his own opinions.

He proved her observations right when he stuck out his chin, eyes flashing. "Why would you stay at a crummy hotel when you could stay with us?"

"Well, Max, I—"

Max frowned at Kari, his gloved hands clenching and unclenching. "Guess Papa's right." Max's breath came in little ragged gasps and tears clogged his throat. "Guess he's right. You don't want us anymore."

Kari tried again. She reached for him. "Max, I need to explain—"

But Max tore himself away and ran down the creek bank toward the bridge. When he started clomping across, Kari could see his chest heaving and his hands swiping at his eyes.

She turned back to Søren—and saw the same pain reflected on his face. Still, she was astonished. And angered.

"You told Max I didn't *want* him?"

"No, Kari, of course not! But it was hard to know what to tell him. So I said you had other things in life you needed and wanted to do rather than live here on the farm with us. I had no idea how he'd interpreted—."

"But that's not completely true! I offered a solution and you—"

"Let's not fight, Kari. Please? You're here and I'm so, so glad. It's too cold out here—will you come down to the house with me? Ilsa left a baked ham in the fridge. I'll make us some grilled ham and cheese sandwiches. Something warm to take the chill off. And we'll talk. Max will calm down."

Kari eyed the toes of her boots. "All right. I don't want to leave at the end of the week with him thinking that I rejected him."

Søren tipped his head toward his truck. "Let me drive you?"

Kari entered the farmhouse kitchen, and even though she knew Ilsa was away, she nevertheless expected to see Søren's sister at the stove, her thick, reddish-blonde braid shimmering down to her waist.

Instead, the house was dark and not much warmer than the out of doors. Kari shivered. "Where's Max?"

"I'm sure he's in his room." Søren looked around. "Um, leave your coat on. I'll get a fire started and then some coffee."

"I can make the coffee."

A while later, hot mugs in their hands, Søren and Kari huddled in front of the wood stove. Its roaring fire was only beginning to radiate heat into the living room, so Kari wrapped her hands around her mug and sipped gratefully from it.

"Kari, what are we going to do?" Søren asked softly.

She stared at the mug. "I don't know. Somehow . . . somehow it feels like the right time for us should be getting closer, but then the circumstances change and appear even more difficult than before."

"I want honesty between us, Kari. I stopped calling you because I felt it best at the time. Yet the moment I saw you standing on the creek bank, I was ready to jump out of that truck and wade across the icy water to reach you faster."

One of Kari's hands left her mug and found a place in his palm. He gathered her fingers into the warmth of his hand and pressed them to his chest.

"This is my heart, Kari. Beating twice as fast because you are here. Do you feel it? Tell me what we are to do, please?"

Kari said nothing, but her thoughts were racing. "I-I will be here until Saturday. It's Tuesday now. Can we agree to talk everything out again?"

He nodded. "Yes, I'd like to. Please forgive me in advance for my frustration. I'm sure you remember how badly it behaves—" he let a wry snicker slip between his words "—and I'm pretty sure you will see it in action again before you leave."

A little sigh escaped from Kari. "But I think you are . . . softer, Cousin. Less adamant? Am I right?"

He drew her fingers to his mouth and breathed warm air on them. "It's been a long, difficult year. I must have reevaluated my life and expectations at least six or seven times."

He pressed her palm against his face and Kari closed her eyes as she felt the stubble of his whiskers prick her.

O Lord, how I love this man! What are we to do?

While Søren went upstairs to speak to Max, Kari made the sandwiches and heated some soup. By the time she called to them, the living room was warm enough for them to shed their coats. They ate off TV trays near the wood stove. Max was quiet as they dipped the grilled sandwiches in mugs of hot, creamy tomato soup.

When they finished, Søren said to Max, "Why don't you tell Kari what you told me upstairs, Max?"

Max shot Søren a look of panic. "I don't want to, Papa."

"I know. It's uncomfortable, but you need to be honest, okay?"

Max dithered until Søren cleared his throat.

"All right. I will." Max looked at Kari, tears glistening in his eyes. "You said you loved us, Kari, but I don't know. I don't think you really do."

Kari, tears in her own eyes, took his hand. "I promise that I do love you, Max. But feelings cannot be everything in this life, can they? Is it more important to follow our feelings or do what is right? Is it more important to follow our feelings or follow God?"

Max's chin dropped to his chest. "God."

"Please look at me, Max?"

The boy sighed and glanced at Kari and then away. He slouched in his chair.

"Max. Let me tell you what I know for certain."

He risked another look at Kari.

"I know for certain that I love your papa. I know that. I know that I love you, too. I know I would like to marry your papa and I would like to be your mom."

"You-you would?" He sounded wary but hopeful.

"Yes, but we have some obstacles. Do you know what obstacles are?"

"Um. Things in the way?"

"Yes, exactly. Things in the way. Let's talk about the things that are in the way, shall we?"

Max looked at Søren, who nodded. "Okay," Max whispered.

"All right. For starters, I have a lot of money. The fact is, I'm rich. Pretty *stinking* rich."

Max's brows shot toward the ceiling and he sat up straight. "You are? You mean, you have more than that fancy house in New Orleans?"

Kari shrugged. "Yes. More by a long shot—but it isn't all, say, *cash* money that you keep in your wallet or in the bank. Most of it is in businesses and factories and hotels and buildings and apartments and stocks and bonds. And, well, *stuff.*"

Kari grimaced inside. *Stuff like oil and gas wells. Mines. And diamonds and gold and platinum.*

"Wow." Max looked unsure now. "But why is being rich a problem?"

Kari thought about how to explain it. "I have prayed a lot about all the 'stuff' I own, Max, all the things God has given me. When I prayed, I felt that the Lord told me I was to learn how to take care of the things he entrusted to me. In particular, I was to make sure they are used in right ways—ways that glorify him.

"Unfortunately, all those 'things' can't be left to run themselves or mind themselves. Even when you hire people to run things, you have to make sure that they are doing their jobs right.

"As an example, I own a factory outside Houston, Texas. When I went there last April to check up on it, I found that the factory manager was treating the workers unfairly and making changes I could not approve of. Why? He was doing those things so he could say that the plant was saving money and then pay himself a big cash bonus. I couldn't let him treat my workers like that, so I had to step in and stop him."

"What did you do?"

"Well, I fired him."

Max's eyes widened. So did Søren's.

"So you can see that I have a great many responsibilities, can't you?"

Max nodded slowly.

"On the other hand, your papa has big responsibilities, too. He owns this farm and works very hard to keep it running. He can't up and leave whenever he wants to, can he?"

Max shook his head slowly. "No . . ."

"So these are obstacles, things that are in the way. I can't be here most of the time, and he can't be in New Orleans most of the time. That's our problem. What do you think the answer to our problem is?"

Max's sad expression deepened. "I don't know."

"We don't know either, Max. I'm hoping things will change for us in the future, but I'm not sure how yet. In any event, I do know that I love you."

Kari lightened her tone at the end, hoping to tease a smile from Max. "I even love your dad."

It worked. The boy ducked his head and grinned. "Bet you love me more!"

"Weeeelll . . ."

Søren's chin snapped up. "Hey!"

Kari and Max pounced on Søren at the same time. "Hay is for horses!"

They laughed easily then, and Kari was relieved. A little.

"But . . ." Max screwed up his face, trying to put his thoughts into words. "Well, why can't you live here part of the time?"

"You mean, why couldn't we get married and I travel back and forth between here and New Orleans?" Kari didn't dare look at Søren—since she had espoused that solution more than once.

"Yeah. Like that."

"If we were to do that—and I say *if*—I would need to be in New Orleans most of the time. Really, for the foreseeable future, I could only be here one weekend a month and a couple of weeks out of the year, like a vacation."

Max frowned. "Well, wouldn't that be better than nothing? And we could go there once in a while, like we did that Christmas, right?"

Kari didn't answer. She was biting her lip.

Out of the mouth of babes?

Søren cleared his throat again. "Kari and I have already discussed that option, Max. I don't think it's a good idea. That's not how married people should live."

Max sulked. "Well, seems like you could figure something out. She's got that big pile of money and all."

Kari swallowed a giggle.

Later Kari couldn't resist goading Søren. "Interesting how Max came up with the same ideas I proposed two years ago, don't you think?"

Søren stuffed his hands in his pockets. "If he hadn't been with me the last two days, I would think you had put those ideas in his head."

"Why, Søren Maximillian Thoresen!"

KARI'S WEEK IN RIVERBEND flew by. Since Ilsa was away, it wasn't right for Kari to stay at the farmhouse, so she continued staying at the hotel down the freeway. And while the contractors poured the foundation for her house, Søren pored over the architectural drawings.

"Four bedrooms. Two baths. All on one level. It's nice. And big"

"I was advised not to build small." A distant ringing caused Kari to turn her head.

"What's that?" Søren asked.

"Oh! I have a mobile phone now. It's in my rental car."

Kari ran to answer it. She stayed on the call from Scarlett for twenty minutes.

"Sorry. That was my associate, Scarlett."

"Problem?"

"No, well, she was confirming something. We, uh, I'm moving Michaels Enterprises into our own offices in December."

"Michaels Enterprises? What's that?"

"I had my last name changed. Changed to what it should be: Michaels. And I'm bringing everything I own under that umbrella. Some entities will retain the Granger name, but the fewer the better, in my estimation."

"And you're expanding? Moving into new offices?"

Kari met his questioning eyes. "Yes. I can do a better job of managing my holdings if I have a complete staff and space of my own. I own the building we're moving into. Scarlett, Oskar, and my new human resources manager are overseeing the office renovations and decor. Scarlett, er, wanted to confirm my paint and paper choices for my office bathroom."

Søren looked away, put his hands on his hips, and took a long, deep breath that raised his chest and shoulders. He let it out slowly.

"Okay. I get it." The words were mechanical, resigned.

"If . . . if I get things in order under this new management strategy, I think it will, in the long run, work better for us," Kari whispered.

Søren nodded and turned back to the plans. "How long does Chuck estimate until the house is finished?"

"At least six weeks. He needs to get the roof and exterior walls done before it gets much colder."

"Then he'd better get a move on."

Søren studied the plans further. "Two-car garage?"

"Yeah. Again, I was advised."

"Sure. So, will you be coming back in six weeks to do the final walkthrough?"

Kari's lips parted in surprise. "I-I actually hadn't thought about that." She scanned around the property, mentally checking her calendar, wondering how she would fit another three days into her schedule. "I am so overbooked as it is. The, um, new offices open December 2, which is right about the same time."

She glanced back up at Søren. "You were hoping I could come back when the house was finished?"

Søren's answer cut deep. "I don't hope for much anymore where you are concerned, Kari."

The blood drained from her face. "I see."

He knew he'd hurt her and tried to backpedal. "Since you can't make the trip, would you like me to do the final walkthrough for you?"

Kari was still blinking, trying to shake off the sting of his reproof.

He touched her arm. "I would like to do it for you, Kari. I would like to do something—anything—for you."

"Truly?"

"Yes, I would. Chuck will deliver a well-built home, but I'll ensure that all the finish work is to your specifications. I'd be pleased to do this for you."

"Thank you." Kari nodded slowly, her voice sounding small in her own ears.

"Søren?"

"Yes?"

"What Max said. I heard what you told him, but could you ever see us, is there a way you could live with that, er, arrangement, for at least the first couple of years?"

He sighed. "I'll think about it some more."

Kari's heart pounded. "And you'll pray?"

"More than you know."

"All right. I'll pray, too."

CHAPTER 23

T he moment Kari returned to New Orleans, she was again caught up in office renovations and staffing issues on top of her already challenging schedule. She, Scarlett, and Bettina attended end-of-year management meetings across the city and state and into Mississippi, Alabama, and Texas.

Kari was pleased when Søren began calling her on a weekly basis again. However, after the first two calls, she detected a difference: They were having difficulty connecting over the phone in the same spiritually intimate manner they had when Kari was in RiverBend.

"Is something wrong, Søren?" Kari finally demanded, even though she figured it was her preoccupation with the launch of Michaels Enterprises. She was surprised by his response.

"I don't know as anything is wrong, exactly," he answered. "I've been praying about us—as I promised—but something is holding me back. Each time I pray, I jump ahead in my thoughts to next spring."

"Next spring?"

"It's as though the Lord is telling me to wait and be patient. Not to push or make any plans until then. So I guess we should . . . back off a little."

He couldn't see Kari nodding slowly. *Maybe by next spring my crazy life will have calmed down.*

"All right. Perhaps you're right. Let's keep in touch, but we won't try to force anything until next spring," she answered.

Then Søren surprised her. "Um, do you have plans for Thanksgiving? You are more than welcome to come here—if you can pull yourself away."

Thanksgiving?

Preparations for Michaels Enterprises' move to its new offices in Decatur Towers were taking every moment of her time. She had no plans to take a single day off between now and then.

"Um, actually—"

"Never mind. It's okay. Well, next spring then." He said goodbye and hung up before Kari could respond.

After that, Kari scarcely noticed when their calls became shorter and less frequent. She spent Thanksgiving again with Clover and Lorene, but returned to work the next day.

So did most of her staff—the move was only days away and the devil was in the details.

The furniture arrived and the movers assembled it. Kari's IT personnel installed computer networking cables, set up the computers themselves, and connected a myriad of peripherals—monitors, printers, copiers, scanners, and fax machines. The phone installers were right behind them.

From November 30 through the first weeks of December, Kari spent ten hours a day in their new offices. She fielded questions and interviews from the New Orleans business media, and took time getting to know her new staff.

Kari was right there with her staff when her two-person IT staff trained them on email, interdepartmental messaging, and the various software packages they had installed. In addition, Kari, Scarlett, and Laurel trained on the HR software. Kari left the accounting and payroll software to Scarlett and the comptroller.

Kari felt like she lived at the office, and Scarlett was drowning in her own responsibilities. Kari started to perceive that she needed some kind of internal "chief of staff," someone who could take hold of the reins so that Kari and Scarlett could do their first job, which was providing oversight to Kari's many holdings.

Oskar volunteered. After consulting with Melanie, Kari had an office set up for him. She allowed him in the office three days a week, no more than four hours a day. Even those few hours made a world of difference.

She began to see the wheels of their new organization begin to turn. And, slowly, she watched as cohesion formed between her staff.

***

A WEEK INTO DECEMBER, Kari received a padded envelope in the mail. The return address was unfamiliar but located in Nebraska. Inside, Kari found two sets of keys.

Dear Miss Michaels,
 Please find enclosed the keys to your new home. The garage door openers are in a drawer in the kitchen. It was a pleasure to build this home for you. Let us know if we can be of further service.
Sincerely,
Chuck Haroldson

***

AND THEN IT WAS MONDAY OF CHRISTMAS WEEK. Christmas Eve was Friday and many in her staff would make a four-day weekend of it.

They more than deserve it, Kari thought, but that weekend loomed before her eyes—three long and empty days.

"What are you doing for Christmas, Ruth?" Kari tried to keep her voice casual. Nonchalant. She needn't have worried; Ruth was caught up in and distracted with her own plans.

"The usual two weeks in New York with Amanda and her brood. I fly out tomorrow. Those four grands are precious but, boy! How they wear me out."

"Of course!" Kari made sure she said nothing to distract her friend. "Have a wonderful time."

"I complain about how they tire me, but to tell you the truth, our new ministry is more demanding than anything I've ever done. Two weeks away from all that pressure will be the refreshing I need."

Kari received enthusiastic weekly reports on Albuquerque's Palmer House. She knew how quickly the program was moving ahead and the good fruit it was already bearing. She was glad for Ruth to take a break.

"Let's have you come for a visit the end of January," Kari suggested. "I'll make us a spa weekend so you can recover from the grands."

"Cookie, you have a deal!"

Kari was laughing when they hung up.

And then she realized nothing had changed.

I'll be spending another Christmas alone.

Lord?

***

KARI'S INTERNAL CLOCK woke her early on Christmas morning. She wandered around the house, ending up with coffee at her desk with her Bible—like any ordinary workday. After she read the Christmas story in Luke, she called Søren and Max.

Max answered. "We're just sitting down to breakfast, Kari," he told her. "Can we call you later?"

"Of course."

She got another cup of coffee and read on in Luke. After she'd read several chapters and done a few word searches in her concordance, she prayed. She prayed for each staff member by name and prayed for Ruth and her family. She prayed for her friends in New Orleans—Clover and Lorene, Oskar and Melanie, Owen and Mercy. She prayed for Søren, Ilsa, and Max.

When she finished, she reached for her briefcase. From habit.

She slowly withdrew her hand. "Lord, if I didn't know better, if I didn't know you'd called me to this work, I'd say my life was getting a tad out of balance."

Max called back. He was enthusiastic over the skateboard she'd sent to him. "Dad says we'll take it to the church later today and I can practice in the parking lot!"

Kari mentally smacked herself on the forehead. *Duh! Søren doesn't have anywhere on the farm where Max can ride a skateboard! What was I thinking?*

Søren and Ilsa took turns talking to her next. Kari apologized over the skateboard.

"Yeah, thanks for that," Søren ribbed her. "I'll be spending hours at any random piece of asphalt or concrete he picks." But Kari could feel he was teasing and relaxed.

Later, after deciding *not* to do any work because it was Christmas, she turned on the radio instead and listened to a Christmas service broadcast.

"Especially during the holidays, it is possible to be out of balance while doing exactly what God has called you to do," one commentator stated.

Kari heaved a sigh and muttered, "Got it. Message received, Lord! So now, I'm something of a workaholic? It would sure be nice if you'd tell me how to get off this hamster wheel."

She took a nap Christmas afternoon and watched a movie that evening. On Sunday, she went to church and joined her friends for brunch.

But at the end of the day, she was restless. Antsy.

The following day, Kari drove herself to work, determined to put the loneliness of the holiday behind her. Her new offices were closed, all the staff out until Tuesday.

The lone security guard who let her in said nothing, but his expression betrayed his surprise at seeing her.

"Good morning, miss."

"Guess we're the only ones here, huh?"

What a sad commentary on my life, Kari added silently. Straightening her shoulders, she turned on the lights she needed and went to work.

She drove home that evening through a dense rain. Storm clouds hung from a leaden sky and she thought she heard rumbles in the distance.

Weary from pushing herself as hard as she could, she skipped dinner. Instead, she filled the garden tub with scented oil and took a long, hot soak. Afterwards, drained and heated through, she climbed into the king-size bed and collapsed into an exhausted slumber.

She was startled out of her sleep sometime deep in the night by pounding on her front door and the incessant pealing of the doorbell. She stumbled from her bed and realized that the wind was howling; rain was beating on her bedroom windows. The sound was deafening.

No wonder I didn't hear the front door—but I can't believe I've been sleeping through this storm!

A blast of lightning illuminated her room; the thunder that followed was immediate and right over them. It shook the house, and Kari shrieked.

The pounding downstairs continued, and she could hear muffled shouting from the porch. Kari threw on her robe and slippers and ran down the stairs.

"Miss Kari! Miss Kari! Wake up!"

Kari turned on the porch light and unlocked and threw open the door. Toller, dressed in a slicker and streaming water everywhere, barged inside and slammed the door behind him. "We have to go! Now!"

Without another word, he unfolded and shook a rain slicker, spattering more water across the parquet floors. He tossed the slicker over Kari's head and began pulling it down over her body, ignoring her protests.

"Toller! What are you doing? What is happening?"

"Tornado watch. Radio says funnel clouds have been spotted not far from here. Gotta get t' the storm cellar!" He grabbed Kari by the hand and dragged her through the living room, dining room, and kitchen.

Kari wanted to demand, "What cellar?" but the word "tornado" glued her tongue to the roof of her mouth.

Toller unbolted and yanked open the back door; the screaming wind nearly tore the door from his grip. He pulled Kari after him and, with difficulty, tugged the door closed behind them. He then led her into the pounding rain. They followed the back of the house until Toller stopped at a small wooden enclosure attached to the foundation. The enclosure was surrounded by shrubs, almost obscured by them. Kari had seen wooden slats peeking through the greenery, but had not thought much about them.

Toller unlatched a gate into the enclosure—as another bolt of lightning crackled overhead. In the flash of the strike, Kari spied what the wooden fence screened from view: The slanted door of a storm cellar leading down, under the house's foundation.

Toller unbolted the heavy cellar door and struggled to lift it. The wind fought his efforts. Kari got her fingers under the door's edge and lent her strength to heft it open.

Holding the door half open with his bent back, Toller handed her a flashlight. "Go!"

Kari switched on the light and descended the steep cement steps. Toller followed and let the door clang shut over them. Kari spun the beam of the flashlight about the tiny room. It was only about six feet in both directions and nearly the same in height.

"Give me some light here," Toller demanded. He was fumbling for something near the door.

Kari aimed the light at him. He located the iron bar he was looking for and shoved it through a clasp on the door and into a hole in the cement wall.

The tiny room was empty with the exception of an old bench. Kari sank onto it. Rain flowed from her slicker and puddled onto the bench and floor. The wind still howled above them but it was muffled from within the cellar.

Kari trembled. She was soaked, freezing, and now half-terrified.

"Will we be all right here?"

"We should be."

"Thank you for coming for me, Toller."

Thunder crashed and shook the cellar door. Dust sifted down from above.

"Will the house survive?" she asked him.

Toller shrugged. "Impossible to say." He jerked his chin at the flashlight. "We should turn that off. Conserve the batteries."

Kari switched it off. She and Toller sat back-to-back on the bench, propping each other up.

In the dark, the noises of the storm seemed more distinct. Thunder crashed continuously and then Kari heard a rumbling sound, a deep growl like a mighty engine. It grew and came closer.

"Wh-what is-is th-that?" She was shaking so badly, her teeth chattered.

Toller's response grated in his throat. "That's a tornado."

The roar intensified. At one point, Kari could not have heard Toller if he had spoken to her or if he had shouted. She huddled on the bench and prayed.

Lord, I thank you for sparing us from this storm. I know that all my earthly belongings are but dust. I place them and I place our lives in your hands.

As chilled as she was, Kari somehow dozed. When she roused, she was shaking from the cold, but light shone from the door.

Toller ducked his head into the cellar. "It's over. We should get out and dry off."

Kari's muscles were cramped, stiff, but she stood up and shuffled toward the cellar steps, not knowing what they would find

Well, Lord, if the house is gone, I guess that's one less obstacle standing between Søren and me, one obstacle I can say you have removed.

KARI SQUINTED IN THE MORNING LIGHT. The first thing she realized was that the wooden fence that had screened the cellar door was gone. Vanished. The lawn was littered with debris. Many of the shrubs had been stripped of their foliage; some were broken, others uprooted. Chunks of wood and masonry cluttered the grass.

She took a breath, turned, and looked behind her.

The house still stood.

"Oh, thank you, Lord," she breathed.

Sodden and shivering, Kari made her way up the steps to the back door and into the house.

I need to repeat that hot bath.

***

"THE ROOF TOOK THE WORST OF IT," Toller pronounced late in the afternoon. He sneezed and drew a hanky from his back pocket to wipe his nose. "Sorry. Caught a sniffle. Half the slate tiles are broken or missing. And the wind busted out a window in one o' your guest rooms."

He sneezed again. "Lotta water damage in that room, Miss Kari. Most ev'rthing ruin't."

"I still count us blessed, Toller," Kari replied. "We're alive. Our homes are standing. We have a dry place to lay our heads tonight. Not everyone does."

Kari had visited the tiny cottage at the back of her grounds where Toller lived and had seen with her own eyes that his home was intact. Then she had walked through her neighborhood where she usually jogged to see how her neighbors had fared.

Marlow Avenue was strewn with broken branches and impassable by car, but Kari had picked her way down the sidewalk, turned a corner and, only half a block away, had seen the devastation left behind. The tornado had touched down twice, inexplicably skipping over some dwellings, but leveling three.

Now she sat at her desk, listening to Toller's report, grateful for the little damage her house has suffered, yet heartsick at the view from her office window.

The doorbell rang. Toller looked up. "Would you like me to come back later, Miss Kari?"

"No; this will likely take but a minute."

She squared her shoulders and marched to the door. When she opened it, she blinked in surprise.

"Miss Em?"

The elderly woman leaned upon the arm of her companion, a woman perhaps twenty-five years younger than Miss Em.

Miss Em offered a tight smile. "Aft'noon, Miss Michaels. This here's my daughter, Doris-Mae, and—"

The younger woman interrupted. "Doris-Mae Jackson, Miss Michaels, Em's youngest. I 'pologize for barging in on you like this, but Mama would not take 'no' for an answer. She insisted I drive her over to see you—and today, of all days, when I can see you have plenty on your plate without us comin' to call at such a time as this."

Despite her protests to the contrary, Doris-Mae propelled herself through the doorway, dragging Miss Em with her.

Kari noted the angry flush that climbed up Miss Em's cheeks, but the old woman held her tongue from the sharp retort Kari figured was lurking behind those pinched lips.

You're a better woman than I am, Miss Em.

"Not at all. Er, please come in." Since they were already 'in,' Kari led them into the living room and bade them sit down.

"Take this seat, Miss Em. I believe it will suit you best. Here—let me put this pillow behind your back."

Kari knew Toller was watching and listening from her office, only steps away.

"Thank you kindly, child." The old woman lowered herself into the chair and plunked her purse onto her lap.

Then Miss Em fixed Kari with a look. "I would not be here right now in the middle of your trouble, 'cept, I know not to ignore a word from the Lord."

Doris-Mae made a small sound under her breath.

Em ignored her. "See, I b'lieve when the Lord speaks to us, we need to be quick to do what he says."

"I agree, Miss Em."

Em slanted a look at her daughter, who rolled her eyes. Em shrugged and settled her purse deeper into her lap.

"See here, Miss Michaels. I had me a dream last night. A'course I have lots of dreams, but this one, this one was special. It lingered and I 'membered it clear as day when I woke up. Been tusslin' with Doris-Mae since breakfast t' carry me over here and tell you."

"Oh?" Kari glanced at Doris-Mae.

The woman emitted a longsuffering sigh. "Oh, yes. Mama has been most insistent."

"Well, I thank you, Doris-Mae, for taking time out of your busy schedule to bring her here."

"Couldn't even get the car down your street," Doris-Mae sniffed. "Had to park and walk an entire block."

Kari stilled. "That must have been very hard on your dear mother."

Something in Kari's tone must have hinted at her underlying meaning, for Doris-Mae flushed and sat back, silenced.

"You came to tell me about your dream, Miss Em?"

"Oh. Yes. And to deliver his message. See, in my dream I saw a great storm brewin'. Now, whiles I was dreamin' I knew deep in m' subconscious that it was a-thundrin' and rainin' outside for real, but that real storm didn't wake me up. I was caught up in my dream, you see?"

"Yes, I understand."

"Then the Lord, he say, 'Tell Kari, they's a storm comin'.'"

Doris-Mae must have recovered from Kari's veiled rebuke, for this time her snort was unmistakable. "Mama, any fool can see there's been a storm."

Em stared at her. "If I am a *fool*, Doris-Mae Jackson, then you are the *daughter* of one. *Hrumph*."

Miss Em turned her back on Doris-Mae and lifted her chin. "Well, when I woke up, the storm had already passed by our house. And the Lord, he didn't say, 'they's *been* a storm.' He say, 'Tell Kari they's a storm *comin'*.'

"It's *comin'*, child." She stared at Kari with such intensity that Kari began to heat under her gaze.

"And in the dream, the Lord showed me a big ol' tree, an old live oak, with its limbs a spreadin' out wide and down to the ground. That tree was bending and twisting in the wind o' that storm until, with a thunderous crack, it split."

Kari's hand flew to her mouth.

"Well, child, at first I thought that tree was split in half, top to bottom. Then the wind died away and I saw, no, it was split in *three* pieces. And the Lord, he say to me, 'Tell Kari when that storm comes, it will break her tree—but she is not to give in to despair.' He say that two times: 'Tell Kari she is not to give in to despair. All will be well.'

"Then he say it all again, like so's I don't forget. 'Tell Kari: They's a storm comin' and it will break your tree, but it will not die. Two branches will grow out of one piece of that broken trunk. Your tree will live—and all will be well.'

"My tree will live . . ." Kari shook her head, perplexed.

"See? That's all stuff and nonsense, Mama," Doris-Mae chided. "All that 'your tree will live' baloney."

Em paid her daughter no heed. "Miss Michaels, the Lord's message is plain: They's a bad storm coming for you, but you are not to despair. Heed the word of the Lord: Even though your tree is broken in three pieces, it will not die. It will live."

Doris-Mae stood up. "All right, Mama. You've delivered your message. Now, let's leave Miss Michaels in peace." Her mouth twisted in a sardonic smile. "I 'pologize again, Miss Michaels."

Miss Em remained seated, her chin jutting forward in a stubborn line. "He tol' me there would be a sign. Here. At your house."

"A sign?" A shaken Kari looked up. "You said you had to park far down the street and walk in. From which direction?"

Doris-Mae and Em pointed together toward the section of Marlow Avenue that ran up to and touched Kari's driveway before the street reached her house.

Kari stood. "Will you both come with me?" She didn't wait for an answer. She went through the front door, down the porch, and across the lawn—away from the driveway. Skirting debris, she led them to the other side of the house

Rhododendrons, azaleas, and hydrangeas, shredded and ripped from their beds, littered the grounds. Shrubs and hedges had been stripped of their leaves. Broken slate tiles from the roof lay scattered amid the vegetation.

Toller took Miss Em's arm and helped her navigate across the grass. Head bowed, Kari waited for them.

The venerable old oak Kari had loved so dearly still smoked and steamed from the lightning strike that had burned its way through the trunk. The blast had cleaved the trunk into three pieces. A full third of it had shattered, and the weight of the trunk's heavy branches had torn its roots from the ground.

The shattered pieces lay upon the drenched grass. Severed. Dead.

Kari knew that the rest of the tree would have to come down, but in the storm's aftermath, the remainder of the trunk, while split in two, stood upright. It supported branches that still overspread the lawn.

"Even though your tree is broken in three pieces, it will not die. It will live," Kari repeated. She lifted her chin. "Since you walked in from the other direction, you could not have seen this. Am I right? Is this sign enough?"

Em's lips quivered. "It's the same tree. I saw it in my dream."

Doris-Mae's mouth hung open as Kari rounded on her.

"Your mother is a woman of God. It might do you some good to heed her." Kari glanced back at the dying tree and swallowed.

"I know I will."

Toller fetched his riding lawn mower and, with Doris-Mae and Miss Em perched on the back, maneuvered them through the debris to their car.

While Toller was gone, Kari folded her hands on her desk and rested her forehead upon them. Visions of disaster and tragedy flooded her mind along with anxiety for those she loved.

Søren. Max. Ilsa. Ruth. Clover. Lorene. Oskar. Melanie. Scarlett.

"Lord, I don't understand what is coming. Miss Em says it will be bad, but I trust you to prepare me for it. When it comes, please help me, O God, no matter what it is, to heed your word and not give in to despair. Help me to cling to you."

$\mathcal{C}$HAPTER 24

JANUARY 1, 1994

T he knock on the apartment door startled Linnéa. She crossed the room and spoke through the reinforced wood. "Who is it, please?"
"Telegram, Miss Olander."

She recognized Gustav's thick voice, but she glanced through the peephole before she unlocked and opened the door.

"I hope it is not bad news, miss."

Linnéa smiled at the rotund man who had been kindness itself so many times. "I'm sure it isn't. Thank you for bringing it up to me."

As soon as she closed the door behind him, the smile dropped from her face. The location of her apartment was as tightly controlled as her phone number. No one in Stockholm but the receptionist and her handlers at Marstead had her address—and they would not send a telegram.

That left only her family back in the States to send a wire via the Marstead operations center.

It was New Year's Day. Stockholm time was two in the afternoon. She calculated the time in Seattle before she ripped open the small envelope.

Five in the morning.

As she read the few short lines, horror gripped her.

> *Stephen and Kelly in accident.*
> *Call soonest. We need you.*
> *Bill.*

Bill Greene was Kelly's father—Sammie's father-in-law. Linnéa swallowed and forced herself to remain calm. *Sam and Kelly were in an accident. A car crash? Are they all right? What about the kids?*

The kids.

An image of Sam and Kelly's beautiful children, ages four years and one year, floated before her troubled eyes.

For the last decade, Linnéa had transitioned to Laynie once a year and had spent her precious leave in Seattle. She always went in midsummer when she and Sam could get out on Puget Sound with his little sailboat. Even after Sam and Kelly married, he and Laynie managed to spend a few days together on the water during Laynie's vacation.

Kelly wasn't keen on sailing, but she understood the strong bond between her husband and his sister. Kelly had always encouraged their jaunts.

And Laynie loved Kelly for that selfless gesture.

Once Shannon was born, though, things had shifted—to Laynie's surprise and Sam's consternation: Laynie found that she wanted to spend every moment of her stateside vacation with her niece. And three years later when Robbie was born?

"I can't pry you loose from these kids," Sam had complained. "It's bad enough that Kelly won't sail with me, but now you? You're drying out! Landlubber!"

"Not even. It's only until Kelly thinks Shannon is old enough to go out with us."

Laynie had been insistent on that point, but Sam had shaken his head. "Riiiight."

So Laynie had made sure to go out with Sam, even though her heart was with the kids.

Laynie hadn't been home since July, and she swallowed, thinking of Shannon's sweet face and Robbie's gummy grin.

"No, he has some teeth now," she whispered, "little, tiny teeth." Kelly had sent pictures.

"They have to be all right," she said, louder. "They have to be."

Not much fazed Laynie. Her parents and her brother and his family represented, perhaps, the only tender place Laynie had left in her heart—so tender that her heart clenched in fear for them.

Laynie threw the sofa cushions to the floor, opened the safe, and yanked out her Marstead-issued mobile phone. She flipped it open, found William and Kathy Greene's number in the phone's address book and, with a trembling hand, dialed through. Bill picked up immediately.

"Hello?"

"Bill, this is Laynie. I received your wire. What is going on?"

Laynie knew the news was bad when Bill sobbed. Laynie's brain turned to icy efficiency, her trained response to danger. In a calm voice she asked again, "What is it, Bill?"

In the background, Laynie thought she heard crying. Toddler crying.

Laynie gripped the phone harder, but she maintained her poise. "Bill?"

Sam's father-in-law gulped. "They-they were coming home from Stephen's company's New Year's party. They were hit by a drunk driver. Kelly . . . Kelly is gone." He sobbed again.

Laynie tightened the rein on her emotions. "I'm very sorry, Bill."

The platitude was automatic. Laynie felt nothing. She would not allow herself to feel. Could not allow herself. "Sam?"

"He-he . . . Stephen's hanging on, Laynie. He's in the hospital."

"How bad is it?"

Bill paused and Laynie felt anger boiling up in her chest. "Don't sugarcoat it. How bad?"

"He has internal injuries, Laynie. He's in critical condition."

Laynie yanked the phone away from her ear and stared into space. Memories of the two of them flooded her: growing up together, the adored children of loving parents, and the unbreakable bond they shared.

She clenched her teeth, all business. She would not allow an iota of feeling to seep outside. "Shannon and Robbie?"

"They weren't with Stephen and Kelly. They were . . . they are here with us."

Some relief washed over Laynie. *The children are all right,* a voice whispered. *The children are all right.*

"Mama and Dad?"

"They are like us. Devastated. But your mother? Gene's worried about her, Laynie. She is so fragile."

"Which hospital is Sam at?"

"Harborview. He's in their ICU. Your parents are with him." He paused and then said all in a rush, "You are coming, aren't you, Laynie? You have to—we need you!"

"Yes. I'll leave as soon as I can."

She closed the phone and tossed it into the safe. Then she picked up her apartment phone and dialed the number for Marstead. Even on New Year's Day, a "receptionist" answered immediately.

"Marstead International. How may I direct your call?"

"This is Linnéa Olander. Mr. Alvarsson, please."

The receptionist paused. "Mr. Alvarsson is not in the office at present."

"I know it is a holiday. Access Alpha seven three three five."

"Stand by, please."

Laynie tapped her foot nervously while waiting for the receptionist to connect her call. When the director came on the line, his tone was brisk. Businesslike.

"Problem, Olander?"

"Yes, but personal. I need to take emergency leave. My brother and sister-in-law have been in an accident. My sister-in-law is dead; my brother is in critical condition. I need to leave for Seattle soonest."

"The timing is bad, Linnéa. You are getting close to Petroff—and that means getting close to the Russians' new laser schematics."

Laynie didn't flinch at her director's unfeeling response. She felt nothing herself at the moment. "The timing can't be helped. I need two, perhaps three weeks."

Alvarsson sighed. "What will you tell Petroff?"

"I will call him and tell him a version of the truth: a family emergency. He will understand—but you'll need to backstop my story. A relative's illness, perhaps."

"Very well, we'll do our part at this end, but don't stay gone long—that man will be the most valuable asset we've had to date, if you can land him. Don't stay one moment longer than needed."

No 'so sorry for your loss.' No 'can we help or comfort you in any way.' Only 'don't stay one moment longer than needed.'

Laynie hung up and called the Marstead emergency number again. "Please book me the earliest flight into Seattle you can get. Arrange appropriate backstop. Approval per Alvarsson."

"Very good, Miss Olander. I will call back with your itinerary and cover."

Linnéa threw the receiver back on the phone and began to pack. While she packed, she began the mental preparations for shedding Linnéa Olander and slipping back into her identity as Helena Portland.

No. I'm Laynie.

CHAPTER 25

The night passed with frustrating slowness. Linnéa packed and repacked until she was satisfied, but she could not sleep.

Sammie. My Sammie! I'm so sorry you lost your beautiful wife, the mother of your children. Your one love.

But please be all right!

Early the following morning, the phone rang in Linnéa's apartment. Gustav's aggrieved voice greeted her.

"Miss Olander? So sorry, but a courier is here. He will not allow me to sign for the delivery and, since he is unknown to me, I will not allow him to bring it up to you. I beg your pardon, but we are at an impasse."

"I will be down directly, Gustav."

The elevator descended to the lobby, and Linnéa stepped out. The courier obviously knew her on sight.

"Sign here, please, Miss Olander."

"Thank you. And thank you for your concern and caution, Gustav." Laynie took the thin package to her apartment. She locked her door before she slit open the envelope and dumped its contents upon her countertop.

Inside was a ticket from Stockholm to London in the name of Linnéa Olander and a terse note telling her where and how to await her contact when she arrived.

Laynie looked at the clock. She had three hours to make her flight.

***

IN LONDON'S HEATHROW AIRPORT, Laynie departed her plane and scanned for the nearest women's lavatory. She entered, went to the sink, and had removed a lipstick tube from her purse when another woman strolled into the busy restroom.

Laynie moved over a little. The woman sidled up next to her to wash her hands, and spoke out of the side of her mouth. "Leave the rest in a stall behind the toilet," she said quietly.

Laynie had slung her purse over her shoulder as directed. It hung between the two women. While Laynie finished applying her lipstick, the woman dropped an envelope into Laynie's purse.

Laynie turned away from the sinks, went into one of the stalls, and latched the door. Inside the envelope in her purse, she found her American passport, Marstead business cards, Washington State driver's license, and credit cards—all under the name of Helena Portland.

She studied the ticket bearing the same name: London to Quebec, then a change of carrier to New York, then on to Chicago and Seattle. The legs from New York to Chicago and then Chicago to Seattle would be tight. A note said that her bags had been claimed, retagged, and sent on their way to Seattle.

Laynie removed all items bearing the name Linnéa Olander from her wallet and replaced them with the Helena Portland license and credit cards. She removed her business cards and replaced them with the identical cards reading "Helena Portland."

All items with the name "Linnéa Olander" she placed in the envelope that the woman had passed to her. She placed the envelope on the floor, behind the toilet.

When she left the stall, the same woman, without any sign of recognition, entered it.

Laynie washed her hands and hurried to find her gate. Within an hour, she had boarded her flight to Canada.

***

RUTH GRAFF DRAGGED HER SUITCASE to an American Airlines ticketing counter at LaGuardia and hefted it onto the scale. "Whew. At least it's not as heavy as it was when I flew in."

The woman at the counter gave her an understanding smile. "Packed all your Christmas presents in this one suitcase, did you?"

Ruth grinned. "Oh, it was worse than that. When I left home, I had *two* suitcases that I lugged to the airport. And the worst part of this trip was not the flight from Albuquerque—it was the drive from here to my daughter's house. Three hours! And she drives this little, tiny economy car. Why, there's scarcely enough room in that trunk for both cases when it is empty. But is it ever empty? No, it's always full of skates and hockey equipment and snow gear!"

She laughed and leaned toward the clerk. "Can you believe it? This suitcase rode in the backseat on the grandkids' laps all the way to their house. Once I got to my daughter's house and unloaded the kids' Christmas loot, I hardly had anything left to pack!

"I consolidated all my clothes into the smaller case, which left the bigger one empty. I put the smaller case inside of the larger case. *Voila!* One suitcase—this one."

Ruth grimaced and waggled her brows. "Weird, right?"

"Not at all. Ingenious. And totally not the weirdest thing I've seen a passenger do."

238

They grinned at each other. The woman pulled Ruth's case from the scale and swung it onto a conveyor belt. She handed Ruth her claim check.

"Have a good flight."

"Thanks. I will."

Ruth, feeling liberated with only a purse to manage, wandered toward her gate. "Now to find a bite to eat and a good book for the trip."

She bought a paperback, paid for a slice of pizza and a soda, and found a seat near her gate. The book, however, didn't immediately hold her attention. Instead, she kept remembering the wonderful time she'd had with her daughter and her family over the holidays.

Lord, this was a good trip. Thank you that even though Hank and Amanda don't live near me, I have the means to visit them. You are so good to me.

She wiped crumbs from her fingers and finished her soda, glancing around at the other passengers starting to assemble for their flight from New York into Chicago. Ruth loved watching people.

A tall, slender woman with dark blonde hair walked at a harried clip to Ruth's gate counter where she engaged the agent in animated conversation. Their exchange ended with the agent handing the woman a boarding pass. The woman turned away, relief momentarily washing her face. Then, her face relaxed into placid lines.

Ten minutes later, the agents began boarding the flight. It would be a short hop into Chicago's O'Hare Airport. From there Ruth would catch her connecting flight to Denver and then on to Albuquerque.

Ruth found her aisle seat and settled into it. *Better not get too comfy,* she told herself. *Someone will be along shortly to claim the window seat, and you'll need to get up to let them in.*

The plane ran rows of two seats down one side and three down the other—Ruth was glad to have only one seat to her right.

"Excuse me. I believe I have the window seat."

"Of course. Let me get into the aisle."

Ruth stood up and came face-to-face with the woman she'd noticed in the boarding area. She smiled, and the woman, perhaps in her late thirties, smiled a strained, practiced smile in return.

When they were both seated, Ruth said, "Hello. I'm Ruth."

But the woman was not in a sociable mood. She mumbled, "Nice to meet you," pulled the in-flight shopping magazine from the pocket in front of her, and snapped it open, effectively blocking Ruth's friendly overtures.

Ruth shrugged and opened her new book, hoping Chapter 2 would be better than Chapter 1.

In the seat beside her, the woman turned pages with aimless intent. When she sucked in her breath, Ruth slanted her eyes onto the magazine.

The page was covered in children's toys—cute and cuddly stuffed animals, mostly.

Nothing special.

Ruth turned her attention back to her book, only to pause, alert, when the unmistakable whiffle of a suppressed sob reached her ears. She kept her eyes on the pages in her lap, but she began to pray.

Lord, whatever is going on, I pray that you draw this young woman to you. If you can use me to comfort her, here I am. I will do what you ask of me.

Ten minutes later, Ruth realized their flight was a little late getting off the ground. That her neighbor was fretting about something was patently obvious.

At last, the airplane taxied to its assigned runway and rocketed down the tarmac until the pilot raised the nose and they were airborne. Ruth buried her nose in her book and, as the action in Chapter 3 picked up, she momentarily forgot about her fellow passenger.

The flight had barely cleared New York airspace when Ruth's neighbor sniffled and dabbed her eyes with a tissue.

As the woman wiped her nose, she saw Ruth watching her. "I'm sorry for disturbing you. It's nothing." She again pretended to be engrossed in the shopping magazine.

Ruth put her head on one side. "Forgive me for disagreeing, but I think you are struggling with something painful. Would it help to talk about it?"

The woman hesitated as though struggling to decide whether to talk to Ruth or not. Finally, she whispered, "My sister-in-law just died." Another soft sob escaped from her.

Ruth, quite naturally, placed her hand on Laynie's. That simple, comforting gesture undid the woman. Her eyes began to water and she looked away.

"We are never ready to lose someone we love," Ruth murmured.

Her seatmate gasped, and then her tears flowed freely. A sob racked her.

Ruth gripped her hand until the spasm of grief had passed.

"My dear, I'm so very sorry for your loss. So very sorry. My name is Ruth."

"Helena," the woman managed, "but everyone calls me Laynie."

She turned in her seat and Ruth got a good look at her face.

She has pretty eyes. Such a soft, unusual shade of blue.

"Laynie. What a delightful name. Well, Laynie, if it would help, why don't you tell me what has happened?"

And Laynie did. In short, choked sentences she told Ruth about the New Year's Eve party, about the drunk driver who killed her brother's wife Kelly, about her brother's serious injuries.

"My dear! You must be worried sick for your brother."

"Yes, I am. I-I need to get to Seattle as soon as possible. Sammie needs me."

"Of course he does."

They talked for a while until Laynie's emotions settled a little.

"Thank you," she said. "You've been so kind to me."

"The Bible encourages us to comfort one another with the same comfort God has given us. I'm glad we were assigned seats next to each other."

The ding of the airline's intercom interrupted them.

"Ladies and gentlemen, we are making our descent into Chicago. Please fasten your seatbelts, make sure your seats and tray tables are in their full upright and locked positions. Please refrain from leaving your seats until the aircraft is on the ground and we have come to a complete stop at our gate."

"Well, thank you again."

"My pleasure," Ruth answered.

As they waited to deplane, Laynie murmured, "Our flight is late getting in and my connection was already going to be tight. I'll have to run to make it."

"Let me help you." Ruth jumped into the aisle and backed up a step, blocking the passengers behind them.

"Go on ahead, Laynie. And my prayers go with you."

With the barest of nods to Ruth, Laynie strode down the aisle, onto the gangway, and was off like a shot. She was long gone when Ruth stepped into their arrival gate.

I'm glad my gate is in the same terminal, not far from here.

Chicago's O'Hare was its usual madhouse. Ruth visited the restroom, bought a small snack, found an empty seat in her gate area, and opened her book.

Another hour's wait, she sighed to herself. But, for some reason, she could not stop thinking of her seatmate on the flight from New York.

Lord, I hope she made her connection, Ruth prayed.

Something else niggled at her, but would not quite come clear.

Lord?

Ruth boarded the flight to Denver. This time she had a window seat. No one came to claim the aisle seat.

***

ONCE INSIDE THE TERMINAL, Laynie paused at the first flight information display and frantically searched for her flight to Seattle. When she spotted it, she groaned inwardly.

It was already boarding—in Terminal 3.

Laynie's flight had arrived in Terminal 2.

"No, no, no!" Laynie flew down the concourse to the first ATS station she saw—the fastest way to get from one terminal to another. The doors were mobbed with people waiting to catch the next train.

Laynie, murmuring "Excuse me, excuse me," elbowed and shoved her way through the crush of passengers and onto a car. She squeezed in behind the doorway so she would be one of the first passengers off the train.

The doors closed and the train lurched forward. Laynie braced herself. While the train sped and swayed along its rails, her mind was on the strange encounter from her last flight.

Forgive me for disagreeing, but I think you are struggling with something painful. Would it help to talk about it?

Laynie had been stunned when the words, "My sister-in-law just died," rolled out of her mouth with no willful forethought.

Ruth.

Laynie frowned and stared at the train tunnel walls as they flashed by. Her seatmate's kindness had dissolved some internal restraint Laynie usually possessed. When she had blurted out those revealing words, Ruth had placed her hand on Laynie's, and that simple, comforting gesture had undone any self-control Laynie had left.

We are never ready to lose someone we love, Ruth had murmured.

As Laynie had wept, she had wondered, too.

Why, I haven't cried in years, she had acknowledged. *Not in years! What will I do if Sammie dies?*

Then she had glanced into the older woman's face and glimpsed something . . . Kindness. Caring. Comfort.

And they had talked more. They had conversed easily. Freely.

How long has it been since I had a normal, unguarded conversation?

The train arrived at the right station. Laynie shoved her way onto the platform and sprinted toward her gate.

But time was not on her side.

Just before their flight was ready to push away from the gate, Ruth heard a small commotion from the doorway, the steward welcoming a late arriving passenger onto the flight. The late passenger hurried down the aisle and slid into the seat next to Ruth.

Ruth's mouth dropped open. "Laynie?"

Laynie gaped back. "Ruth! Wow. What are the odds?"

"Yes, er, *wow*! But what happened?"

Laynie's brows knit into a crease. "We came in from New York ten minutes late—and of all the bad luck, I had to change terminals. My direct flight to Seattle was already on the runway when I got to the gate."

She sighed. "They rebooked my tickets and sent me here—and I still barely made it. So, instead of nonstop to Seattle, I'll fly into Denver and catch the next flight to SeaTac. I may arrive three hours late, but that's better than the nine it could have been."

"When did your day start?"

Laynie snorted. "My *day*? I've been traveling for fifteen hours already. I'm not sure what *day* it is. And I couldn't sleep the night before I left."

"Goodness! Where did you fly in from?"

"I live and work in Stockholm. I started there."

"Stockholm? Sweden?" Ruth smacked her forehead. "*Duh!* Well, of *course*, Sweden. But what a long way to come when time is so precious."

Laynie's face fell in on itself. "I forgot . . . the horror of it all for a moment. It's like I'm hearing it again for the first time."

Ruth nodded. "Why don't you try to get some sleep, dear? We have close to two hours' flight time before us." She held out a tiny airline pillow to Laynie.

"Thank you, Ruth. I'll try."

Laynie put her seat back, rolled her head to one side, and tucked the pillow between the seat and her cheek. She slept deeply and only woke when a stewardess gently shook her.

"Miss? I'm sorry to disturb you, but we're beginning our descent into Denver now. Please return your seat to its full upright position and fasten your seatbelt."

Laynie blinked sleep from her eyes and did as requested. When she looked at Ruth, the older woman was smiling.

"I think you needed that, Laynie."

"Must have."

They were companionably quiet as the flight dropped into Denver. Then they were on the ground, taxiing to their gate.

"Ruth, thank you again for your kindnesses to me."

"Don't mention it, Cookie."

Laynie shrugged. "I'm still kind of amazed that we had seats together twice. What a coincidence."

"I don't believe in coincidences," Ruth said softly. "When the airline assigned you the seat next to mine—not once, but twice—I figured God had put us together. I promise that I will be praying for you."

Laynie stared at Ruth, something flickering behind her soft blue eyes. "I think God gave up on me a long time ago, Ruth, but thank you for caring. It meant a lot to unburden my heart."

Ruth looked back at Laynie, a quizzical expression on her face, and Laynie felt suddenly exposed. Her guard clicked into place. "What is it?"

"I don't know. You kind of remind me of someone but I can't think who."

The rest of the passengers had deplaned, leaving Ruth and Laynie as they finished their conversation. Laynie picked up her handbag and started to rise.

A tiny itch persisted in Ruth's mind.

"Laynie—may I trouble you for your card?"

The woman's milky blue eyes pooled into blankness. "My card?"

"Your business card. So that I remember to pray for you by name." Ruth conceded to herself how lame her explanation must sound, but the prompting of the Holy Spirit was not to be ignored.

Laynie opened her handbag and fished a silver card carrier from it. She withdrew a card and handed it to Ruth. "Thank you again."

The woman rose from her seat and walked with stately grace down the aisle toward the exit.

Ruth studied the card. The white cardstock was simple, the embossed letters elegant.

Helena Portland
Marstead International

A telephone number with an international prefix followed.
Helena Portland.
No, not *Hel*ena, He*len*a.
She put the accent on the second syllable, like "Laina," but she called herself "Laynie."

Something nagged at Ruth, something tiny and "prickery," as her grandkids called it.

Prickery like a little sticker that wouldn't stop bothering her.

This must be important, Lord. Your Holy Spirit wouldn't be so insistent if it weren't. I just don't know why *it's so all-fired important.*

"Ah, well. I'm sure you will tell me soon enough."

Ruth lifted her shoulders in resignation, but opened her purse, unzipped an inner compartment, and slid the card inside.

She was on her flight from Denver to Albuquerque, dozing in her seat, when the threads came together.

One moment she was dreaming of Kari's last visit to Albuquerque. The next moment, she was wide awake.

This Laynie woman reminds me of Kari. Not the eyes, exactly, but something else.

Laynie.

Laynie Portland.

Portland?

Why is "Portland" significant?

Gooseflesh rippled down Ruth's arms.

"Portland? O Father! No, it couldn't be! It couldn—

"Wait. Could it?"

CHAPTER 26

"Anthony, it's Ruth Graff. I need to see you right away." Ruth kicked off her shoes and rubbed one tired foot while holding the phone. "It's about Kari's sister. I think I met her. On the plane coming back from New York."

She listened. "No, I'm not kidding. Please come right away."

Anthony listened to Ruth's recitation with a jaundiced eye. And then Ruth handed him the woman's business card. "Look at her name, Anthony."

"Helena Portland. So?"

"No, not *Hel*ena Portland. He*lena* Portland. A long 'a' like 'Lena'—as in Lena Horne."

"Yeah?"

"And she calls herself *Laynie* Portland."

Anthony muttered some Spanish word under his breath. "Ruth, Ruth, Ruth. I'm hearing you, but I'm not following you."

"Kari's sister's name is *Elaine*. Sounds a lot like He*lena* and *Laynie*, yes? Laynie's last name is Portland. So what was the *one word* written in Marge Showman's ledger under the date Kari's parents died?"

Anthony frowned and muttered, "Portland. It was Portland."

"See, now, those two coincidences wouldn't impress me, Anthony, but the Holy Spirit kept at me. That woman had a look about her that reminded me of someone, and I couldn't figure it out. Then I took a little nap on the airplane and had a dream—and you want to guess who figured in that dream? Kari! When I woke up, *bingo*! It all came together."

Anthony was still frowning. "Let me see that card again."

An hour later, they were on a conference call with a skeptical Owen Washington.

"Let me recap, then. This woman's name is He*lena* Portland. She calls herself Laynie. She bears a small resemblance to Kari. That's it?"

Ruth bristled. "No, that's not *it*! The Holy Spirit is *it*."

Owen sighed. "This Helena Portland works in Europe but her brother lives in Seattle?"

"Well, he must. Laynie said he and his wife were in a bad accident—and her sister-in-law died. She wouldn't be flying from Europe to Seattle if her brother *wasn't* in Seattle, now would she?"

"All right, all right. Let me think."

Ruth looked at Anthony. When she raised her eyebrows in a question, he shrugged and mouthed, "I dunno."

They waited.

Finally, Owen spoke again. "I can think of two things we can do to test this out. First, I'll call my friend at the FBI office here in NOLA. Ask him to run a background check on Helena Portland and this Marstead International.

"The second one I'll give to you, Anthony: Call your contacts and the major newspapers in the Seattle area. Ask around about a car accident involving a couple named Portland."

"Kelly. Her sister-in-law's name was Kelly."

"Okay. A fatality is always newsworthy. You could contact the ME's office, too. Did this woman mention her brother's name?"

Ruth thought a moment. "I think she called him Sam. Sammie."

Anthony stared at Ruth. "Are you serious?"

"Why wouldn't I be?"

"Owen, you caught it, didn't you?"

"Yeah, man, I did. Kari's brother's name was Samuel."

***

BETTINA PUT HER HEAD into Kari's office. "You have some visitors, Miss Michaels."

Kari did not look up. "Who?"

"Um, your friend, Ruth Graff."

"Ruth?" Kari did look up then. Bettina stepped away and Ruth walked in—followed by Anthony and Owen.

The repressed excitement in their expressions made Kari's mouth go dry. "What is it?"

"Where can we go to talk?"

Kari gestured to the small round table in the corner. "Right here."

Owen closed the door. Ruth gave Kari a long hug before they sat down together.

In as few words as she could manage, Ruth told Kari about her flight home from New York. Kari's mouth grew drier still as Ruth described the woman she called Laynie Portland. "Tall, dark blonde. Beautiful, milky blue eyes. A strong chin and manner. Her name is Helena, but she called herself 'Laynie.'"

Ruth did not mention the accident that drew Laynie to Seattle.

"Portland? Her last name is Portland?" Kari grew lightheaded. "Are you suggesting that Portland wasn't a city? It was a name?"

"That's what I thought, so I called Anthony as soon as my flight landed and I got home. We called Owen together."

Anthony spoke next. "For the past six days we have been following the leads Ruth gave us—the only new leads we've had in two years. We called the number on her business card first, and asked for Helena Portland."

"The number was, as she told Ruth, a number in Sweden. The receptionist who answered would only say 'Miss Portland is out on emergency leave and is unable to return our call.'"

"That makes sense," Kari muttered. "She's here in America. But what emergency, I wonder."

Owen took over. "Um, see, then it gets a little crazy. Since I have friends who are agents assigned to the NOLA FBI office, I called in a favor and asked one of them to run background checks on this woman, Helena Portland, and her company, Marstead International. I asked this agent friend to find out what kind of company Marstead is, what they do."

"And?"

"And my friend, rather than calling me back, took the time to cross town and pay me a visit. Highly unusual. So was what he told me.

"He looked me in the eye and said, and I quote, 'Owen, we've been friends a long time and I respect you. So I'm going to say this one time and one time only: Don't ask about this woman or her company again. Leave it alone. *I'm serious.*'"

Kari's jaw went slack. "What? What does that mean?"

Anthony and Owen exchanged troubled looks. "It means that the federal government doesn't appreciate anyone digging into Helena Portland or Marstead International, Kari."

Kari was flummoxed. "I still don't know what that means."

Anthony said softly, "I would take it to mean that Helena Portland is either WITSEC or something else."

"WITSEC?"

"Witness Security Program, also known as Witness Protection."

Kari moved her head side to side. "But if she's working openly in Europe . . ."

"Right, so probably the 'something else.'"

Kari stared at Anthony.

"We did our own—discreet—digging into Marstead International. Public records, newspapers and the like. So, Marstead is a big, high-tech aeronautics and technology acquisition firm with a large office in Stockholm."

"That agrees with what Helena—Laynie?—told Ruth."

"Stockholm is not far from St. Petersburg," Owen added, "and Marstead has a large office there."

"In Russia?"

He nodded. "St. Petersburg is a hive of Russian R&D. Lots of stuff going on in the new Russian economy—and Marstead is all about emerging technology."

"But, what does that mean? What 'something else'?"

"We think CIA or some shirttail cousin."

"You've got to be kidding. That's . . . that's so farfetched, so implausible."

Owen cleared his throat. "Not if I read my FBI friend right. Helena Portland may be this woman's real name, but I'd bet a plate of beignets that she lives under another name in Europe."

"But then, if she's . . . how would we . . . " Kari's voice trailed off.

"How would we find her? We still had her American name, Helena Portland, and Portland was the notation in Marge Showman's ledger. And Laynie was headed for Seattle. So, we went looking, and here is what we've uncovered in the last six days."

Kari leaned toward Owen, her heart racing.

"In 1958, a couple by the name of Gene and Polly Portland adopted an infant boy and a three-year-old girl. After that, I had a friend in Olympia dig for the birth certificates of their adopted children. We found two—for Helena and Stephen Portland."

"Elaine? Samuel?"

Anthony nodded. "Yes. So now, the single word 'Portland' in Marge Showman's ledger makes sense. We are certain that the children they adopted were Samuel and Elaine."

Kari was breathless. Giddy. "Were they . . . were the Portlands good people? Did they give Sammie and Elaine a good home? A real family?"

"From what we've uncovered so far, yes. Gene and Polly Portland were a childless couple in their late thirties who paid well for what they believed was a legal, private adoption."

Anthony added, "The Portlands likely had no idea that the adoption was illegal, Kari. Marge Showman provided the broker with good documentation purportedly of a 'closed adoption.'"

Owen looked at Anthony, who nodded. Owen sighed. "There's more, Kari. The reason Helena Portland was flying to Seattle."

Kari flinched when Owen hesitated. "It's bad news, isn't it?"

"I'm sorry, Kari, but it is. We were able to locate the Portlands and conduct research into the adoptions only because we first found their names listed in a Seattle obituary."

Kari blinked and frowned. "Obituary? Who? Who died, Owen?"

Owen's voice dropped. "Kari, Stephen Portland and his wife Kelly were in a car crash on New Year's Eve—ten days ago. Kelly passed away from her injuries on scene. It was her obituary we found. Her husband, Stephen, was critically injured, but lingered."

Owen looked away. "I'm sorry to tell you this, Kari, but Stephen Portland passed away two days ago."

Kari's face crumpled. Her mouth worked silently until she was able to speak. "Are you sure?"

"Yes."

Kari kept blinking as she processed Owen's words. "Stephen Portland is Sammie. He died two days ago. I missed him by two days?"

Anthony and Owen exchanged glances. Anthony touched Kari's arm. "In the middle of this tragedy, there is still something good, Kari."

It took a moment for her eyes to lift to his. "What do you mean?"

He shrugged. "We might not have found them if not for the accident. Not ever."

Kari's glazed eyes sharpened—as did her tone. "What good does finding them do if they are already dead?"

Owen spoke up. "But all is not lost, Kari, don't you see? *Laynie.* Laynie is not dead! She told Ruth she was returning home due to a family emergency."

Laynie.

Elaine.

"She was returning to Seattle because her sister-in-law had passed away. She said that her brother *Sammie* was still clinging to life at that time—that he needed her."

"She called him *Sammie?*"

Ruth nodded. "I heard her."

Kari's thoughts were racing. "When did . . . when did you say Sammie died?"

"Two days ago."

"Have they—"

"His funeral is tomorrow, Kari. In Seattle."

"Tomorrow? Then-then if I can get there in time—"

"Bettina has already booked your flight."

Anthony cleared his throat. "We don't feel that you should go alone, Kari. It's why we are here. Ruth and Owen and I will accompany you."

Kari nodded.

"We have taken care of all the details. Go home now and pack. Our flight leaves at 3:15. Ruth and I will meet you and Owen there."

Kari stood. "Thank you. I—" Her voice cracked. "I don't know how to thank you."

"Let me drive you home, Kari," Owen suggested. "I will wait until you've packed and then we'll go to the airport together. Scarlett or Bettina will make sure your Caddy gets home."

"Yes. All right."

All Kari could focus on was that Owen and Anthony had found her sister. She would be at Sammie's funeral.

Sammie's funeral?

Kari could not breathe.

Sammie! I wanted to find you. I tried! I did!

Owen took Kari's car keys from her purse and handed them to Bettina. He guided her from her office to the elevator and down to the parking garage. Then he placed Kari in the front seat of his car and pulled away from the offices of Michaels Enterprises.

They were silent as they rode to Kari's house until Owen cleared his throat. "We uncovered one more piece of information about your brother, Kari."

Kari turned her head toward him. "Yes?"

"Stephen and Kelly Portland left behind two children."

"Oh!" Kari's chin began to tremble. "How old? How old are they?"

"Shannon is four. Robbie is one."

Kari clapped a hand to her chin to make it stop quivering. "Those poor babies! O Jesus, please help them!"

CHAPTER 27

A slow drizzle met them at the funeral home, but the parking lot was packed. Anthony slid their rental car into a slot at the far end of the lot.

"So many people are here already," Kari murmured.

"There is a viewing prior to the service," Owen reminded her.

"Oh. Of course."

"Ready?" Ruth asked Kari.

"As I'll ever be, I suppose."

Ruth and Kari got out and walked together toward the double doors of the building. Owen and Anthony followed behind. When they reached the entrance, Owen opened the door and Kari and Ruth stepped inside.

The lobby was clogged with mourners milling about, some greeting each other, some whispering. The crush of the crowd overwhelmed Kari. As she signed the guest book, she felt her heart would jump out of her chest.

A funeral director greeted them in soft, sober tones and handed them folded service programs.

Owen motioned him aside and asked, "Could you point out the parents of the deceased, please?"

"Yes. They are seated at the front to greet friends during the viewing. The Greenes are on the left; the Portlands are on the right."

"Thank you."

Owen gently tugged Kari's arm. "The Portlands are in the front row, right. Kelly's parents are on the left," he whispered.

Kari nodded.

"Anthony and I will keep our eyes open for Laynie," he breathed into Kari's ear. "If the opportunity presents itself, we'll ask for a private word with her after the service."

Again, Kari nodded. She was numb. Shaky.

With Ruth at her side, Kari walked up the center aisle. Her legs felt like rubber, as if they had no bones. Ruth took hold of her arm.

In the left front row, a couple who looked to be in their sixties and a younger, very pregnant woman huddled together. A man stood with his hand resting on the pregnant woman's shoulder.

Kelly's parents, Kari thought. *And her sister and husband?*

Kari's footsteps slowed as she approached the two caskets. Kelly's casket was closed, and Kari pushed away thoughts of the accident that had killed her outright—and the damage the accident had to have caused.

The other casket was open. With Ruth supporting her, she made her way to it.

Kari stared down at the body of the stranger lying there. At first, she saw only light brown hair, a strong chin, and closed eyes. As she struggled to see some resemblance to the baby brother she'd known but briefly, Ruth murmured, "Look at his hair, Kari."

"What?"

"It is the same as yours. Light brown. Shimmers of gold. And Kari, look! Look at this."

Ruth gestured to the large color photograph centered on the table between the two caskets. Kari glanced at it and stopped, stunned.

A happy couple, arms interlocked, smiled out of the frame. But Kari could only stare at the man—and his very familiar, very blue eyes.

"Kari, he has your eyes," Ruth whispered.

Like Søren's. Like mine.

Every doubt drained away. Kari had found her brother.

"Sammie," she gasped. "Sammie!" Kari pressed a tissue to her face to hold back the tears. Through the sheen over her eyes, she tried to memorize Sammie's face.

"Okay, come on, Cookie." Ruth took Kari's arm and steered her away—only to come face to face with the man the funeral director had identified as Sammie's father.

He took in Kari's emotional state and wiped his own eyes before asking, "Did you know Stephen well?"

Ruth slid her eyes toward Kari, wondering how she would respond.

Kari sniffed and fumbled for the right answer. "I hadn't, um, seen him in a long time," she managed, "but-but he was . . . very dear to me."

"Please come meet my wife," the man said, "Stephen's mother." He took Kari's arm and led her to the first row of chairs.

Kari blinked when she took in the frail African-American woman slumped in a wheelchair. "Hello," she whispered.

"Thank you for coming, child." The words were spoken by rote and broken by weeping. "I apologize. I can't seem to stop crying."

Polly Portland lifted her grief-stricken face to Kari. "Seems like I'm done and then it just starts all over and—Oh! Oh, my!"

The woman looked to her husband. "Gene?"

"I apologize. I didn't get your names."

"I'm Kari. Kari Michaels. This is my friend, Ruth."

"Gene and Polly Portland."

Polly took Kari's hand and peered into her face. "But, Gene? Look at this girl." She was insistent.

Kari turned toward Gene Portland and let him examine her.

"What is it, Polly?"

"She-she reminds me of Stephen. And Laynie."

Gene looked at her again. "I—yes, I see what you mean."

"It's her eyes, 'specially." Polly gripped Kari's hand harder. "Like Stephen's." The tiny woman was shaking a little.

Kari could think of nothing else to say that would be appropriate. It wasn't the right time or place. "Please, Mrs. Portland. Don't upset yourself."

Ruth nodded her agreement. "We are so very sorry for your loss. Is there a reception afterward? We might speak to you again then."

She disentangled Polly's hand from Kari's and pulled Kari down the aisle. "This isn't going to be easy," she muttered.

Kari couldn't answer what she was thinking, *No. It isn't.*

They found seats in the very back but Kari kept turning her head, searching.

Lord, where is my sister? Please, Lord!

"Do you see her? Do you see the woman you sat next to on the plane?"

"No, not yet." Ruth swiveled to the right. "Yes! There she is," Ruth whispered.

Kari's hungry eyes sought and fell upon the tall, graceful woman. Her hair was lighter than Kari's, a dark blonde with natural highlights. She wore it up in a sophisticated twist.

Elaine!

Kari and Ruth observed the woman as she paused and greeted mourners on her way to the front of the room. She had a composure about her that seemed unshakable—polite, calm, collected. They saw Anthony and Owen position themselves so that the woman would come upon them naturally.

Kari and Ruth watched the exchange.

Laynie shook their hands and listened to something Anthony said. She studied Anthony and Owen in turn. When Anthony spoke again, her lips pursed slightly. Other than that, nothing in her expression marred her poise.

Finally, she gave a curt nod and stepped away from them, continuing to work her way to the front of the room until she reached the two caskets. She stared at the carpet a long moment as though preparing herself and then stood next to the open casket where her brother lay.

When she drew herself up and turned away, her expression was unchanged. She took the seat beside her parents.

Anthony and Owen joined Kari and Ruth as the auditorium began to quiet.

Kari searched their faces. "Well?"

"I told her we wished for a few minutes of her time following the service. That we had some important information regarding her brother."

"How did she respond?"

Anthony grimaced. "Hard to say. I couldn't get a read on her."

He looked to Owen for confirmation. Owen shrugged. "Me, neither."

"Well, did you find out anything about the children?"

"We asked around. Apparently, Kelly's parents have hired a nanny. She has the children in another room during the service. The nanny has Kelly's sister Talia's three boys, too."

That was all they had time to report before the minister came to the lectern and the service commenced.

"We are here today to celebrate the lives of Stephen and Kelly Portland—but more importantly, to celebrate their home going. For the Scriptures tell us emphatically, 'that to live is Christ, and to die is gain.' Yes, we have lost them temporarily, but Stephen and Kelly, who loved and lived for Jesus, have gained their eternal home with him."

Kari hadn't known what to expect. Being preoccupied with the news of Sammie's death, she hadn't given the service any thought. At the opening words of the minister, her soul began to lift.

Sammie and his wife know Jesus! They know him!

She heaved a sigh and a wave of relief flowed through her chest. Ruth gripped her hand.

"Our God is so good," Ruth whispered. "So good!"

Tears of joy mingled with Kari's tears of grief.

O Lord! You are faithful to your promises!

The assembled mourners stood and Kari stood with them, not having heard the minister's instructions. And then the attendees' united voices, raised in sweet triumph, rolled like warm, healing ointment over Kari's heart.

When peace, like a river,
attendeth my way,
When sorrows like sea billows roll;
Whatever my lot,
Thou hast taught me to say,
It is well, it is well with my soul.

It is well with my soul,
It is well, it is well with my soul.

And Lord, haste the day
when the faith shall be sight,
The clouds be rolled back as a scroll;
The trump shall resound,
and the Lord shall descend,
Even so, it is well with my soul.

It is well with my soul,
It is well, it is well with my soul.

Yes, Lord. It is well with my soul, Kari acknowledged.

When the hymn ended, she was able to listen with a calm mind as friends, fellow church members, and business acquaintances shared their memories of Stephen and Kelly.

I am so glad we are here, Lord. For the rest of my days I will cherish this little bit of Sammie they are sharing, Kari thought. *I will hold fast to the tiny glimpse into Sammie's life offered by those who knew him best.*

The last person to share was Elaine.

My sister! Kari's heart said again and again.

"Good morning. My name is Helena Portland, although those of you who know me well know that I prefer Laynie."

Laynie? Kari frowned as hazy memories intruded. *Did I call her Laynie? Yes, I think I did.*

"I want to speak for a moment about my brother Stephen—although, again, if you know me, you know that my pet name for Stephen was Sammie."

Sammie! Under the ripple of laughter that ran through the room, Kari wrung Ruth's hand.

"Sammie and I were very close growing up—closer, I would say, than most brothers and sisters. We had a bond that I cannot describe except to say that, when I think of home, I think not of a place, but a face. You see, Sammie and I were adopted, and my earliest, most precious memories— memories earlier even than those of our beloved Mama and Dad—are wrapped up in him."

Laynie! Do you have any memories of me? Of Mommy and Daddy?

Laynie addressed Kelly's family. "Mr. and Mrs. Greene, when Sammie met Kelly, we all knew she was perfect for him, and I was so happy for both of them. But I also loved Kelly from a purely selfish perspective. You see, she was never jealous of my bond with Sammie.

"I have lived and worked in Europe for more than fifteen years, returning home to Seattle on leave only once a year. Thirty precious days. I must cram all my family time into that one short month—time with Mama and Dad, but also time with Sammie, especially out on the water in his sailboat, *The Wave Skipper*.

"Kelly had a generous, loving heart, and she never begrudged me time alone with Sammie during that month. I loved her for that, and I loved her more for the two beautiful children she gave Sammie. Shannon and Robbie are—"

Laynie's voice cracked and sniffs around the room joined her. Kari and Ruth wept with every mourner present.

"Shannon and Robbie hold my heart," Laynie managed to say, "and that heart breaks for them today, for they do not yet understand that their mommy and daddy are not coming back.

"Please pray for them," Laynie finished, her voice dropping so low that Kari had to strain to make out the words.

Laynie gathered herself and concluded, "I, my parents, Gene and Polly Portland; Kelly's parents, Bill and Mary Greene; and Kelly's sister, Talia, and her family thank you for coming today to honor Stephen and Kelly."

The minister prayed a closing benediction and then announced, "Thank you for coming today to celebrate the lives of Stephen and Kelly Portland. The burials will take place this afternoon with only family in attendance. Please join us now in the reception hall for a light lunch."

Kari, Ruth, Owen, and Anthony waited for most of the crowd to leave the room before making their way to the reception hall. Kari was trembling and faint from the emotional strain.

"Sit here," Ruth instructed. "I'll get you some punch."

Owen found Kari a chair, and she relaxed into it, so exhausted. Then the hum of chatter dropped as the nanny they'd hired to help with the children brought them into the hall. Kari strained forward as a little girl with light brown hair raced toward Polly Portland.

Talia's husband corralled his boys and took them to get something to eat. Robbie, however, was wrapped in a blanket in the Nanny's arms, presumably sleeping.

Ruth brought Kari a glass of punch and a plate of finger foods, but Kari had no appetite except to study Sammie's children or Laynie. She watched and waited, hoping Laynie might, by some miracle, feel drawn to her.

More than once, the woman turned or faced in her direction. Kari felt certain Laynie would look at her, that their eyes would meet and some spark of recognition would ignite, but Laynie's soft blue eyes remained preoccupied with her parents or those who came to offer their condolences.

Each time Laynie passed where Kari was seated, Kari thought surely they would make eye contact—only to be disappointed when Laynie's gaze passed over or through her. As the reception wore on, Kari's hope that Laynie might, by some miracle, recognize or be drawn to her grew dimmer.

After two hours, the crowd of memorial attendees began to disperse until only a few knots of mourners remained. The Portlands and Kelly's parents sat at a table together speaking in hushed tones.

Kari saw that the nanny was reading the girl a story. She sat next to the nanny on a bench, the boy's sleeping form curled on the bench on the nanny's other side. He was still wrapped in a blanket, his thumb planted in his mouth.

"I think now is our best shot," Owen suggested.

Anthony again waited off to the side for Laynie to notice him, Kari, Ruth, and Owen not far away. When Anthony signaled Laynie, she approached him. "You said you had some information for me regarding my brother."

Kari, Ruth, and Owen loitered close enough that they could make out the woman's words, but far enough away and facing a little to the side, that they hoped the woman would not think they were listening in.

"Yes," Anthony answered. "A personal matter."

"So you said. However, is this really the appropriate time? My parents and I are in mourning."

Anthony nodded and the lines between his eyes deepened. "We do understand and sympathize with you. If you decide to do this later, we can. However, we've come quite a distance and would hate to miss this opportunity while the family is together. The funeral director has provided a private room for us to talk."

Laynie studied Anthony. "Are those two women with you? That one," Laynie gestured toward Kari with her chin, "has been fixated on me for some reason."

Anthony, as surprised as Kari and Ruth that she had noticed them, said simply, "Yes."

Laynie's gaze looked past Kari and fastened on Ruth—and did a double take. "You!"

Ruth nodded. She and Kari and Owen moved to join Anthony and Laynie.

In the seconds it took them to walk over, Laynie's momentary surprise disappeared. In its place was cool detachment.

"We sat together on the plane. New York to Chicago and then Chicago to Denver. Just who are you? What is this about?"

"We would be happy to explain," Anthony assured her, "but in private would be best."

"Then let's get this over with." She stared at Anthony with raised brows. "I hope, for your sake, that you aren't selling anything."

"I assure you I am not. This way, please." He motioned to the others to follow and led Laynie down a hall toward the room the funeral director had given them.

They settled uneasily into a small circle of chairs.

"My name is—"

"Anthony Esquibel. So you said."

"Yes; and I should tell you that I am a private investigator licensed in the State of New Mexico."

Laynie showed no surprise, only a glimmer of curiosity. "Oh? And your friends are?"

Anthony moved his hand in Ruth's direction. "Ruth Graff. Owen Washington. And my client, Kari Michaels."

Laynie nodded to Ruth. "Yes, Ruth. You were . . . very kind to me on the plane." She glanced at Kari and Owen. "All right. Now what?"

Anthony hesitated a fraction of a second. "Miss Portland, you said in the service that you and your brother were adopted."

Laynie blinked her eyes. They glittered for a moment and then turned a soft opaque, as though blinds had come down. "Our parents have always been candid with us about our adoption."

"But the adoption was a closed one? You never knew who your birth parents were? Never knew their names?"

"No."

"And were you three years old when you were adopted?"

"Yes. I hope you are coming to a point here."

Anthony pursed his lips for a moment. "I don't wish to overwhelm you. Perhaps I may relate a story to you?"

Laynie sighed. "If you must." She glanced at Kari and Ruth. As she examined Kari, a split second of uncertainty crossed her face—and disappeared as quickly.

She turned her attention to Anthony as he said, "Miss Portland, on the night of October 8, 1958, a married couple, Michael and Bethany Granger, were on their way to Albuquerque when their automobile broke down.

"The road was narrow and had no shoulder to speak of, so the Grangers took their three children from the car. They placed the children on a blanket a safe distance from the car while they attempted to fix it.

"It was a very dark night and the road out there in the desert was not lit. Not long after the Grangers moved their children, a semi tractor-trailer swept down upon them, hitting their vehicle, killing them both."

Kari saw Laynie shiver and frown. Laynie glanced at Kari and Ruth again and this time she focused on Kari. Her frown deepened.

O Lord, please help me to hold it together! Kari prayed.

Anthony was saying, "The police picked up the three children and took them somewhere nearby. The tale becomes a bit complicated at this point, so I will skip all but the pertinent facts.

"The two younger children, a girl, approximately three years of age, and an infant boy, about six months, were handed over to an adoption broker. I can tell you that the transfer was an illegal one, but we are not here to dwell upon that point. I only wish to provide you with a sequence of events.

"A girl age three. A boy six months." Laynie's voice was mechanical.

"Yes." Anthony waited, knowing how the year 1958 and the children's ages would be striking her.

However, when Laynie said nothing and kept staring at her hands, he asked, "Should I continue?"

After a moment, Laynie nodded, and Anthony resumed.

"The oldest child, a girl age six, saw her parents die. As you can imagine, it was a horrible experience, and she was, for a while, unresponsive to the police and to those involved in the illegal adoption. When the, er, adoption 'broker' arrived to take the two younger children, their sister snapped out of her unresponsive state and protested her siblings' removal.

"The unscrupulous people involved slapped and threatened this little girl. They vowed to drown her little sister and brother if she ever told anyone what had happened—if she ever spoke of them or even *thought* of them again. The horrors she experienced so traumatized her, that it was thirty-two years before she remembered the events of that night and the days that followed."

"Stop." Laynie was breathing hard. "Stop, please. Let me think."

No! You can't take them away! You can't take them!

Laynie shook her head, trying to dispel the voice. "*Care . . . Care said*," she murmured, distracted and somewhere else.

Kari started, but Anthony shook his head as Laynie asked, "What-what were their names? What were the children's names?"

"The boy was Samuel. The girl was Elaine."

"Samuel. Elaine . . . *Care* said *Laynie*." The woman was floundering, and Kari could stand it no longer.

Ignoring Anthony, Kari knelt by Laynie's chair. "Laynie, I'm Kari. I was the oldest of the three children."

Laynie searched Kari's face. "*Care . . .*"

Kari nodded and placed her hands upon Laynie's. "Laynie, I am your sister, Kari. You and Sammie are my brother and sister."

Laynie stared at Kari. "*Care . . . Kari.*"

Kari was weeping. "Yes. You called me Care. I called you Laynie. I had forgotten! But I remember . . . I remember always calling Samuel 'Sammie.'"

Laynie blinked back tears of her own and shivered. After a long moment, she withdrew her hands from Kari's and stood up.

"I-I need some air."

Without another word, Laynie stood and left the room, leaving Kari weeping into the chair Laynie had vacated.

CHAPTER 28

The remainder of Stephen and Kelly Portland's friends and coworkers had departed. Only family lingered at the funeral home—family and Kari's little entourage.

Kari and Ruth sat at the back of the auditorium. Owen and Anthony waited outside where their presence would be less intrusive.

The family was viewing Stephen's body a last time.

Kari was trying her best to behave in an inconspicuous manner, hoping no one would ask them to leave, but when the funeral workers closed up Stephen and Kelly's caskets and readied them for transport to the cemetery, she clutched Ruth's hands and moaned.

Kelly's sister and her family went on ahead to the cemetery. "The boys need to burn off some energy," Kari overheard her say to her parents, "And I could use a stretch myself. We'll meet you there."

That left the grandparents and the nanny to care for the other grandchildren. Robbie was awake now, and he and Shannon chased each other up and down the side aisle of the room. Robbie shrieked with glee and toddled on chubby legs first toward Shannon and then away when she chased after him.

Kari devoured them and their antics with hungry eyes.

Sammie! You have such beautiful children! They look so much like how I remember you and Laynie.

Gene Portland, himself filled with anxious energy, paced near his wife. He noticed Kari and Ruth at the back and said something to Polly. Polly lifted her weary head and twisted to look at Kari. Then she said something to her husband.

"I don't know how you intend for this to play out," Ruth murmured. "I mean, I've been in awkward positions before, but this takes the cake."

Kari lowered her head. "I can only let the Lord lead, Ruth. It won't be easy or convenient, but I can't let Laynie just fly back to Europe."

They both glanced up as Laynie, now quite composed, strode into the room. She glanced at them and nodded once but continued up the center aisle to her parents. She said something to them and they nodded their agreement.

Laynie then spoke to the funeral attendants, who began to wheel the caskets toward the door and the waiting hearses.

Kari and Ruth stood up as the caskets rolled by, and Kari wiped away more tears.

Even though I won't see Sammie again until the resurrection, I thank you, Lord, for using his death to cause Laynie and Ruth to meet. I acknowledge that their encounter was a miracle.

I also confess that I don't understand why you didn't allow me to find Sammie before he died! But I cannot deny your sovereignty in bringing Laynie and Ruth together like that. And so I give myself to your will, Lord. Blessed be your name.

Kari sniffed. "Come on. We'll go to the cemetery and watch from afar." She pulled Ruth from the pew and they followed the family out.

The rain-swept skies were clearing when they arrived at the cemetery. Within the wrought iron gates, they found a lush, tree-lined park. The grounds glowed a vivid green, washed clean by the latest shower.

Kari spied Kelly's sister and her family and pointed toward her. "Over there, I think."

Talia wandered slowly over the grass, reading grave inscriptions. She held her bulging belly protectively. Her husband and the three boys played tag, keeping to an as-yet unused section of cemetery lawn.

Not far away a tent had been erected over two open graves. The mounded dirt beside the graves was covered in green cloth.

"Shall I park here?" Owen asked.

"Yes, thank you. Ruth and I will wait in the car until the service starts."

A full half hour passed before the family and the minister were assembled.

"Ready, Kari?" Ruth asked.

"I guess I am."

Anthony opened the back door for them and patted Kari's shoulder when she stepped out. "We are here for you, Kari."

"Thank you. I'm so blessed to have the three of you as friends."

Ruth and Kari crossed the grass but stopped yards shy of the small assembly. Perhaps fifteen souls, counting children, stood around the graves. Gene and Polly, Bill and Mary Greene, and Talia sat in the short row of chairs. Laynie stood directly behind her mother, one hand on Polly's fragile shoulder.

Kari stared at the two caskets and the small family circle of which she was not part. She was surprised and relieved that the exclusion did not pain her.

She looked down with gratitude at the grassy, emerald green beneath her feet and prayed.

All my life, up till the last three years, I had felt alone, Lord. I had no family, no abiding home, no one to call my own. My heart was an open, bleeding wound.

How I thank you for allowing me to find Rose's journal! It was your divine provision to save and heal me. Through her words, I found you, discovered my family's roots—and, at last, remembered the sister and brother I had forgotten.

And so I thank you for the Body of Christ and the large extended family that welcomed me. Because of your grace toward me, I can stand here today, an outsider looking in, and yet a whole and healed person. Thank you for your never-ending mercy.

Kari had not noticed two individuals walking from the graves toward them until their shadows fell upon her feet. Her head jerked up.

Sammie and Laynie's adopted father observed her. Laynie at his elbow, was silent. It was Gene Portland who spoke. "Miss Michaels, is it?"

"Yes. But please call me Kari."

Even when they ask me to leave, it will be all right, Lord.

Gene's gaze intensified. At last he spoke. "Kari, were you aware that this service is for family only?"

Kari raised her chin. Her tongue stuck to the roof of her mouth, but she managed, "Yes, I was aware."

"Are you family, then?"

Kari's answer was calm. Steady. "Yes. I am."

Laynie's expression gave nothing away, but Gene looked from Kari to Laynie. "She looks like Sammie, doesn't she? Same hair. Same brilliant blue eyes."

Laynie offered a minute nod of her chin. She, too, studied Kari, but from behind a mask of detachment.

With tears pooling in his eyes, Gene held his hand out to Kari. "Please, Kari. Polly and I wish you and your friend to sit with us . . . and with your sister while we . . . bury your brother."

Kari's breath caught and next to her, Ruth sobbed.

O Lord! Your unexpected, unmerited favor!

"Th-thank you."

Gene tucked Kari's hand in his arm and led her to the graveside. Curious and speculative eyes considered Kari but, at Gene's request, the mourners moved down one seat, making space for Kari next to Polly. Laynie returned to her place behind her mother. Ruth stood behind Kari.

Polly took Kari's hand and searched her face. "We would like you to come home with us afterwards. We have a lot to talk about. Will you come?"

"I-I would be honored."

***

GENE AND POLLY'S HOME was modest, plain, and comfortable, a home to be lived in rather than displayed. Friends from church were waiting and had prepared yet another meal that Kari knew she would not touch. She and Ruth sat in a corner of the living room while the family and a few close friends mingled and talked in low tones. Owen and Anthony had gone to a restaurant and would return for them when Kari or Ruth called.

Shannon ran past their chairs. She chortled as Robbie careened along behind her—but he crashed into an ottoman and fell to the floor where he burst into tears. The nanny, showing the fatigue of the day, picked him up.

"Come along, little man."

He screamed louder over her shoulder until he caught sight of Kari. He shushed and poked a thumb into his mouth and, with the other hand, pointed to her.

"Da-da."

He pointed and strained toward Kari.

"Da-da."

Kari was on her feet before she knew what she was doing. "May I take him for a while?"

The nanny was grateful to relinquish her charge, so Kari hefted the boy from her shoulder, amazed at how solid he was. She plopped back into the overstuffed chair and smiled at the boy.

"Hello, Robbie."

"He's beautiful, Kari," Ruth whispered.

"Isn't he?"

Robbie touched Kari's face and studied her with serious eyes. Bright blue, familiar eyes. Then, of his own volition, he leaned against her chest. As Kari's arms curled about him, tears welled again and dribbled down her cheeks.

"He's gone out like a light," Ruth murmured a minute later.

"Poor boy. He has to be so confused and tired."

From the corner of the living room, Laynie watched, her expression unreadable.

***

ALTHOUGH IT WAS ONLY EARLY EVENING, winter darkness had fallen when Gene Portland addressed his guests. "Thank you all for your love and support this day. Our family and the Greene family appreciate everything you have said and done for us on this difficult day.

"As much as our Lord has kept us strong through today's ceremonies, they have taken a toll on us, but especially on Polly. I hope you'll understand if we draw this gathering to a close."

Kari saw what he meant: The tiny woman sagged in her wheelchair, exhaustion written in the slump of her shoulders. Nevertheless, as Gene mentioned her name, she lifted her chin and smiled at Kari, weary grief intermingled with hope.

And Kari felt Bill and Mary Greene's eyes upon her, as well as Talia and her husband's. They remained where they were while Gene and Laynie saw friends to the door.

Laynie or Gene has told them who I am, and they expect to hear from me. Kari shifted Robbie's sleeping body a little and prepared for the long conversation ahead.

Lord, please help me.

Gene returned and sighed. "Yes, we are all exhausted, but before we disperse, we need to talk. As a family."

He addressed the nanny. "Mrs. Brown, would you be so kind as to take the boys and Shannon upstairs?"

Gene wheeled Polly's chair close to Kari. Polly's sweet smile was pained as she observed her grandson sleeping soundly on Kari's lap.

Kari's thighs had gone numb from the weight of the toddler and now, with little fanfare, she was the object of everyone's attention. She tried to shift again.

"He's heavy, isn't he?" Polly asked.

Kari nodded. "It's all right. I'm just not used to children."

Gene cleared his throat. "Miss Michaels—I'm sorry, Kari—your appearance today has given us quite a shock. Laynie related a little of what your private investigator told her earlier."

He looked around. "Does anyone doubt that Kari is Laynie and Stephen's sister?"

No one disagreed, although Talia's husband, Don, looked unconvinced.

Under Gene's questioning, Kari related an abbreviated version of her life. She directed much of her tale toward Laynie who, despite everything, remained distant. Remote.

"After I recovered my memories, I actively searched for Sammie and Elaine. My investigators ran down every lead we had—even though they were precious few. They traced Sammie and Elaine to an unlicensed adoption broker, but then the trail ran cold. We had the broker's name, but he had died. We also had what we believed was the name of a city: *Portland.* We never dreamed it was a *name.*"

Excited murmurs ran across the room.

"And because we thought 'Portland' referred to a city, my investigators told me that the search was over. Hopeless. I-I confess that I was devastated."

A sob broke from Polly, interrupting Kari. "Gene and I wanted children so badly! But back then, no one would give a baby or a child to a mixed-race couple. We-we were forced to seek out a private adoption—but we had no idea! No idea it was illegal. No idea someone had stolen those precious babies."

She broke down and wept and Kari rubbed Polly's arm and shoulder, hoping to soothe her. "It's all right, Polly. I understand. And-and I'm so grateful for you and Gene . . ."

"Grateful?" Gene asked, bemused.

"Yes, Grateful. Grateful that you loved Sammie and Elaine and that you are Christians, that you raised them to know Jesus. When the service today began and the minister talked of Sammie and Kelly's faith, my heart was thrilled and comforted because, you see, Sammie and Elaine and I come from a family whose faith is everything."

Kari looked from face to face and saw their amazement. "Through them I have learned—and have seen them live out—this precious principle, that our lives here last only a moment. In the end, Jesus is everything. To know that Sammie and Kelly are with *him,* that I will meet them some day in heaven? That gives me such comfort. So I am grateful, so very grateful."

"Amen," Mary Greene whispered.

Kari saw damp eyes and agreement. She also saw Laynie. Still standing, apart from the others, staring at the floor.

Please tell me what is going on in Laynie's heart, Lord, Kari prayed. *Something is very wrong.*

"Go on, Kari. Finish telling how you found us?" Gene asked.

"Well, as much as it pained me to do so, I had to surrender the search for Elaine and Sammie to the Lord. It was one of the hardest things I have ever done—but I trusted that the Lord would honor his promises.

"Two more years went by—and then out of the blue, *you*, Laynie, sat down on the plane next to my good friend Ruth—not once, but twice."

Kari choked up and could only point her chin in Ruth's direction, so Ruth took over the narration. "I felt something special about you as we talked, Laynie, but it wasn't until we were seated together for a second time, on the flight from Chicago to Denver, that the Holy Spirit broke through and impressed upon me the need to know your name and have a means to reach you later."

Ruth smiled at Laynie. "You gave me your card, remember?"

"I did." But Laynie's eyes narrowed in silent warning.

Ruth put her hand over her mouth and feigned a cough to give herself a moment to think.

If Owen is right about Laynie, she will not thank me for theorizing aloud as to why her card led us down a rabbit hole, Ruth realized.

"Do you need a sip of water, dear?" Polly asked. "Laynie, please fetch Ruth a glass of water."

"Um, no. No, I'm fine. Really." Ruth nodded to Laynie and hoped she understood. "Where was I? Oh, yes.

"While Laynie and I sat together on the plane, I could see that she was distressed. I asked if I could help, and Laynie told me she was going home to Seattle because of a family emergency."

She glanced at Laynie again. "She told me her sister-in-law had passed away and that her brother *Sammie* was in critical condition. I told her I would pray for her and for her family.

"That night after I returned home, I dreamed about Laynie, only in my dream I kept confusing her with Kari. Again and again, Kari intruded into my dream—as did the word 'Portland.' When I woke up, it hit me: Laynie's last name was *Portland*. It came clear to me in a rush that *Laynie* was Kari's sister *Elaine*. I knew that meeting Laynie was an encounter arranged, not by chance, but by the sovereign hand of God.

"I rushed home and contacted Kari's investigators. Those few pieces of information she had mentioned to me? Her last name of Portland, the city, Seattle, and the car accident? Those were enough. Kari's investigators found reports of the accident."

Ruth slipped a glance toward Laynie. The woman nodded, once, as though acknowledging Ruth's discretion.

Ruth concluded. "By the time the investigators located Kelly's obituary, Sammie—*Stephen*—had also passed away. The investigators found out about today's memorial service only yesterday morning. We told Kari and made arrangements to fly here yesterday afternoon knowing Kari would not have such an opportunity to meet her sister again."

The room settled into quiet as the listeners digested Ruth's story.

"So we're clear, Stephen and Kelly didn't leave any money," Don said. His tone was even but challenging.

"Don!" Talia stared aghast at her husband, as did the Greenes and Portlands.

"We shouldn't ignore the elephant in the room," he persisted. He directed his next comments to Kari. "What little money Stephen's insurance policy pays out, goes to his children."

Gene started to protest, but Kari lifted her hand. "I understand your concern, Don. I would feel the same, were I in your position. However, I can assure you that I have no designs on any of Stephen's estate. In fact—"

"Then, let's move on to the next topic," Don said. "Who is going to take custody of Shannon and Robbie? Because, as you can see, Talia is pregnant and due in about five weeks. We will have four children in a three-bedroom house. We are in no position to take two more."

He pointed to Laynie. "You are their aunt. You should move home and raise them."

Every eye followed his finger. Laynie did not flinch; her placid expression did not alter, but inside all was turmoil.

Alvarsson would not allow me to quit. Marstead would not allow it. I am on the cusp of my relationship with Petroff, and he is too important an asset. And besides—

The old voices returned in force.

And besides, you are beyond redemption, Laynie. What would Sammie think of you, a spy and a whore, raising his children? He would want them raised as Christians—and you are the last person who could do so.

You made your choices years ago. It is too late to unmake them.

Kari, stunned at the turn in the conversation, stared with everyone else as Laynie said nothing and gave nothing away.

Moments ticked by before she answered.

"No. I'm sorry, but that will not be possible."

"Really?" Don's face reddened. "Not possible? You're an executive—you can work anywhere! Isn't it that you choose not to—"

Laynie leveled a sneer that quelled him. "I said it is *not possible.* It isn't. Do not question my motives, Don."

Bill and Mary blinked and looked to each other. "Then I guess we will take them," Bill murmured. He addressed Gene and Polly with kindness and resignation. "We know you would offer if you were both younger, if Polly were well. We know that you'll help out as you can."

He turned to Talia and Don. "We don't fault you. We understand that you can't take them. Your quiver is already full with four children."

Mary wiped her weary face. "We've had them since the accident anyway, but we'll need to hire a permanent nanny."

Mary looked around. "The days have not been too bad for the children, but we're not spring chickens anymore, you know. Bill is closer to seventy than sixty and his heart is not what it used to be. Chasing active children around takes a toll.

"But the nights? They are not good. We are concerned. Shannon has had nightmares ever since the accident and Robbie wakes up crying for hours. He misses his mommy. It's too much for us at our age."

She sighed. "And frankly, if we have to hire a live-in nanny, I don't know how we'll handle the expense. The insurance Stephen left should be put in Shannon and Robbie's college fund."

"I'll handle the expense," Kari said.

Don's mouth twisted in skepticism, but the others looked curious. Hopeful.

"Whatever you need, I will provide," Kari added. "In fact—and I was just getting to this when Don raised the issue of custody and money—our great-uncle left his estate to us."

She added no details. *Forgive me, Lord, but I can't foist the saga of our father's abduction on these poor people tonight.*

"The three of us—Elaine, Samuel, and I—are our great-uncle's heirs. That means Shannon and Robbie will inherit their father's portion when they are old enough to inherit outright. I am the estate's administrator and can provide for them until they inherit."

Gene and Bill exchanged looks. Gene asked, "Is their share of the estate enough to support them to adulthood?"

"More than adequate." Kari didn't want to get into particulars in front of Talia's husband, to whom she'd taken a strong, sudden dislike.

"As the estate administrator, I will send monthly checks for their support." Kari gestured toward Bill and Mary Greene. "We can discuss how much Shannon and Robbie will need before I go home."

Heads nodded, but Kari didn't care for the calculating expression growing on Don's face. His next words cinched her opinion of him.

"If there are sufficient funds available, perhaps Talia and I could reconsider," he smiled.

The look of loathing Talia turned on her husband reflected Kari's sentiments exactly.

Laynie came to life. "As the children's grandparents, the legal authority falls to Bill and Mary and Gene and Polly to determine who is best suited to have custody of Shannon and Robbie."

Kari telegraphed a glint of approval toward Laynie and, for a moment, *for the first time*, their eyes communicated: On the subject of Shannon and Robbie, they were in accord.

Kari nodded to Laynie and a smile touched her sister's lips and then was gone.

Laynie spoke again. "I believe they have made their decision, Don. The children go to Bill and Mary." Her tone brooked no argument.

Laynie is tough, Kari thought. *Formidable.*

Bill Greene still had doubts. "Are you certain you understand how much a nanny will cost? Certain you can afford to help out, Kari?"

"Yes. I will write you a check for the first six months tonight. And the custody issue will need to be approved by the courts. It will accrue legal costs. Let me pay those expenses also."

Don's indignation bled through. "This is the first we've heard of you and your cockamamie story! Who are you to dictate to us? If the children have inherited any money, what gives you the right to decide how it is spent?"

Talia dragged herself to standing. "You know, sometimes you disgust me," she hissed to her husband.

She turned to her parents and the Portlands. "I am so sorry." She fixed on Kari. "I do believe that you are Stephen and Laynie's sister. Thank you for your generosity. Don't let anything my husband said today influence you—he is usually a decent man. *Usually*. We didn't plan on another baby and it's put some financial pressure on us, but we'll be fine."

She huffed and glared at him. "Please get our sons. We're going now. I'll be in the car."

She kissed her parents and left by the front door while Don trudged up the stairs to fetch his sons. Their departure left the living room in silence.

Ruth, who had been a mute witness to the unexpected family drama, smiled cheerfully and jumped up. "Well! May I freshen anyone's coffee?"

Polly sighed her gratitude. "You are a dear. Yes, thank you."

Robbie woke then and clambered down from Kari's lap. He wobbled, a little unsteady and sleepy, then ambled over to pick up a plastic truck sitting on a shelf. Kari hadn't noticed the little collection of toys sitting there, but Robbie was obviously quite familiar with them.

He's played here at Gene and Polly's many times.

271

Kari stood, stretched her stiff muscles and, at Bill and Mary's beckoning, went to sit beside them.

Bill didn't mince words. "Kari, are you positive that you have the money to do everything you said?"

"If you can keep this information to yourselves, yes. Shannon and Robbie will be independently wealthy when they reach their majority."

Mary shook her head, a little in awe. "You are a godsend, Kari. Popping up out of nowhere like this."

Kari bit her lip. "I'm sorry it took Kelly and Sammie's deaths to bring us together. And I hope—" She paused. "One second."

Kari found her handbag next to the chair she'd been seated in and pulled out three business cards. She scribbled her mobile and home phone numbers on the backs.

"Please," she handed one to Bill and Mary, "if you need anything, anything at all, call me. Day or night."

She handed a card to Gene and Polly but spoke to both sets of grandparents, "I would like to be part of Shannon and Robbie's lives, if that is all right with you. I could come visit, when it's convenient. I-I would like to hear more about Sammie—I mean Stephen—and have the children know me as their aunt. Would that be all right?"

"More than all right," Bill answered. "You will be a blessing to them."

The nanny brought Shannon downstairs and into the living room. The girl ran directly to Polly. "Grammy, I'm hungry."

"What would you like, Little Duck?"

Shannon grinned. "Milk and Grammy crackers!"

"Now, did you ask nicely?"

Shannon bounced on her tiptoes. "May I have milk and Grammy crackers, please?"

"Of course, child." Polly looked to Kari. "Kari, would you like to help Shannon?"

Kari flushed. "I'd love to."

Shannon stared at Kari. "Who're you?"

Kari stooped down so they were eye-to-eye. Shannon did not have the bright blue eyes that Robbie had—her eyes were pale and softer, more like Laynie's eyes—but her shoulder-length curls were brown and gold.

Like mine.

"I'm your Aunt Kari, Shannon."

The little girl blinked, perhaps absorbing Kari's name. "Do you know where Grammy keeps her Grammy crackers?"

"Could you show me?"

In response, Shannon took Kari's hand and tugged her toward the kitchen.

Before Kari and Ruth left the Portlands' home that evening, Kari cornered her sister. They watched each other, deep, unspoken feelings churning beneath the surface.

"Could we meet, the two of us, tomorrow?" Kari asked. "I want to spend a little time with you before you . . . go back."

"Lunch?"

"That will work."

I have a lot of questions for you, Laynie.

"All right."

But Laynie's veiled expression told Kari the conversation would likely be one-sided.

And that's all right, Laynie. I have lots to say.

CHAPTER 29

Kari and Laynie settled into their booth on opposite sides of the table. They studied each other in silence. Kari had spent long, sleepless hours praying for wisdom, asking for help to somehow connect with her sister. She had left New Orleans in such a rush, that she had not packed her Bible.

In the hotel room nightstand, she looked for and found a Gideon Bible. She found some comfort in a seemingly obscure and unrelated passage from Jeremiah. In the archaic King James prose, the verse read,

> *Be not afraid of their faces:*
> *for I am with thee to deliver thee,*
> *saith the Lord.*

Kari had whispered the first line in more familiar language. "Don't be afraid of their faces."

It was Laynie's face that troubled her.

Don't be afraid of her face?

That unnaturally blank expression.

That deadness?

How do I break past that, Lord, and reach the real Laynie?

She had reread the verse. *For I am with thee to deliver thee.*

"You don't want me to be afraid of her face. You will be with me. You will deliver me." Kari sighed. "What I want is for you to deliver *her*, Lord. Something feels so wrong. Please help me to help her."

The waitress arrived to take their orders.

Since it would be a battle to get Laynie to open up, Kari decided upon a frontal assault, hoping to breach the walls between them. So she stared into Laynie's milky blue eyes and refused to look away.

"How about salads and iced tea?" she suggested.

"That would be fine." Laynie's response was cheerful. Detached. Fake.

Kari seemed to be able to see past the façade that others, apparently, could not.

The waitress departed and Kari plunged in.

"Laynie, I'm not going to beat about the bush. I have missed you terribly, and I want us to be sisters again. We don't have much time and I really don't care to engage in meaningless chitchat, so I'm willing to risk a few things to get us off on the right foot."

Laynie's shuttered visage was disturbing, but Kari chose not to let it move her.

"My investigators called the number on your business card, but the receptionist on the other end would only say that you were out on emergency leave and she would pass on our message."

Kari paused for Laynie's response.

"And so they did," Laynie answered. "Of course, I've been a bit preoccupied."

She smiled, but Kari was not fooled.

"Yes, but we were frantic to find you *now* rather than after you returned to Sweden. So Owen, one of my investigators, turned to a friend in the FBI. Asked him to run a background check on you."

Something flickered in Laynie's expression.

Whoa. Did I imagine that?

Keeping her eyes locked on Laynie's, Kari forged ahead. "His FBI friend came to see him. Personally. Drove across town. Strange, don't you think? And do you know what he told Owen?"

Laynie blinked. "How could I?"

"Ah, but I think you do know what he told Owen. He told him to forget checking up on you, that if Owen knew what was good for him, he would give up trying to dig up info on you."

Laynie feigned surprise and grinned. "Wow. That's wild. I have no idea why he would say such a thing."

Kari did not falter nor did she break eye contact, even for an instant.

"Owen thinks his FBI friend warned him off because you work undercover for some intelligence agency. He says nothing else makes sense."

Laynie laughed softly and shook her head, but tension crackled between them.

Kari persisted. "At the service I heard you say how you loved Sammie. 'When I think of home, I think not of a place, but a face,' you said. You have no idea how deeply that touched me, Laynie. And about Sammie's children? You said, 'Shannon and Robbie hold my heart.' Sounds like love to me—and yet you can't move home to raise them? 'It's not possible,' you said."

Laynie's mask tightened. Her face was immobile, without expression, but she answered with mild matter-of-factness, "Kari, I work for Marstead International. Have you heard of them? They do aeronautics and technology research and transfer all over the world. It's important work, and I am engaged in a very difficult piece of negotiation at the moment."

Kari drew in a fortifying breath. "Well, I think this Marstead company makes for a good cover. And if you're doing any tech transfer, you're doing it in Russia, aren't you?"

Kari leaned closer to Laynie. "I think *you are a spy* and possibly a very good one. I think you are so deep undercover in Sweden, that they—whoever 'they' are—don't want to let you out. I think you feel obligated to stay and feel a patriotic duty not to quit—even to raise your brother's children."

The waitress arrived. She placed the salads and glasses on the table, looked from Laynie to Kari, and stepped away without a word.

"Laynie, you say you love Shannon and Robbie, but isn't your work for this agency the real reason 'it isn't possible' for you to move home and raise our niece and nephew?"

Something in Laynie shattered and Kari glimpsed pain, deep pain, before her sister gathered up the fractured pieces and slapped them back into place.

"You don't know me," she breathed. "You don't know a thing."

You don't know what I've done to steal the secrets our government wants. You don't know the things, the horrible things, I've done.

"But I want to, Laynie. I want to know you. And I love you. I have loved you since you were born. I was only three, but when Mommy and Daddy showed you to me, I gave *you* my heart like you gave your heart to Sammie—to Shannon and Robbie. *Please*. Please trust me."

Kari glanced away to wipe her moist eyes. When she looked back, the real Laynie was staring back at her.

"Laynie! Elaine!" Kari reached for her sister's hands and they gripped each other. "I have longed for this day."

Laynie blinked back her own tears. "*Care*. All my life your name and your voice have both haunted and eluded me. I-I wouldn't let Mama and Dad call me anything but Laynie, because I could hear your voice in my head. I thought . . . I thought I'd done something wrong and that's why you left me."

"How could you have done anything wrong? You were a baby! I'm here now, Laynie. God has brought us back together. I won't ever be far away again."

Laynie did not relinquish her hold on Kari's hands, but she stared at the table. "I wasn't lying when I said you didn't know me, Kari. You don't know . . . what I've done . . . for our country."

Kari's heart stuttered as the possibilities—the awful possibilities—sifted through her mind.

Laynie squeezed Kari's hands and released them. "And we may never speak of this again, Kari. Never."

"I-I understand. But—"

"No buts. I'll stay with Mama and Dad through the end of the week. Then I'll go back."

"But, Laynie!"

The old, unreadable Laynie was back. "Let me be clear, Kari. Even if there were a way for me to 'get out,' Sammie would not thank me for raising Shannon and Robbie. I'm not like you. I'm not like him. Not like Mama and Dad."

"You mean you aren't a Christian." Kari said it as a statement.

"Yes. I never took to it like Sammie did because, even from the beginning, I knew I was different. Flawed. I don't fit."

"I've only been a follower of Jesus for around three years, Laynie. I always had these . . . internal voices telling me that I did not belong. That I would never belong."

Laynie snorted. "We should compare voices sometime. I have my own demons."

Conviction rose in Kari. "Well, those voices lied to me. They lied about God. About myself. They lied to me, like they are lying to you."

Kari was halted by Laynie's icy retort. "I only wanted to explain myself, Kari, not engage in a theological debate."

Kari nodded slowly. "I apologize, but you need to know that nothing, *nothing*, can change how I feel about you. Not one iota. You are my sister. I love you. I would give my life for you."

Laynie licked her lips and the shutters fell away again. "And I for you. I thought Sammie was my last link to whatever it was I was missing, but—"

"But God, at just the right time, brought us back together."

One side of Laynie's mouth tipped up. "Sammie and I learned to 'agree to disagree' on the subject of God and Christianity. When we were out on the water in the sailboat? Then we could say anything. We were two hearts in a little boat bobbing on the water. I will miss that but . . ."

"But?"

"But perhaps you and I can find a boat for our two hearts?"

Laynie smiled. Kari smiled back. They picked at their salads then, saying little, both processing the emotions that bound them together.

Before they left, Kari said, "You don't know this, but I've become something of a businesswoman. I run a large conglomerate—an assortment of businesses and holdings to which you have one-third ownership rights. You will be a multimillionaire when the dust clears, Laynie."

"When the dust clears?"

"We'll go through probate again. Since you'd been missing so long, the courts awarded the estate to me. Technically, it is all mine; however, I insisted that your names remain in the court documents, should you ever be found. We'll go through probate again and, somehow, split it all up.

"One-third will be split between Shannon and Robbie, although I will petition the court to make me the administrator of their holdings until they are each twenty-one."

"No."

"Hm?"

"No, you can't do that." Laynie gripped Kari's hand again. "It could be dangerous for my name to come out in open court documents, in newspapers. If a journalist sought me out? Wanted an interview or photos? It could lead back to me and my other, er, persona. It could be dangerous if *that person* was connected in any way to *Stephen's* name. My agency made certain my name was left out of Stephen and Kelly's obituary; in fact, you would be hard-pressed to find Helena Portland in many public documents these days. However, it would be more difficult to keep it that way if lawyers get involved."

She scanned the room, but the lunch crowd was gone and the tables around them were vacant. "Listen to me, Kari. You are the only person on American soil, outside of my handlers, who knows what I do. It needs to stay that way."

The intensity in Laynie's eyes became grave. "The people I, er, interact with in . . . that country you mentioned? They have curious, probing minds and long fingers. My coming home for Stephen's funeral on only a moment's notice set my handlers' teeth on edge. No one must ever trace my cover's movements here. No one must ever associate *her* with Helena Portland. Not ever."

Kari shivered. "So, what should I do about the estate?"

"Keep it as it is. Perhaps in ten or fifteen years, when I'm not young and attractive enough for this work, things may be different."

Laynie laughed and, to Kari's ears, it was an ugly, ragged sound. "Who knows? Someday I may be allowed to retire. You can provide for Shannon and Robbie, on the side, so to speak, but nothing must *ever* come close to connecting the woman I am in Stockholm with this estate you manage— because it could link Shannon and Robbie to me."

She tightened her hold on Kari's hand. "You understand what I'm saying? Shannon and Robbie make me vulnerable, and certain . . . individuals would exploit that weakness."

Laynie lapsed into silence, her thoughts far away.

A man such as Vassili Aleksandrovich Petroff. He would use them against me in a heartbeat. I must be careful. So very careful.

"Laynie?"

Laynie gathered herself.

"Keep my name out of the estate, Kari. Keep it out of your life. For Shannon and Robbie's sake."

Kari shivered again. "You have my word, Laynie."

CHAPTER 30

"Go on home ahead of me," Kari told her friends late that evening. "I will stay another week and spend some time getting to know Laynie, Shannon, and Robbie."

Ruth, Owen, and Anthony bid her a reluctant goodbye and departed for the airport in a cab the following morning. Kari called the office and spoke at length with Scarlett and Bettina.

"If I encounter anything I can't handle, I will call you, Kari," Scarlett assured her.

"Thank you."

"We're all very sorry about your brother," Bettina said softly. "But are you also getting to know your sister?"

"Yes. Thank you for asking."

Laynie's warning tingled across Kari's skin. *Don't add any detail, Kari,* she cautioned herself.

"Please do not publicize that I've found my sister," she directed. "No one in the office or outside my confidence need know. It-it is important."

"All right, if that's what you want, Kari," Scarlett assured her. "You can count on our discretion."

Kari drove the rental car to pick up Laynie from the Portlands' home. Polly invited her to breakfast. Seeing how her presence seemed to lighten Polly's grief a little, Kari stayed and, in a way, felt that she was seeing the Portland family as it had been before Sammie and Laynie grew up and moved away.

"You've made me feel very welcome," Kari said as she and Laynie prepared to leave. "Thank you."

Polly reached up and drew Kari toward her, searching Kari's face with hungry eyes. She kissed Kari's cheek before she let her go.

"Where shall we take them?" Kari asked as she and Laynie headed to the Greenes' to pick up the children.

"It's not too cool today. Union Lake Park would be nice. Lots of boats, houseboats, even seaplanes taking off from the lake and landing."

"Robbie will love that!"

"It's where . . . it's where Sammie keeps his boat. I paid for the slip, and he paid for the boat's maintenance. We would motor through the locks and out into the sound."

She looked bleak. "They will sell the boat now."

"But they haven't yet, have they? Take me," Kari said impulsively. "Not while we have the children today, but before you leave? Take me sailing?"

Kari thought that every part of Laynie softened. She smiled at Kari. "Nothing you could have said could be more right than that. Thank you."

Kari lifted one shoulder. "Well, don't thank me yet. I have no idea if I get seasick or not."

"What's all this stuff?"

The Greenes' nanny had piled coats, hats, mittens, a diaper bag, a large lunch pouch, blankets, and two car seats on the floor near the Greenes' front door.

Laynie smirked. "Welcome to the world of kids. First, we need to install these car seats in your rental. Have a degree in engineering, by chance?"

When they had the seats properly installed, Kari and Laynie went back for the children.

Shannon again stared at Kari and asked, "Who're you?"

"We met at your Grammy Polly's house day before yesterday, remember? I'm Aunt Kari."

Laynie grinned. "Aunt Kari. I like it."

Robbie, on the other hand, toddled up to Kari and reached out his arms. Kari lifted him up and he patted her face with both hands. With enthusiasm.

"Goodness! You haven't missed many meals, Sir Robert!" She hefted him to her hip. "He's built like a tank."

Laynie smirked.

The day was perfect—except for having to pursue Robbie nonstop as he chased and tormented seagulls. He never failed to scream in delighted abandon as he hounded the scavenging birds.

Yes, the day was perfect. Except for Shannon's sixteen questions every sixty seconds. Except for snacks and bottles and lost mittens and potty breaks.

Except for diapers.

"Ugh! That is so disgusting," Kari exclaimed.

"Bet you don't see many of *those* in your high-flying board rooms," Laynie quipped.

***

LAYNIE AND KARI SPENT PART OF EVERY DAY with the children except for the day Laynie took Kari sailing.

"Dad is buying an ad to sell Sammie's boat after I leave," Laynie explained. "I'm glad we're taking her out. One last time." A wistful sadness settled on her.

"Um, won't it get a little cold out on the water? It being January and the middle of winter and all."

"Well, sure—this isn't the Gulf Coast, you know. So we'll dress for it. Bundle up."

Kari had never been sailing and, even though it had been her idea, she was more than a little terrified. "Well, what if, I mean, what if I fall overboard or something.?

Laynie sent her a superior look. "Spoken like a true landlubber."

Then she arched one brow. "Not to worry. The good news is you'll be wearing a lifejacket and be tethered to the boat. The bad news is I'll be hauling in a Popsicle."

"Gee. So reassuring."

***

LAYNIE AND KARI SAT SIDE-BY-SIDE on a bench in the stern of the boat, lunch and a thermos at their feet, the tiller between them. Kari was impressed by how effortlessly Laynie handled both the tiller and the two sails mounted on a single mast. She used the boat's motor when they entered and left the locks and managed the small boat as though born to the sea.

"It's funny sailing here in January," Laynie confessed. "I'm usually here in July or August."

"You said you could only come once a year. Why is that?"

She shrugged. "Security concerns. It's a big deal, transitioning back to the States. Something of a risk. Many precautions. A lot of effort."

"Oh." Kari didn't know what to say.

Lord, she must live under such pressure!

"Don't know how I'll spend my next leave with Sammie gone."

"Perhaps I'll make sure to be here when you come. We could spend time with Shannon and Robbie together like we have this week?"

Laynie, quiet and remote again, nodded. "That would be nice."

And then they were in the open water. Laynie, one hand on the tiller, the other on the lines, laughed and sent them racing across the frothing waves of the sound. The little craft, like its name, skipped over the tops of the waves, barely bouncing, and Kari laughed, too.

They were flying. One with the wind.

"Sammie and I spent entire days out here," Laynie shouted. "I thought I would never sail Puget Sound again, especially in his boat."

She looked at Kari. "I guess I'm trying to thank you for suggesting this. And I'm glad you're here with me today."

It was while they were sailing in calmer waters off a little island that Kari began telling Laynie of the events of the past three years, beginning with her divorce and the letter from Brunell & Brunell. She told Laynie how she had found a journal in the garage attic of the house she had inherited from Peter Granger.

"It was written by a woman named Rose Thoresen and covered a period of two years, April 1909 to April 1911. She and her daughter, Joy, had been given a house in Denver they called Palmer House. They rescued women from forced prostitution and brought them to this house where they helped them . . . get their lives back together."

"That was very noble of them."

"Uh huh." Kari intentionally steered away from talking about Jesus. For the moment.

"The way Rose wrote about their work, about the girls and their, er, transformations, caught hold of my heart. I was captivated by Rose's words, by her life. After I finished reading her journal, I decided I wanted to see if I could find Palmer House."

When Laynie had digested those details, she went back to Rose's journal.

"So you drove all the way to Denver to see if an old house was still standing?" Laynie wrinkled her forehead. "After how long?"

"Eighty-some years? I guess I wanted to *see* the house. You know, with my own eyes, not merely see if it was standing after eighty-some years. And not only was it there, looking exactly as Rose had described it, but someone from Rose's journal still lived in it."

"What? Who?"

"A woman by the name of Shan-Rose. She was the daughter of one of the girls Rose and Joy had rescued."

"So what happened when you found this 'Palmer House' and Shan-Rose? She had to have been old when you met her, right?"

Then Kari began the long, slow telling of how Shan-Rose introduced her to the descendants of Rose's friends, how they told her about Rose and Joy, and even showed her the grave of Grant Michaels, Joy's first husband.

"Then they invited me to see Rose's homestead in RiverBend, Nebraska. Said that her husband's relatives would be glad to meet me. It felt odd, but they were so sweet, and I really did want to see Rose's homestead, so I went."

"You went? To stay with strangers?"

Kari fixed Laynie with an intent look. "My story is going to get a lot 'stranger' in a minute, Laynie, and that story is important. To us—to you and me and even Shannon and Robbie."

Laynie frowned. "If you say so. Go ahead, then."

"All right. So I went to RiverBend and I met a man named Søren Thoresen first. You might say that we 'ran into each other.' A bale of hay fell off his truck and landed on my car. I had to stay with Søren, Ilsa, and Max until it was fixed.

"They put me to work on their farm—mucking out stalls, feeding chickens, milking goats, working the garden and canning—and I stayed more than two weeks. It was nice, actually. Søren showed me their family cemetery. It goes back generations. Rose's grave was there. So was Joy's and her second husband's. Even though my visit had started out feeling uncomfortable, I was glad I'd come."

Kari sighed. "And then, at the end of the first week, a horde of family and friends showed up. A parking lot's worth of cars, RVs, and vans drove onto the farm. They set up a huge, white tent, and unloaded a bunch of chairs—like a big family reunion. It was kind of weird."

"People just showed up? How many?"

"Would you believe a couple hundred? Maybe more? Lots of them live in Nebraska and Kansas, more in Colorado. Søren said that when 'the family' heard through the grapevine that I'd found Rose's journal, they all wanted to meet me."

"No, now that's more than weird. All over an old book? I think I would have run for my life."

"I might have—except I didn't have a car and they promised to tell me more about Rose."

Laynie wrinkled up her nose. "Dunno. Seems like you are a bit obsessed with this Rose woman."

Kari smiled. "Yeah, I guess I am. Well, I should cut to the chase now. This is the important part.

"Three old gentlemen—who said they were Joy's sons from her second marriage—sat me down in Søren's living room with a few other people hanging about. Matthew, the eldest of the three, said they had some of Rose's family history to tell me, history that I didn't yet know. Of course, I wanted to hear anything and everything about Rose, so I was keen for him to tell me.

"First, he asked to see Rose's journal. When I showed it to him, he and his brothers looked it over and became very emotional. Then they agreed that it was Rose's writing and gave the journal back to me.

"Remember that I said Rose's journal ended in April 1911? Matthew began by saying that on April 12, 1911, Rose had put Joy's baby son, Edmund, and Mei-Xing's daughter, Shan-Rose, in a baby buggy and taken them for a walk in a park not far from Palmer House."

"Shan-Rose. The woman who lives at Palmer House?"

"The very same. Rose's grandson, Edmund, was about three months old. Shan-Rose was a few months older. Are you with me so far?"

"I think so. Rose, two babies in a buggy. Walk in the park."

"Yes. Then Matthew said a car full of hired thugs pulled up to the curb. He said Rose had been—"

Kari choked up and could not get the words out. "I'm sorry."

"It's all right. Take your time." But Laynie watched her, concerned.

"They said Rose had been . . . shot."

"*What?*"

A stiff gust of wind heeled the boat over and Laynie hurried to adjust the sails. For the most part, Kari stayed out of her way—and made sure the straps of her life vest were snugged.

Tight.

When the boat settled on another tack, Laynie turned to Kari. "Wait. Rose was *shot*?"

"Yes. The hired men killed her guards and shot her. Rose didn't die, of course, but the thugs took Joy's baby son, Edmund."

"Took him? No." Laynie shook her head. "How sad."

"This next part might get a little confusing. The kidnapping was really about Shan-Rose. Her paternal grandmother, Fang-Hua, had hired these men to snatch her grandson—except Shan-Rose was a girl, not a boy. The kidnappers thought Fang-Hua's grandchild was a boy and, faced with two babies, they took the boy. They took the wrong child.

"Now, the head thug, the man who reported to Fang-Hua, was a man named Dean Morgan. Apparently, there was bad blood between Dean Morgan and Joy Thoresen. Some of the girls Joy and Rose rescued 'worked' in a brothel owned by Dean Morgan. Morgan was arrested because of Joy's efforts to bring down the brothel, but later escaped from jail."

"This reads like a western soap opera," Laynie groused. "Are you certain it's important?"

"Yes, very." Kari's shoulders twitched as she laughed behind one hand.

"It had better be. Now get on with it. The suspense is killing me."

"Okay. Well, when Dean Morgan realized his men had taken the wrong child and that Fang-Hua's grandson was actually a granddaughter, he knew what Fang Hua would do to him. So he changed plans.

"He decided to run from Fang Hua and, at the same time, pay Joy back for all the trouble she had caused him. He decided to pay her back by keeping Edmund."

Laynie cursed under her breath. "Despicable!"

"It truly was. He even sent a letter to Mr. O'Dell, the Pinkerton detective and Edmund's namesake, telling him so. Mr. O'Dell searched for Morgan and for Joy and Grant's son for months. Years. But in reality, the trail went cold only days after the abduction."

Kari was quiet, grieved all over again for Joy and Grant, for Rose. For little Edmund.

"Kari, you said this is important to us? How? How is it even remotely to do with us?"

Kari wiped her eyes. "Sorry. It's easy for me to get teary-eyed when I tell this. You see, when Matthew told me all of this, everyone in the room also got teary-eyed. And then Matthew told me."

"Told you what?"

Kari sniffled. "Told me that the kidnappers had accidently snatched up Rose's journal in Edmund's baby blanket and taken it with them."

"But you found—you found it." Laynie's face froze in consternation, horror, and unthinkable inferences.

Kari nodded at her shock. "Yes, I did. Did I mention earlier that Joy's married name was *Michaels*? I had my name legally changed, and it is *your* name, too, Laynie.

"Dean Morgan took baby Edmund—Edmund *Michaels*—to New Orleans. Morgan changed his own name to Peter Granger and changed Edmund's name to Michael Granger.

"Baby Edmund was our father, Laynie. I found Rose's journal, and it led me back to our family."

She watched Laynie try to process what she'd been told, saw the many doubts and questions flashing across her face.

"But, if all this is real, then that would make this Rose and her daughter Joy . . ."

"It would make Joy our grandmother and Rose our great-grandmother."

"Is it true, Kari?"

"Yes. All of it. More than I could tell you today. Or at least more than you'd be able to take in."

They sailed on in silence for an hour or so. Kari let her reflections wander. Mostly she marveled at how God had, in his timing, arranged for her to be sitting in Sammie's little sailboat with her sister.

Laynie managed the boat out of unconscious habit, too wrapped up in her own thoughts to speak. And then Kari saw that Laynie was nosing their craft toward a small island, into a little cove.

Sand grated on the boat's hull. Laynie, on sure feet, skipped to the boat's bow and out onto the sand. She grabbed a line and started to pull the boat up onto the sandy beach.

"Give a hand? Thought we could eat lunch here."

Kari grabbed their lunch bag, clambered to the bow, and jumped off. She grabbed the line with Laynie and, together, they brought the boat farther up the beach. Laynie tied off the line on a beached log.

"You don't handle yourself too badly for a landlubber."

"Hey, I'm impressed that I haven't been puking over the side all morning."

"Ugh. Me, too. Let's eat!"

Kari pulled a blanket from the lunch bag. They spread the blanket on the sand and Kari parceled out the sandwiches and fruit.

"Tell me more about this Søren and his wife, Ilsa? Are they cousins, then?"

"Um, Ilsa isn't Søren's wife; she's his sister. But Max is his son. Søren's wife passed away years ago. And, yes. They are half-cousins, a bunch of times removed."

Laynie mouth curved into a sly, knowing smile. "Hmmm. Do I detect something in you for Søren? How old is he? Are you sweet on him?"

Kari blushed. "If you must know, we've been, oh, I don't know what to call it, exploring the possibility of marriage for a couple of years. The thing is, we're both dedicated to our lives—him to his farm in Nebraska and me to my businesses in New Orleans. We haven't figured out how to make it work."

"Well don't wait forever, Kari. Sometimes we think we have time, and then, one day, it is too late."

Kari got momentarily stuck on what Laynie said.

Have Søren and I waited too long? Is it too late for us?

"Don't go all morose on me. Tell me the rest of the story."

While they ate, Kari told Laynie about a lifetime of nightmares and panic attacks. She recounted her last nightmare—the moment *The Black* was defeated and Kari remembered. Remembered the accident that took their parents. Remembered the little sister and brother who had been stolen away.

Laynie was a good listener; still, the complexity of Kari's narration forced her to, more than once, ask Kari to stop and repeat herself.

So Kari took her time, filling in details and being transparent about her struggles, including her lifelong disgust with Christians—only to be told that their own father was not only a Christian but also a missionary.

"A missionary?" Laynie was stunned.

"It seems that you and Sammie were born in Central America," Kari told her, "one more reason it was so easy to adopt you out illegally—no American birth certificates. Apparently, not that many people here in the States even knew about you and Sammie—only the missionary organization our parents belonged to.

One letter from Marge Showman to the organization saying that Michael Granger's children had been claimed by his uncle was all it took to remove the organization's concerns about us."

Laynie chewed on a sandwich, thinking. "What did you think—no, what did you *feel*—when they told you . . . told you your father had been kidnapped as a baby?"

"You mean *our* father?"

Laynie grimaced. "Right. Wow—it's tough believing that this is sort of my story, too."

"I understand. Well, our uncles—our half-uncles from Grandma Joy's second marriage—they were so kind, so loving as I struggled to absorb what they'd told me. I didn't know they were my uncles when I met them, mind you, only that they were Joy's sons, Rose's grandsons.

"Anyway, I understand how difficult all this must be to take in, the whole, 'Oh, by the way, your real father was kidnapped and you have like a bazillion relatives in Nebraska.'"

"I never knew anything about my ancestors, where I sprang from," Laynie said in wonderment. "Now I have all these relations?"

Kari chortled. "First, I haven't even started on all our 'relations.' Second, I find it ironic, humorous even, that you are passing yourself off as a Swede."

"Why is that?"

"Well, because Rose's husband, Jan Thoresen, emigrated from Norway. You aren't Swedish, but you *are* one-eighth Norwegian—with the Scandinavian height and features to prove it."

"That explains a lot. But did you know that Dad—Gene's— grandparents are Swedish immigrants? As a child I told myself—and I realize how foolish this must sound—I told myself that I got my looks and language aptitude through them even though I was adopted."

Kari ginned. "Oh, yeah? How? By osmosis?"

"Right? Kids believe the craziest things, you know. Tell me . . . tell me again about how this Dean Morgan guy got away with kidnapping Edmund?"

"From what we've pieced together, Morgan took Daddy and the wet nurse Fang-Hua had hired for her 'grandson' by car from Denver to New Orleans. There Morgan changed his name to Peter Granger, bought a house, and began a financial consulting business.

"He was quite a gifted money manager and had many wealthy, influential clients. He never went back to a life of crime. Instead, he made a legitimate fortune and raised Daddy as his nephew.

"When he died, he left everything to Daddy, but he and Daddy had quarreled years before. Guess why? Because Daddy became a Christian—and Dean Morgan hated Christians."

Laynie's brows drew down into a frown. "Every time I turn around, someone is becoming a Christian. I am loathe to side with this despicable Dean Morgan/Peter Granger jerk, but, well . . ." She shrugged.

"Funny you should say that. I felt exactly the same. When I learned that Daddy had become a Christian, I was disgusted."

"And yet?"

"And yet I learned through Rose's journal that being a Christian is much different than I'd been led to believe. Later, I had, um, an encounter with Jesus myself, and gave my life to him."

Laynie sniffed. "Yeah, okay. Sure. But getting back to your story . . ."

"All right, getting back to my story."

Kari smiled inside. *Laynie is right where I was, Lord. And* you *know exactly how to draw her to you.*

"Uncle Matthew told me all of this in Søren and Ilsa's living room. He said that after Morgan took Edmund and left Denver, Rose, Joy, their family, and all their good friends made a pact. They vowed to never stop praying for Edmund. They agreed to never cease believing that God would bring him home—that in God 'the lost are found.' That's when I realized that Uncle Matthew was saying baby Edmund had never been found."

"So, despite all their prayers, despite all their 'believing,' he *wasn't* found."

"No, but the thing is, Laynie, even the way Daddy was raised to mock Christianity? In spite of all that, *Jesus* still found *him*. Now he is in heaven, and every individual who prayed for him will be reunited with him."

Laynie waved one hand in dismissive scorn. "That's like answering a question with another question. Christians believe in promises but when those promises don't pan out, they have another answer."

Kari studied Laynie, saw the hardness settle on her face. "Eternity is real, Laynie. When this life ends—and it always does, for every person—eternity takes over. When people limit God's answers only to this life, they miss the truth that God inhabits eternity and can fulfill his promises when and where he chooses."

Laynie's derision was evident. "Again with the circular thinking."

Kari's answer was calm but pointed. "All right, but consider this, Laynie: Edmund wasn't found—and yet *I was*. After all those years, I 'just happened' to find Rose's journal, happened to decide to look into her life and find out what became of her. Just happened to knock on the door of Palmer House after eighty-odd years—and just happened to meet people who, to that very day, were praying for Edmund's return.

"And think of this, too. I spent upwards of three hundred thousand dollars looking for you and Sammie. I used every resource available to me, all for *nothing*. The task proved to be impossible. Futile. And then you 'just happened' to board a 'random' airplane—not once, *but twice*—and happened to be assigned the seat—again, not once, but twice—next to the single individual in this world who, other than myself, would realize who you were.

"All of God's promises are true, Laynie, because he is true. One way or another, he will work those promises into reality. He is God, and he will have his way."

They cleaned up their lunch remains, packed the blanket, bag, and thermos into the boat and pushed the boat out into the water. Laynie motored them out of the cove and they, again, flew before the wind.

Kari and Laynie lapsed into companionable silence until Laynie asked, "And so you never once thought of Sammie and me during all those years you were growing up?"

"I tried to. I knew I'd forgotten something—something truly important—but each time I tried to remember, it would trigger a panic attack."

Kari tried to laugh, but it ended on a groan. "You've never lived until you've experienced a full-on panic attack."

"Then I've never lived," Laynie snorted. She did a 360° sweep around them, even though they were bobbing across the choppy waves of the inland waters, and dropped her voice. "I've been in some very tight places—tight enough that I'm surprised I *don't* have anxiety attacks, some tight corners that could easily have ended with me in a Russian interrogation room. The day I ever have such an attack? I'll be finished in my present line of work."

She shook her head. "Not that the end of my 'career' would necessarily be a bad thing. For me, anyway."

Kari studied her sister for a long while. "You know, Laynie, I think we're beginning to bond or something. That's the most open you've been with me."

Laynie faced the water in profile to Kari, and her blonde hair, much of it pulled from her ponytail by the stiff breeze, caught the light and glistened like spun gold. When she turned and smiled her acknowledgement, Kari's heart soared.

She has let her guard down. For me.

Laynie's gaze swept the water and the weather in the distance. She wasn't looking at Kari when she said, "Would you know what I meant if I said that I'm not really the 'girlfriend' type? You know. The 'girly-girly, slumber party, call-your-bestie-six-times-a day, let's do lunch and get our nails done together,' type?"

"I think I would. I might be the same way. Until I met Ruth, I had no close girlfriends. I've maybe been more comfortable alone or with men rather than with other women."

"Yes. That's what I mean."

"And?"

Laynie turned her head toward Kari but still stared out into the distance. "And it's different with you. Talking with you. Being with you feels . . . natural. Comfortable. Like it was with Sammie."

She sniffed. "In spite of our glaring differences."

Kari agreed. "I know! It's like, like there are no barriers between us. And I like that we can talk about real stuff and not get bent out of shape when we don't agree." She waggled her brows and giggled. "Even share secrets."

"But only because we're in a boat out on the ocean, far from prying eyes and eavesdropping ears!"

Kari grinned at Laynie and then sniggered. "Remember when you said, 'maybe our hearts can find a boat'? Well, check this out. Do you know what someone told me the word 'fellowship' means?"

"I'm sure you'll fill me in."

Kari snickered again. "Fellowship is like two fellows—*wait for it!*—two fellows sitting together in the same ship. Get it? Fellow-ship—and here we are. Together."

Laynie groaned. "That is . . . terrible."

But she laughed. And Kari laughed. And they laughed together.

Laynie turned the boat in a wide sweeping arc and began the long sail home.

"You know . . . you're all right, Kari Michaels," Laynie said softly.

"I love you back, Laynie Portland."

How I thank you for this precious time, Lord God. How I thank you for your faithfulness.

***

AS THE WEEK DREW TO A CLOSE, Kari felt as though she'd always known Laynie, that they had never been apart. She was welcomed in the Greene and Portland homes, loved by Kelly and Stephen's parents, accepted without reservations as 'Aunt Kari.'

Shannon and Robbie poured unexpected affection upon Kari—but Kari wondered if it was more than simple acceptance and affection. Since Polly had commented on the marked resemblance between Kari and Sammie, Kari wondered if Robbie, in particular, recognized his father in her.

On the other hand, despite the good times that week, Kelly and Sammie's loss was ever-present. Grief often overtook the Greenes and Portlands. It came in waves that crashed and receded. Crashed and receded.

Laynie fretted over Gene and Polly. "All this stress could cause Mama's MS to flare up. And Dad acts strong in front of everyone, acts so strong for Mama, but he's getting older, too, and he-he . . ."

"And he needs to be able to grieve. He's not Superman," Kari agreed. "I'm so sorry—sorry that you must go back to Sweden next week."

Another problem crept on them during the week. One morning Mary Greene burst into tears when Kari and Laynie came to fetch the children.

"I'm so concerned about Shannon," she sobbed. "She keeps having bad dreams, and she wakes up screaming in the night. And Robbie? If Shannon wakes up, we calm her and she goes back to sleep, but Robbie does not. He cries and cries. All night.

"I don't know if I can do this," she whispered.

"I will pray for you, Mary," Kari promised. "Hopefully the children will settle in soon."

***

KARI HAD STAYED LONGER than she'd planned, knowing she would pay the price when she returned home. She stayed until the day Laynie's flight left for Stockholm.

"I've booked my flight on the same day. I can drive us to the airport," Kari offered.

Laynie nodded but said nothing. Kari was saddened to see the curtains come down upon Laynie's eyes, as though she were mentally preparing to return to her other life and a role she regretted.

They said their goodbyes to Gene and Polly and drove to the Greenes to bid the children farewell.

"Goodbye, Shannon," Kari whispered. "Be a good girl for Grandma Mary, okay?"

"Where are you going, Aunt Kari?" Shannon's eyes were wide with alarm.

"Aunt Laynie and I need to go home now, but I'll come back for a weekend in about a month."

Shannon looked from Kari to Laynie and back. "No! I don't want you to go home!"

Kari hugged her close. "You may call me on the telephone anytime you like, okay?"

But Shannon pushed herself out of Kari's embrace and stomped her foot. "No! I don't want you to go!"

When Laynie and Kari reached for the door, Shannon threw herself on the floor screaming and kicking. Robbie, taking his cue from Shannon, screwed up his face. His sobbing wails, even around one finger in his mouth, followed Laynie and Kari down the walkway to the car.

"This is so hard," Kari whispered.

"I know," Laynie answered. "I know."

Kari pulled up to the departure curb for Laynie's airline.

"You'll visit the children like you promised Shannon?" Laynie asked.

"I hope to fly in once a month. You have my card?"

"Yes—for the third time. And you have mine. But don't call unless you really need to. Send letters. They will reach me through back channels."

Laynie nodded and opened the door.

"Wait! Laynie—"

And then their arms were around each other. Kari sobbed into Laynie's shoulder but Laynie showed no emotion except to grip Kari as tightly as Kari gripped her.

"Be safe, little sister," Kari sniffed. "I've only just found you."

Something sad—something wounded?—flickered across Laynie's face.

"I'll do my best."

"If-if you need him, the Lord will hear you call on him, Laynie."

Laynie nodded once and climbed from the car.

❧ ✳ ☙

CHAPTER 31

K ari tried to throw herself back into her work, but it was obvious to those who knew her best that she was distracted. Preoccupied. "Anything of note happen in the last ten days?" Kari asked Scarlett.

Scarlett launched into a detailed account, only to pause midway when she saw Kari staring into space.

"Kari?"

"Yes? Oh. I apologize."

Scarlett pressed her lips together. "Nothing of note, really. All is well."

"And Granger Mills? How was your last visit?"

"I think things are going to smooth out soon. The employees are pleased with the transparent wage scale. They know the piece rate they should be earning and, for many of them, it means a wage increase."

"Good." Kari lapsed into silence again.

"I can report something of a personal note."

"Yes?"

"Cadie's aunt passed away unexpectedly. Well, of course, she's been ill for a few years, but she died in her sleep last week. Cadie and her sister were not prepared."

"I am sorry to hear that. Did we send flowers?"

"Bettina took care of it."

Kari's attention sharpened. "Do you think we'll lose Cadie, now that she doesn't need a job close to her aunt's house?"

"I sure hope not. We need her there. Of course, she's making a salary now that is more in line with her education and previous experience."

"Double check that, would you, Scarlett? I want Cadie Bryant to remain a Michaels Enterprises manager. She's an asset we can't afford to lose."

Scarlett nodded and left Kari's office. Kari fingered the card on her desk, the one Laynie had pressed into her hand on that last day.

I don't have a direct line in Stockholm, Kari. It's . . . complicated. But if you call this number and leave a message, I'll get back to you as soon as I can. And I'll be sure to check in from my end from time to time.

Kari looked at the card. "Marstead International," Kari mouthed.

She had the number memorized.

***

"SØREN? I HAVE SOMETHING TO TELL YOU. Something immense." Kari had been home a week and had not yet had the time or heart to tell him.

I haven't had time to eat. If it weren't for Bettina and Azalea, I would probably have starved by now.

He was concerned. "What is it, Kari?"

"We-we found Elaine and Samuel."

Silence on the other end and then, "Are you certain?"

Kari poured out everything to him and, while she did so, grieved again for Samuel, the brother she had lost, not once, but twice.

"I am so sorry, Kari. And he left two children?"

"Shannon and Robbie. Kelly's parents will raise them. And, Søren! Sammie—Stephen—and his wife, Kelly, were Christians. That is the only thing making his loss bearable."

"I understand—and completely agree. What about Elaine? Er, Laynie?"

"We spent some wonderful time together, Søren. And she remembered me, if only a little. She said she remembered me as *Care* and that I had called her Laynie. She remembered me screaming for them not to take her and Sammie away."

Søren sucked in his breath. "That is remarkable. It all—the entire thing—is remarkable. Her sitting next to Ruth on the plane? That was a miracle."

"Yes. It surely was."

***

MID-FEBRUARY, SOONER THAN SHE'D PLANNED, Kari flew into Seattle and spent a short forty-eight hours with Shannon and Robbie. Bill and Mary apologized for not asking her to stay in their home.

"With a live-in nanny and the children, we don't have a bed to spare."

Kari was distressed to see new lines in Mary's plump face. "It's all right. Gene and Polly are delighted that I'll be staying with them. I'll come fetch the children early tomorrow and give you, Bill, and your nanny a much-needed break. How does that sound?"

"We will appreciate it, Kari. Frankly, we're all exhausted."

"Is Shannon still having nightmares?"

"Yes, and they are awful. I wish we could separate the children at night, for once Shannon starts screaming, Robbie wakes up, too, and will be up, crying his heart out, for hours."

Since Kari was staying with the Portlands, she did not witness the night episodes Mary Greene described. Instead, when she arrived, the children rushed to her and covered her with sweet kisses and hugs.

Over the weekend, Robbie even learned to say "Aunt Care." He would climb up in her lap and, as he had before, stare into her face as though searching for something and then, with a gentle hand, pat her cheek.

It was when Kari said goodbye Sunday afternoon that she witnessed the behavior Mary said lasted for hours on end each night.

As soon as Shannon realized Kari was leaving, she threw herself into a tantrum. To Kari's dismay, when she tried to assure Shannon that she would be coming back in a month, Shannon bit her hand.

"Ow! Shannon! I can't believe you *bit* me!"

"I hate you! I hate you, Aunt Kari! Go 'way!"

Shannon ran for the stairs, sobbing.

And Robbie crumpled onto the floor and could not be consoled.

Kari stared at Mary. "Is this what it's like every night?"

Mary looked away, unshed tears glistening on her lashes. "And worse."

***

KARI WAS DEEPLY ASLEEP WHEN THE PHONE rang at three in the morning. She had been back in New Orleans only a week.

She fumbled for the receiver. "Hello?"

"Kari, it's Bill Greene. I apologize for calling in the middle of the night."

Kari found her alarm clock. *It's midnight in Seattle.*

"Don't give it another thought. What can I do?"

And then the fog of sleep lifted a little and she heard hysterical screaming in the background.

Shannon.

"The thing is, Kari, we're at the end of our rope. We've talked it over, Mary and I, and we've spoken to Gene and Polly, too. We are agreed . . . we think you should take the children."

Kari's mind couldn't process the words. "I'm sorry—*what?*"

"I'm sorry, too, Kari, but it's become urgent. Mary will have a complete collapse if the children are not removed from our home. Soon."

When Kari didn't immediately respond, Bill added, "Don . . . wants to take the kids. We all know it's too much for Talia—particularly with a four-week-old baby! But Talia is beginning to think it would be better for Shannon and Robbie to live with them—she's seen what it's doing to her mother.

"No. That's not a good idea."

For more than one reason!

"But Don is pressing us, Kari. Please. You are as much Shannon and Robbie's aunt as Talia is, as Laynie is. You're young. And we think you can help them—they see Sammie in you, Kari. And you are all Shannon talks about anymore."

"She talks about me?"

"She talks to herself, Kari, and says things like, 'Aunt Kari loves us. She is coming back soon.' But then she gets angry and says, 'Aunt Kari doesn't love us. She's gone away like Mommy and Daddy.'"

"O dear Jesus! Oh, our poor girl."

"We are deadly serious, Kari. If you don't take them, I don't know how much more we can take or how long we can hold out against Don. We love Shannon and Robbie with all of our hearts, but—"

His voice broke. "Please say you'll take them, Kari."

Kari climbed from her bed. "I will, Bill."

She wiped the sleep from her eyes. "I-I'll be there sometime tomorrow. And please . . . tell Shannon that Aunt Kari loves her. Tell her I am coming."

***

GENE AND POLLY WERE WAITING with Bill and Mary when Kari's rental pulled up in the Greenes' driveway. Mary had the nanny lift Robbie up to the window. His arms and legs pumped and waved when he caught sight of Kari. Shannon was already pulling open the front door.

They know me. They are happy to see me, Kari realized. *And I am overjoyed to see them.*

With Robbie ensconced in her lap, Shannon at her knee, and both sets of grandparents looking on, Kari talked one-on-one with Shannon.

I need to remember that Shannon is almost five. She's learning the hard way that words have real meaning.

"Shannon, honey. I need to ask you a question, a really important question."

Shannon gave Kari her most grave look, and the nod with which she replied, made her pigtails shake. "Okay, Aunt Kari."

"Auntkareeeee!" Robbie echoed. He jounced in Kari's lap until she thought her left kidney would burst.

She snugged him to her side and held him tight so he couldn't jump and asked, "Shannon, would you like to come and live with me?"

Shannon's lower lip began to tremble. "Wouldn't Robbie come, too?"

"Well, of course he would."

"Will you ever go away?"

"No, sweetheart. If you come live with me, the three of us, you, me, and Robbie, will live in my house together. I will go to work each day, but I will come home every night."

"Promise?"

Kari bit her lip. *This is it, Kari. There's no going back from here. And you know what else it means, what it implies.*

She nodded, answering her own question.

"I promise, Shannon. You and Robbie will live with me, and I will never go away."

"Okay."

After the nanny took the children off to play, Kari looked at the Portlands and Greenes. "I know this has to be very hard for you, but if you are all in agreement, I will have my assistant book a flight for tomorrow."

Four sadder adults Kari had never seen.

"We realize we are asking a lot of you, Kari," Gene murmured. "We . . . you've never had children. It will take more out of you than you imagine."

Kari wondered how it could possibly be more than her imagination was already painting it. Her expression must have reflected her doubts.

"The Lord will never leave you, Kari. He will be the Helper you need. Just . . . do you promise to love them?"

"I-I already do."

"You see, they are mine and Gene's only grandchildren," Polly added in a whisper. "All we have left of Stephen. Could you . . . could you bring them to see us once in a while?"

Bill and Mary added their hopes to Polly's request with nods.

"Of course. As often as I can. And I'll have them call you—all of you—regularly."

Mary wiped her eyes. "All right, then. I will start gathering up their things."

"I will help you, dear." Bill took her hand and they went up the stairs together.

Kari sat thinking of how she would manage two children on the airplane. Where they would sleep when they arrived home. How she would find a nanny to care for the kids while she worked.

"Kari."

"Yes?"

Polly crooked her hand at her. "Come here, child. I want to say something to you."

"All right."

Kari knelt on the floor next to Polly's wheelchair. Polly grasped her husband's hand. With her other hand she caressed Kari's hair and then her face, following the contours of her cheek and jaw with gentle fingers.

"You look very much like our Stephen, you know. Like Laynie's Sammie. I knew in my heart you were his and Laynie's sister the moment I laid eyes on you."

Kari didn't know what to say. Moisture was gathering in her eyes and she tried to blink it back.

"Gene and I, we know you lost your mama and daddy a long time ago, Kari. We hope you won't take 'fense, but we feel, well, we feel that the sister of our b'loved son and daughter should, by rights, be our b'loved child, too.

"You are Stephen and Laynie's blood, so we consider you to be ours now. Will you . . . would you allow us to call you our daughter, Kari? Will you allow us the great honor of being mama and daddy to you?"

Gene and Polly leaned toward Kari with loving expectation.

O Lord, I did not expect this! This wonderful, this immense blessing!

"I . . . yes. Oh, yes!"

Kari buried her face in Polly's lap and wept.

She wept for joy.

CHAPTER 32

Toller and Azalea met Kari at the airport in Toller's old station wagon. While Toller fetched their luggage, Azalea tried to introduce herself to Shannon and Robbie.

They were having none of her or anyone else.

It had been a long trip made more difficult by Kari's inexperience with children and the paraphernalia they required. Kari's fellow passengers had stared daggers at her when Robbie wailed for thirty minutes nonstop after takeoff.

The flight had *started* well: Kari had put the tray table down and given Shannon the new coloring book Mary had slipped into her knapsack. Then Robbie had grabbed a crayon and shoved it into his mouth—which elicited a shout of rage from Shannon, the forcible removal of crayon pieces from Robbie's mouth by Kari, and the thirty-minute screaming fit on Robbie's part.

Kari had fixed a bottle to soothe him; Robbie had pushed it away. And as soon as Kari had returned the bottle to his diaper bag, he had reached for it, throwing his weight against Kari's tired arms.

Screaming the entire time.

I'd dose your bottle with knockout drops if it wouldn't land me in prison, mister, she had warned him silently.

Now, in the midst of the New Orleans airport, surrounded by crowds and confronted by two more strangers, Shannon clung to Kari's leg and Robbie tightened his death-grip on her neck.

"Please take us home," Kari begged.

At Kari's request, Azalea had purchased a crib and a twin bed and Toller had set them up in Kari's room. The bed and crib were made up with fresh linens—Shannon's bed in a princess theme, Robbie's in a Pooh Bear print.

Kari put Robbie down and let go of Shannon's hand. The children stared round the room with sullen faces.

"Shannon, do you know what I made this morning?" Azalea asked.

Shannon ignored her and fingered the Tinkerbell pillow on her new bed.

Azalea went on as though Shannon had answered her. "Well, now, I made some cookies, I did. Chocolate chip cookies and sugar cookies,"

Robbie pulled a finger from his mouth. "Tookie."

"The cookies are downstairs in the kitchen in the cookie jar. And I have a fresh gallon of milk in the refrigerator."

Shannon glanced at Azalea and back to Tinkerbell.

Robbie looked at Kari.

"Tookie."

Kari smiled a weary smile.

"Who would like to go with me downstairs and find the cookie jar?" Azalea asked.

Robbie looked to Kari again.

She nodded. "If you'd like a cookie, go with Azalea."

He took a few steps toward Azalea and glanced back.

"It's okay, Robbie," Kari said quietly. "We're home now."

Home. Kari thought with longing of the deep garden tub in her bathroom.

"Hey, Shannon. Want to see my bathtub?"

Robbie went downstairs with Azalea, and Shannon, enthralled with Kari's wading-pool-sized tub, begged for a bubble bath. Somehow, the afternoon and evening passed and Kari began to relax.

Azalea stayed longer than usual, cleaning up after a late supper. "I have those phone numbers you asked for, Miss Kari," she said as she prepared to leave.

"Nanny numbers?"

"Yes'm. Three, but I think you only need the one. Mrs. Birch. 'Bout your age, maybe a little older, raised three children of her own, and still has lots of energy left in her."

"You know her?"

"Went to school with Toller, she did."

"Thank you, Azalea. For everything."

"You have a mighty big row to hoe, Miss Kari, but don't you worry. We'll be 'round to help out, Toller and I."

The next evening, Kari placed the call she had been dreading.

"Søren?" Kari's hands on the phone shook. "This is Kari. I-I need to tell you something."

Is this how dreams die, Lord?

***

IT WAS THE DEAD OF NIGHT, and Robbie was awake.

Again.

Crying and inconsolable.

Night after night, he repeated the pattern Bill and Mary had described. Not much had changed since the children's move to New Orleans.

Not with Robbie anyway.

Kari had thought having the children sleep in her room until they settled in would ease the transition to her unfamiliar house. She also hoped to help Shannon wake up quickly whenever a nightmare came.

So far, that part of her plan had helped, if only a little.

Whenever Shannon began to whimper in the dark, Kari would rise and gently shake her. As soon as she opened her eyes and saw Kari, she would calm and, within minutes, go back to sleep.

Robbie was another story. Night after night, at two in the morning—like clockwork—he woke up. Sobbing. Shrieking.

I may be a lot younger than the Greenes, but after two weeks of this? I'm wiped out.

"Your little sleep clock is broken, my sweet Robbie," Kari whispered. "Let's ask Jesus to fix it."

As Kari prayed over him, she smoothed his silky hair and attempted to snug his blanket around him. He resisted, kicking the blanket and her hands away, wailing harder. Louder.

She lifted him from his crib, placed him against her shoulder and, with the blanket loose about him, descended the dark stairs. After many nights of this, Kari knew the best place to walk with him was her office.

She paced the carpet between her desk and the window. "You're having such a tough time, aren't you, little man?" Kari cooed. "But you're getting used to me, right? Getting used to your new home? Soon you'll get past this. I know you will."

She hoped he was adjusting, if only a tiny bit.

Please, Robbie. You just have to.

And then he sobbed softly on her shoulder rather than struggling against her and throwing himself to the floor in a screaming fit as he had many times before.

As Kari walked, she sang. She stroked his back and breathed kisses onto his chubby neck. After a while, she resorted to a rhythmic patting on his bottom that seemed to soothe him.

Kari put on a good face at work and at home, but she was fearful of the steep wall of compounding problems mounting against her.

I don't get enough sleep. When I'm at the office, I'm thinking of Shannon and Robbie. I'm not keeping up. And when I'm here, I feel helpless. Inadequate.

As Azalea had suggested, Kari had liked Mrs. Birch and hired her right way. She came early in the day and stayed with the children while Kari worked. If Kari stayed later than she'd intended, Azalea kept the children while she fixed dinner.

They liked Mrs. Birch and Azalea well enough, but . . .

Even though the children like the nanny and Azalea is worth her weight in gold, I can't keep my mind on my work. Things are slipping through the cracks. Scarlett is flagging under the load, drowning in responsibility, and I'm not helping her enough.

Kari walked faster.

Her breathing grew ragged, anxious.

Did Peter Granger ever walk my father in this very room? Did he ever calm Daddy's fears?

The questions came out of nowhere, blindsiding her. An image of her father as a bereft infant flooded Kari's mind—an infant weeping for his mother.

With no warning, a single sob broke from her mouth. Kari was astonished at how raw her pain was.

Robbie ceased his pitiful mewling and pushed himself up to look at Kari. In the lamplight from Kari's desk, he considered her with sober eyes.

"I'm sorry, little man." Kari wiped her eyes and sniffed.

Robbie, still with serious face, placed one fat hand upon Kari's cheek and patted it. Once. Twice.

A wail of anguish burst from Kari's mouth.

All I can think is that I'm not enough. Not good enough, not strong enough, not 'present' enough for these children. Even my love is not enough! I'm so afraid I will let them down!

"O Robbie! I am a poor substitute for your mama! I'm so sad your daddy can't be here! I'm so sorry, little man. O Jesus, please help me. Please help me to help these precious little ones!"

Robbie laid his head over her shoulder again. Kari wrapped her arms about him and wept against his blanketed back.

Lord! I don't know if I can do this! Please help me. Show me what to do.

Dawn was rising. Kari didn't know how long she had walked, only that she had cried herself out and Robbie had, too. He was fast asleep, snuggled against her chest, the inevitable finger in his mouth.

Kari's arms about Robbie were wooden, frozen in place, her legs and feet lead weights. She dragged herself to the window and rested bleary eyes on the garden where her beloved tree had bowed its majestic branches to the ground.

The garden will never be the same. I made them leave the remains of the trunk, but my beautiful tree—and all its majesty—is gone and has left such a void.

No matter what I do, another will not grow here—not in my lifetime.
Kari blinked.

They's a storm comin'.
Miss Em's words came rolling back upon Kari.

And in the dream, he showed me a big ol' tree, an old live oak, a'bending and twisting in the wind o' that storm until, with a thunderous crack, it split.

Kari gasped.

Well, child, at first I thought it was split in two pieces. Then the wind died away and I saw, no, it was split in three pieces. And the Lord, he say to me, 'Tell Kari when that storm comes, it will break your tree—but she is not to give in to despair.'

He say that two times: 'Tell Kari: You are not to give in to despair.'

Then he say it all again. 'Tell Kari: They's a storm comin' and it will break your tree, but it will not die. Two branches will grow out of one piece of that broken trunk. Your tree will live, and all will be well.'

Kari's knees buckled and she dropped to the carpet, Robbie still clutched in her arms.

"A trunk broken into three pieces! Me! Laynie! Sammie! And two branches will grow out of one piece of that broken trunk . . .

"O God! O God! You have saved these two little branches, Shannon and Robbie, to continue our line. Our tree. Our tree will live!"

Kari curled on the floor, Robbie's breath warm and steady against her neck.

Our tree will live. Yes. It will.

Robbie slept and Kari slept, Miss Em's words washing her heart.

Tell Kari: You are not to give in to despair.

As Kari slept, her heart settled.

All will be well.

CHAPTER 33

Kari looked around Oskar's rec room, seeing with new eyes the tiny table and chairs. She took in the toys and games he and Melanie provided for their grandchildren.

Funny how a month with two tiny tyrants can change a perspective forever.

"You wanted to talk to me, Kari?" Oskar was concerned, Kari could tell.

"I'm sure Scarlett has mentioned how . . . distracted I am."

"No one can fault you, Kari. You found a long-lost sister. You lost a brother before you could know him. And now you are raising his children. That's a tremendous amount of change. A lot to adjust to."

"I . . . yes, it is. Thank you for not judging me."

"Judging you? I admire you more than you know."

Kari winced under the unexpected praise. "I don't know. I'm not doing a good job at the office. Or at home."

"It is a dilemma that frustrates every working mom."

Kari frowned. *Did he just call me a mom?*

Oskar was still talking, but Kari's attention was fixed on that one word: *mom.*

I wanted a home. A family. David promised me both—and broke his promise and our wedding vows.

And Søren. He talked about us having babies . . . but I'm going on forty-two. Too late for babies, in all practicality.

Kari studied the little table and its miniature chairs.

Huh. So am I a mom now?

"Kari?"

"What? Sorry."

"I was saying, perhaps it's time to take on more help at the office, time to give some of your responsibilities to another pair of capable hands."

Kari put her elbows on the table, her chin on her palms. "So, what then? Would I take less of a management role? Work only part-time?"

"Would that be so terrible? Haven't you proven to yourself and the world that you are the head and heart of Michaels Enterprises? That you are more than capable of guiding and growing your conglomerate?

"If you were to, say, step away a bit more, wouldn't you still be able to check up on how your people are managing and know for yourself the state of things?"

Oskar looked with frank fondness on Kari. "Take some time to pray about what to do, won't you?"

"Yes, I will. Thank you, Oskar."

"Good. I'll be praying also."

***

MORE WEEKS CRAWLED BY. Shannon's nightmares were becoming less frequent.

And Robbie had actually slept the night through. Once.

Miracles are real, Lord, Kari sighed. *I'm a believer now!*

On the other hand, Kari's internal clock—having grown accustomed to mid-sleep interruptions—woke her in the night and kept her up for hours. She used the time to catch up on the pile of back work that, despite her efforts, was morphing into a mountain.

After one such sleep-deprived night, Kari slept late and missed her morning devotions. She hustled the children into their clothes, got them downstairs to the breakfast Azalea was making, met Mrs. Birch at the door, and dragged herself into Michaels Enterprises.

She nodded and smiled at those who greeted her, but went directly to her office. She closed the door behind herself and leaned on it.

Lord, I can't go on like this. I need you. And I need answers.

Scarlett and Bettina knew that when Kari's door was closed she was not to be disturbed. Kari sat down at her desk, folded her hands upon its surface, and leaned her forehead upon her hands.

Father, if ever I have required your guidance, it is today. I promised to raise Shannon and Robbie, to do my very best. For their sake—for my sake—I need to know how to do that.

She prayed for Shannon. She prayed for Robbie. She prayed for the Greenes and the Portlands. She prayed for Laynie.

Then she was praying for Søren, for Max, for Ilsa.

I have a house in RiverBend.

I have a house in RiverBend, and I haven't even seen it—not since the contractor laid the foundation. It is sitting empty.

What a waste.

"Lord," Kari whispered, "what I need—what I would dearly appreciate—is a solution. Father, you can do anything! If it pleases you, could you just make it fall into my lap? Please?"

Since Kari's door was closed, she was surprised to hear a timid knock.

"Oh, well. Whenever you're ready, Lord." Kari sat up and blotted her face.

"Come in."

Bettina peeked her head around the edge of the door. "I apologize, Miss Michaels. Cadie Bryant is here. She . . . she is insistent upon seeing you."

"Cadie!" Kari got up. "Thank you, Bettina. Please send her in."

With a somewhat sheepish greeting, Cadie said. "I know you weren't expecting me, Miss Michaels. Thank you for seeing me anyway."

"Actually, I'm delighted, Cadie, but I was sorry to hear about your aunt."

"You are so kind. We miss her terribly, but at the same time? My sister and I are free to live our lives again."

Kari nodded. "And how goes The Battle of Granger Mills?"

Cadie smiled, and Kari saw new confidence in the woman—in the glow on her high, ebony cheekbones, in her bright grin. Kari motioned her to a chair and they sat together.

"The battle? I believe we have routed the enemy and the battle is won, Miss Michaels. We hired a new comptroller last month—a wise and experienced gentleman. I trained him myself and know he will work out well."

"Trained him? But isn't Comptroller *your* job?"

Cadie grinned again, and Kari did not miss the mischievous twitch of one shoulder. "I, well, I was actually a little bored, Miss Michaels." She opened both hands wide. "You asked how the battle goes, but I'm wondering if you need another lieutenant to help win the war?"

The wheels in Kari's head started turning slowly, but within seconds, they were moving along at a good clip.

"Do you mean to tell me that you quit your job at Granger Mills and came here hoping for a new one?"

Cadie answered Kari's question without flinching. "I would prefer something with a little more, um, 'scope for imagination' than a textile mill and sewing shop."

Kari bit back a snicker at the reference to *Anne of Green Gables*. "And you think Michaels Enterprises would provide more, er, scope for imagination?"

One of Cadie's long legs bounced. She shifted in her seat and buzzed with pent-up energy. "I've been researching your holdings, Miss Michaels. In manufacturing alone, you are diversified in so many interesting directions! Durable medical equipment and surgical implement manufacturing; electronics, semiconductors, lighting; tools and hardware. Textiles, of course. And it's not solely your manufacturing side that intrigues me."

She looked Kari in the face. "What I'm really saying is that I want to work for *you*. With you. What I saw last April at Granger Mills? I want to learn how to lead like that."

Cadie jutted her chin as she made her pitch. "I'm willing to work wherever in your organization you have a need."

"I see." Kari sat back and gave free rein to the possibilities.

This woman has the best grasp on facts and figures I've encountered. She's brilliant. Her education and experience are top notch. She is loyal and ethical.

Another quality rose in Kari' mind. *And she's certainly courageous. Quitting her job and showing up here?*

And then it hit her: *Father, you can do anything! If it pleases you, could you just make it fall into my lap? Please?*

"Oh, wow."

Kari wasn't aware she'd spoken aloud until Cadie fidgeted.

"I meant no disrespect, Miss Michaels."

Kari laughed softly. "I saw none, Cadie. I was, um, thinking aloud." She drummed her fingers on the arm of her chair and then reached a decision.

"Would you mind following me?"

Kari swept out of her office without waiting for an answer. She knew Cadie would be right behind her.

Kari tapped on Scarlett's door. "Have a minute?"

"Sure! My place or yours?"

"Here is good." She waved Cadie in, "Look who came knocking a minute ago."

"Good to see you, Cadie."

Scarlett was not as surprised at Cadie's unannounced visit as Kari expected her to be. Scarlett nodded in Cadie's direction and looked back to Kari.

"Yes?"

Kari's eyes narrowed.

Scarlett has been visiting Granger Mills every other week for months.

"You knew she was coming here today."

Scarlett smiled. "Not today. Just the 'coming here' part."

"Okay, obviously you've been giving this some thought. What are you thinking?"

"I'm thinking Cadie and her skills are what we need right now."

Kari marched to Scarlett's desk, put her hands on it, leaned toward her with a menacing air, and whispered, "Are you angling for another bonus, Miss Brunell?"

"A raise would be more appreciated," Scarlett whispered back.

"You're planning on Cadie taking the load off me?"

"I'm planning on Cadie taking the load off *me*—where it's been for weeks now."

"Are you complaining, Miss Brunell?"

"I never complain, ma'am. I find solutions."

So smug!

"Huh. You're thinking we bring her on board and divide the work in thirds?"

"Fifths would be better. Two-fifths me, two-fifths Cadie, *one-fifth* you."

"I believe you are conspiring with Oskar."

"Certainly."

"I see."

"You're welcome."

"Harrumph."

Kari stood up and spoke at her regular volume. "And furthermore, Miss Brunell, I'm going to dock two weeks from your paycheck for collusion and insubordination."

"*As you wish*, Miss Michaels."

"My left foot!"

Scarlett grinned and Kari pivoted.

"Cadie, come this way, please."

Kari marched about ten feet down the hallway and threw open the door of an empty office. "When can you start?"

***

FIVE WEEKS LATER, at her weekly Monday morning meeting, Kari looked over her staff. Her heart was at peace.

This is going to work, Lord. You are making a way.

"As you all know, I've had to cut back on my schedule since my niece and nephew came to live with me. The loss of their parents and the move here, away from their grandparents, has been very difficult for them.

"Many of you, Scarlett and Bettina most of all, have had to shoulder the responsibilities I let slide. With Cadie joining us, things are smoothing out. It is because this office is running so well, that I have the confidence to announce . . . that I intend to scale down my role with Michaels Enterprises even further. To that end, I will be limiting my in-office schedule to a few days a month. Effective immediately."

A round of murmured comments answered Kari. Scarlett, Bettina, and Cadie, who had already been told of Kari's decision, said nothing, but they nodded.

Kari held up her hand. "That is not to say that I will be unavailable. I will attend, via conference call, weekly staff meetings when I am out of the office and keep in close contact with my management team. Once every quarter I will spend a week in the office. And Mr. Oskar Brunell will join the staff as a part-time employee at *one-half* time—that's twenty hours a week, four hours a day, five days a week."

She glared at where he sat at the end of the table. "Anyone willing to attest to Mr. Brunell's being here more than twenty hours in any given week will earn the bonus of their choice: a two-hundred-dollar gift card or a day off—on the house."

"I'll see your two hundred dollars and raise you fifty!" Oskar growled.

The laughter and good will echoing around the room did a lot to cheer Kari.

It's still not easy letting go, Lord, but I will adjust. I'm confident in the people you've given me. Thank you.

You said you had "something else" for me? Well, I'm pushing into it.

Later, Kari and Oskar spoke alone in her office.

"What are your plans, Kari? What do you have in mind?"

"It will take me a few weeks to prepare, but I want to go home, Oskar, home to my roots on the prairie. It is peaceful there. I will have the time— and we will have the open spaces—for these children to heal and for us to become a family.

"I'll need a nanny for the few days I'm in the office, but I'll always bring the children back and forth from Nebraska to Louisiana with me."

Oskar studied Kari. "You're going to Søren, aren't you?"

Kari's smile was faint. "If he will have me. If he is willing to accept my brother's children—*my* children—as his own and help me give them an intact family."

She laughed a little. "My children. Who would have thought?"

❧ ✳ ☙

ℰHAPTER 34

MAY

T hey arrived at her house in RiverBend early in the evening, when dusk was overspreading the prairie. Kari parked the rental car in the empty garage and, leaving the children buckled into their seats, unloaded and hauled their luggage into the house. Then she carried Robbie and led Shannon by the hand inside.

The interior designer Kari had hired had furnished the house with the basics and stocked the cupboards and fridge. Kari had selected a few special or needed things from her house on Marlow Avenue and had them shipped. They would arrive in due time.

It took her an hour to put linens on Robbie's crib and Shannon's bed, unpack their bags, find their PJs, and fix the children something to eat.

I will sorely miss Azalea, she realized, as she rooted through the cupboards, familiarizing herself with what was there.

After Shannon and Robbie were fed, she bathed them and bedded them down. They were exhausted.

Robbie was particularly fussy, so she wrapped him in his favorite blanket and, perched on the edge of Shannon's bed, she rocked him, singing softly until his whimpering changed to relaxed, even breathing. Shannon slipped off, too.

By the time she tucked Robbie into his crib, it was fully dark, and a large moon was rising in the east.

Kari poured herself a cup of coffee and wandered onto the covered porch. She sat down, weary in heart and body. *Lord, thank you for getting us here safely. I pray you guide me over the next few days. If I didn't think this was what you were telling me to do, I'd have to say I was nuts.*

From where she sat, Rose and Jan's house, off to the left, was in full view. She'd planned her own house's location that way, so that she could always see the little house's profile.

She stared hard across the creek and Søren's fields. A few lights glimmered in the windows of the farmhouse.

Is he still up? Or has he gone to bed? Kari wondered. *Will he have noticed the lights over here?*

As weary as she was, Kari was restless. She left the remains of her coffee on the railing and wandered into the yard. Tonight's moon cast a glow upon the land. She had no difficulties picking her way toward Rose's house. She stepped up onto the wide porch Jan had built Rose and sat upon the old bench facing east.

This. This was the view Rose had of Jan's land. Did she yearn for the man who lived in that farmhouse as I am yearning this night?

A breeze skittered across the porch, and she listened to the prairie's night sounds: the sweep of an owl's wings as he hunted the fields, a coyote's call and, in the distance, the deep low of a cow.

It is so peaceful here, Lord.

Her eyes followed the long stretch of lawn that led away from Søren's house, that ran up the sloping hill and into the aging apple orchard. Kari knew that the orchard hid the Thoresen family plot.

Kari could not see the little cemetery, screened as it was by the trees and the night, but nearly three long years ago, she had often visited the Thoresen graves. Much of each visit had been spent kneeling near the grave of her great-grandmother.

Thinking.

Seeking God's guidance.

Hoping for answers.

Long ago, Rose stared across this same creek. She sat where I am sitting and studied these very same fields, that same barn, that house, and the origins of the Thoresens' apple orchard.

More than one hundred years ago, she was a stranger in this land, as I am. She had to have felt lost and afraid many times, Father. Did she ever question your wisdom and direction?

Did she wonder if the man who lived in that house was your provision for her? As I am wondering?

Lord, could this finally be our time?

Eventually, Kari began to nod off. She shook herself awake and walked back to her house.

As she stepped up onto her own porch, a shadow shifted. She jumped, and Søren moved into the moonlight.

"I didn't mean to frighten you, Kari."

"I-I wasn't expecting you."

"We've seen all the activity over here the past week—a moving van, furniture being hauled inside, a landscaper clearing up the lot, laying sod, planting flowers. And I saw the lights over here this evening when you arrived."

He shrugged. "I waited until I figured you had the children in bed before I walked over. You did bring them, didn't you?"

"Yes. I-I won't leave them with anyone except the nanny, and only for a few hours at a time. They are a little fragile."

"I hope it's okay that I came?"

"Of course. I mean . . . well, of course it is."

He grunted softly and said nothing.

He is waiting for me to make the first move.

Well, all right then.

"Søren, I . . . have cut my involvement with Michaels Enterprises to the bone. I will take the children there once a month for a few days, a week once a quarter. The rest of the time I, that is we, will be living here."

"Living here?" He was curious.

"Yes. Shannon and Robbie need a full-time mother. A place where they can roam and play outdoors. Cousins."

Kari couldn't see Søren's face in the porch's shadows. Couldn't see his expression.

"So, this is a permanent move?" He sounded aloof, skeptical.

Kari gave him the best answer she could.

"I hope so."

***

IT WAS STILL EARLY. Kari woke to a light tapping on her front door. She was groggy, but sat up and checked the children—they were sleeping, their breathing regular and deep. She pulled on a robe, shuffled to the door, and opened it as quietly as she could manage.

"Max!" She almost forgot to whisper.

"Hi, Kari." He hugged her and she wrapped her arms about him, amazed that his head lay on her heart.

"You've grown."

"Yeah. Gonna be as tall as Papa." He had taken Kari's cue and spoke in a low whisper. He looked past her into the house. "Are your niece and nephew still sleeping?"

"Well, it *is* only six in the morning."

"Yeah?"

Kari snickered. The day began at four in his house.

"Oh, hey." Max let go of Kari and stared behind her.

Kari turned. Robbie stood there in his little sleeper pajamas, the kind with attached footies and rubber soles, a zipper up the front. He rubbed his eyes, looked from Kari to Max, and pointed at him.

Kari scooped him up. "Good morning, my sweet Robbie. This is your cousin, Max."

Max waved. "Hey, Robbie."

Robbie grinned—and buried his head in Kari's neck.

"He likes you, Max, but he plays shy at first. He'll get used to you."

"Aunt Kari?" Shannon peeked from the hall into the living room.

"Here I am, Shannon."

Shannon scampered to her and peered around Kari's legs at Max. "Who's that?"

"This is your cousin, Max."

Shannon looked at Kari, crinkled her nose, and grinned.

"You have lots of cousins here, Shannon, but Max is a very *special* cousin. And guess what? He lives on a farm. They have animals on the farm. If you ask nicely, perhaps Max will show you the animals some time."

"What kinda animals, Aunt Kari?"

Kari didn't answer; she looked at Max.

"Hi, Shannon. Do you want me to tell you what kind of animals we have?"

She grinned up at Kari again.

"Do you want Max to tell you about the animals?"

Shannon dithered and then nodded. "Yes, please."

"Well, we've got chickens. And we've got cows and horses. And—"

"Horsies!" Shannon was astounded.

"Yeah. We've got two horses."

"I wanna see the horsies, Aunt Kari."

"Yes, perhaps later today. Ask Max what else they have."

"What else, please?"

"Well, we've got a lot of goats. Pigs, too."

"Pig!" Robbie hollered in Kari's ear. He jumped up and down in her arms, so she promptly set him on the floor—and rubbed her ringing ear.

Robbie joined Shannon on the backside of Kari's legs.

"Hey, Robbie." Max wiggled his fingers at Robbie, who laughed and, again, hid his face.

"Would it be all right if we came over this afternoon when you get home from school, Max?"

"No school today, Kari. It's Saturday."

"So it is. Seems that I've lost track of time."

"Aunt Ilsa asked me to come over and invite you to breakfast. I could show the animals to the kids afterwards."

"Why . . . why, that would be lovely."

"Okay. Ilsa said seven, if you can make it." He studied the two heads that poked out from behind Kari's back.

"They sure look a lot like you, Kari."

Max was cheerful as he said it. Maybe a bit too cheerful. A little forced?

"Tell Ilsa thank you. We'll be there," Kari said.

Max went away with a wave of his hand, trotting down the path toward the bridge.

Ilsa pulled Kari into the kitchen and hugged her long and hard. "I'm so glad to see you, Kari. So glad you're here." She backed away from Kari and tried to see Shannon and Robbie, but they were shy and clung to Kari like stickers to socks.

"It's okay, Ilsa. They'll get used to you—especially if you have food." Kari smiled at Søren and Max. They were already seated at the table, waiting for their breakfast.

"Do I have food? *Do I have food?* Come and see if I have food. Sit there, Kari, however you'd like to arrange yourself and the children."

Kari carried Robbie and tugged Shannon with her to the long, planked table. She sat down on the bench near Max and plopped Robbie between them. Shannon climbed onto the bench on Kari's other side.

Then Ilsa brought on the food: Fried bacon, sausages, ham, and potatoes; pancakes, eggs, and hot syrup. Muffins, fruit, juice, and milk were already waiting on the table.

When Søren bowed his head to pray, Shannon and Robbie stared at him with round eyes. Kari bowed her head with Max and Ilsa.

"Lord, we thank you for this food, for all your provision, for bringing Kari, Shannon, and Robbie to us safely. We love and honor you, Lord. Amen."

"Amen," Ilsa, Kari, Max, and Shannon echoed.

"MEN!" Robbie yelled.

Laughter floated around the table and Robbie bounced on his bottom, unconcerned that he was the center of attention. He was hungry.

"BAKE!"

"Ah, spoken like a true farmer," Søren laughed. He placed two strips of bacon on Robbie's plate. Robbie grabbed one up and gnawed on it.

Ilsa studied Shannon and Robbie. "Goodness, Kari! Max said they looked like you, and they most certainly do."

Ilsa held out a plate of muffins. "Shannon, I'm Ilsa. Would you care for a muffin?"

"No, thank you."

"What sweet manners you have. What would you like to eat, dear?"

Shannon's eyes gleamed. "Pancakes, please."

"CAKES!" Robbie roared.

Søren grinned at Kari. "I like this boy!"

Max stared from his father to Robbie and then to his plate.

After breakfast, Max and Kari took the children down to the barn. Kari carried Robbie while Max held Shannon's hand.

Shannon asked to see the horses first so Max showed her the big bays. She was enthralled when one put his head over the stall door and stared down his nose at her.

Kari was impressed with the care Max took for the children's size and their safety.

"Don't ever walk up to a horse's backside, Shannon. Always let them see you. Stay by their head so they don't kick you." He guided her hand to the bay's soft nose.

"He's got whiskers!" she exclaimed in wonder.

She put her hand in Max's and let him lead her to the chicken pen. He unlatched the gate and took her inside.

"Hens usually aren't mean, Shannon, but roosters can be. Take a handful of this here grain and throw it right out there. See? They like that. Pretty soon they'll know you on sight and even that ol' rooster won't bother you."

When they got to the goats, Shannon fell in love. "They are so tiny! Here, baby goat! Max, I wanna pet the baby goats!"

"They aren't all babies, Shannon. They're little goats, even the grownup ones."

The goats came to Max, anticipating he would pet them. He rubbed and scratched their knobby heads and guided Shannon's hand to a gentle she-goat.

"Here, rub this one right here."

Shannon, glowing with excitement, did so—and then threw her arms around the goat's neck in a bear hug. The startled goat jerked back and ran, jumping and cavorting, to the other side of the pen.

"Whoa! That ol' nanny wasn't expecting that," Max laughed.

"How's it going?" Søren's voice came from behind Kari.

"They are loving it. Robbie seems content to watch from up here, but he is very engaged."

"I take it Shannon is more hands-on?"

They chuckled as Shannon ran from goat to goat, trying desperately to hug one of them. Max, laughing, trailed behind her.

"Cow." Robbie pulled a finger from his mouth and pointed. Three cows with wondering eyes stood at the fence at the top of the pasture.

"Yup. Do you want to see the cow?" Søren asked.

Robbie considered him and then turned away. "Cow." He pointed again.

Søren held out his arms. Robbie stared at him and then leaned toward him. Søren scooped him up and they made their way toward the fence. Kari followed them.

"Cow! Cow!" Robbie bounced and strained toward them.

The bossies, however, trotted off as soon as Søren approached the fence. They made a beeline for the rest of the herd grazing far down the pasture.

"Cow!" Robbie burst into wails.

"How about a pig, Robbie," Søren suggested. "How about a big ol' fat pig?"

He walked to the other side of the goat enclosure and leaned on the pigpen's rails. "Look at that one, Robbie."

Kari followed them and leaned on the wooden slats, too. A sow, with eight piglets rooting along her belly, had to have been eight hundred pounds. Kari was suddenly breathless with fear.

"Oh, my goodness! We mustn't ever let Robbie down! If he climbed in there—"

"Right. Even more reason to train them, starting now, as to what is safe and what is dangerous. Max has known since he was two to stay away from the pigpens. Especially the boar."

They wandered the barn and the stock sheds, looking at all Robbie showed an interest in. Thirty minutes later, Robbie leaned from Søren toward Kari. His eyes were drooping.

"He needs a nap," Kari said.

"Let's take him in the house. He can sleep on the guest bed." Søren slanted his eyes toward Kari. "You know where that is."

"Yes, I do." She craned her neck for Shannon and Max.

"Looks like they've gone up the hill toward the apple orchard. Don't worry about her. Max will take good care of her."

"All right."

Kari put Robbie on the bed and laid an afghan over him. When she left the room, he was already asleep.

"I think that's more excitement than he's had in a month," Kari whispered. "Tuckered him right out."

Kari accepted a cup of coffee from Ilsa and the three of them sat down at the kitchen table. "That reminds me. He has a birthday coming up."

"He'll be two?" Ilsa asked.

"Yes. And I haven't a clue what to do."

"We can have his party here," Ilsa announced. "I know all about little boys' birthday parties."

Kari stole a glance at Søren.

He was stirring his coffee.

Deep in his own thoughts.

CHAPTER 35

The first two weeks passed in a pleasant fog. Kari organized the house and set up an office area for herself including computer, phone, and fax. She placed her favorite photograph of Rose on her desk and liked to look at it when she was on the phone with Scarlett, Bettina, Oskar, or Cadie.

She'd had another photograph reproduced: The portrait of Stephen and Kelly that had sat on the table between their caskets. Kari placed that framed photo on the coffee table in the living room where Shannon and Robbie could see and handle it.

Shannon often picked it up, pointing to it and telling Robbie, "That's Mommy. That's Daddy. They are in heaven."

Kari also ordered a swing set and had it delivered and set up. At the same time, she had a chain link fence erected to surround it, the house, and the newly laid sod.

"That creek is too enticing for a toddler," she told Ilsa.

The kids loved it all. She played outside with them, pushing them on the swings, waiting at the bottom of the slide, showing Shannon how to hold onto the monkey bars and swing across, one hand at a time.

Kari took Ilsa and the children shopping for groceries and other necessities. Ilsa directed her through RiverBend to the freeway.

"We only shop at the neighborhood grocery in town when we run out of something," Ilsa explained. "He doesn't have much selection. The best thing is to make the forty-mile trip to the nearest town and use the Shop and Save."

"That's a hike! I'll have to train myself to shop no more than once a week."

Kari bought enough food to keep them for a month, if necessary. Afterwards they went to a large department store and selected cake decorations and party favors for Robbie's party. While there, Kari wandered into the baby section.

"Looking for anything in particular?" Ilsa asked.

"I need a highchair for Mister Messy. Left his in New Orleans."

"Great idea. And since you're so all-fired filthy rich, why don't you get two and keep one at our place?"

"Great idea!"

"I just said that."

Lulled by the long drive home, the kids fell asleep in their car seats. And Ilsa asked the questions Kari had been anticipating.

"So, Kari, do you think you'll stay long in RiverBend?"

"That's the plan for now. Shannon will start kindergarten in the fall. Say, where is the school? Where do I register her and when?"

"The school is on the outskirts of town. You register there. Max takes the bus; Shannon can ride with him"

"Wow. That's unsettling—Shannon riding a school bus by herself?"

"But she won't be by herself."

"All right." Did Kari detect something defensive under Ilsa's remark?

"I'm sorry. I was a little sharp there."

"Um, it's okay. Are you worried about something?"

Ilsa sighed. "A little, I guess. You coming back here. It's sort of upset the applecart. Not that it was a *happy* applecart before you came back, mind you, but it was a stable cart. Content, after a fashion. You know, all the apples, um, not wondering if they were going to be dumped . . . out."

"Or just dumped?"

"Yeah. Maybe that."

"You want to know if my intentions are honorable?"

"Come to think of it, yes."

"Well, I'll let you in on a secret, Ilsa. I came here husband shopping."

"Ah. Did you, now?"

"Yes, but I'm shopping for a father, too. And a big brother."

"Well, I know a boy who would be relieved to know that."

"What about the prospective husband/father?"

"All's quiet on that front."

"Yeah. I thought so."

***

ROBBIE'S PARTY WAS A ROUSING SUCCESS. He decided he liked being the center of attention. He sat, enthroned in one of his two new highchairs, tearing into gifts like a pro.

Kari gave him puzzles. Ilsa (and Søren by default) gave him bath toys. Max, though, from his own pocket, bought Robbie a big yellow dump truck.

"Truck!" Robbie loved it. He ran the wheels over his highchair tray and then wanted down.

"Max, that was the sweetest thing," Kari told him. "Your gift is the big hit."

"Can I take him outside to play with it in the dirt?"

Kari nodded slowly. "Yes, if you'd like. You are a wonderful cousin, Max."
"Yeah."

There it was again. That sort of sad expression that flickered across his face.

Kari said nothing. She thought she understood what was going on in Max's head. In his heart.

Lord, we need you.

Kari washed cake from Robbie's hands and face. She helped him down the back steps with his new truck. Max took him by the hand.

When she came back into the kitchen, Shannon stood on a chair helping Ilsa wash the dishes. Kari took a rag and began wiping chocolate frosting off the highchair. Then she saw Søren, hands in his pockets, watching her.

"Guess we never saw this coming, did we?" Kari murmured.

"Not in a million years. I had imagined this scene, yes, but it was a whole lot different."

"Guess God really threw us a curve ball, huh?"

"Us?" Søren studied Kari with pain in his eyes. "What is it you want from me, Kari?"

She flushed and kept cleaning, too hurt to answer him.

Ilsa, on the other hand, turned around and hissed, "Do you mind?" She tipped her head toward Shannon. The little girl's expression was a mix of curious and wary.

"Sorry." Kari put the washrag in the sink and hurried outside.

Søren did not follow her.

She found Max and Robbie in the yard playing under the pump. Max had made some roads in the moist dirt and they had a little hand shovel that Robbie was using laboriously to fill the truck.

"That's good, Rob. Now drive it over and dump it."

Robbie, his entire being engrossed in the process, got up and leaned on the yellow truck. He rolled it ahead of him to a spot where Max had drawn an 'X.' Once he got it there, he looked to Max.

"Hep. Hep, Max."

"Sure thing, buddy." Max made a show of lifting up the truck's bed, complete with sound effects. Robbie danced about, squealing in delight as the dirt poured out.

"'Gain! 'Gain, Max!"

"Having fun, Robbie?"

"Fun," Robbie repeated. "'Gain, Max!"

"I think it's time to go home, Robbie." Kari hated it. Hated tearing Robbie away, but the atmosphere in the house was too charged.

Robbie, as though she had not spoken, pushed the truck back to the pump and started digging. Max looked up at her and then Robbie. He got to his feet and walked up to her. "Kari, can I ask you something?"

Kari nodded, wondering at the hurt on Max's face.

"Do . . . do you remember when you and Papa and me talked about obstacles and stuff?"

"Yes. Of course."

She looked closely. Max was nervous. Afraid? "What is it, Max?"

"Well, you said . . . you said you loved my dad and wanted to marry him. Said you wanted to be my mom."

"I did, Max. I still do."

He looked a little relieved—but not completely.

"And you said you had to live in New Orleans. But now you live here, right?"

Kari nodded, watching for what was truly bothering him.

"'Cept now you have Shannon and Robbie. Are they new obstacles? Or . . ."

"Or what, Max?"

"Or am I an obstacle? 'Cause you have them now? Maybe you don't need more kids, now that you have them."

Kari felt like she'd been punched. "You, an obstacle? You could never be 'an obstacle' to me, Max. I love you. I will always love you."

He blinked. Something was still there.

"But do you love me like-like a-a cousin? Not like you love Shannon and Robbie? Not like a-a son?"

There it was. Kari closed her eyes for a moment against Max's pain.

She reached for him and hugged him with a fierceness that only grew stronger when he sobbed against her breasts.

"Max! Max, I love you in the same way I love Shannon and Robbie. As my own child. As my *son*. I have room in my heart for all three of you. Forever. If God allows me to marry your papa, it will make me your mom for real—but you are already as dear as a son to me right this minute."

"Really? Truly?"

"Really and truly."

"Will you tell Papa? Tell him you're ready to get married?"

Kari closed her eyes again. "I can't tell him, Max. Not yet anyway."

"Why not?"

Kari fumbled, trying to say it in the best way. "You know how you wanted to be sure that I would love you like a mom?"

"Yeah."

"Well, your dad has barely met Shannon and Robbie. He doesn't know them very well yet, and they don't know him, either. Before I tell him I'm ready to get married, I have to be sure that he can love them as a dad. I-I wouldn't want him to marry me and then realize he couldn't feel the same about them as he feels about you. I can't do that to Shannon and Robbie. Do you understand?"

"Oh." It was a revelation to Max, a different way of looking at the problem. But he got it.

"Well, he will. He'll love them. I know he will. Why wouldn't he? They're the best kids ever!"

Kari thought her heart would burst. Max could not have expressed his acceptance of Shannon and Robbie better.

"Then we'll be patient, all right? Until your papa falls in love with them. In the meantime," she planted a kiss on his forehead, "I love you to the moon and back, Maximillian Thoresen, and—Oh! Robbie!"

Robbie looked up, all innocence, but his face was caked in mud.

And he was chewing.

***

THE NEXT MORNING, Kari dressed the children for church. She had skipped church the first two Sundays they had been in RiverBend, figuring that Shannon and Robbie didn't need to meet another group of strangers quite yet.

The late May morning spoke of warmth to come as the day lengthened. She put the children in the car and drove the now-familiar road toward RiverBend's small community church.

She saw Lars and Dalia Thoresen and their active brood visiting with other church members on the grass. She directed the children to where they were standing.

"Hi, Dalia. Lars."

"Hello, Kari." Dalia smiled and bent toward Robbie and Shannon. "And who are these precious children?"

"These are my niece and nephew, Shannon and Robbie."

Dalia was clearly confused. "But I thought—"

"They are mine now," Kari murmured.

"Yours?"

Kari nodded. "We can speak of the details another time."

"Well, it's good to see you. I see you're staying in your new house. Are you planning to be here long?"

"Actually, we've decided to put down roots here."

Lars stepped in, kept Dalia from asking more questions.

"Service is about to start."

"I'm sure we'll see each other often," Kari said as she moved toward the church.

Reluctant to push herself onto Søren and Ilsa, Kari picked her own place to sit in the church—and not knowing how the children would behave, she chose seats on the back row.

She saw when Søren, Ilsa, and Max entered the building—particularly Max. He was searching for Kari, neck craning, eyes darting around the church.

That boy will crimp a knot in his neck, Kari laughed to herself. She waggled her fingers at him and he relaxed, a giant grin stretched across his face.

After church, Ilsa found them, too.

"Please come to Sunday dinner," she begged. "I know you were at our place yesterday, but Sunday dinner is for family."

"Is it all right with Søren?"

Ilsa bristled. "Well, of course it is."

"All right. We'd love to. We'll go home first so I can change the children into play clothes."

Dinner would have been a relaxed, pleasant affair—except that Robbie was more interested in skipping lunch and playing outside with his truck. He bounced in his highchair. He fidgeted. He refused to eat. He kicked the chair's legs. If the chair hadn't restrained him, he would have been long gone.

In other words, dinner was a battle.

"No, Robbie. Not until dinner is over," Kari warned him for the fourth time.

She sighed. "Is this the Terrible Twos?"

"Want down! Down!" he yelled. He began kicking the highchair nonstop.

"Doooowwwwn!"

"ROBBIE!"

Søren's voice boomed in the kitchen, bringing all activity to a halt. Robbie stared at Søren with wide, startled eyes.

"Robbie, stop kicking and eat your lunch," Søren instructed in a bit softer voice.

Robbie turned his head to Kari. Kari shook her head and shrugged.

"Robbie, look at me," Søren demanded. "You will behave at the table. Now, finish your chicken."

Robbie's chin trembled, but he picked up the chicken leg on his tray.

Dinner resumed and, five minutes later, Robbie held out the chewed drumstick to Soren. "All gone, Sor."

"You are a good boy, Robbie."

"Down?"

"Down, *please*."

He nodded vigorously. "Down peas."

"Robbie," Ilsa interrupted. "Do you want cake first?"

He dropped the drumstick onto the tray and clapped his hands. "CAKE!"

When dinner was over, Shannon, Robbie, and Max went outside to play. Kari and Ilsa did the dishes and cleaned the kitchen. Søren took a cup of coffee into the living room.

Soon after, Søren wandered into the kitchen again, ostensibly to refresh his coffee.

"Thank you for your help with Robbie at lunch," Kari offered.

He cleared his throat. "They seem to be adjusting. Getting used to being here."

"Yes. I'm glad I can give them a fairly stable routine."

Ilsa spoke up. "Speaking of routine, you mentioned you will travel to New Orleans once a month. When do you go next?"

"That's a good question. Probably next Sunday. Travel Sunday, work Monday and Tuesday, back on Wednesday."

Søren frowned. "And you'll take the kids with you? That's a lot of disruption for them."

"I don't see another way around it. We will have to roll with it. Work it out."

"And while you're at the office?"

"Mrs. Birch took a permanent position elsewhere. Azalea has recommended another nanny to watch them for me."

Ilsa huffed. "Well, why can't they stay with us?"

Søren shot her a cautioning glance, but she ignored him.

"They know us now." Under her breath she muttered, "They don't need yet another stranger in their lives."

The back door flew open and a whirlwind of three wild children blew in.

"Aunt Ilsa, we want cookies!" Shannon shouted it the way a highway robber demands all valuables.

"Tookie! Tookie!" Robbie echoed.

"Shannon and Robbie! Walk when you come into the house—and no shouting. If you want a cookie, you must ask. Politely," Kari told them.

"May I have a cookie, please, Aunt Ilsa?"

Robbie walked over to Ilsa and stared straight up at her face. "Tookie peas Ilza."

Kari heard Søren snort a laugh and grinned with him. "Ilsa has volunteered for four days of *this* next week. Are you all right with it?"

He looked down and then met Kari's eyes. "I'll adjust."

It wasn't the most enthusiastic reply, but Kari would take it anyway.

"Shannon, I have to go to work next week. You can come with me on the plane or you can stay here. Would you like to stay here with Ilsa?"

Shannon, holding a cookie in each hand, looked from Kari to Ilsa and back. "No."

She pointed a cookie at Max. "Max."

Max let out a whoop. "Ha! She chose me! She chose me!"

She pulled on his shirt. "Max. I wanna play with the baby goats."

Robbie grinned. "Goats! Goats!"

"Okay, buddy, but first you need t' wipe your mouth." Max grimaced in Kari's direction. "Gosh, Kari. This kid slobbers worse'n our old mama cat."

Kari laughed. "He's teething, Max. Molars."

"Ugh." Max pulled a disreputable kerchief from his back pocket and proceeded to wipe Robbie's mouth and chin. "There ya go, Rob. Come on, then."

He held the children by the hand and led them down the back porch steps toward the barn.

CHAPTER 36

K ari felt horrible when she left the children in Søren and Ilsa's kitchen early the following Sunday morning. *They are such a part of me now. I will miss them. Terribly.*

Apparently, the kids would not miss her as much as she would miss them. They ran to Max. Robbie tried to climb up his leg.

"Shannon and Robbie, Max has chores to do. Let him go," Ilsa scolded them. "Kari, would you like to put their things in the spare room upstairs?"

Kari did so, hanging their church clothes in the closet and laying out their pajamas. When she came back, Shannon and Robbie had disappeared.

"Where did they go?"

Ilsa pointed out the window. Kari looked and what she saw caused a lump to form in her throat.

Striding toward the barn were Max and Søren. Shannon skipped and bounced but clung to Max's hand. Robbie sat on Søren's shoulders. Robbie waved his hands in the air. Even through the window, Kari could hear Robbie's screaming laughter.

Kari put a hand over her mouth to stifle a sob.

Ilsa said nothing.

***

WHEN KARI ENTERED HER HOUSE on Marlow Avenue that evening, it felt like another world—a world devoid of life. Azalea had left her a simple meal in the fridge. Kari heated it up and took it to her office.

As she ate, she wondered how this life so barren of little children had ever appealed to her.

It hadn't. Not really. Oh, I was content doing what God required of me—but only until Shannon and Robbie needed me.

"The truth is," she whispered into the air, "I will go into the office tomorrow and enjoy the work I need to do. But I will be counting the minutes until I go home again. Home to my little family."

She sighed. *Lord? Will you speak to Søren while I'm gone? Our little family needs a daddy. And a big brother.*

***

KARI PULLED INTO SØREN'S YARD Wednesday afternoon. She didn't have to wonder where the kids were—all three of them were digging in the dirt not far from the pump, making roads and bridges, hauling loads and dumping them.

Max had found a few more vehicles—a grader, a front loader, and a dated sports car. Shannon was dirty, but Robbie was coated in mud. They were utterly engrossed in their play and having the most fun Kari had seen them have.

When they saw Kari drive up, they ran to her. Within seconds, Kari had been hugged, squeezed, and kissed by three sets of filthy hands and lips.

"Aunt Kari! Aunt Kari! You're home!"

"Auntkareeee! Auntkareee!" Robbie plastered a particularly muddy kiss on her cheek.

"I should call you Pigpen," Kari laughed.

Ilsa suggested that Kari shower Robbie off in the guest room. "Best way to keep the dirt contained," she cautioned.

"Thank you, Ilsa." Kari hauled the screaming toddler into the guest bath and showered him clean, liberally soaking herself at the same time. When they emerged, a cleaner Shannon was sitting next to Ilsa, and Ilsa was reading to her. Robbie scampered over and climbed into her lap.

Shannon looked up. "Aunt Ilsa is reading Pooh Bear to us."

"Aunt Ilsa is pretty neat, huh?"

"Yup."

Søren came to Kari. Stood near her, his back to Ilsa.

"How did it go, Søren?"

"I think we need to talk. The two of us."

Kari's heart thumped so hard she found it hard to answer.

"All right. Could you come over this evening? After the children are in bed?"

"Yes."

Søren knocked on the door at eight. Kari let him in and, while she made a pot of tea, he wandered the living room looking at her things. When she came back, he was standing by her little office area holding Rose's photograph.

"Where did you get this?"

"Uncle Matthew. When my photographer left here, he went to Emporia next. That one is special to me. I kept it on my desk in my New Orleans' house."

"I guess I didn't notice it. It's a wonderful likeness of her."

"I love it. It captures the woman I came to know through her journals. That expression . . . O'Dell captured the patient hope on her face."

Søren walked to the coffee table and picked up the photo of Stephen and Kelly. "This has to be your brother and his wife."

"Yes. I put it where the children can see it as often as they like."

"Your brother . . . he looks a lot like you. Same coloring, but mainly the eyes."

"Our eyes, Søren."

Søren studied the image again. "Yes. It's remarkable. He's definitely a Thoresen."

"So are Shannon and Robbie."

Søren nodded. "Come out on the porch with me, Kari?"

They went outside and stood at the railing. And Søren took her hand. It felt so good! Her hand in his large, strong one.

"Max told me about the conversation you two had. About obstacles."

"Oh?"

"He said . . . he said you were ready to get married. Is that right?"

Kari's lips would hardly move. "Yes."

"But then he told me . . . that *I* was the last obstacle. Is that what you think?"

"I-I told Max I had to be sure you could love Shannon and Robbie the way I love him— as my own child."

Søren was quiet for a bit. "I have nothing to offer you, Kari. I probably have less now than when we first met. You are the wealthiest person I know. What can I possibly give you that you don't have or cannot buy?"

Kari shook her head. "It is not what you have, Søren, it is who you are that I love and need. I need a husband, a godly man who will be a father to Shannon and Robbie. I cannot buy that. I can only turn to God and ask him to provide."

"What if I told you that having Shannon and Robbie these last few days proved to me that I can love and accept them as my own?"

"In my mind, it would remove all doubt. Would remove the last 'obstacle.'"

"But what about . . . What about all your 'holdings?' Stewarding it all? Will you change your mind and want to move back to Louisiana?"

"I have responsibilities in New Orleans, yes, but I don't want to raise Shannon and Robbie there. I want them to know their heritage, their prairie heritage. I want them to know the faith Rose and Jan left all of us. I intend to keep on top of things back there but remain here the majority of the time."

Søren looked away into the distance. "I've missed you, Kari. Every moment of every day since we parted, I have missed you."

Through the gathering shadows, Kari saw Søren's jaw working. Saw him struggling.

"I watched Max grieve for you, Kari, and I wondered, time and again—had I made the single biggest mistake of my life? Had I placed too high of an estimation upon my own ways?"

He shook his head and sighed. "But now I understand why, whenever I prayed last year, all I heard was *spring. Wait until spring.* It could have thrown us into a tailspin if Shannon and Robbie had come into our lives after we'd married. Might have been even more difficult for Max to accept."

"Because neither of you would have had the opportunity to choose them?"

"I guess so."

"Do you choose them now, Søren?"

"Yes, Kari. Yes, I do."

"And I choose you, Søren. You and Max. For always."

Kari went to his arms. Søren cupped her chin and they kissed—a long, tender, satisfying kiss—a pledge of commitment, a seal of promise.

Kari was breathless when their lips parted. "Goodness!"

Søren grinned, and Kari loved how his even, white teeth gleamed in the twilight.

She took his hand. "Come in the house. We have a wedding to plan."

They had no more than sat down when tiny plastic-padded footsteps pattered into the living room.

"Uh-oh!" Kari whispered. "What are you doing up, little man?"

Robbie didn't answer. He shuffled to Søren, clambered into his lap, laid his head on Søren's chest, and closed his eyes.

Søren shook his head and smiled a crooked smile at Kari. "How could I not love this?"

***

"HAVE YOU DECIDED TO GET MARRIED, THEN? At long last?" Ilsa stood with both hands on her hips looking from Søren to Kari.

"Yes," they answered at the same time.

"God be praised! Thought we'd all be moldering in the grave before you two figured things out. So when? When will you do it?"

Kari looked to Søren. "September, I think. Is that right?"

"September seems too far off for me, but yes. September. The season when I'm *most* at my leisure."

Kari and Ilsa burst into laughter.

Max opened the door and let Shannon and Robbie inside.

"What's so funny?"

"Well, we were trying to figure out when to have a wedding," Søren grinned.

"A wedding? Oh, boy! *Finally!*"

"Come here, Shannon and Robbie. Max. Let's do this right."

Søren sat on a bench and gathered the children to him. "Shannon? Robbie? Max? I have asked Kari to marry me. That would make us a family."

Robbie squirmed and climbed up on his knee, oblivious to the conversation, but claiming his place nonetheless. However, Shannon studied Søren, unsure of what was happening.

"Shannon, if Aunt Kari and I get married, then I would be your new father. Max would be your new brother. What do you think of that?"

Shannon looked at Kari. "What about Mommy and Daddy?"

"They will always be your Mommy and Daddy. Always. You can pick a name for Søren that isn't Daddy."

"I call him Papa, Shannon," Max told her. "You can call him that if you want to."

"Okay."

"Does that mean it's okay for Aunt Kari and me to get married?"

Shannon nodded vigorously. "Yes. Cause then you'll be Papa Søren. And Max will be my brother. I like Max."

"And when they get married, then Aunt Kari will be my mom," Max added.

But this confused Shannon. "How can she be Aunt Kari and your mom, too?"

"Well, she could be your new mom like Søren is your new father. If you want," Max suggested.

Kari knelt by Shannon. "I'm not your mommy, but I would like to be your new mother. Would you like to pick a name for me that isn't Mommy?"

Max touched Kari's arm. "I want to call you Mama, if that's all right."

Tears sprang to Kari's eyes. "I would love that, Max."

"Well, then I want to call you Mama Kari," Shannon announced. "Papa Søren and Mama Kari."

Søren grinned. "It sounds like we have a plan."

"Hallelujah, Lord!" Ilsa muttered. "I thank you, Father, for answered prayer. And before Jesus comes back, too."

❧ ✺ ❧

CHAPTER 37

SEPTEMBER 1994

Kari looked from her bedroom window toward the sunrise. It was going to be a glorious day—sunny and warm with a slight breeze. "What do you want for a wedding?" Søren had asked her. "A big church wedding or something simpler?"

Kari didn't need to think long. "I want to be married surrounded by poppies, Søren. I would like our lives to be joined down on the creek bank, where our lands join—surrounded by poppies and all the people we love."

"All the people we love? *All* of them?"

"I'm filthy, stinking rich, remember? And I guarantee this is the last time I'm getting married. I'll pay for airline tickets for all our friends and family—or charter a plane, if that is easier. I'll buy out an entire hotel for the festivities and feed all of RiverBend if necessary. But I want *all* our friends and family—including Shannon and Robbie's grandparents, including my one and only sister—to be with us as we commit ourselves to this new family."

"And poppies, eh? They grow wild around here, you know," he smiled.

"Yes, I know."

"But they're gone by September."

"Well, then it wouldn't hurt to plant some."

And he had done just that. In late July, he had driven his tractor from the top to the bottom of his field and mowed a wide path from the driveway to the creek bank. Then he had plowed a wider swath along the creek.

And, Max had informed her, "Papa ordered a big sack of poppy seeds—the tall red kind—and broadcast the whole sack of 'em along the creek bank!"

Søren had watered daily during the heat of July and August and—utterly past their natural season—they had grown. Now they were flowering and had transformed the other side of the creek into a glorious red haze.

"Mama?"

"Yes, Shannon?"

"Is today the wedding?" She had asked the same question every day for a month.

"Yes, darling. Today is the wedding. Finally."

"Finally!" Shannon hopped on one foot and then the other. "And I get to wear my wedding dress! And you get to wear your wedding dress!"

"Me, too! Wed' dress!" Robbie shouted.

Shannon corrected him. "Boys don't wear wedding dresses, silly."

Robbie screwed up his face, but Kari grabbed him up and tossed him in the air before he could wail.

She giggled. "You get to wear your wedding *suit*, Rob, my son. You and Søren and Max get to wear wedding *suits*!"

"Me an' Søren! Me an' Max!"

"Yes, and today Søren gets to be your Papa and Max gets to be your brother. What do you think of that?"

Kari asked the question often. She wanted to be sure that the children wanted this big change. As much as possible, she wanted to be certain that they understood what bringing the two families together would mean.

Both kids hollered their approval. "Papa! Papa! Papa!"

A knock sounded on the door— the children raced to it. Shannon yanked it open.

"Hi, Aunt Ilsa! Today is the wedding. I get to wear my wedding dress!"

"Yes, you do, sweet Shannon."

"What is that?"

Ilsa carried a paper-wrapped package. "A present for your mama and papa on their wedding day."

Many such packages had arrived in the weeks leading up to the wedding.

"Who's it from, Ilsa?"

"Not sure. The postmark is foreign and it's marked urgent and sent express mail, so I thought I should bring it over."

Kari's fingers on the paper wrapping slowed. She examined the postmark and nodded. "I . . . it must be from Laynie."

Kari had sent the invitation two months ago. And Laynie had replied. She was supposed to arrive early this morning.

Laynie, where are you? You promised to be with me today.

She removed the paper and cut open the stout packing box. The box was filled with packing peanuts. Kari dug down and found a smaller box wedged inside. As she pulled it out, Styrofoam bits went everywhere. Kari let them fall—she needed to know what was in the smaller box.

Ilsa helped her to clear the table so that Kari could cut open the box. Inside, nestled in tissue paper, was a small envelope. Below that, Kari glimpsed a tiny sailboat. She lifted it out with tender care.

"It-it is a replica of-of Sammie's boat. An exact replica."

Kari's fingers traced the tiny stern and the bench across it, the miniscule tiller in the middle. "This is where we sat when we went sailing together. Laynie handled the tiller and the sails almost all by herself. I held the tiller steady once or twice."

Kari felt the salt spray and the wind on her face, saw again Laynie's hair flying free . . . and the joy on her sister's face.

Laynie! My sister! Where are you?

Every part of the boat was crafted with extreme attention to detail—it was a perfect copy of Sammie's boat.

"What's the boat's name?" Ilsa asked.

"Oh, it's the—" Kari stopped when she read the tiny red script flowing across the stern. She swallowed against the emotion that rose in her throat.

"What is it?"

Kari whispered, "Sammie's boat was *The Wave Skipper*. This boat is the *SS Fellowship*."

Fellowship is like two fellows— wait for it!—two fellows sitting together in the same ship. Get it? Fellow-ship—and here we are. Together.

You know . . . you're all right, Kari Michaels.

I love you back, Laynie Portland.

"It's a sweet gesture, but why would she send it ahead? Why wouldn't she bring it herself?"

Kari picked up the little envelope, but did not break the seal on it right away. "Because she's not coming, Ilsa." Kari knew it before she had finished opening the parcel.

Ilsa frowned at Kari, hurt and indignation reddening her face. "Not coming to your wedding? Her only sister's wedding? But she promised!"

Kari tried to smile. She lifted one shoulder. "I had a feeling she wouldn't be able to come."

"But . . ."

"She couldn't come, Ilsa. Please don't fault her."

Kari placed the little boat on the shelf above her desk. "I'll keep it close, Laynie," she whispered. "I'll keep you close, too."

She turned to Ilsa. "I don't want you to think badly of me for asking so late, Ilsa, but it seems I am short a maid of honor."

Ilsa stretched to her full height. "Laynie's loss is my gain. I would be, well, *honored* to be your maid of honor."

"The wedding starts in two hours."

"Yikes! I still need to shower. See you then." Ilsa ran to her car and sped away.

Kari sighed and ran her finger under the envelope's glued seal. She pulled out the card and read the simple lines.

Kari,

As it turns out, I am unable to attend your wedding. I am sorry. You know I would be with you if I could. And so I send the most fitting gift I could think of, a token of our day together. I think of it—and you—often.
—LP

Kari chewed her lip to keep from crying. *O Lord, wherever Laynie is, I pray you watch over her. Keep her safe and draw her heart to you!*

Kari slid the card back into the envelope and tucked it into her desk drawer. Then she sniffed back her sadness and called Shannon and Robbie.

"It's time! Shall we put on our wedding outfits?"

An hour and forty minutes (and much primping) later, the sound of tires crunching on gravel alerted Shannon and Robbie. They ran to the window.

"Who is it, Shannon?"

"It's Grandpa!"

"Grandpa Gene and Grandma Polly have come to drive us to the wedding. Are we all ready to go? Line up and let me take a look at you."

Shannon and Robbie stood tall and solemn while Kari made a show of checking them over.

"Everything seems in order. That is a *very* nice bow tie, Robbie. I love your dress, Miss Shannon. Oh, and your shoes are adorable.

"Now. How do *I* look?" Kari stepped back and let them see her dress— a lacy ivory Gunne Sax special edition that flowed from a high Empire waist and ended mid-calf in frothy flourishes. Peeking from underneath her hem were ivory calfskin boots trimmed with lace that matched her dress. Kari's long hair curled around her shoulders from under a short veil.

Shannon smiled in awe. "You look beautiful, Mama. Like a princess."

"P'incess!" Robbie repeated, bouncing up and down.

Slow footsteps sounded on the porch steps.

"Shannon, would you like to open the door for Grandpa Gene?"

Gene Portland stood in the doorway, beaming at Shannon and Robbie. "Grammy will be so glad to see you two! And Kari! Don't you look wonderful! Come on, now. Take this old man's arm and let me drive you to your wedding."

He had parked Kari's red Caddy so that Polly's window faced the house. Gene led Kari down the steps and through the gate and paraded Kari in front of Polly. Shannon and Robbie—after much previous practice—held hands and preceded them in solemn procession. That is, for half a minute. As soon as they saw Polly smiling from the passenger seat, they raced to her.

"Grammy! Grammy!"

"Ohh, my sweet grandchildren! You are the most beautiful sight I have ever seen!" She grasped their hands and showered kisses on them.

"Now, step back a mite and let me see my daughter Kari. Go stand with her so I can take it in all t'gether."

The children ran back to Kari and stood next to her.

"What a picture you all are. I shall never forget this day."

"Kari's gonna be our new mama, Grammy. And Søren's gonna be our new papa," Shannon shouted.

"Papa!" Robbie shouted.

Polly raised a tissue to her eyes. "What a blessed, blessed day this is. You have turned my sorrow into joy, O Lord!"

Kari leaned into the window and kissed Polly's damp cheek, and Polly clasped Kari's hand.

"Kari, have you seen our Laynie? Is she here yet?"

"I, um, I received word a bit ago, Mama Polly. She won't be able to come. I'm so sorry."

"I see." Polly was silent a moment, and then her creased brow smoothed. "I'm sorry, too. Sorry that we are going to celebrate this blessed day without her. But celebrate we shall! Come on, now. Everybody in this big ol' car! We need to get the bride to her weddin'!"

Kari and the children climbed into the back seat of her Caddy, the two children on either side of her. Shannon grinned and fluffed her skirt. Kari grinned back and fluffed her skirt as well.

Shannon giggled.

It took only four minutes for Gene to deliver them to the top of Søren's pasture. Three adjoining white tents were arranged on the grassy lawn. Through the tied-back folds of the nearest tent, Kari spied round tables already laid with snowy cloths, silverware, china, and crystal. Caterers scurried about, preparing for the reception.

The upper pasture was filled with guests' vehicles. Gene parked in the spot designated for him. Lars and Dalia were waiting. With little effort, Lars lifted Polly onto a seat on a golf cart and Dalia held her steady while Lars drove them down the pasture to Polly's front row seat.

More than two hundred guests waited at the bottom of the pasture for the wedding to start. Their chairs faced the creek and a sea of poppies. The rich harmonies of a harpist, three horns, and seven strings players wafted in the air.

"Here is your bouquet, Kari," Ilsa grinned. Søren's sister was radiant in pale yellow. Her red-blonde braid, hanging below her waist, glowed with the poppies twined into it.

Kari caressed her bouquet of red poppies, white lilies, and trailing golden wheat. "Thank you, Ilsa."

"I'm sorry your sister isn't here."

"But you're my sister, now, Ilsa. And I'm so glad *you* are here."

As they embraced, the strains of *Jesu, Joy of Man's Desiring* floated to them.

"That's our signal. Shannon, here is your basket of petals." Ilsa handed the large basket to Shannon.

"You and Robbie hold the basket together, like we practiced, and scatter the petals on the way down to the creek. See Søren and Max and the pastor down there? Keep walking until you get to them. It doesn't matter how long it takes. Let everyone enjoy watching you, okay?"

Shannon nodded. She was all business now. "Come on, Robbie. Hold the basket handle with me."

The two of them set off, and Shannon began to scatter scarlet rose petals along the way. Robbie wobbled like one of his toy Weebles, but he kept up with Shannon.

Ilsa turned to Kari. "Guess it's my turn. I-I'm so happy for you and Søren—"

"Please don't cry, Ilsa! If you set me off, I won't be able to stop!"

They chuckled. Ilsa sniffed back the tears and lifted her chin. "Here I go, then."

Swaying gracefully, Ilsa began her walk down the sloping pasture.

Arm in arm, Kari and Gene watched Shannon and Robbie's progress ahead of Ilsa. The children were nearing the rows of assembled guests when Robbie let go of the basket.

"Oh, dear," Kari murmured.

Robbie, apparently called aside to see some Wondrous Sight, veered off in the direction of the barn. His departure was followed by Shannon's outraged, "No, Robbie!"

And then they heard Max's voice. "Robbie! Over here, buddy!"

Robbie changed course instantly. He "raced" on his stubby legs toward Max. With only a few yards of the sloping path left, Robbie's forward momentum overcame his short legs' ability to keep up.

Kari and Gene sucked in their breath as Robbie tumbled, end over end, and came to a halt face down in the mown pasture grass. The assembled guests inhaled as one.

After a breathless pause, Robbie raised his head and bellowed out a wounded protest of which Kari was certain half of Nebraska took note.

Amid laughter that drowned out the music, a large number of guests rose to their feet to help Robbie, but Max—resplendent in an ivory tuxedo—was faster. He sprinted up the slope, scooped up Robbie, and raced back to his spot next to Søren. Robbie, still bawling, reached out for Søren, who took him and kissed away the "injuries."

The guests' mirth floated to the top of the pasture where Gene and Kari, too, were gasping with laughter. Shannon, who had finished her journey as rehearsed, now stood between Søren and Max. Ilsa was approaching them.

"Think we should get moving, Kari?" Gene asked. "I'm not sure how much longer that boy will hold out."

"That's our signal, Papa Gene," Kari murmured. She shivered as the horns of Mendelssohn's *Wedding March* resounded in the open air followed by the combined strings.

Gene and Kari began their long march down to the creek.

Unexpected and unanticipated, Kari's thoughts turned toward Laynie. *Elaine. My little sister. I'm so glad we found you at last.*

The sadness against which Kari struggled when she thought of her sister glistened in her eyes.

Lord, Laynie's heart is damaged in ways I cannot imagine . . . but you will draw her back to us. I know you will. And Lord? I am leaning upon you to bring her all the way. All the way home to you.

As Gene and Kari came down the pasture, the guests' faces became clearer. Kari struggled to keep her composure as those dear to her smiled, nodded, and wept tears of happiness.

On Søren's side, Thoresen relations and friends abounded: Uncle Matthew and Aunt Linda. Uncles Jacob and Luke and their families. Sean Carmichael. Alannah Carmichael.

On Kari's side, precious friends: Ruth. Clover and Lorene. Owen and Mercy. Oskar, Melanie, and Scarlett. Bettina, Cadie, and a raft of Kari's management team. Anthony and Gloria.

And then, in the front row on Kari's left, Polly Portland. Bill and Mary Greene. Talia, Don, and their children.

Immediately behind them, frail and failing but adamant about attending, sat Shan-Rose Liáng. On one side, supporting Shan-Rose, was her brother Quan; on the other side, sat Mixxie.

Kari nodded to Mixxie and, for the first time in Kari's acquaintance with the girl, Mixxie smiled.

And then there was only Søren and the children.

Søren stood tall. Solemn. His close-cropped red-blonde hair gleamed in the sun. Like Max and Robbie, Søren, too, wore an ivory tuxedo. The ivory accentuated Søren's deep tan and piercing blue eyes. From within Søren's jacket peeped a crimson cummerbund that matched the poppies at his feet.

O Father, my Søren is so handsome!

Søren!

And Max.

Shannon.

Robbie.

Our children.

Kari's entire world.

Standing together in an ocean of swaying poppies.

Waiting for her to join them.

And over their shoulders, beyond the creek . . . Rose's tiny house.

Rose! How I thank you for your courage. Your faithful walk with God.

"Stop, Papa Gene."

Startled, Gene slid his eyes her way.

"Stop. Please." She pulled on his arm a little, and he slowed to a halt.

The music played on, but a collective murmur ran through the ranks of the guests.

Kari didn't care. She wanted to take in this image, burn it into her heart where she could hold it forever.

She smiled her reassurance to Søren and he nodded. *He understood.*

Kari looked up at the wide blue sky and back to the sight that she would never have enough of. She filled her eyes with it.

"O God! How I thank you!"

Next to her, Gene sniffed, and Kari turned her smile on him.

"I . . . I just needed to savor this moment. I'm ready now."

He cleared his throat. "Well, then . . ."

And they finished their walk into the field of poppies.

Before God and the assembled witnesses, Søren and Kari pledged themselves to each other.

It wasn't a typical ceremony.

Søren and Kari held hands—with Shannon and Max squeezed between them. Robbie, perched on Søren's shoulders and gripping Søren's short hair in one fist, waved at his grandparents and anyone else who smiled and wiggled their fingers at him—which was, actually, quite a large number.

"I, Søren, do take you, Kari, as my wedded wife. To have and to hold, from this day forward. For richer, for poorer, in sickness and in health, till death do we part."

He cleared his throat. "And I, Søren, do take you, Shannon, and you, Robert, as my daughter and my son. I pledge to love you and raise you as my very own. From this day forward, till death do we part."

Through her tears, Kari replied, "I, Kari, do take you, Søren, as my wedded husband. To have and to hold, from this day forward. For richer, for poorer, in sickness and in health, till death do we part.

"And I, Kari, do take you, Max, to be my son—"

Kari's voice broke. Shannon turned around and stared up at her. She patted Kari's dress in a very adult manner.

"It's okay, Mama. It's okay."

"I know, honey. I'm j-just s-so happy."

Kari swallowed the lump in her throat and looked into Max's tearful face. "Max, I pledge to love you and raise you as my very own son. From this day forward, till death do we part."

Max crushed Kari in a hug that no one was expecting.

"I love you, Kari—I mean *Mama!*"

Kari raised her eyes to Søren's as the pastor said, "In the presence of Almighty God and these witnesses, I now pronounce you husband and wife. Søren, you may kiss your bride."

He did.

It went on a long time.

Shannon squealed and covered her face.

Max blushed red. "Oh, man . . ."

The crowd stood and roared its approval.

And Robbie toppled off Søren's shoulders.

Later, as they sliced into their wedding cake, Søren murmured into Kari's ear, "I was sorry when Ilsa told me Laynie wasn't coming, Kari. I know you had your heart set on her being here, on being part of our wedding. Our lives."

Kari nodded. "I was disappointed, of course, but Rose said something in her last journal that I cling to. She said that God's promises are the only things of which we can be certain—and they are certain because they are eternal, not subject to time, death, or decay.

"I believe that the Lord will continue the work he has begun in Laynie. And I believe he will bring it to completion. Someday she will be restored to him and to us."

"I will believe with you, Kari Thoresen."

Kari lifted her face to Søren's.

"Søren. My husband. It took us long enough, didn't it?"

"It took as long as was necessary." He smiled and kissed her fingers.

"As Rose said, God's promises are timeless."

ᕼ ❀ ᕼ

THE END

Thank you, my dear readers, for going with me on this amazing journey. I love and appreciate you.

To God be the glory.

—Vikki

ABOUT THE AUTHOR

Vikki Kestell's passion for people and their stories is evident in her readers' affection for her characters and unusual plotlines. Two often-repeated sentiments are, "I feel like I know these people" and "I'm right there, in the book, experiencing what the characters experience."

Vikki holds a Ph.D. in Organizational Learning and Instructional Technologies. She left a career of twenty-plus years in government, academia, and corporate life to pursue writing full time. "Writing is the best job ever," she admits, "and the most demanding."

Also an accomplished speaker and teacher, Vikki and her husband Conrad Smith make their home in Albuquerque, New Mexico.

To keep abreast of new book releases, sign up for her newsletter on her website at **http://www.vikkikestell.com/** or connect with her on Facebook at **http://www.facebook.com/TheWritingOfVikkiKestell**.

Faith-Filled Fiction™

www.faith-filledfiction.com | www.vikkikestell.com

Made in the USA
Columbia, SC
25 April 2017